HOW
THE
OTHER
HALF DIE

Rachel North was born in Scarborough and studied English Literature at Oxford University. She has worked as a cleaner, a receptionist, a kitchen designer, a market researcher, a company director, a celebrity shopper and a victim support volunteer. She has an MA in Creative Writing. Under the name Caroline Bond, she is the author of six novels, including two Radio 2 Book Club picks, *The Second Child* and *The Day We Left*. She lives in Leeds with her husband and one of her three children ... the other two having grown up and escaped.

Also by Rachel North

Happily Never After

HOW THE OTHER HALF DIE

RACHEL NORTH

CORVUS

Published in Great Britain in 2025 by Corvus,
an imprint of Atlantic Books Ltd.

1   3   5   7   9   8   6   4   2

A CIP catalogue record for this book is available from the British Library.

Paperback ISBN: 978 1 80546 057 2
E-book ISBN: 978 1 80546 058 9

Printed in Great Britain by CPI Group (UK) Ltd, Croydon CR0 4YY

Corvus
An imprint of Atlantic Books Ltd
Ormond House
26–27 Boswell Street
London
WC1N 3JZ

www.atlantic-books.co.uk

Product safety EU representative: Authorised Rep
Compliance Ltd., Ground Floor, 71 Lower Baggot Street,
Dublin, D02 P593, Ireland. www.arccompliance.com

MIX
Paper | Supporting
responsible forestry
FSC® C013604

FSC
www.fsc.org

With love to Suzie B

Chalice Family Tree

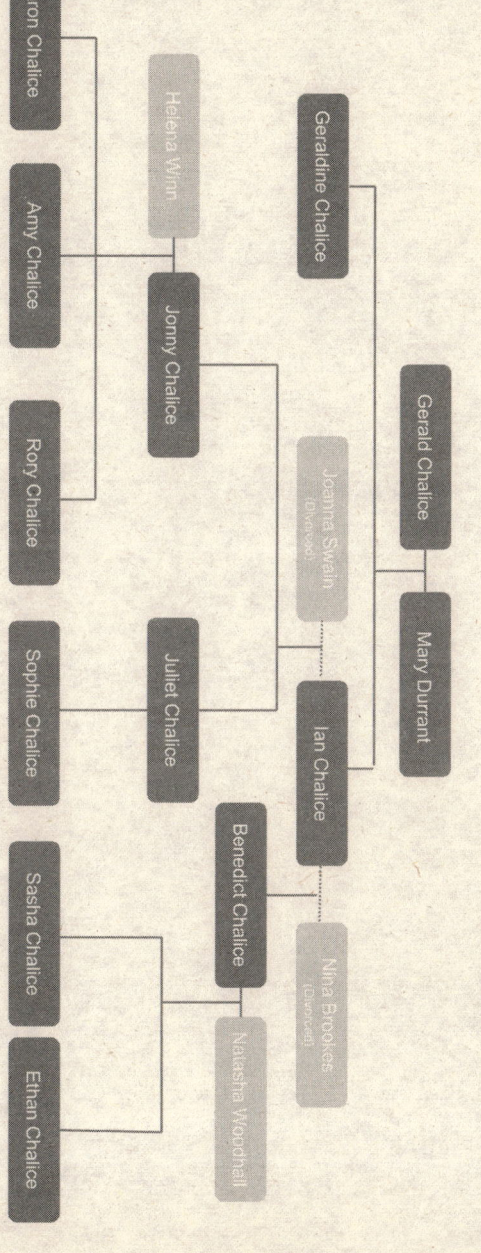

Prologue

One minute the sea breeze is ruffling my hair and the sun is hot on my face, the next I'm falling.

It's a fast, merciless descent. I flail, grasping at thin air, but there's nothing to hold on to. I manage one deep, desperate breath.

I hit the water. It feels like concrete. Bones snap. I black out.

When I come to, the sea is breathtakingly cold. Blood surges through my heart. I open my eyes. The salt water stings. I can see the eddies of foam where the waves are smashing into the island. Having survived the fall, I'm now in grave danger of having my brains dashed out on the rocks, but I'm powerless to resist. The sea throws me around like an enraged child with a damaged toy. My arm smashes into my face, breaking my nose. My legs are yanked in different directions. I'm being ripped apart. Mercifully, the assault doesn't last long. The pummelling and tumbling eases, then stops. The current carries my battered body away from the jagged shoreline. I've been granted a reprieve.

Free of the pull of the island, the sea's power is muted. It's a blessed relief after so much violence. I drift, suspended in a quiet, calm underwater world. I can see for miles. Shoals of silver fish tilt, turn and flash away from me. I sink further, moving slowly, twisting and twirling away from the light. My limbs waft, liquid and useless as the water darkens, deepening from sky blue to cobalt. My lungs begin to burn. The cold gnaws at my bones. I can't hold out much longer. As much as I know it will be the death of me, I start to panic. The water deepens from lapis to indigo. Even the fish have deserted me. There's no air, but the compulsion to breathe is overwhelming. I simply have to.

I gulp.

There's a burst of bubbles – my last breath leaving my body – and I'm done for.

The sea rushes in, forcing its way down my throat like a fist. It packs into my lungs, stretching them, filling up every last bit of space. I'm waterlogged. I plunge faster. Indigo turns to denim. Still I stare. The living, breathing, sunlit world is long gone. The sea is suffocating me.

My lungs burst and the panic melts away. My body relaxes and I accept my fate.

I'm grateful that it's over – all of it.

I'm no longer cold, no longer hurting, no longer fighting. I watch denim blue deepen to slate grey. The darkness beckons me. I briefly wonder whether I'll ever reach the bottom.

My last conscious thought is the realisation that I'll never know.

Five Weeks Earlier

Chapter 1

JONNY

It was Saturday night and Jonny was watching the Grand Prix highlights on his laptop, a tumbler of whisky in his hand, his kids asleep in bed and his wife upstairs with a book – all was well in his world. Well, perhaps not everything. Helena was still only speaking to him when the children were present, but at least she no longer looked like she wanted to murder him. Her jealousy was becoming a problem, again. She went through these cycles of insecurity, the start and end points of which were hard for Jonny to fathom. His recent spate of business trips obviously hadn't helped, but he suspected that her age and hormones were also playing a role in her mood swings. Helena's niggling suspicions were wearying and unjust. Jonny didn't have the time or the inclination for emotional entanglements outside of his marriage; there were already too many within it. But this was not Jonny's first rodeo. He and Helena had been together for seventeen years and during that time he'd learnt that sometimes you simply had to smile, buy flowers and hang on in there until things settled down. Jonny finished his drink, poured himself another one and watched Lando Norris try to chase down Max Verstappen.

During the ad break Jonny glanced at his inbox. In among the usual barrage of business correspondence and rubbish there was one email that caught his eye. It was from Geraldine, his aunt – who also happened to be head of the Chalice Group and, therefore, his boss. Time sent 23.29 p.m. Did the woman ever switch off? He opened it.

To: JC888@gmail.com
From: Geraldine.Chalice@thechalicegroup.com
Cc: Alice.Baxter@thechalicegroup.com
Subject: 70th Birthday

Dear Jonny,
I've decided to celebrate my birthday with family this year.
Propose we get together on Isola dei Delfini, 9th–12th May.
It's during termtime so I'm not expecting the children to come, or Helena for that matter. I assume she'll already have plans.

It will be an opportunity for us to talk about the future.

Alice will be in touch re arrangements.
Yours,
Geri

WTF. It wasn't an invitation, it was a summons. The arrogance was breathtaking, even by Geri's standards. So his aunt expected him to totally upend his schedule, at incredibly short notice, to accommodate a trip to Italy – *and* not bring his family with him. And the dig about Helena *having plans* was low. Geri simply couldn't understand that being a mother was a job, and a valuable one. That's what came of never having a family of your own. Geri had sacrificed everything for her career. It had worked. She had made it, and made it big, but there had been consequences – for herself and everyone around her. Jonny stared at the ashy logs in the wood burner – despite it being April it was still cold enough for a fire in rural Hertfordshire – and his thoughts drifted to Isola dei Delfini.

Rich as he was, Jonny was still cognisant of the fact that owning an island off the Amalfi coast was a privilege. His grandfather, Gerald Chalice, had bought Isola dei Delfini over thirty years ago; an overt 'fuck you' to everyone who had ever doubted or disrespected him, and there had been quite a few of them. A bald, fat baker from Scunthorpe was not your usual multimillionaire. Jonny had spent many happy holidays on the island as a teenager. He still visited as frequently as he could – often combining business and pleasure. Frigid investors had been known to thaw rapidly in the warm waters that surrounded their rocky little lump of paradise. But the thought of spending three days there with his aunt was not something he relished. In truth, Jonny couldn't remember the last time he'd been on the island with her. Geri rarely visited Isola dei Delfini; she was too busy, too uptight, too averse to enjoying the fruits of her considerable labour.

Jonny reread her terse message. Irritating as it was, it was interesting and timely. So fly to Italy, as demanded, he would – not because it was Geri's birthday, but because of her seemingly innocuous comment about *discussing the future*. It was the first time Geri had directly acknowledged that things were going to have to change – and that was huge. Jonny had been waiting long enough for her to realise that her reign couldn't last forever. She was sixty-nine, for Christ's sake. Sure, she was still as sharp as a pickaxe, but questions were being asked and that was never good, for any business. Jonny felt the long-suppressed anticipation that had lived in his stomach for years stir and stretch. Was Geri finally going to step aside after nearly twenty years as CEO of the Chalice Group? He switched off the Grand Prix and fired back an immediate 'yes'. It would do no harm to come in first and fast.

Chapter 2

JULIET

To: julietelizabethchalice2@gmail.com
From: Geraldine.Chalice@thechalicegroup.com
Cc: Alice.Baxter@thechalicegroup.com
Subject: 70th Birthday Celebration

Dear Juliet,
I hope you are well.

You'll be pleased to know that your absence is being felt around the business.

I wanted to let you know that I've decided to celebrate my birthday with family this year. I propose that we get together on Isola dei Delfini, 9th–12th May.

It will be an opportunity for us to talk about the future.

Alice will be in touch re arrangements. If you have special requirements for the baby, please let her know and she will sort.
Yours,
Geri

Juliet read the email from her aunt at 2.15 a.m. on the Sunday morning. It only served to add to her already considerable distress. Crying was the wrong word for what newborn babies did. What they did was bleat – frantically and insistently. At least, that's what her daughter, Sophie, had done, with little pause, since arriving in the world, red-faced and furious, four short but interminable weeks ago.

Juliet had known that becoming a mother would be a huge adjustment. Having been childless for so many years, she'd been nervous about the realities of actually having a baby. But she hadn't dreamt it would be like this. She'd never known tiredness like it. She felt disabled, undone, inadequate at even the basics of life, never mind motherhood. She also felt totally alone. Harry, her ex-husband, was gone. Christ, what would he think if he could see her now? Not that he would be thinking about her. He'd currently be tucked up in bed with Fleur, his two flaxen-haired children slumbering peacefully in a distant corner of their immaculately converted barn. Juliet still hated to do the maths on that particular equation. Three years to create a whole new life; complete with wife, kids and a dog – it was going some. Support from her own relatives? No, that wasn't an option either. The Chalices were not that sort of family. The only person who had expressed any interest or kindness had, somewhat surprisingly, been Jonny's wife, Helena. But as she'd said when she'd called round with an outfit for Sophie and a pamper hamper for Juliet – she understood how tough having a newborn was, having been there and got the milk-and-tear-stained T-shirt three times herself.

Juliet rocked the still-crying Sophie in her arms. The impossibility of Geri's request sat there in black on white, backlit for emphasis, on her phone screen. *Any special requirements for the baby*. Geri hadn't even used Sophie's name. It was too much. She was being asked to get dressed, brush her hair and clean her teeth, pack everything a baby travelling abroad for the first time would need, then drive to Heathrow, get on a plane and fly to Naples. From there she would have to navigate the airport with the three tonnes of baby paraphernalia and get a car to Positano, where she would be expected to board a boat that would, in theory, take her and her daughter across the sea to a lump of rock in the middle of the Med.

It was some sort of terrible joke. The timing of which was perfectly appalling. After nineteen years of non-stop dedication, after establishing beyond doubt that she, Juliet Chalice, was as good as, if not better than, both of her brothers, never mind the legion of middle and senior (mostly male) managers she'd worked for, then managed; after expanding the business into new, exciting areas and demonstrating that such expansion was worthwhile and hugely profitable, at precisely the point she was on the cusp of proving that her vision for the future of the Chalice Group was the correct one, in fact, the only one – Geri had decided to kick the hornets' nest.

Why couldn't Geri have waited a few measly months? Why call a family meeting to discuss the future now, when Juliet was away from the business on maternity leave, coping alone with a baby that simply refused to sleep?

Juliet set off on what felt like her thousandth circuit of the bedroom. Her suspicion that the timing was deliberate made her want to weep. At best it was unhelpful, at worst it was sabotage – at precisely the point Juliet was least able to defend herself. As Sophie cried and Juliet paced, her fears mushroomed. Perhaps, despite all Geri's protestations about the need for equality, despite her position as one of the most influential role models for women making it in the upper echelons of the corporate world, she was, deep down, unwilling to hand control of the business over to another woman? Fuck! Fuck! Fuck! Her struggle to become a mother had cost Juliet her marriage; now it looked like it was going to cost her even more. It was too much. Juliet gave in to her emotions and joined her daughter in sobbing. That was the only benefit of being a single parent – there was no one around to hear you scream.

When they were both howled out Juliet put an exhausted Sophie in her cot – a third of the way down, on her back, with the blanket no higher than her tiny shoulders so that there was no chance of it restricting her breathing, as instructed by the baby books – then she crept out of the nursery. She crossed the landing and went through to the wreck of her en suite. There she had the pee that she'd needed for the past three hours. As she sat on the toilet she gave herself a talking-to. Solutions, not problems – that was her forte. At least, it used to be. She might not be in control of her emotions, but she could be in control of her circumstances, and she needed to if she was going to make it to Isola dei Delfini in a month's time She took a deep breath, hoisted her knickers up over the ruche of skin where her toned stomach used to be, and flushed the toilet. Then she washed her hands and face, avoiding the mirror as she did so. Her postpartum struggles were, when you boiled it down to the basics, primarily a resource and expertise issue. What she needed was help. And given that her family were not going to provide it, she was going to have to go 'out of house' and buy it in. For the first time since Sophie's birth Juliet felt her synapses firing. Perhaps Geri's email had inadvertently done her a favour. It was amazing what a tight deadline could do to clarify your thinking.

Back in her room, Juliet grabbed her laptop and climbed into bed. She emailed a curt acceptance to Geri and set about googling nanny agencies.

Chapter 3

BENEDICT

Ben finally made it home at about 11.30 on Sunday morning.

First step – strip and shower. Next step – pop a couple of benzos and sleep. He set his alarm for 7.00 p.m., then on second thoughts changed it to 5.00 p.m. It had been another heavy weekend, but with the Nielson meeting at 9.00 a.m. the following morning he knew he'd need the evening to get his shit together. And people said he was irresponsible! Once in bed, Ben was comatose and snoring within seconds.

Only after he'd woken, eaten spaghetti hoops on toast – his go-to hangover cure – and updated his Insta did Ben check his emails. He was surprised to see his aunt's name on the list. Geri was very much of the 'why have a dog and bark yourself?' school of thought when it came to the business, and her terrier of choice, Ms Baxter, normally did most of the yapping.

To: Benedict.Chalice@yahoo.co.uk
From: Geraldine.Chalice@thechalicegroup.com
Cc: Alice.Baxter@thechalicegroup.com
Subject: 70th Birthday Celebration

Hey Ben,
Given that everyone keeps insisting that seventy is some sort
of a milestone – apart from you – I've decided to celebrate my
birthday properly this year. I'm sure you'll approve – I know
how you love a party.

I propose that the family get together on Isola dei Delfini,
9th–12th May. No kids, no spouses. Although Juliet will,
obviously, have to bring Sophie.

It will be good for us to have some time together.

It will also be an opportunity for us to talk about the future,
which I know is the subject of much frenzied speculation at
the moment.

Alice will be in touch re the arrangements.
Love,
Geri x

A trip to the island! Now there was a pleasant thought
on a wet Sunday evening.

It had been a while since Ben had been to Isola dei
Delfini. Work got in the way of so many things – use of the
beautiful house, the clifftop pool, and the private yacht
that provided easy and very stylish access to the many bars

of Capri and Positano, being just some of them. Ben wondered, with increasing frequency these days, whether it was all worth it. What was the point of being stinking rich if you didn't have the time to enjoy it? Maybe his father had had the right idea after all. Perhaps stepping off the treadmill mid-sprint, at the relatively young age of forty-seven, hadn't been a typically random act of Ian Chalice madness, but a rare example of sanity. Although from what Ben had gleaned from his father's bitter rants, it was more a case of being shoved off rather than stepping off, and by his big sister Geri, of all people! Sibling rivalry was obviously hard-wired into each generation of the Chalice family.

It was time that Ben had a little R & R at the family's Italian hideaway. His bloody brother was there all the fucking time. Jonny seemed to view Isola dei Delfini as his own private retreat. If it wasn't holidays with Helena and the kids, it was business trips with potential investors or one of his many 'strategy sessions' with his team. Why such meetings needed to take place in the middle of the Med was anyone's guess. Ben felt so energised by his resentment that he hauled himself off the sofa and went to get dressed. As he pulled on a pair of linen trousers and a jumper he reflected on how Jonny always managed to get more than his fair share – of everything. Even if Jonny hadn't been his brother . . . well, half-brother . . . Ben could quite easily have hated the complacent prick.

The thought of Jonny on holiday with his family stung. Ben hadn't seen his own children, Sasha and Ethan, for over a month. It wasn't for the want of trying – although, come to think of it, he hadn't responded to the most recent email from his solicitor yet. He'd do that tomorrow, after the Nielson meeting. His own kids, and he was reduced to haggling like some cash-strapped junkie for whatever his dealer was prepared to part with. A wave of self-pity washed over Ben. He looked around his stylish, sound-proofed, silent apartment and yearned for the mess and noise of the house in Fulham. The house that he was still paying for, but wasn't permitted to set foot inside without prior permission, and even then Natasha only allowed him as far as the hall. Sensing the emptiness of a long evening ahead, Ben briefly considered calling Charlie or Khalil and meeting them in the Mayfair, but he resisted the urge. See? Concrete proof that he was behaving himself, and there wasn't even anyone looking.

Instead of heading out Ben wandered into the kitchen and opened the fridge. Savoury or sweet? Krystyna, his housekeeper, knew what snacks he liked and kept the shelves stocked accordingly. Feeling a craving for sweetness, he went for the pack of Belgian chocolate eclairs. He ate the first where he stood, musing on what his favourite hag was really up to.

Geri had been dangling the Chalice crown in front of them for years, assessing just how high each of them was prepared to jump to snatch it, but this was new. Normally Geri liked to keep them apart while she made them dance. She ran them like a stable of mistresses, rationing her attention and her patronage, sowing seeds of mistrust by casually mentioning time spent with one or a decision influenced by another. Divide and rule – it was a strategy that had worked well in the past. That Ben was the 'mistress' who got the most attention was precious to him, and not only because it put Jonny and Juliet's noses out of joint. Ben genuinely had a soft spot for Geri. Odd as it obviously seemed to his siblings, and to everyone else, the two of them had a connection that went beyond business and blood. In truth Ben wasn't one hundred per cent sure what Geri's fondness for him was based on, but he was happy to roll with it. It was nice to have someone who liked him. But gathering them all together on the island was a different tactic – more risky and much more likely to result in open warfare. Maybe Geri really was planning her succession. Ben prised another eclair out of the box and took a bite. The other two would be wetting themselves at the prospect of her finally making a decision. They'd been vying with each other to become Geri's successor for years. Or perhaps the old witch was simply bored. Either way, it would be interesting, and it was always fun to run a little interference.

Eclair demolished, Ben licked his fingers and picked up his phone. He found an old shot of himself silhouetted against the sunset on the terrace at Mira Capri and typed, *Heading back to my spiritual home in a few weeks' time. Can't wait. Bring it on!* Then he texted Geri a thumbs-up.

Chapter 4

ALICE

The Chalice siblings were so predictable it was almost funny. Jonny coming in first, fast and formal, with Juliet close on his heels a few hours later followed, eventually, by Ben – way off the pace, as per usual. But at least they'd all confirmed that they would be attending Geri's birthday celebrations. It was game on.

Alice kept her own email to Geri brief and purely professional, which was exactly the way her boss preferred things.

To: Geraldine.Chalice@thechalicegroup.com
From: Alice.Baxter@thechalicegroup.com
Subject: 70th Birthday Celebration

All confirmed, as of 20.19 p.m. on Sunday.

Will copy you in once itineraries are finalised.

See you tomorrow.
Alice

It was as much a part of Alice's job to know what was going on within the family and to keep Geri apprised of it, as it was for her to run Geri's office and her diary. It was such deftness, diligence and discretion that had secured her a job with the company in the first place. Not her current role, of course. Hell no, it had taken Alice three years to claw her way up through the interminable strata of the Chalice Group head office hierarchy to get close to the seat of power. Another eight months before she got to cross the polished parquet of the executive floor into the inner sanctum of Geri Chalice's office. Add a year, and finally she'd made it. She was Geraldine Chalice's PA. On her way up Alice had made it her business to find out as much as she could about the Chalices – past and present.

As with all 'great' dynasties, it was a rags-to-riches tale. The Chalice empire began with a small bakery called the Bread Basket that opened near the market in Scunthorpe on Monday, 13 March 1960. Gerald Chalice, Geri's father, made the loaves and Mary, his wife, ran the counter. But from the outset Gerald didn't really want to make bread, what he wanted to make was money. So when his father, unexpectedly and somewhat fortuitously, died at the age of forty-five, Gerald sold his parents' house, moved his mother into the flat above the shop and invested the proceeds of the sale in another shop. With the profits from the Bread Basket and the new bakery he then bought another shop. And so on . . . and so on. The acquisition of a catering supplier four years later marked Gerald's transition from baker to businessman, and he never looked back. Nor did he ever stand still. His business model was simple and very effective: low production costs, high margins and healthy profits on unhealthy products, the majority of which he ploughed back into his rapidly growing business. Gerald's later, much-repeated claim – that he never borrowed a penny in his life – wasn't strictly true, but it wasn't far off. Gerald was all about keeping control financially as well as strategically. That the Chalice Group was still family-owned was testament to the power of that mantra.

As planned, Gerald made his first million by the time he was thirty-five, his second before he turned forty. He stopped counting the million milestones after that, but he never stopped striving for more. Gerald's success transformed his and Mary's lives. Scunthorpe became little more than an origin story. The couple were living in a huge house, with staff, in Holland Park by the time they had their children. Geraldine was born first, followed two years later by Ian. The children grew up surrounded by wealth and privilege, but dominated by their father. He invested in a private education for both of them – up to the age of eighteen. There would be, Gerald knew, benefits from eradicating the last traces of his children's northern roots and in them picking up some well-off, well-connected London friends, but eighteen was the cut-off in terms of 'book learning'. Gerald certainly didn't believe in university; he thought it 'fostered idleness and odd ideas'. Instead, first Geraldine then Ian joined the family firm on the first Monday after they finished sixth form.

By then the business had expanded massively, to encompass an extensive retail operation, a chain of in-store bakeries in supermarkets, a very lucrative catering supplies network and some own-label contracts.

But although the Chalices' wealth was now eye-watering and the circles they moved in unrecognisable compared to their 'humble' beginnings, Gerald still held onto some very traditional values – which was where the trouble began.

By all accounts – and there were still stories doing the rounds within the business even when Alice joined – Gerald's decision to nominate Ian as his heir, rather than Geraldine, poisoned the family well from the beginning. According to legend, Geri always had the better brain. Her maturity, application and business acumen trumped her younger brother's hands down, but she lacked one essential attribute – she wasn't a man. Years of rivalry and rancour ensued, with the siblings vying for Gerald's attention and endorsement. Tensions came to a head when Gerald finally retired after forty-five years in charge – and made Ian CEO. The business held its collective breath, but to everyone's surprise feisty, fierce, formidable Geraldine appeared to accept her father's decision. She carried on working as hard as ever and even more effectively. It was under Geri's direction that the business ramped up its own-label division. A division that went on to deliver huge profits for the Chalice Group.

That Geraldine was also working equally hard on unseating her brother only became apparent five years later when, in a swift, effective and some would say brutal coup, the Board turned against Ian and he was out on his ear. The bitter legal battles and Ian's very public journey from business tycoon to rich waster in the years that followed made the Chalice family a favourite with the press, gutter and financial, but through it all

Geraldine pushed the business and the bottom line to new heights.

The one surprise was that Geraldine's feud with her brother did not extend to his children. All three of them joined the business and rose through the ranks – in at least two cases to the Board – in double-quick time. Some saw this as noble of Geraldine, a sign that she didn't lay the 'sins of the father' at the feet of his offspring. Others said it was a cruel tactic to take away not only the business from her brother, but his children as well.

Well, they weren't children any more.

Geri's decision to make Jonny, Juliet and Ben her heirs did, obviously, carry the risk of history repeating itself, but as many insiders told Alice when she started work at head office, family businesses were different; the politics far more personal, the rivalries more intense and the risks and rewards so much higher.

That Alice was being trusted to play a role in this next chapter of the Chalice family saga was exciting. She had done her homework, she knew the players and, most importantly, she was privy to the thoughts and wishes of Geri.

What she was going to do with that trust they were all about to find out.

Chapter 5

GERI

Geri read Alice's email before her evening swim. On seeing that they'd all confirmed she felt little, other than glad that things were finally in motion. Geri was used to people doing as she asked.

She walked down the stairs to the basement. The lift had not been her idea, but the pool was. She dropped her robe on the side, dived in and began powering up and down. The only sounds were her own breathing and the small splash as she executed her tumble turns. Geri swam her sixty-nine lengths in just over an hour. She added a length every birthday. It was a good way of keeping her stamina up.

How did she stay so fit in mind and body?

It was simple – commitment. Geri always fully committed to everything she did. You had to, if you wanted to stay on top. A healthy eating regime, and regular exercise, including her swimming, daily yoga and very little downtime, took care of her body. As to her mind, well, that was as sharp as ever. Running a business worth an estimated two billion tended to be all the workout your brain cells needed. It was undeniable that ageism was rife, in business as in life,

24

especially with regard to women, but Geri had no intention of falling victim to it. She'd spent a lifetime building up her reputation and her profile precisely for this reason. Power and wealth were the ultimate protection and she had accrued a lot of both. But with each passing birthday Geri had felt the spectre of other people's prejudices drawing nearer. There was the increasing interest in her 'future' every time she gave an interview, the whispers among their commercial partners, the occasional rumour in the City that she was going to step down at the next AGM, or perhaps the one after that – the vultures were most definitely circling. Including the ones in her own family. Of course, her nephews and niece had a massive vested interest in her plans. They, and their offspring, were her heirs. She could almost smell the desperation to see her retire emanating from them like BO. No amount of expensive cologne could mask it. Why else had they all agreed to drop everything and come to Isola dei Delfini at her request? They weren't coming to celebrate her birthday, they were coming to claim their birthright. The irony that she'd chosen not to have children so that she could focus on the business, only to have to hand it back to one of her brother's line, was not lost on Geri.

Unsettled by the ghost of past decisions and the spectre of impending choices, Geri towelled off and went through to her yoga studio. She slipped on some leggings and a vest and settled into Padmasana. Eyes closed, she began her Bahya Pranayama breathing. Geri's Sankalpa was difficult, but clear. If it was the last thing she did as CEO, she was going to ensure that the next generation of the Chalice family got what they deserved.

Day One

Chapter 6

BENEDICT

Ben wasn't the least bit surprised when Jonny and Juliet decided to come down to meet Geri with him. The thought of him being the one to welcome her to the island was obviously unacceptable to them. And so it began, the jostling for the spotlight.

They walked down to the helipad in single file. Once they reached the terrace they instinctively arranged themselves by age order along the low wall and looked out at the distant horizon. Ben wondered, not for the first time, where Juliet's freakish height came from. Perhaps Geri would be wise to ask for DNA tests on all of them before she chose her successor. Although given their father's reputation, perhaps it would be safer to leave that old dog sleeping – for all their sakes. Watching Jonny and Juliet standing together, leaving a gap between them and him, brought back some uncomfortable childhood memories for Ben. He'd known from being very young that there was no love lost between his half-brother and sister, but that regardless of their personal animosity they would always put up a united front when confronted by him. It had been that way since they first met. To be fair, it had, somewhat inauspiciously, been on the day that Jonny and Juliet buried their mother, but that had hardly been Ben's fault. As a trusting ten-year-old, how was he supposed to know that their father would use the occasion of his ex-wife's death to try to reintegrate himself, and Ben, back into the family? It had, understandably, been a tricky few hours all round, so when Ben had seen his grief-ravaged but still beautiful eighteen-year-old half-sister finally look at him and approach, bearing a plate of much-needed food, his little heart had lifted. Only to be crushed. Juliet had set the plate down on the table, stood over him and without any preamble whatsoever asked, 'Why are you called Benedict?' Ben didn't know, so he'd politely and simply replied, 'I don't know. Why are you called Juliet?' Juliet had smiled, with zero warmth, and said, 'Our mother chose mine and Jonny's names specially. We're both J's because she was called Joanna. She did it so that we would always be connected whatever happened.' She'd swallowed. Ben remembered it as a painful sound. Then she'd said, 'And what happened was, your father left her and us.' And with that she'd walked back to Jonny, her real brother, and not looked at or spoken to Ben again for the rest of the day.

That powerful need to put him in his place had dominated their relationship ever since.

The same silence surrounded them now. There was no asking after each other's kids, no small talk about their journeys, no chat about their current projects and absolutely zero speculation about Geri's plans. But Ben knew that it was what was *not* said that mattered most when it came to his siblings. That neither of them considered Ben a contender was no secret; in their eyes, he was an irrelevance. Their much higher-profile roles within the Group and their seats on the Board bolstered them in their smug complacency. Both of them had had stellar trajectories within the business.

After stints working on the Advertising and Marketing side of the business Jonny had, astutely, moved over into Finance where he was now a director, which was as close to God as you could get in many people's eyes. Not Ben's, obviously. Because despite his Savile Row suits, his full head of silver-tinged hair and his strong jaw, what was Jonny really other than a broker? Well, sharp, greedy, self-obsessed bastards were ten a penny in the City. Why would Geri choose him to head up the organisation that she had poured her life and soul into? Jonny had never cared about the business really, all he was interested in was the money.

No, in Ben's humble opinion, it was Juliet the Giantess who was Geri's natural successor.

Juliet was, and had always been, a slave to the company. She'd worked her way up from the actual shop floor, learning the ropes the old way. Geri's way. And his aunt must have been impressed. Why else would she have entrusted Juliet with the core bakery business at the tender age of twenty-six and put her in charge of Acquisitions by the time she was thirty? Acquisitions was known as the *future of the company* division internally. Under Juliet's stewardship, and with Geri's blessing, the acquisitions team had made real inroads into precisely Ben's wheelhouse – health and well-being. The Chalice Group now owned a number of branded spa hotels, a large chain of gyms, and a successful yoga and meditation franchise, and had recently launched a very lucrative well-woman product range. Not too shabby for a company whose roots lay in churning out cheap, unhealthy fast food to the masses. Oh, how Ben would have loved Juliet's gig. But no. When he'd joined the business he'd been stuck in the Research division, and he'd never left. He'd moved no further than one floor up, in the same building, in the past eight years. Sure, Geri had appointed him Head of Consumer Insight after he'd moaned about his lack of progression and she'd given him a bigger office, but he wasn't even a full director. It sucked.

Why shouldn't he be in with a shout? Long shots provided the best returns. He was younger than Jonny or Juliet, he understood the modern world that the Chalice Group now operated in and he was the only one who appreciated the power of social media in global brand-building. He had relationships with some of the best digital houses and links with the most successful influencers. If Geri really wanted to appoint someone who could lead the Group not just into the next decade, but into the 2040s and beyond, then he was her best option.

Was he trying to convince himself? Yes, of course he was, but he needed to, no other bugger was going to.

Ben sensed Jonny looking at his Breitling, as impatient as ever. Juliet was also getting restless. She was shifting from foot to foot and sighing, very audibly.

'I thought you said she'd be here by 5.00 p.m.,' Jonny huffed.

Ben stretched and yawned, an OTT gesture specifically designed to irritate his brother. 'I did.'

'Well, it's quarter past. I'm not standing around here like a tool for much longer, if we don't how long she's going to be—'

Ben interrupted Jonny – it was another thing that his brother hated. 'Things to do, bro?'

Jonny hesitated. 'No. Not really.' That was unlikely. Jonny always had something on the boil. 'Can't you check?' he snapped.

Ben refused to rise to his rudeness. 'I could, but Alice's message, all of ten minutes ago, gave their ETA as 17.00.' She'd actually said 17.30, but what was the point of having more information than the competition unless you used it – even it was for the petty entertainment of ticking off your rivals; sorry, siblings.

Jonny glanced at his watch again, but he didn't move. Being absent from the line-up would look bad. To signal his displeasure he started pacing up and down the terrace. Juliet continued to shuffle on the spot, her eyes glued to her phone. Her silent agitation was as oppressive as Jonny's pissed-off restlessness. And the pair of them wondered why he avoided them as much as was physically possible. Given there was time to kill, Ben decided to go fishing – metaphorically, not literally, obviously. 'What do you two make of all this, then?'

'What do you mean?' Jonny.

'This.' Ben waved his arms around to encompass them, the island and Geri's imminent arrival. 'Her sudden desire to "celebrate"' – he made air quotes with his fingers – 'her birthday with family.'

Jonny stared at him, his impatience shading into irritation. 'As you know full well, it must be about succession planning.'

Ben grinned. 'Succession planning. Is that what we're calling it?'

33

Juliet finally pitched in. 'I don't think we should be calling "it" anything. Trying to second-guess Geri is like trying to predict the weather – only much more difficult.' It was on the tip of Ben's tongue to point out that with any decent weather app it was dead easy to know whether you were going to have sunshine or a storm, but he didn't get the chance.

Jonny got in first, as he so often did. 'Oh, come off it, Juliet. Let's not pretend. The only reason we've all made this trip is to finally get some clarity about what she's planning. God knows it's about time. Why she's decided to do it here, I don't know. I can't remember the last time she set foot on Isola dei Delfini.'

It was too good an opportunity for Ben to miss. 'That could be because you're always in residence.'

'Do you have to be such a dick?' Jonny snapped.

'Me?' Ben's laughter drifted out to sea and was quickly lost. 'It's not me who's the big dick around here.'

'Can you two please pack it in? Look. She's here.' Juliet pointed to the horizon and there, sure enough, was a small black dot that was growing bigger by the second.

As the helicopter closed in on the island, the throaty *tack tack* of the blades filled Ben's ears. Soon the trees were thrashing back and forth and full of dust. There was nothing understated about arriving by chopper. Ben slipped on his shades, all the better to watch the landing. He'd seen helicopters land on Isola dei Delfini before, but each time it was impressive. The landing pad was small and the jagged rock face unforgiving. Any descent had to be pinpoint accurate. Geri's helicopter slowed, turned sideways and manoeuvred into position. The swirl of debris increased. The chopper hovered fatly for a couple of seconds then sank heavily from the sky. There was a point when it looked like the pilot had misjudged the landing and flown too close to the cliff, but after a brief ungainly wobble it touched down perfectly, bang in the centre of the small landing pad. Then, instead of slowing, the roar of the blades appeared to speed up and get louder. Ben could feel the power surging through them. For a second or two, it looked as if the force was going to pull the helicopter off the small concrete ledge into the sea. But gradually they lost momentum until they finally came to a complete stop. The engine died. Everything settled: the dust, the noise, the turbulence. The pilot removed their headphones, unhooked the door and climbed out. Their aviator sunglasses glinted in the late afternoon sun as they looked briefly up at the terrace. Then they set off, striding up the steps two at a time.

It was time to say hello to Geraldine Chalice, their aunt and current CEO of the Chalice Group. The woman who had run the company, impressively and ruthlessly, since ousting her elder brother, their father, twenty years ago. A woman with huge power and influence and a personal wealth that ran into the tens of millions. A woman with no children of her own. A woman who, contrary to her appearance and energy levels, was about to turn seventy. And, most importantly, the woman who held their future in her tight, some might say choking, grip.

Chapter 7

GERI

Geri got a serious buzz out of flying. The control, the freedom, the perspective. Flying allowed you see the whole picture, the adjacencies, the connections and the distances between places and people, and Geri liked to view things in their entirety. Flying was also a skill, an impressive one. It required mental acuity, knowledge, astute judgement. To do it well you had to monitor a myriad of ever-changing conditions and master a very powerful machine. The slightest lapse in concentration could easily result in you killing yourself and everyone travelling with you.

People were always shocked to discover that Geri had her pilot's licence and that she used it. And Geri liked nothing better than surprising people. Her capacity to confound expectations had been integral in helping her to transform a successful retail and food services business into a multi-million, multicountry food and lifestyle empire.

There was also, she was more reluctant to admit, the image factor. A self-piloted helicopter, a private island, the town house in Chelsea, the property on St Barts and the apartment in New York; they were the necessary assets of a dynasty. As much as Geri was personally indifferent to such status symbols, she knew that they were important to the Chalice brand – Ben didn't talk shit all the time. Even the uber-rich needed to flaunt their power, if they wanted to keep hold of it.

Geri was relieved that she'd nailed the landing. She'd had to concentrate hard on the approach. The crosswinds and the presence of a wall of sheer rock behind the awkwardly positioned landing pad made for a tricky descent. Isola dei Delfini might look idyllic, but to held dangers for the ill-prepared. It was also an age since she'd last visited. She simply didn't have the space in the diary and . . . ? Well, the 'and' was more complicated. Family matters often were. Emotions, in Geri's experience, took an inordinate amount of energy, and although she was ridiculously cash-rich she was extraordinarily time-poor. Which was why she'd made the considerable effort and investment in carving out the time from her busy schedule for this trip. You could bury a whole host of emotions – disappointment, resentment, shame, anger – but that didn't necessarily mean they died.

It was only after she'd switched off the engine that Geri noticed her audience. They were lined up on the terrace like a set of mismatched Russian dolls. Jonny, Juliet and Ben, her closest relatives and the future of the Chalice Group.

Mismatched. It was a tag that aptly described her nephews and niece. The first time Geri ever saw the siblings together she knew there was never going to be an easy or harmonious dynamic between them. And once again the blame for that could be laid fairly and squarely at Ian's door. Who, in their right mind, decides that their ex-wife's funeral is *the* ideal moment to introduce their new son to the kids from their previous marriage? At the time, Geri remembered being relieved that Ian hadn't gone the whole hog and brought Nina, his new wife, along as well. As Ben told the story, years later, he'd been totally unaware that it was a funeral. Ian had apparently told him that he was going to a very serious grown-ups' party and that if he was really good then he might get a slice of chocolate cake, and the chance to meet his big half-brother and sister. What the hell had Ian been thinking? The best way he could have paid his respects to Joanna would have been to stay away. But no, he rocked up with a wide-eyed, suited and booted ten-year-old Ben in tow and everyone had been too shocked and embarrassed to say anything – to his face, at least.

Jonny, to his credit, had handled his father's appearance and the day itself with a maturity well in advance of his twenty-two years. He'd been dry-eyed and remarkably in control throughout. His eulogy had papered over Joanna's mental health challenges and the cruel nature of her death with real skill. He even managed to include one short, polite reference to Ian, which must have been a last-minute addition. Juliet, who was already reeling from her mother's death, had coped less well. Geri had never seen anyone cry so much or so steadily at a funeral. Although to her credit, after the service, when they returned to the hotel for refreshments, Geri had spotted an interaction that had stayed with her for years afterwards.

While Geri was circulating, as one must at these sort of events, she'd spotted Ben sitting alone and miserable at one of the tables. It looked as if he hadn't moved since his father had abandoned him to go and speak to some of his friends in the bar. Even way back then, there was something about Ben that had made Geri feel protective. She'd been about to excuse herself and go to his rescue when she caught sight of Juliet. She was standing with Jonny and some other people across the other side of the room, but she was staring at her half-brother. Given her niece's volatile state Geri had been concerned. But she'd had no need. Because after a moment Juliet stepped away from the group. She walked over to the funeral tea, loaded up a plate and carried it over to Ben. The look of desperate delight on Ben's face when Juliet silently set her peace offering down in front of him had been touching. *Step, blended, nuclear* – all families were complex, whatever their composition.

See, this was what happened when they got together away from work; it tilled the soil covering the memories and emotions that Geri tried so hard to ignore. And this visit there was a new ingredient in the mix – fear. Not of her nephews and niece – Geri wasn't afraid of anything or anyone – but *for* them.

Chapter 8

ALICE

No matter how often Alice flew with Geri, she was always relieved when they were back on solid ground. It wasn't anything to do with her boss's skill as a pilot – in that, as with so many other areas of life, Geri was highly proficient – it was a question of size. Private jets and helicopters, for all their kudos, were small, and small did not equate to safe in Alice's mind. Added to which, the landing pad on Isola dei Delfini was little more than a shelf tacked onto the side of a sheer cliff. Alice's shredded nerves were going to take a while to settle after that knife-edge landing. Hence she took her time undoing her harness – even the restraints in a helicopter were designed to make you think about crashing. Not so Geri. She was, as always, straight on to the next thing. She unhooked her belt, removed her headphones and was off without a backward glance. Alice watched her go, content to be left with the luggage and her shifting stomach. Besides, she had no desire to be present for the welcoming ceremony that Ben had arranged. Nor was she needed. She was unimportant within the Chalice universe – in the opinion of Jonny, Juliet and Ben.

The flight and the precarious landing weren't the only things making Alice feel on edge. As much as she'd prepared for this moment, being on the island was unsettling. The mainland might be only five or six miles away, but Isola dei Delfini felt far more remote than that. Its isolation was, and always had been, an integral part of its appeal.

A loud bang on the side window nearly brought the contents of Alice's stomach back up. She fumbled with the tricky door latch and only managed to release it after a few attempts. Flustered was the last thing she wanted to be seen to be. Standing next to the helicopter was a young man. He wasn't tall, but what he lacked in height he made up for in muscle. He looked like a boxer: wiry, strong and poised. He had wavy black hair, worn long and tied back, steady dark eyes and an impressive array of tattoos. As Alice tried to calm her jitters he stood placidly by, awaiting her instructions. This must be Luca, Carla's nephew. Boat hand, porter, all-round shifter and fixer for the next few days. He'd been hired, at very short notice, on Carla's recommendation, after the regular guy cried off. To be fair, a heart attack was a reasonable excuse, but it had been one more problem for Alice to solve.

'You want me to take the bags?'

So Luca wasn't one for chit-chat. That was fine with Alice. 'Yes, please. That would be a help.'

Together they pulled Geri and Alice's luggage out of the hold. The ratio was 10:1. Although Geri wasn't much of a clothes shopper, she knew the role of appearance in influencing people and perceptions. Power dressing might no longer rely on designer suits and shoulder pads, but what you wore and what it cost did still matter, especially if you were a woman. Alice suspected that Geri had planned her wardrobe for this weekend as meticulously as she did everything. Simple, deceptively casual quality was Geri's style. She was living proof that there was a tangible difference between a pair of £500 white linen trousers and a £50 pair. Geri had, of course, also brought her working life with her: laptops, files, the two satellite phones that she'd had Alice source – connectivity could still be a problem on the island and Geri simply could not tolerate being off-grid for a second. The press comparisons with Margaret Thatcher were no exaggeration – four to five hours' sleep per night were her maximum. Plus there were the two crates of champagne and the hamper of expensive goodies that needed hauling up to the House. Alice instructed Luca to take the tech first, then come back for Geri's personal luggage, then the food and wine. Knowing Geri's priorities was a big part of Alice's job. On Luca's third trip she accompanied him up to the House. She carried her own bag.

At first glance the main residence on Isola dei Delfini looked modest, but looks could be, and in this instance were, deceptive. Low-key by name and frontage, the House kept its glories hidden from anyone not invited across the threshold. The property, along with the island on which it nestled, had been owned by a series of rich, famous men who obviously valued their privacy highly – to the tune of millions. It had originally been owned by an exiled Russian emigré who went bankrupt. He sold it to Enzo Barone, one of the first big stars of motor racing, in the 1940s. Barone apparently sank all his winnings, and a good chunk of his inheritance, into transforming the island. The end result was a stylish, Moroccan-inspired enclave created for the sole purpose of entertaining his famous, glamorous friends. After his death in a car crash the island had been bought by another style icon, Gore Vidal. During his tenure Jackie Onassis and Nureyev were apparently regular visitors, as attested to by the black-and-white photographs that lined the staircase. It was this aristocracy of wealth and celebrity that Gerald Chalice had bought into when he acquired it, as a present to himself, on his sixtieth birthday. (At the time Gerald bought it, the island was actually owned by a hedge fund, but that detail didn't quite fit the legend so it tended to be skirted over.) The Chalice family had been using Isola dei Delfini's class and style to seduce people ever since.

Hence, as Alice stood in the large entrance lobby and looked through the arches at the large, airy reception rooms beyond, she saw almost exactly what Barone and Vidal's famous guests would have seen all those years ago. Namely, thousands of dark-blue, iridescent Moroccan tiles, acres of art deco glass and much of the original furniture, tastefully augmented with touches of modern luxury. The House now boasted lots of sympathetically installed and disguised mod cons: power showers alongside the original roll-top baths; a temperature-controlled larder; a screening room, etc., etc. Nineteen-forties and fifties glamour was all well and good, but no one could be expected to holiday without decent water pressure and air con. And then there was the icing on the top of this amazing wedding cake, because as lovely as the accommodation was, it was the views that took your breath away. The Le Corbusier-designed terrace faced Capri, the bedrooms looked out across Positano and at the back of the House there was nothing but mile upon mile of the sun-tipped Mediterranean.

Having distributed the luggage to the appropriate rooms as directed, Luca melted away down the narrow staircase that led to the kitchen, leaving Alice alone. All she could hear was the sea, all she could feel was the breeze blowing through the House, all she could smell was the scent of the lilies in the huge glass vase on the intricately inlaid table and all she could see was herself, reflected in the massive, ornate mirror that dominated the hallway. For a glorious moment it was as if everyone else had been vaporised. But that fantasy was soon shattered by the sound of a door opening and closing upstairs and footsteps on the marble staircase. The House was not a place that was easy to creep around. Alice knew by the tread that it was Juliet. Jonny and Ben both made a lot more noise.

She appeared at the head of the stairs, saw Alice and shouted, 'Alice! A word.'

Alice, who'd had no intention of moving, suddenly felt the urge to be somewhere, anywhere else. It was a familiar feeling whenever she encountered the next generation of Chalices, although to be fair Juliet wasn't the worst. But Alice could tell by her expression that there was an issue. When wasn't there, with this lot? High standards or low tolerance – it was all a matter of perspective. Alice hadn't seen Juliet in person since the birth of her daughter. There had, however, been plenty of correspondence. She smiled. 'Juliet. It's lovely to see you.' They didn't shake hands or hug or air-kiss. There wasn't a physical interaction eti-quette for their type of 'relationship'. Technically Alice was only at Geri's beck and call, but the siblings obviously saw it differently. A family-owned and run business of the size and success of the Chalice Group was totally unlike normal business environments – there were the hidden agendas, far more personal and the jockeying for position more intense. 'Is everything to your satisfaction?' It should be. Juliet had sent a very long list of requirements in advance of the trip and every single item on that list, from the top-of-the-range cot to the Brezza baby-milk preparation machine, had been secured, shipped and installed as per Juliet's instructions.

'Yes,' Juliet said, but then she hesitated. 'It's just . . . I'd assumed I'd be staying in the Cottage . . . with Sophie,' she clarified.

Alice apologised immediately. It was always best, even when it was unwarranted, with the Chalice siblings. 'My apologies if I didn't make that clear in my correspondence, but Geri' – it was also good to use the 'key that opened all doors' early on in any and every situation – 'asked me to have a room prepared for you in the House. She wanted you all to be together.' That was true, but it wasn't the whole truth.

'Ah.' Juliet looked uncertain. This was new. Juliet was never uncertain, about anything. Alice found herself warming to her, ever so slightly. Sophie was only nine weeks old. Juliet must still be getting over the birth. Travelling a thousand miles to an island in the middle of the Med couldn't have been part of the plan for her maternity leave. And separating a new mother from her baby was a strange thing to do, cruel even. But Geri had been clear – they must all stay in the main house, and what Geri wanted, Geri got. Then Juliet ruined the moment by saying, 'Yes, I suppose it makes sense. We do have a lot to discuss over the coming days.' So Juliet would rather be close to the seat of power than with her own child. Motherhood had obviously not changed her one iota.

'Is there anything else I can help you with? I'm happy to go and check that everything is in order at the Cottage, if you would like me to,' Alice toadied.

'No. No, that won't be necessary. Lena has got Sophie settled.' Of course, the child would be farmed out to staff, as most things were by the Chalices. 'I'm on my way there now.' Still Juliet didn't move, so Alice did. As she walked away Juliet added, 'Besides, it'll be a treat to get an uninterrupted night's sleep.' Alice was glad that she had her back to Juliet at this point. It meant she could avoid having to make the fished-for sympathetic response. As much as Alice had been around the wealth and entitlement of the Chalices for a while now, she still struggled to get her head around how differently the other half lived.

Chapter 9

JONNY

Jonny's phone pinged. It was a text from Alice, reminding him to be in the dining room **no later than 7.30 p.m.** It pissed Jonny off being ordered around in his own home, by his aunt's PA. Okay, the island and everything on it, was technically owned by the company, but it was his as much as anyone's – beside Geri, of course.

When Jonny came to Isola dei Delfini he was normally able to relax, be himself, shake off the constraints of life in London. He usually did what he liked, when he liked. That was a huge part of its appeal. But this visit he felt anything but relaxed. What he felt was tense. Geri's presence and her cryptic clues about who was going to succeed her were uppermost in his mind. Jonny was fully aware that Juliet was never going to let him become CEO without a fight, nor was Geri going to give it to him without making him sing for his supper first. It might look like a holiday, but this was, most definitely, a work trip; possibly the most important one of his career. And on top of that he had Helena to worry about.

Jonny had decided to ask Helena to come along as a peace offering. He knew that she had mixed feelings about

Isola dei Delfini. For her it was both the location of many happy family holidays and somewhere he withdrew to, leaving her alone and resentful. Jonny had worried that she might use his request as another opportunity to punish him, but to his surprise she'd agreed to come without much discussion. He'd been reassured to see how willingly she'd rejigged her schedule and sorted out cover for the kids. Her mother was coming to stay for a few days. She'd also gone shopping for some new clothes for the trip. All of which he took as indicators that her feelings towards him were thawing. Actions, not words, that's what his darling wife had demanded of him. Defying Geri and bringing Helena along for the ride would hopefully go some way to proving that he was invested in their marriage, and in her. The sun, the pool, Carla's excellent, if simple, cooking, and his plan for a rather special early celebration of their fifteenth wedding anniversary the following day would all help to get them back onto the same page. Jonny needed a wife who supported him. As CEO he would need that support to be unequivocal.

He tapped on the bathroom door. Courtesy, that was another thing Jonny was working on, at Helena's request. He heard her muted 'Come in', and opened the door. She was leaning over the sink, putting the finishing touches to her make-up. Jonny guessed that the dress was new. It clung to her curves nicely. The signs that hostilities were coming to an end were stacking up. 'You look great.' Helena could still look top-notch, when she tried. She met his eyes in the mirror, questioning his interruption. 'We've been summoned by her royal highness.'

'Geri?'

'No, Alice, the ferocious mouse.' Helena turned her face one way then the other, checking her reflection in the mirror. 'Seriously, you look beautiful.' He meant it. For a brief moment Jonny contemplated stepping up behind his wife, cupping her generous arse in his hands, squeezing the soft flesh beneath the slippery material of her dress, maybe even pressing himself against her. He yearned for such simple confirmation of his standing in her life – sex was a shorthand that Jonny understood – but the expression in her eyes stopped him. Instead he smiled, channelling patience, and held out his hand to her. 'Ready?' The perfect gentleman.

Helena picked up her bag, set her shoulders and said, 'As I'll ever be.'

The dining room looked classy. There were candles everywhere. An ice bucket had been set out on the side. In the sitting room the windows had been thrown wide open. There was music playing softly in the background: Stevie Wonder, 'My Cherie Amour'. Ben had obviously put on his playlist. The sunset was so perfectly framed by the French doors that it looked unreal. Jonny ushered Helena over to one of the sofas and went to fix them both a drink. Ben was already out on the balcony, taking photos – correction, selfies. They didn't acknowledge each other; Ben, because he was impervious, Helena because she was pissed off with Ben. Helena was normally good at concealing her feelings, but her already low opinion of her brother-in-law had sunk even further since his split from Natasha and as a result her dislike had risen to the surface. Women talked – something that Jonny was very aware of.

49

Juliet appeared as Jonny was pouring Helena's white wine. She walked briskly across the room, her low heels clacking against the wooden floor. His sister had always had a thing about her height. The irony was that in trying to mask it, she drew attention to it. Juliet's dress was a muted, but no doubt expensive, slim-fitting mustard affair. It was hard to believe that she'd given birth only two months previously. There wasn't a sliver of spare flesh on her. She was all collarbone, sternum and hipbones. It was impressive how quickly she'd got back into shape, but the sad truth was that tautness was not a good look on her. As always, she'd gone too far, too fast. Helena had kept her yielding post-baby flesh and big breasts for months after the twins and Rory were born. Even now, twelve years later, her body was still softer, less defined than when they had met and married.

'Drink?' Jonny waggled the wine bottle at Juliet. She looked past him at the extensive alcohol selection on offer on the drinks trolley, shook her head, and reached for a tonic water. His little sister had certainly hoovered up all the self-denial genes in the family, for which he supposed he should be grateful. 'Did you get the summons from Alice as well?'

'Yes.'

'Being so close to the throne is going to that girl's head.'

Juliet took a sip from her cut-glass tumbler of nothing. 'Woman,' she corrected him, then without another word she went and sat next to Helena.

So the sisterhood extended to the staff, did it? Jonny was, privately, sick and tired of the incessant drumbeat of feminism. There was always someone banging on about it. Even Chalice now had a Diversity and Inclusion team – grandfather Gerald would be spinning in his grave, if his huge belly allowed it. Jonny had his doubts about how deep-rooted Juliet's feminism really was. Sure, it was a useful banner to march beneath given Geri's own much-flaunted advocacy of equal opportunities, but Jonny had seen little evidence of Juliet applying affirmative action on behalf of anyone other than herself. Still, it was another factor at play and Jonny made a mental note to watch himself over the next few days. Being white and male in today's febrile climate was a positive disadvantage at times. His sense of being encircled by the fairer sex was heightened when he saw how easily Helena and his sister slipped into a conversation. Previously their relationship had always been awkward, Helena the home-maker having little in common with Juliet the high-flier, but watching them chatting away together on the sofa you'd think they were best buddies. It was amazing the impact motherhood could have. It was a swift and bemusing turnaround. Juliet had spent most of her life telling anyone who was stupid enough to ask that *the business was her baby*, so her untimely about-face on motherhood had come as a shock to everyone.

A shift in the light drew Jonny's attention away from the thorny thicket of his family to the world outside. The sun was sinking on the far horizon. Mauve and crimson streaks rippled through the sky. The swirls shifted and reformed like a psychedelic storm. Even Ben lowered his phone and watched as nature threw in one last, impressive encore before darkness descended. The stage was well and truly set. All they needed now was the leading lady.

Chapter 10

GERI

Geri finished with a few humble warriors. She was aware of the irony, but strength and flexibility were important, and not only because of her age. She skipped the savasana. She didn't have the time to be imitating a corpse, she had a dinner party to go to.

She showered quickly, dried herself briskly. As always, she took pleasure in her toned body and her cropped platinum hair. A couple of rubs with a towel and she was good to go. Her make-up took a little longer. The trick was to give the impression that she wasn't wearing any. Carla had laid out her outfit for the evening. Geri appreciated the gesture. Carla was a busy woman, and finding time for such small acts of kindness took thought and effort. Geri could have had extra staff brought in; they did it when they hosted bigger parties or had business associates staying on Isola dei Delfini, but she had wanted the team to be small and trustworthy for her birthday celebrations and their fall-out. Tonight Geri had chosen to wear a midnight-blue trouser suit with wide-legged palazzo pants and a close-fitting top. Clothes that looked good on her. Her exercise regime helped, but Geri knew it was pure luck that she was naturally lean. Thankfully, it was Ian, her brother, who'd inherited her father's heft and her mother's chest. Geri suspected that her success would have been even harder won if their genetic inheritance had been the other way round. A fleshy woman in business was always going to find it difficult to impress. Simple diamond stud earrings and a swipe of plum lipstick completed her look. She glanced in the mirror – not out of vanity, but to check that she'd hit the right note. The next few days were going to require some play-acting and Geri, who was used to being her undiluted and unapologetic self, felt in need of a little assistance with her upcoming performance. Such tactics were normally beneath her, but when you were deciding the fate of a multimillion-pound company, and determining the prospects of your nearest and dearest, some misdirection was advisable.

When she entered the sitting room they all turned to look at her, as planned. Ben jumped to his feet and came forward to offer her his arm as if she was some sort of decrepit royal. For a moment she wanted to laugh. It must be nerves. It gave her pause – it was a long time since Geri had felt anything resembling uncertainty or anxiety. She told herself to calm down, remember who she was. Jonny rose to fix her a drink. She stopped him. 'I think champagne is in order. Would you be kind enough to fetch a couple of bottles up from the kitchen, please, Ben?'

But there was no need; Alice was already on it. She materialised from behind the door: 'I've set it up in the dining room.' Ben looked momentarily disappointed. He really needed to drop the errand-boy performance if he wanted her, or anyone else, to view him as a serious contender.

Lured by the prospect of chilled Taittinger, they all drifted through the arch into the adjoining dining room. Candlelight flickered across the domed roof; the best cutlery and crockery gleamed on the table; through the open window the waves hitting the island provided the perfect mood music. The overall effect was magical. Alice handed out the delicate flutes of champagne and they gathered around Geri like moths to a flame – except for Alice. She stood back, in the shadows.

'First of all I want to thank you all for coming.' They murmured their varying degrees of happiness, willingness, joy even at being there. The insect analogy strengthened in Geri's mind. The stress was making her fanciful. 'It was important to me that you should all be here, for my birthday.'

Ben, as was Ben's wont, chipped in. 'But that's not until tomorrow.'

Geri smiled at her youngest nephew – although thirty-two was hardly young. 'No, you're quite right. I do have another twenty-four hours before I hit that next big headstone.' Ben laughed. No one else did. To be fair, she wasn't known for her comedy. She carried on, undeterred. 'Seventy? It hardly seems possible, does it?'

There was another awkward pause. They obviously had no problem seeing her as an old woman for whom retirement was long overdue. Twenty years at the helm. To her it felt like she was just getting started. They were still waiting, dutifully hanging on her every word. It pleased her to frustrate them. 'Tonight I want us to simply relax and enjoy each other's company. Other matters can wait.' Geri saw disappointment flicker across all their faces. Jesus, they really couldn't wait to see the back of her, could they? She kept her own smile stapled to her face. She indicated the empty chairs. 'Shall we?'

Geri had learnt early on in her career that where people choose to sit, in meetings and within families, was revealing. Tonight the table was laid with a setting at the top, three places on one side and two on the other. They hesitated. She took her rightful place at the head of the table, freeing the rest of them to make their move. Ben nearly tripped himself up in his haste to secure the seat to her right, but then there was a pause. The dynamic was tricky. If only the three of them had managed to stay married to tolerable spouses then there would have been a more natural balance. Juliet was the next to move. Impatient of old-school etiquette, she took the seat next to Ben. Jonny was therefore forced into the end space. Siblings unite! Helena said something sharp and low to Jonny then took the chair opposite him as far away from Geri as possible. There was no love, or more importantly respect, lost between Geri and Helena. Geri simply didn't know what the woman did all day, every day. Alice slipped into the space to Geri's left without looking up. The dance was complete, they had their places – for the time being.

Chapter 11

JULIET

Juliet didn't think she was going to make it. Her head was banging. They'd finished the fish course, but there was still pudding, cheese and coffee to go. Her brothers seemed to be having no such difficulties. She watched Ben help himself to another spoonful of polenta and felt queasy. She checked her phone, again – she'd instructed Lena to send updates every hour, on the hour. The presence of a phone at the table drew a look from her aunt, but she ignored it. Juliet was a mother now. Her phone was no longer simply a business tool, it was a tether to a whole world of new obligations and anxieties. There *was* another message. Juliet tilted the screen so that she could read it in the wavering candlelight. Sophie was apparently still sleeping. That would be four hours straight. Something very strange was happening. The trip seemed to be having a soothing effect on her normally fractious daughter. Juliet wished the same could be said for herself.

She rejoined the conversation, but was disconcerted to find Geri still looking at her. Her aunt's expression appeared pleasant enough, but her eyes were flinty. Juliet was finding it impossible not to conclude that she disapproved of her decision to embrace motherhood so late in life, although forty was hardly ancient in this day and age. As far as Juliet could tell, Geri didn't inherently dislike children, but her aunt wasn't a fan of divided loyalties. Geri was old-school. In her day a woman had a choice – work or family. And the women she admired chose the former. Why else had she scheduled the trip slap bang in the middle of Juliet's maternity leave, and why had she insisted that she stay in the House rather than in the Cottage? It was all obviously a test of her commitment and her focus. Jonny was banging on about politics, or more accurately Westminster. He threw the names of ministers and undersecretaries around as liberally as he had pepper on his tuna. Ben looked bored. He had finished eating now, but not drinking. Juliet watched as he reached clumsily across the table and poured himself another glass of wine. Given how hard he banged the neck of the bottle on the rim of the delicate wine glass, it was a surprise it didn't shatter. Juliet felt a wave of tiredness crash over her. She didn't know why they bothered to go through these happy, or at least civil, family charades when they didn't have an audience. Why couldn't Geri have simply told them who was taking over at a meeting in London?

Carla silently appeared and started to remove the dirty crockery. Juliet was glad. Perhaps it would move things along. As Carla lifted one of the big serving bowls, Jonny reached out and stayed her hand. He helped himself to the remaining polenta and added the surviving roasted vegetables. Only then did he let her clear the dishes. Another wave of fatigue sluiced through Juliet. Would this evening never end?

Jonny was still pontificating. Ben kept trying to butt in, and failing – to be fair, Jonny in full flood was unstoppable. With each failure Ben glugged down more Barolo. Helena yawned like a cat, openly and none too politely. Juliet could see the bumps on her tongue. In the middle of it all sat Geri, still and upright. Juliet let herself float. It was nicer than being present. Even their voices became muffled. Or perhaps she simply wasn't concentrating any more. The only sound was the regular thud of the waves. No, there was another sound. Footsteps on the kitchen stairs. Not Carla's. She was light and quick on her feet, as was her nephew. These footsteps were slow and ponderous. Perhaps it was the sound of her own heartbeat in her ears. But the footsteps grew clearer and louder. They must be real because conversation around the table petered out and everyone listened. Juliet was concentrating now. The heavy footfall was joined by heavy breathing. It sounded like some sort of huge beast was lumbering up the stairwell. Juliet looked at Geri, and was unnerved to see that instead of the usual glacial calm, she looked concerned. 'Are we expecting anyone else?' Juliet asked.

'No.' Geri rose to her feet.

The footsteps stopped. The doorway was filled by a large, heavy-headed figure.

'Well, isn't this nice.'

'Dad!' Their three voices chimed discordantly together.

The fug in Juliet's head was blown away by a blast of pure anger. How long was it since Juliet had last seen her father? Three years? Four? A long time. But not long enough to make her forget just how much she hated him, and nowhere near long enough for her to have forgiven him. What the hell was he doing turning up on Isola dei Delfini?

The old bastard glanced around the room, taking it all in. Juliet noticed that his eyes skimmed over her. A sign of shame? Uneasiness? Guilt? No. That was unlikely. Juliet understood her father well enough to know that he was a stranger to any impulse other than self-gratification. 'I assume my invitation got lost in the post.' He spied the drinks trolley and made a beeline for it. They all watched as he uncorked a bottle of bourbon and poured himself a measure. He held the heavy-bottomed tumbler up to the light, decided he'd short-changed himself, and poured some more. No one said a word. What could they say? The time for challenging him on his behaviour and for hoping for something . . . for anything . . . different was long gone. He was their father in name only.

Juliet watched with disgust as he turned to face them and raised his drink in a mock salute. 'To family! It's good to be together, at long last.' No one joined him in his toast. 'May we never go to hell, but always be on the way!' He took a deep swallow then paused. 'Come along. You know how much I hate drinking alone. And besides, we need to wet the head of the newest Chalice.' *Now* he looked at Juliet. Slowly, the rest of the table lifted their glasses. Juliet didn't touch her smeary glass. That didn't deter him. 'To Sophie. May she have her mother's brains, her aunt's ambition and her father's . . . whoops . . . silly me . . . her uncle Jonny's charm and her uncle Ben's' – he paused – *'joie de vivre. Saluti!'* He was a total bastard.

Spectacle made, he took a turn around the table. 'It looks like I've got some catching up to do.' Suddenly the room felt cramped and overcrowded. Despite her over-whelming desire to leave, Juliet stayed in her seat. If her father was on the island, he would have his reasons, and she wanted to know what they were.

Mid-prowl, he paused. 'What, no seat at the table for the prodigal brother and father?' His attention snagged on Alice. He moved to her side and leant over her. 'Apologies, my dear, but I haven't a scooby who you are. Are you Ben's new companion?'

Juliet watched Alice flush an unsightly mottled red. 'No!' It came out sharp and loud. 'I'm Alice Baxter. Geraldine's personal assistant.' She began to get to her feet, but Geri gestured at her to sit down. No one else offered Ian their chair. Only a fool would insert themself into that long-running war. The atmosphere stiffened. To Juliet's surprise, it was Ben who rose to his feet. 'Here, Dad, have my seat.'

'No,' Geri snapped.

Ben faltered, but stood his ground. 'Give me a minute and I'll go fetch another chair.'

Their father's face was transformed when he smiled, the ghost of the attractive man he used to be resurfac-ing. 'That's very kind of you, my boy.' The awkwardness endured as the chair was brought. In the intervening silence Juliet could hear Geri's breathing.

Ian took the chair from Ben and placed it, with unnec-essary care and deliberate intent, not in the empty space between Helena and Alice, but at the far end of the table, directly opposite Geri. It protested as he sat on it. Geri took her seat as well. They were like chess pieces setting them-selves down on the board, readying for the opening attack. It was Juliet's father who made the first move. 'Ah, lovely.

That's better. I'd forgotten how many stairs there are in this place.' He sighed and took another mouthful of his drink. 'But I suppose it has been a while.' He surveyed the cleared table then asked, seemingly without guile, 'Might there be some food left for the late arrival?'

Geri, who looked calm but was obviously simmering with repressed anger, said nothing.

'No?' He swung his big head around and spotted Carla, who stood, frozen and forgotten, over by the sideboard. If it were possible, she seemed to shrink even smaller under his gaze. 'Ah, Carla. Whatever's left is fine. You know me, I'm not fussy.' She didn't move. 'Thank you, my dear.' His assumption of her compliance released her. She was staff; a member of the family had issued a request, and she was coded to respond. They all listened as she scampered down the stairwell.

Finally Geri spoke. 'How did you get here?'

He sat back. 'The usual way. By boat.'

'You chartered a boat?'

'No, silly. I texted Luca and he came and collected me.' Juliet winced at the 'silly'. It sounded like a throwaway comment, when in reality he was being deliberately provocative.

Geri seemed determined to stick with the facts. 'And how, might I ask, did you get hold of Luca's number?'

Ian took another swig of bourbon and swallowed extravagantly before answering. 'Carla gave me it.'

'Why on earth would she do that?' Geri's eyes were glittering.

Their father smiled another lazy smile. 'Because I asked her to.'

Juliet briefly pitied poor Carla; that act of disloyalty would not go unnoticed. Geri moved her interrogation on. 'When did you arrive?'

Ian's answer was laconic, but surprising. 'A couple of days ago.'

'Sorry? What?' Juliet could hear the struggle to control her emotions in Geri's voice.

'I got down to the coast earlier than planned so I thought I might as well hop across the water and have a look around the old place before the rest of you arrived. So many happy memories. And there seemed no point in paying Positano prices for a hotel when there was a whole island lying empty.'

'Where have you been staying?' Geri asked.

'The Hut.' The basic overflow staff accommodation, down by the landing stage. It had once been a fisherman's hut, hence the name. So he'd been there when they landed – he must have watched them disembark – and he'd been around as Juliet shuttled between the House and the Cottage visiting Sophie, yet he'd not announced his presence until now. The thought made Juliet's skin crawl. Who spied on their own family?

Geri seemed to be losing patience. 'You're not supposed to be here, Ian —'

He cut her off. No one cut Geri off when she was talking. 'And yet here I am.' He held his arms wide as if he was the top prize in a raffle.

For once, Geri seemed lost for words. It was at this moment that the door that led down to the kitchen squeaked open and Carla entered carrying a plate piled high with prosciutto, mozzarella, tomatoes and focaccia.

She placed it in front of their father like a child feeding a python, and he set to as if he was ravenous. They all watched, appalled and fascinated. After a few mouthfuls he looked up from his overflowing plate. 'What? Don't mind me. Carry on.' He waved his dirty knife about. 'I'm interested to hear all your news. I confess, I feel slightly out of the loop.'

But there was no way that things were going to go back to normal now that their father had reappeared, after all these years, and at precisely the point when the future of the business was about to be decided – and every single one of them knew that.

Chapter 12

JONNY

With their father at one end of the table stuffing his face and Geri at the other quivering with anger the centre simply couldn't hold. But Jonny understood Geri well enough to know that there wasn't a cat in hell's chance she would rise from the table before Ian did. Power balances were just that – finely calibrated high-wire acts. Geri had successfully driven Ian out of the business long ago; there was no way she was going to tolerate him turning up to cause trouble at this delicate moment. No, they were going to duke it out and Jonny wasn't going to miss that for the world.

The others seemed less keen to stay around for the showdown. As their father shovelled food into his mouth Juliet rose from the table and claimed – Jonny suspected falsely – that her daughter needed her. From the little Jonny had seen, the child was better off in the hands of the doe-eyed young nanny, Lena, than with her own mother. Jonny was reassured to see that Juliet obviously still detested the old sod as much as he did. He didn't want any little side plots springing up over the next few days.

Once Juliet had signalled her intention to retire for the night, Helena jumped ship as well, claiming she had a headache. Jonny flinched. His darling wife could have opted for a less loaded cliché. Thankfully the others appeared not to hear her, but then they never did pay much attention to what Helena said. Within Jonny's social circle wives were for decoration, not for listening to. After 'the girls' had departed there was an awkward pause into which a distinctly inebriated Ben announced that he needed *a piss*. Given the amount he'd put away during dinner, Jonny wasn't surprised that his bladder couldn't stay the course. Ben rose clumsily to his feet and wandered out of the dining room. It was almost as if his half-brother was trying to sabotage things for himself. As much as Geri undeniably had a soft spot for Ben, Jonny simply didn't believe that she would pass control of the business over to someone who had so little control over themselves.

When they heard Ben crash into one of the big jars in the sitting room Geri turned to Alice. 'Would you be kind enough to make sure that Benedict gets back to his room in one piece, please, Alice?'

Alice said calmly, 'Of course', but Jonny could have sworn that he caught a momentary glint of anger in her eyes.

Jonny pondered the officious Ms Baxter as she made her reluctant exit. Never in her wildest dreams could she have imagined that she would end up as Geri's PA; flying around the world, sitting in on high-powered meetings, liaising, on Geri's behalf, with the great and the good. So quiet, so demure – butter wouldn't melt. But just because Ms Baxter didn't cast much of a shadow that didn't mean she was harmless. Who knew what she was really thinking behind those unflattering specs of hers? Jonny, for one, would dearly like to know; she must have her myopic eyes on all manner of confidential, commercially sensitive, useful information.

Jonny was brought back to the tussle at hand by his father reaching out to pour bourbon into his wine glass. He covered it with his hand. Jonny was as drunk as he wanted to be. Alcohol loosened inhibitions and led to mistakes, and Jonny had no intention of making any missteps over the next few days. His father shrugged, clearly signalling his disappointment in his son's feeble appetite for booze, and instead turned to Geri. She had no such qualms. She sat, unmoving and unsmiling, as he stretched awkwardly over the table and sloshed a huge measure into her glass.

Scene set, glasses filled, Jonny sat back and waited for the battle to begin.

Chapter 13

BENEDICT

Alice snuck up behind Ben so quietly that he nearly had a fucking heart attack. She was like some sort of smart-suited, bespectacled ninja – in the pay of his aunt. They stared at each other for a moment or two. Ben didn't feel inclined to help her out. 'Geri wanted me to check that you're feeling okay.' There it was – the implication that he'd had a skinful. Even people who had no right to have an opinion about his drinking, never mind voice it, frequently did.

'Me? I'm grand. Having a wonderful time with the famalam. You?'

She looked uncomfortable, as well she might. She was the interloper, the odd fish in the tank. 'It's lovely to get a chance to see the island,' she replied. So a diplomat and a ninja . . . and a fish. No wonder Geri employed Ms Alice Baxter, the girl was a whole separate species. Ben indulged in imagining Alice as a guppy with a human face, complete with specs, swimming around with hundreds of other tropical fish in a softly lit aquarium. From the dining room there came nothing but an ominous quiet and the dull thud of full glasses hitting the tablecloth. The fish-tank mirage dissolved. Ben knew he should have stayed at the table. Letting Jonny have space to expand was never a good idea; he was a 'give him an inch and he'll take a mile' merchant. But Ben had simply had to get out of there. Despite having grown up surrounded by conflict, Ben was bad at it. He didn't have thick enough skin. At least, that's what his mother used to say, when she cared enough to notice his distress. Being trapped between the conflicting expectations of his aunt and his father in the dining room had brought back painful memories from his childhood. Ben had realised, very early on and to his cost, that in pleasing one parent you were doomed to piss off the other. Did wanting to avoid such conflict make him a coward? It did inside the barbed wire of the Chalice family. Whoever said that families fucked you up, was right.

Alice was still standing there watching him. He burped – tasting Carla's cheesy polenta. That didn't seem to bother her, she merely blinked. He'd had enough! 'Well, if you'll excuse me, Alice. It has been a lovely evening, but I desperately need a piss.' He headed into the hall and for the staircase. To make sure she didn't follow him up it, he added, 'Unless, of course, you intend to escort me up to my bathroom and provide me with some of your renowned personal assistance.'

As Ben set off up the stairs he could've sworn that he heard the guppy say, 'In your dreams, you self-indulgent arsehole.'

Chapter 14

JONNY

Geri made her move when the bottle was down to the last dregs. She sliced off his father's ramblings about 'how nice it was to see good old Carla again after all this time' with a direct question. 'Who told you we were coming to Isola dei Delfini?'

His father smiled sloppily. 'No one. I just spotted the smoke rising. And, as the saying goes, there's no smoke without fire.'

Geri wasn't buying it. 'Cut the crap, Ian. You arrived before everybody else. Someone told you we were coming and I want to know who.'

He drained the last of his bourbon and his bonhomie. 'I'll bet you do.'

'You have no right to be here . . . and no reason.'

'Oh, but I do, dear sis. And you know it.'

Geri spoke slowly, concisely and coldly. Jonny had to stop himself from leaning forward in anticipation. He'd heard so much about their hatred of each, but he'd never seen it up close and this unfettered before. 'Not this again.' She pulled herself up to her full height – even seated she looked tall. 'The deal was scrutinised ad infinitum by your lawyers. You agreed to the terms and to the financial settlement. And you have profited from it, handsomely, ever since. You cannot reappear twenty years later, simply because you smell blood in the water. There's nothing to discuss. Nothing to negotiate. This has nothing to do with you.' She was impressive.

His father's response was pantomime concern. He swung his big head to and fro. 'Is someone injured? Quick! Call a doctor! We can't have the glorious head of the Chalice Group bleeding out on this rather beautiful parquet flooring, can we? Oh, thank God! You were talking figuratively.' He clasped his hand to his chest. 'For a moment there, I thought my beloved big sister was on her way out.' Then he smiled lazily and tilted back on his chair. Jonny was convinced that he was going to fall, but the old bastard had surprisingly good balance. He crashed forward at the last minute, narrowly averting disaster. The glasses on the table rattled. 'But perhaps I do detect a slight iron taint in the air.'

'Ian!' Geri's voice rose a notch. She was obviously tiring of his one-man show.

'Okay. Okay. Let me explain.' He held his hands up. 'My children . . . or at least one of them, the one with a beating heart' – bloody Ben, Jonny might have known – 'thought that I should be present, given what you're going to be discussing.'

'We aren't discussing anything,' Geri bit back. 'We're here to celebrate my birthday.'

His father smiled. 'Bullshit, Geri. You've dragged them all here to do one last song-and-dance routine for you before you deign to tell them who's going to be crowned

70

your successor . . . at long bloody last.' The oily, ingratiating tone was gone now. His father's voice was pure, distilled dislike. He straightened up in his seat as well. It did little to improve his overall dishevelled appearance, but Jonny could tell that his father was gearing up to throw his hand grenade.

The incendiary turned out to be a tatty sheaf of papers that he withdrew from his jacket pocket. He unfolded them and pushed them across the table. 'All I'm saying, my dear sister, is that you might want to take a shufti at that before you go promising anything to anyone. I haven't just been tanning my arse this past year.' Geri glanced at the scruffy bundle, but did not pick it up. She simply waited for an explanation. His father obliged. 'You were going to have to retire at some point and you don't need to be a member of Mensa to guess that hitting seventy might make even the indestructible Ms Chalice think about hanging up her whip. So I had a corporate lawyer friend of mine – oh, don't look so surprised, I do still have some friends – take another swing at our agreement. I gave him the context, something that you were very keen to keep quiet, weren't you, Geri? I told him all about my fragile mental health around the time of the negotiations – poor Joanna, such a waste' – Jonny went cold at the mention of his mother – 'and the aggressive tactics you employed to pressurise me into signing, and he reckons that I have a case. His actual words were, "a strong case for substantial restitution".' The only sign that Geri was furious was her flaring nostrils. Indifferent to the danger he was in, his father continued, 'And his expert opinion, which I'm inclined to agree with, is that any challenge that I might bring could cause you real problems in terms of your authority to appoint the next CEO. The legal fine print on something as important as this would, after all, have to be beyond reproach. And even if it's not upheld, my claim would, at the very least, delay things. Probably for a considerable period of time. You know what lawyers are like . . . why take a year when you can take a decade?' He sat back and smiled. 'And just think of the adverse publicity! The press will be all over it. They do so love a juicy family feud.'

Silence descended. His father had thrown his grenade, without – as always – a moment's thought about who might get injured by the blast, including his own offspring.

There was a reason they all hated him.

Chapter 15

BENEDICT

Ben hadn't been joking about his bladder; he only just made it into his en suite. As the urine poured out of him he braced himself against the wall. Was excessive peeing an early indicator of prostate cancer? He had being having a spot of trouble getting it up recently. Not often. Just on the odd occasion. With the wrong girl. Nah. Maybe he should just cut down a bit. Yeah, he would – when he got back to the UK and back to work. His drug and alcohol use was largely recreational; weekends mostly, with the occasional bump during the week if he was at a social event, or he was especially tired, or stressed. And, of course, he was on holiday, so a little overindulgence tonight was only to be expected. He finished up, kicked his trousers into the corner of the bathroom and wandered through to his bedroom. He starfished onto the bed, letting the room and his head spin. It wasn't an unpleasant sensation. It reminded him of the headrush he used to get as a kid when he rolled down a grass bank and ended up flat on his back, with no idea where he was.

Which in a sense he still didn't know. He knew he was on Isola dei Delfini with his fractious, fighting, fucking awful family, but where he was 'at' in life and where he was heading was less clear.

Ben was under no illusions. He knew he was the second-tier heir. He was only here on the island as a courtesy; even the Chalices made an effort to keep up appearances, sometimes. His 'crime'? He was the progeny of the affair that killed Jonny and Juliet's mother, Joanna. Or, at least, that was the family mythology. The problem was less that Ian had been unfaithful – that seemed to have been expected – more that he 'lost his head', left Jonny and Juliet's mother and, subsequently, married Ben's mum, Nina. Which meant, rather inconveniently for his siblings, that Ben couldn't be dismissed as the illegitimate by-product of a brief fling. He was, undeniably, a Chalice. That Ian had subsequently left Ben's mother when Ben was thirteen and gone on a seemingly never-ending spree with a parade of interchangeable, increasingly young women made no difference. Why? Well, because Joanna was the only one of his father's litany of discarded women who went on to develop serious mental health problems that culminated in her taking her own life. Juliet had, unfortunately, been the one who found her. You wouldn't wish that on your worst enemy, would you? But Joanna's death had been a good eight years after the divorce, so perhaps his dad had been right when he said that her fragility had been there long before he met her.

Ben got it. He really did. His father . . . correction, 'their' father . . . he had a habit of leaving a trail of angst in his wake, and he was a bit of a shit when it came to women, and he had been a rubbish dad, but that was hardly Ben's fault, was it? They'd all had a rough time growing up. The money hadn't protected any of them from that. Jesus! Affairs, betrayal, blame, the legacy for the next generation! The dysfunctional Chalice dynasty would be fascinating and endlessly entertaining – if it weren't his own life.

Ben knew he was *wallowing*. That was a Natasha phrase. But as much as his estranged wife could be a heartless bitch, she wasn't often wrong. That's what had made living with her impossible. Who wanted a clear-sighted wife? No one. What Ben wanted was someone who would agree with him, even when he was talking shite. Someone kind and softly spoken who would give him unconditional, unwavering love and support, no matter what mistakes he made. Wasn't that what everyone wanted, deep down?

Ben gave himself a slap. A real one. The sting helped. He needed to climb out of his 'pity pit' and fast, if he was going to get back in the game. And to do that he was going to need help.

Resolve strengthened by his whack in the face, Ben rolled over to the edge of the mattress, reached under the bed and prised free the loose tile. Inside his hidey-hole there was a thick wad of cash, his stash and his burner phone. He retrieved the phone and switched it on. Some calls you really didn't want to be traced back to you.

Chapter 16

LUCA

Luca walked through the darkness. He wanted to put as much distance between himself and the Chalices as possible. He never liked being in the House, that was their domain. The island was small, but it was big enough to find peace and solitude, should you desire it. Unfortunately, on this visit the family had spread out further than usual. The baby and the nanny were in the Cottage, which meant the path up to the Ledge was off limits, and much to Luca's discomfort, Ian Chalice had commandeered the Hut. Having him living so close had ruined the cove and boatyard for Luca. He could see the lights on in the Hut from his bedroom above the Boathouse and when he lay down to sleep he could sense the old lech lumbering around inside, plotting whatever it was he was plotting.

When Luca had received the summons to go and collect Ian from Positano he'd considered deleting it, but he hadn't. Instead he'd sought Carla's advice. She'd flushed and squirmed and hummed and hawed and advised Luca to do as asked. Her argument was that the Chalices were paying his wages and, consequently, that ignoring a direct request, even one coming from a deposed and disgraced member of the family, was unwise. And she should know – she'd been working for them most of her life. Thirty-seven years. People got less for committing murder. Carla was right, of course. One act of defiance could easily result in Luca being thrown off the island, and he simply couldn't risk that. What was bugging him was why Carla was still in touch with her old employer after all this time and why she'd given him Luca's mobile number. It was almost as if she wanted the old goat on the island.

Whatever the truth of the situation, Luca had had no choice but to go and collect Ian Chalice and get him secreted in the Hut, two days before the rest of the family arrived. That he wanted his presence concealed from the other guests was weird – if you could be bothered to be curious about the behaviour of a bunch of spoilt, entitled rich folk. Their infighting, jealousies and perversities were so removed from Luca's life that it was like observing the antics of a different species. Was Ian Chalice any worse than the rest of them? It was hard to say, but watching Carla run around, making sure that the old bastard was comfortable and had everything he needed, had made Luca feel furious and impotent in equal measure. It was a dangerous mix of emotions. Carla might not have to wear an apron and curtsey whenever a Chalice entered the room any more, but she was at their beck and call twenty-four hours a day. Added to which, Luca was aware that having him around was making her more anxious than normal. Hence, her suggestion that he go and get reacquainted with the island for a few hours while they drank themselves into a stupor was both a gift to Luca and a way of easing the pressure on herself.

Luca walked fast, relieved to be outside. Alone and unobserved, he was finally able to breathe. The glitter of the sea in the moonlight and the endless star-pocked sky were welcome after the narrow confines of the House. At the old rowan tree that he used to climb, he stepped off the path and started to make his way up to the vantage point at the northernmost tip of the island. The scent of the basil as he crushed it underfoot released a wave of memories.

Luca had had plenty of practice in keeping out of the Chalices' way as a child. Carla had allowed him to stay on the island whenever she could arrange to get him over for a few days, and always for the long summer holidays. She understood how difficult Luca found school on the mainland – the religion, the rigidity, the endless and, to Luca, pointless rules used to crush his spirit – so she did her best to provide him with as much freedom as possible when he was on the island. From a very young age he was allowed to roam free while she worked – just so as long as he promised to stay away from the cliff edge and the family, if they were in residence. As a result, Luca got to know every inch of Isola dei Delfini as a child. He discovered the best places to get into the water to swim, the shadiest spots for when the sun was at its height and would burn the skin off your back, and the hidden 'paths' through the dense undergrowth that a small child could traverse, but no adult could even see, never mind take. He'd spend days on his own, perfectly content; swimming and exploring and napping. Carla used to call him her 'happy little savage' when he returned to their rooms above the Boathouse, hungry and tired, his hair full of grass seed and his legs laced with sea salt. Those glorious months of freedom every year had had a huge effect on Luca. They helped him to work out who he was and what *he* wanted out of life. And to recognise what he'd known all along: that his dreams and aspirations were very different to those of other people.

When Luca could walk no further, not without plunging to his death, he sat down. He swung his legs over the cliff edge, saying 'sorry' in his head to Carla as he did so, then he lit a cigarette and inhaled. He looked out at the blackness and listened to the hypnotic thud and crump of the waves far below. He tried to return to the 'happy savage' he'd been as a child. Free. Strong. At one with himself and the world.

But the sad truth was that his inner peace was being sorely tested by being around the Chalice family again. Geri's superiority, Ian's creepiness, Juliet's coldness, Ben's fake friendliness, Jonny's supreme arrogance – in their own ways they were as bad as each other. And Luca knew, to his cost, that having that much privilege concentrated in one place could be dangerous. However hard he might try, he was never going to be able to hold himself totally separate and untouched when he was around them. He took another drag on his cigarette and waited for the nicotine to kick in. Peace might be a pathetically small ambition compared to the grand aspirations of the Chalice family, but it had been Luca's. It was typical that they had now stolen even that away from him.

The full moon on the water, the black sheen of the sea: the view was as beautiful as ever, but it no longer held the power to soothe. Luca was awake now and watching and the Chalices had better be on their guard.

Chapter 17

HELENA

Heels, dress, stockings, underwear, earrings, make-up – the reverse engineering was Helena's long walk back to freedom. Stripped of her costume, she went through all five phases of her skincare regime – wrinkles were the enemy. Age held at bay, with expensive lotions and effort, for a little while longer, Helena got into bed with her book. Happy as she was to be released from her wifely duties, at the same time she was angry to be excluded. Such conflicting emotions were very familiar, but they were no less irritating. Being married to a Chalice had many advantages: the houses, the cars, the freedom not to have to work, the holidays, this island, etc., etc., but although Helena rarely paid for anything, there was a cost.

Helena hadn't been surprised when Jonny hadn't come upstairs with her. She was used to leaving, or more accurately being left, at the end of the evening. Once the wining and dining was done she was surplus to requirements. Helena had lost count of the number of times she'd been driven home, alone, while Jonny stayed on to talk shop. Normally she was happy to exit stage left; business dinners were, by and large, a total bore. But tonight she'd thought it might be different. This was family business, after all. Fraught and ugly as it was, she had hoped that Jonny had brought her with him to the island to be part of it for a change.

Helena was fully aware of the deep well of jealousy that bubbled just beneath the surface whenever the siblings got together. She knew that it spoke of childhood rivalries made worse by the intense competition in their adult lives. The fact that they all worked for the family firm was an obvious recipe for, if not disaster, then at least some very thinly veiled discord. Their intense rivalry had clearly been fuelled by Geri playing them off against each other for years. And Ian turning up! That was *not* going to help. Helena put her unread book aside and, not for the first time, reflected on how wealth seemed to exacerbate the worst traits in people, selfishness among them. As always, the thought made her anxious.

Helena loved her life and enjoyed all the benefits of a ridiculously high standard of living, but it was all dependent on her marriage. Hence her dedication to keeping her own family functioning and together. If that required some sacrifices, then so be it. That she believed Jonny had, on occasion, been unfaithful was one such sacrifice. A difficult one, but not impossible. Or so Helena had discovered over the past fifteen years. It was amazing what you could accommodate given time and enough compensations.

When Jonny still hadn't put in an appearance an hour later, Helena took a pill and snapped off the light. She went to sleep swiftly, like falling off a cliff.

She was woken by clattering in the en suite. Jonny's

presence was always asserted, no matter where they were or what time it was. And it was, obviously, late. But now that she was awake Helena knew that the zolpidem still sloshing around in her system wouldn't help her get back to sleep, just make her groggy and thirsty. She sat up, had a drink of water, lay back down, then rolled onto her side with her back to the bathroom door and listened to her beloved husband pissing like a bull elephant.

When Jonny had finished, he crept into the bedroom, banging the bathroom door behind him. Deliberately? She was never sure whether Jonny was inconsiderate or simply unaware. He thumped down on the mattress. Helena bounced, but she said nothing. She heard him take off his watch and go to put it on the bedside table. There was a loud clank as it hit the floor. 'Shit!' This was followed by a pause, probably him checking that his Breitling wasn't damaged. Finally there was another gentler noise as he put the watch carefully aside. She rolled over. 'Really?'

'Did I wake you?' He lay down beside her.

'Yes.'

No apology was forthcoming, but he was obviously in the mood for a chat. He sometimes was after a night of ulterior-motive socialising. She gave in. He loved her because she listened, or least that's what he used to say. 'Go on, then, how did it go?'

To her dismay Jonny sat up and clicked on the lamp. She had brought this on herself. Resigned, she sat up as well. 'It was a bit of a shit show. But it was interesting. My father is up to his old tricks.'

Helena yawned. 'Meaning?'

'He's hoping to gouge some more cash out of Geri.'

Helena truly didn't care. Surely there was enough money to go round them all, ten times over. 'And?'

'Geri was incandescent, though as always it was hard to tell, but what was clear was that she's not having any of it.'

'Why does your father turning up matter?'

'Well, it probably doesn't, but he's been talking to the lawyers and it's obvious that he's intent on causing trouble. And that could be bad news, given the timing.'

'You mean the decision about who's going to be the next CEO?'

'Precisely.'

Helena's heart sank. She really couldn't take much more of Jonny-in-waiting. His impatience was like a bomb that couldn't be disarmed. Only Geri stepping down and making him CEO would stop the ticking. 'Is there anything you can do?'

Jonny hesitated before answering, then he smiled. 'Oh, there's always things I can do, if I have to. Don't you worry about that.' He didn't actually say the words 'your pretty little head', but Helena heard them. 'Anyway' – he patted her leg – 'enough about me. Did you have a nice time?'

Helena sometimes wondered if they had really been married for nearly fifteen years. She opted for a bland, 'It was a lovely meal.' Jonny probably hadn't even noticed. He ate well and greedily, but Helena had her doubts about whether he tasted what was put in front of him.

'It was nice to see you having a catch-up with Juliet.'

What rabbit was Jonny chasing now? 'Yeah.' With any luck he'd be happy with that.

No such luck. 'You seemed to be having a good old chat in the sitting room.'

83

'Well, she is the only one who actually speaks to me about anything other than you.'

'And?'

'And what?'

'What did she say?'

'Look, if you're fishing for info about her thoughts on this CEO race, forget it. Juliet doesn't talk to me about the business. She never has. You know that. It's only since she got pregnant that we've had any common ground.'

Still he wouldn't let it go. 'So what *were* you talking about?'

'Life in general. Kids. Having a newborn.'

'How do you think she's coping?'

'Like most new mums.'

'So she's finding it tough?'

'I didn't say that.'

'But it can't be easy at her age, on her own and so soon after her break-up with Harry.'

'It was her choice.'

Did Jonny actually lean forward a touch? 'The baby or the divorce?'

'Well, both, but I meant having Sophie. It was absolutely her right to pursue it.' Helena was feeling woozy. She listened to the sea, wishing herself asleep. She hoped that her silence would silence him. It didn't.

'Has she ever spoken to you about how she got pregnant?'

Helena studied her husband through drooping eyelids. This wasn't a casual late-night chat – he was trying to sniff out any signs of weakness in his sister that he could exploit. It was what he did. Family, friend or foe, it really didn't matter to Jonny; in that at least he was egalitarian. Oh, how he would love it if Juliet had, to use his charming phraseology, 'got knocked up on a one-night stand'. He would have a field day with that. Helena's tired irritation finally got the better of her. She smiled at him. 'She has, actually.' She paused. It was nice to have more information than him for a change. Juliet had, in fact, told Helena what she'd done, in confidence, months ago. It had been a surprise – both the news of her pregnancy and the confiding in her bit – but it had made Helena realise that Juliet was human and that she saw Helena as such as well. Since then they'd kept in touch. Having a child could be a lonely process. Helena knew that all too well. Jonny was waiting. What harm could there be in him knowing? There was no gossip, there were no tawdry details that he could use against Juliet. His sister had behaved, as she always did, with discretion and efficiency. 'It was all planned. A clinic in Switzerland, the last viable embryo, and Bob's your uncle – a pregnancy and a child, without any of the usual complications.'

'Like a man.'

'Well, there obviously was a man, but at a remove.'

Jonny laughed suddenly and loudly. 'Yes, of course, when you think about it, it makes perfect sense. Sexless conception is right up Juliet's street.'

He was such a shit sometimes. Helena closed her eyes and let the tiredness, the wine and the zolpidem swirl through her brain. She stopped herself from saying any more. It was none of his business what Juliet did in her private life. To discourage any further discussion Helena lay down and pulled the sheet up to her chin. He took the hint, turned off the light and settled down beside her.

But he wasn't quite done with her. 'She's a cute little thing, isn't she?' Helena said nothing. 'Does it make you think?'

'Think what, Jonny? It's nearly 1.00 a.m. and I desperately need some sleep.'

Jonny sighed softly and gently touched her arm. Then to her horror, he said, 'About having another one.'

Chapter 18

JULIET

The house was finally silent; bedroom doors closed, lights switched off. They had obviously called it a night. Juliet imagined them all settling in their comfortable beds. They'd be asleep in seconds, anaesthetised by alcohol and their own self-righteousness. Not her. She paced. She couldn't settle. Her father's capacity to provoke simultaneous rage and need in her was as disorientating as ever. That he could make the effort to travel to Isola dei Delfini when he thought there might be something in it for him, but he couldn't be arsed to fly back to the UK to see his own granddaughter was classic Ian Chalice behaviour.

His response to Sophie's birth had been pathetic: a bouquet of tacky pink flowers that had arrived three weeks late, with a brief note. She remembered the wording exactly, 'Congrats. So happy for you. Love Dad x'. The abbreviation had infuriated her. He'd abdicated from every role that had ever demanded anything from him. First as a husband, then as a father, then as CEO and finally as a grandparent. And yet here he was assuming that he could simply walk back in, pull up a chair and carry on as if he'd merely stepped out of the room for a moment.

As Juliet wandered around her bedroom, finding no outlet for her anger, she felt her phone vibrate. Her first thought was that it would be Lena with another update on Sophie, but it was a text message from an unrecognised number. Juliet clicked on the contact. It read, **Isn't she lovely?** What appeared on the screen next made her stomach contract.

It was a photo of Sophie. An extreme close-up. It had obviously been taken on the island because in it Sophie was lying on the patterned beach blanket that Lena had suggested Juliet buy at the airport, in the shade of the fig tree that grew at the side of the Cottage. She was wearing the pale-yellow dress that she'd travelled over in. Her legs and tiny feet were bare. She looked small, vulnerable and, as the text said, *lovely*. The rational voice in Juliet's head told her that the photo could only have been taken by Lena. But this was not Lena's number, and why would Lena be sending Juliet random photographs at this time of night?

Another, more disturbing thought bubbled up. Perhaps this was her father's crass way of trying to worm his way back into her life? Maybe he'd been sneaking around the island hoping to catch a glimpse of his new granddaughter, while Juliet had been down on the terrace waiting for Geri to arrive? Had he come across her daughter and Lena and asked if he could take a picture? But why on earth had Lena not told Juliet, and why had she said yes? Juliet had been very clear with her about safety protocols. The rules were designed to protect her daughter from precisely this sort of thing. Being on the island made no difference. Ian being Sophie's grandfather made no difference. Lena's job was to watch Sophie like a hawk. Juliet scrutinised the picture again, looking for clues. Unless Lena didn't know anything about the photograph? Jesus, had Lena left Sophie unattended for some unfathomable reason? If so, Juliet would sack her – the minute they got back to the UK.

Juliet chest tightened. She didn't want her father anywhere near her daughter, whatever his motivation. She texted Lena for an update and got an immediate response saying that Sophie had been fed, changed and was fast asleep.

Alone in her lovely room, with the window thrown open and the sea stirring and restless out there beyond the cliff edge, Juliet felt a queasy churn of unease and fatigue. Sleep, that's what she needed. Just one night of unbroken sleep, then she would feel more herself. Stronger, less emotional, less likely to be freaked out by a manipulative photo and a text from her father.

She climbed into bed and clicked off the lamp. She left the shutters open, not wanting to feel hemmed in. The moonlight was reassuring, far preferable to the absolute darkness that descended when the shutters were closed. In the morning she would confront him, tell him in no uncertain terms that covert photographs and cryptic messages were not the best way to start building bridges. Whether she wanted to bridge-build – well, that was another issue altogether. Too much water had flowed through the gaping hole of the past two decades to make thoughts of a reconciliation with her father appealing. He had abandoned her twice, and Juliet knew that if she let him back in, he would do it again. Tired of it all, tired of them all, she lay down and closed her eyes. But despite the soft moonlight and the soothing sound of the sea, the sleep that Juliet so desperately craved would not come. She tossed and turned and stared at the shimmering tiles on the ceiling. She threw the pillows on the floor, pushed down the covers and tried to get more comfortable, but couldn't. Exhausted as she was, her mind raced – not with speculation about what she was missing downstairs, but with anxiety about Sophie. Fifteen minutes passed, twenty. It took until the thirty-minute mark before the ludicrousness of the situation struck Juliet. She wasn't a child confined to her room. She was a mother with a child of her own. She got up, pulled on a creased T-shirt with a pair of shortie pyjama bottoms, shoved her feet in her slippers and headed downstairs. She crossed the hall, opened the heavy front door, slipped outside and ran up the path to the Cottage.

She let herself in and crept up the stairs. There was music playing softly in Lena's room. Juliet unlocked the nursery door with care. She was pleased to see that Lena kept it locked, as per instructions. So the girl had stuck to some of the rules. Why Juliet was creeping around she wasn't too sure; it just felt right to go undetected.

Sophie was there, in the nursery, fast asleep – as Lena had confirmed. Juliet took off her slippers, put them down carefully by the door and tiptoed across the room. The monitor was on. She didn't want Lena hearing her footsteps, coming in and taking over. Sophie was breathing softly and rapidly as if she'd been running a race. Juliet found the regular puffs of air reassuring. Her daughter looked tiny inside the huge cot that Alice had had shipped over from the UK, at Juliet's request. She stirred in her sleep. Perhaps she could sense her mother's presence. Juliet prayed that she wouldn't wake. She simply wanted, no, she needed, to be with her daughter – to be at peace with her, if only for a few minutes. After some wriggling, Sophie stretched out her arms and made tiny starfish with her fingers. It looked for a moment as if she was waving. The sight made Juliet's still-tender womb pulse. Was this the first sign of the much talked-about maternal instinct taking root? Juliet desperately hoped so. She wanted to be a good mother. She wanted her daughter to feel loved and safe in a way that she never had.

She just didn't know how.

Day Two

Chapter 19

JULIET

Juliet nearly dropped Sophie. What the hell was Geri doing in the kitchen of the Cottage at four-thirty in the morning? And how had she known that Juliet was there? Sophie started with some low-level whimpering that was usually the precursor to full-on screaming. Geri's 'I didn't mean to startle you' didn't help. Juliet's heart banged inside her ribcage. As if telepathic, Geri answered both of Juliet's questions with her first breath.

'I wanted to have a word with you, in private, before everyone else surfaces. We didn't really get a chance to talk last night, what with all that nonsense with your father. When I saw that your room up at the House was empty I deduced that you must be here.'

Juliet heard reproach in her voice. She busied herself getting Sophie's bottle ready. It was awkward doing it one-handed. Geri didn't offer to help and Juliet didn't ask. Besides, it meant that she could justifiably turn her back on her aunt. Juliet felt, as she so frequently did nowadays, at a disadvantage. Even at this ungodly hour and after a long night spent drinking and no doubt arguing with Ian, Geri looked good. She was wearing a black one-piece swimming costume underneath a beautiful, sheer kaftan. A crack-of-dawn swim was obviously next on the agenda. By way of contrast, Juliet knew she looked half dead. She was wearing just her creased T-shirt and pants, no pyjama bottoms, her hair was a mess and she was jittery after a night spent dozing off and jerking awake, having been driven to rise multiple times to check on her child.

The machine beeped. The bottle was ready. Juliet suddenly realised that she had no idea how long the silence between the two of them had gone on for. 'Sorry. You were saying.' Juliet sat down opposite Geri, tugged her T-shirt down, and tried to feed a now fretting Sophie. But hungry as her daughter was she still fussed, twisting her head to and fro in distress. Juliet took a couple of calming breaths and gently stroked the side of her daughter's cheek with the bottle teat, the way Lena had shown her. To her huge relief Sophie responded. Once plugged in she began to suck down the milk quite happily. Thank God.

With Sophie settled and silenced, Geri cut to the chase. 'I know that you're concerned that this is not the best juncture for us to be discussing the future of the business.' Too damn right. It was disastrous timing – for Juliet. Geri acknowledged as much by not waiting for her to respond. 'But there have been a number of developments over the past few months that have forced my hand.' That was bullshit. Nothing and no one could make Geri do anything she didn't want to. 'And as a result, I simply can't leave the issue unresolved any longer. It would damage the business, and the family. It is important to me that you know that.'

Juliet gifted her aunt a small nod. It was all she could manage. At the same time, her slowly clearing brain began to wonder what *developments* Geri was referring to. There hadn't been any big news within the Group nor anything of note with regard to their key competitors while she'd been off – Juliet had made it her business to know. She might not have come into the office much over the past couple of months, but that didn't mean that she hadn't still been working. The only logical conclusion was that Geri was talking about the candidates themselves and their suitability for the top job. But any change in her views on that score was not good news for Juliet. Up until Sophie, Juliet hadn't put a foot wrong. As if she needed reminding of the impact of her daughter, Sophie chose this moment to unlatch from the bottle and start making those distressed creaking noises that signalled discomfort in her tummy. Milk poured out of her mouth, soaking the front of her Babygro and Juliet's T-shirt. Shit. She'd forgotten to wind her. Juliet put the bottle aside and hoisted Sophie onto her shoulder. As she gently rubbed her daughter's back Geri watched them intently.

'How *are* you finding motherhood?'

Geri expressing interest in Juliet's well-being was *not* normal, or welcome. This is what happened when you had a child; people instantly assumed that you were weakened – which you were, you'd just carried and given birth to a whole new human being, for Christ's sake – but you sure as hell didn't need reminding of it. Juliet needed to chop off that line of questioning as cleanly and quickly as possible. Sophie could not be seen as a hindrance. If she was, then Juliet's chances of becoming CEO would be torpedoed. 'Fine,' she replied. Geri wasn't going to enquire how Ben's drug use was going or offer Jonny some friendly advice on his marriage, was she? No, her brothers' private lives were just that, private. 'We're getting into the swing of things nicely. And I think that, with some guidance, Lena is going to fit the bill as Sophie's primary carer. I will, of course, be getting in additional help when I return to work.' The clear message being that she, Juliet Chalice – the most proficient and dedicated sibling – hadn't changed, which meant that she was still the best candidate for the job. And they both knew it.

At least, Juliet hoped Geri did.

'That's good.' Geri finally stopped staring at Sophie and regained her usual brisk tone. 'I want to reassure you that whatever my decision, it will be made solely on the basis of who is best placed to take the business forward. My personal feelings will not come into it.' It was interesting that Geri hadn't even mentioned Ian turning up and what impact that might or might not have on her plans. So her father was an irrelevance to Geri. Juliet was reassured by that. On cue, Sophie burped and immediately started demanding the rest of her bottle. Geri used it as the perfect opportunity to rise to her feet. At the doorway she paused. 'I'm sure the sacrifice will be worth it, in the long run. She is lovely.'

Juliet watched her aunt leave, none the wiser as to her intentions, but determined to find out whatever she could before it was too late.

Chapter 20

GERI

The water was shockingly cold, but that was its appeal. Geri surfaced from her dive and began her sixty-nine laps. Her technique was good. Clean, quiet, fast. Unlike yoga, swimming was not a mental respite for Geri, it was a workout. As she swam up and down in the early-morning darkness she reflected on the past twelve hours. Christ, was it really only yesterday afternoon that she'd landed on the island? It felt much longer. But time was like that; it contracted and created pressure at precisely the moment you most needed space to think.

Uppermost in Geri's mind as she swam was her brother. Ian's arrival had brought far too much heat and noise to the island. She had downplayed her concern in front of the others, but his presence was a threat, and one that she could do without. If she was to proceed as planned then that threat would need to be neutralised, and quickly. Geri executed an inelegant tumble turn and smashed her foot into the end of the pool. As she swam on, the throb in her toes neatly reflected her frustrations.

That Ben had seen fit to let Ian know that they were meeting on the island hurt. Because who else could it have been? He was the only one of the three of them foolish enough to think that blood trumped self-interest. There was certainly no love lost between Jonny, Juliet and their father. None whatsoever. People thought it odd that all three of Ian's offspring stayed on in the business after his acrimonious departure, but what did 'people' know? Your closest relatives were often your greatest adversaries. Jonny and Juliet had always been very clear-sighted about which side their bread was buttered. Sadly, it would appear that Ben was yet to learn.

Juliet. There was another concern. Up until a year ago Juliet had been the most worthy contender for Geri's job. A businesswoman moulded in her own image; dedicated, sharp, respected, capable of playing hardball when needed, and it often was within the Group and the family. But since Harry had upped and left her, Geri had noticed that Juliet had slowly, incrementally and – to Geri at least – inexplicably, begun losing focus. Then the baby! This is what happened when you let your private life matter more than your career.

Which left Geri with Jonny. Reliable, ambitious, high-profile, City-friendly Jonny. He could never be accused of letting his private life get in the way of his career. Geri picked up the pace, foregoing elegance for speed in a bid to leave all thoughts of her family behind.

When she was done she hauled herself out of the deep end and sat on the side of the pool, her head bowed. Blowing hard, starved of oxygen and flooded with lactic acid as she was, she felt good; invigorated, ready for the challenges ahead. She was Geri Chalice and she had wrangled her fighting, feral, dysfunctional family into shape before, and she would do it again.

It was only as Geri got to her feet that she noticed that the sun had risen and flooded the sky with gold while she'd been thrashing her way up and down the pool. It was as good an omen as she was going to get.

Chapter 21

JULIET

It was a new day and a new dawn and Juliet was determined to start it with a new attitude.

First item on the agenda. Lena.

After Geri left, Juliet took Sophie upstairs. She laid her down in her cot and walked away before the crying could start. Then she crossed the tiny landing and banged on Lena's bedroom door. There was a delay before Lena opened up. She'd obviously been asleep because she was only wearing a vest and a tiny pair of pants and her cheek was creased from the pillow.

Their conversation was terse. Juliet dominated it. She cut off Lena's apologies for having overslept – she hadn't, it wasn't yet 6.00 a.m. Juliet went in hard, with little explanation, but with a lot of concern that Lena wasn't being vigilant enough. Muzzy with sleep, the girl defended herself staunchly, but politely. She denied all knowledge of the photo being taken and swore that she'd never left Sophie alone – not even for a second. Juliet fell silent and for a moment or two they stared at each other. Thankfully, it was the girl who had the good grace, and the good sense, to look down at her bare toes. Satisfied that Lena was contrite, Juliet reiterated that her sole duty was to take care of Sophie and to be alert to all and any threats to her safety. Lena nodded her understanding. Juliet also said that she would be dropping by the Cottage at regular intervals, as and when her commitments permitted, across the course of the day.

Lena chastised, Juliet headed back up to the House. She had a power nap and followed that up with a cold shower. She decided to skip breakfast. She still had a few pounds left to lose and the thought of a hung-over Ben drinking gallons of black coffee, or more likely – given the hour – a rambunctious Jonny chewing his way through a fry-up, held little appeal. Feeling more in control and, therefore, more equipped to rejoin the fight, Juliet stepped outside of her room, but she didn't go downstairs, instead she headed upstairs, in search of Alice.

The top floor of the main house had always been set aside as the private quarters of the owner of Isola dei Delfini, and despite Geri very rarely setting foot on the island from one year to the next she maintained the tradition. It was another marker of her position at the tip of the apex. The third floor comprised her extensive personal suite, her study, a general admin office, that for this week was doubling as Alice's base, a washroom and a door that never seemed to be unlocked, but which Juliet assumed was a storage cupboard.

Alice looked up from her keyboard at Juliet's approach. 'Hello.'

Economical, that was a good description of Alice Baxter. She was also efficient, hardworking and as close to Geri as anyone. And she was female. Juliet had detected a glimmer of solidarity between the two of them on occasion. The sea of suits in which they both swam was, with a few very notable exceptions, adorned with paunches and penises. Despite Geri's advocacy of equality, men still heavily out-numbered women in the senior managerial posts within the Chalice Group and the Board was still all male, with the exception of Geri and Juliet. Geri was one of *the most* successful woman in business in the UK, but she was no feminist. Juliet wandered into the office as nonchalantly as she could manage, and perched on the edge of Alice's desk. 'Well, last night ... that was a bit intense, wasn't it?' There was no response. 'You've not met my father before, have you?'

'No. I've not had that pleasure.'

See. Juliet was right, there it was – that spark of sarcasm. 'I wondered if you'd like a coffee? I can have Carla bring you one up.'

'There's no need.' Pause. 'But thank you ... for the thought. Is there anything I can help you with?' Again, was that a dig about who really had to service the needs of the Chalices on the island, and in life?

'No. I'm good.' Juliet didn't move.

'You sure?'

'Yes, really.'

'Okay.' There followed an awkward pause. 'Well, if you don't mind. I've got quite a lot to get through before the meeting tomorrow.' She went back to her keyboard.

Polite chit-chat was getting Juliet nowhere. It was too painful to endure any longer so she cut to the chase. It was Alice who had brought up the meeting, after all. 'So she is serious, this time?'

Impressively, Alice didn't stop typing. 'Yes. She is.'

That was very direct, but still Juliet pushed. 'Are you sure? She's dangled the prospect of her retirement over us for years.'

Finally, Alice sat back and took off her glasses. 'I wouldn't know about that.' That was true. Alice had only been in post for eighteen months, although it felt longer given the speed with which she had become Geri's trusted right-hand woman. 'I think her birthday has focused her mind.'

Juliet kept her own tone light, but insistent. 'You and I both know that she could go on for years, if she wanted to. Turning seventy isn't going to put much of a dent in her. She's Teflon.' Alice made no comment. Her lack of response forced Juliet to push even harder, which she knew was risky; Alice would no doubt report this conversation back to Geri. 'I presume you know who she's going to give it to?'

Alice didn't so much as blink. 'That's an odd way of putting it . . . "give".' The emphasis she put on the word made Juliet feel uncomfortable. Alice continued, 'I think she'll choose the best person for the job. But' – she replaced her glasses, rolled her shoulders and went back to her work – 'what do I know?' Exactly. What did she know? She might do Geri's bidding, but she wasn't privy to her thoughts. No one was. Juliet stood up. This was pointless, as in her heart she'd known it was going to be. Alice was loyal and discreet. It was a prerequisite of her job. But as Juliet was leaving Alice did toss her a scrap. 'All I can tell you is that she's approached the issue with the same diligence as she does everything else. And that certain factors that have come to light recently have influenced her thinking.' Was

Alice enjoying this? Proving that she was in the know or at least more in the loop than Juliet? Her last word on the subject, or so Juliet thought – it was difficult to hear above the bash of her fingers on the keyboard – was, 'Quite markedly.'

As Juliet walked back along the empty hallway her mood darkened. She felt no clearer as to Geri's intentions, but simultaneously more concerned. What did Alice mean by 'certain factors coming to light'? Geri didn't simply stumble across things – she went looking. And 'factors' meant facts. Christ, if Geri had been digging into each of them, what had she found? They all had their sins and secrets. Reputation was everything to Geri, as she'd clearly demonstrated when she so coolly and efficiently removed their father from his post. On the landing Juliet paused and looked out of the huge picture window over the terrace towards Positano. If what Alice had said was true, then the future CEO of Chalice Group might well be determined by who had buried their skeletons the deepest.

Chapter 22

BEN

It was a delicious day. Sunny, but with the occasional drift of high white cloud. Ben had no problem with a morning spent lounging by the pool. Geri certainly seemed in no rush to put them out of their misery, which just went to show that misery was a very elastic concept.

Ben took a couple of arty shots of the pool with the bougainvillea-smothered house in the background and posted them on Insta to provoke Natasha, then he settled down on a sun lounger and put his earbuds in. He scanned through the playlist on his phone and opted for some John Legend – he was having a run on the classics – then he leant back and looked at the miles of glittering sea. He vaguely remembered his father telling him that Sardinia was out there somewhere. Or was it Sicily? Ian was the only Chalice who actually enjoyed sailing – which was ironic when you thought about it. A private island with a beautiful antique yacht at their disposal and there wasn't a sea leg between them, apart from his father. Some passions were obviously not passed on through your genes. Ben had very clear child-hood memories of his father striking out into the wide blue yonder whenever he got the opportunity. He used to call

107

it having 'adventures'. He would often be gone for days on end, with no communication whatsoever. The concept of a 'family' holiday had never meant much to him. Perhaps his father's regular disappearing acts, and Ben's childish but very real worry that he might never return, were the reason he preferred his yachts securely moored in harbours, preferably with professional catering and a good crowd on tap. The truth was that one beautiful place was much like any other after a while – it was the company that made the difference.

Tired of the view, Ben looked closer to home. From behind his sunglasses he watched his brother thrashing up and down the pool. Jonny was slapping at the water as if it had done something to personally offend him, his big, fat, fancy watch flashing like a beacon in the sunlight on every second stroke. Being Jonny must be so fucking exhausting. Petty as it was, Ben was pleased to note that he was the only one paying his brother any attention. Geri was sitting at one of the tables in the shade, working away on her laptop; Helena had her head in a slim book and a broad-brimmed hat; and Juliet's nanny had settled herself on another sun lounger under one of the big umbrellas, away from them all. She had Juliet's baby propped up on her knees. The nanny was singing softly to Sophie. Juliet herself was MIA. Ben suspected that his sister would be up in her room memorising chunks of her presentation for the following day. Maternity leave or not, Juliet was never going to be anything but overprepared. He wondered if she realised that her eagerness to impress sometimes came across as desperation.

Having known that they had a free pass for the full day,

Ben had dabbled a little after breakfast. Only a few grams. It was, on one level, a holiday, after all. Once they got into it tomorrow, it would inevitably kick off, so why shouldn't he enjoy the chilled vibe while it lasted?

Ben had been filled with a warm swell of nostalgia when he'd lifted the loose tile beneath his bed and reached into the hole that he'd dug out with a butter knife when he was a teenager. Some traditions mattered, and your first stash pit was one of them. But Ben's rosy glow had dimmed somewhat when he'd looked inside the pouch. He could have sworn that his personal pharmacy was light. But who could have found his hiding place and, even more unlikely, who would have helped themselves to its contents? As the ket kicked in, Ben indulged in a fantasy of Carla, high as a kite, floating around the House stark naked, with a feather duster in one hand and a joint in the other. The vision made him laugh out loud. That drew a glance from Geri. Fuck it. Letting go of your inhibitions every now and again was good for you. He was sure that secret toker Carla would agree. Who knew what their loyal, self-effacing house-keeper got up to when she was on the island on her own? In reality, he was probably misremembering how much he'd got through the last time he'd been on Isola dei Delfini. Now *that* had been a good weekend, not that he could remember it very clearly. It was no sweat. He'd message Aldo or Dante and restock when he was over in Positano. Luca would run him across. That was what he was there for, after all. But he'd do it later. For now, Ben couldn't be arsed. He tilted his head back and closed his eyes. Lena's lullaby drifted across the pool underscored by the slap slap slap of Jonny in the water. Ben let the sounds blend and ripple over him. He felt the warmth on his skin and the fizz of the ket in his bloodstream. The sun put on a lightshow inside his eyelids. Pleasure. He sometimes wondered whether he was the only Chalice who could feel it.

Some time later, Ben heard his father approach. It was impossible not to. The puffing, the shouted, 'Hello there. Lovely morning for it, but when is it not on Isola dei Delfini?', then the finale, the scream of metal across concrete as he crashed into one of the sun loungers. Ben opened his eyes. Maybe being sidelined within the business, and the family, at the very point that he was king of the hill was the reason his father felt compelled to make a grand entrance wherever he went. Jonny mid stroke, Helena mid page-turn and Lena mid verse – all paused and clocked him. Only Geri didn't react. It was impressive, but there again, having the self-discipline to ignore Ian was just one of Geri's many and varied ways of demonstrating just how much she despised him.

Ben waited for his father to make his way over to the empty sunbed next to him and begin spilling the beans about the previous evening – he owed Ben an update – but no, the old man glanced around then made a beeline for the far side of the pool. Ben felt his heart stutter. It was painful, like being struck in the chest with the butt of a knife. Ben watched as his father circled around Lena and the baby like a lazy old shark for a minute or so, then lowered himself heavily onto the sun lounger next to them. Sitting sideways, knees spread wide, really wasn't a good look for a sixty-seven-year-old man, in shorts, with a paunch. In response Lena sat up straighter and took hold of Sophie's little fists in her hands. A circle complete. A fragile barrier erected.

Ben couldn't hear every word of their conversation, but it appeared that his father was asking Lena questions about Sophie. The nanny responded with a brevity that his father seemed to find less than satisfying. Ben's chilled-out mood evaporated. It was, on the surface, a cute scene – the grandfather getting to know his new grandchild – but it was also a provocative one. Ian Chalice already had five grandchildren who he barely saw. Ben couldn't remember the last time his father had spent any time with Sasha and Ethan. That was hardly the behaviour of a doting family man. When Ben saw his father lean forward and take hold of Sophie's little fist in his big paw, he was ashamed to feel another stab of pain in his chest. Or was it jealousy? Either way, it made his eyes water. Thank Christ for sunglasses. The next thing Ben heard was Lena's raised voice, 'But it's time for her nap.'

His father was obviously not to be deterred. He lumbered to his feet, bent over Lena and lifted Sophie off her lap. The expression on the nanny's face was dark. Ian was oblivious, or feigning it. He cradled the baby in the crook of his arm and set off. Lena scrambled inelegantly to her feet and followed him. 'Mr Chalice, please. Ms Chalice has been very explicit that Sophie must be with me at all times.'

Ian stopped. He spun around so suddenly that Lena nearly crashed into him. They stood, nose to nose, glaring at each other over the baby. It was a virtual tug-of-war that his father was always going to win. With everyone now watching, Ian raised his voice and slowed his words; the effect was as chilling as it was patronising. 'My dear. Please stop with all this unnecessary twittering. I simply want to have a little chat with my granddaughter. I can assure you that she will come to no harm. I do know what I'm doing.' Then, as swiftly as he'd turned menacing, he switched back to saccharine politeness. 'It's a beautiful morning. All work and no play makes Jill a very dull young lady. Why don't you take a break? Catch a few rays. I'm sure my daughter won't really object. Her bark is worse than her bite. This little one will be perfectly safe with her grandpa.'

Lena held her ground for another second or two then accepted the inevitable, but to her credit she made her feelings clear by following Ian over to the sunbed next to Ben. She made quite a performance of dragging a parasol into place above his father's head and angling it so that Sophie was in the shade. All the while his father watched her, smiling his snaggle-toothed smile.

His father only spoke when Lena had removed herself to sit, bolt upright, three sunbeds over. 'Jeez, where did Juliet find her? Not the back pages of *The Lady*, that's for sure.'

Ben made no comment. Criticising staff was not something he indulged in. It never ended well; pissed-off staff were far more likely to take unflattering photos and sell them to the press or post them online than politely thanked and well-tipped ones, in Ben's experience.

'You're a little cutie, though, aren't you?' His father bent low over Sophie and took a deep breath. It sounded as if he was trying to inhale her whole. 'God, new babies. Don't you just love 'em?' He held Sophie up and stared into her eyes. Juliet's daughter didn't seem overly concerned about being manhandled like a lion cub, but Ben was finding his father's display of familial affection nauseating. 'You had best be on your guard, my little princess. Your relatives may look like normal people, but I fear you've been born into a nest of vipers.' He glanced across at Ben and added, 'The only one you'll ever be truly safe with is your Uncle Benny.' Ben smiled. A sliver of praise, at last. But then his father ruined it by adding, 'He may very well lead you astray when you're older, but he's the only one who is exactly what he appears to be. Totally and utterly harmless.' His father then held his new granddaughter to his cheek as if she was the most precious thing in the world.

Ben had to look away. The weak third wheel: pointless, directionless, wifeless, useless. It was how they all viewed him, even his own father. And harmless? Well, they would have to see about that.

Chapter 23

JULIET

Juliet only got as far as the entrance hall.

While she'd been talking to Alice another message and another photo had arrived. Juliet's stomach contracted. This time it was a long-distance shot of Sophie resting happily on Lena's bare legs. It had been taken over Lena's shoulder. The painful blue of the pool was visible at the end of the sunbed. Sophie's outfit in this shot was the all-in-one cotton suit with the rabbit motif that Juliet had put her daughter in that very morning. Message: **Isn't she wonderful?** As Juliet stood with her phone gripped tightly in her hand another message arrived. **But life isn't a Stevie Wonder song, is it, Juliet? Sophie is not made of love. Quite the opposite! Your precious daughter is made of something much less sweet. She's made of deceit.** Juliet ran to the door. Another message appeared as she yanked it open. **You know it.** Juliet rushed outside. **And now, so do I.**

Juliet raced across the courtyard and looked down at the terrace. She located Lena immediately, but Sophie was not with her. Juliet scanned the garden and the pool. Panic bloomed inside her. Where the hell was her daughter?

The answer – in the meaty paws of her father.

Juliet flew down the steps and raced around the pool. She snatched her daughter out of her father's hands – much too violently. Sophie gulped and started crying. Her wails rang out across the garden. Her father stared at her, with a deeply hurt expression on his face. Ben was also studying her, but his opinion was irrelevant. Then Juliet felt Lena step up beside her. Wordlessly, she offered to take Sophie from her. How dare she? No! No one should be holding her daughter, taking photographs of her, being anywhere near her – not without Juliet's permission. Sophie belonged to her. She was her child. And Juliet would not let anyone say otherwise. But her child was currently yelling and squirming in her arms and Juliet didn't know how to make her stop. As much as she shushed and rocked Sophie, it made no difference. If anything, her cries increased in volume and intensity. Next Jonny appeared, nearly naked in his tiny swim trunks with his arms outstretched, as if he intended to take Sophie from her as well. Juliet swung around in order to get away from him and saw Geri over in the shade. She was getting to her feet. They were all judging her and finding her wanting.

In the midst of the noise and the panic Juliet felt a hand on the small of her sweat-drenched back. The steady, gentle pressure helped to ground her. Common sense returned. Her daughter was upset because *she* was upset. Sophie would calm down if she calmed down. Juliet took some deep breaths and loosened her grip. Ignoring all the questions and concern, Juliet focused on Sophie. She whispered reassurances to her daughter that she had no confidence in, but knew were needed, and miraculously it worked. Sophie's crying slackened. Juliet allowed the hand on her back to guide her towards a chair on the lawn in the shade. She lowered herself into it and raised Sophie up onto her shoulder. It was her favourite position. The crying mutated into snuffling. The weight of her daughter's head was calming. Finally Sophie relaxed in her arms. Her baby did not hate her. Juliet met Lena's inquiring gaze and said, 'Thank you.'

Lena flushed and looked down at her feet. 'I'm so sorry. He wouldn't take no for an answer. I did try.'

Juliet realised in that moment, with absolute clarity, that Lena was the only person on the island that she could trust. She managed a small smile. 'It's okay, Lena. He never does.'

Chapter 24

JONNY

As Jonny watched Lena steer Juliet away he wondered if his sister was suffering from some sort of postnatal breakdown. It wouldn't be surprising, not with everything that had happened.

Up until a year ago Juliet had been the epitome of the successful career woman. Her life had been one long, impeccably scripted performance since the day she'd joined the business at the tender age of eighteen. In all that time there'd been no hitches, not a single one. More's the pity. Which was why the implosion of her personal life had come as such a surprise.

First there was the separation from her husband, Harry. Jonny had thought that mild, moderate, supportive, boring-as-sin Harry was going to hang around forever, sponging off Juliet. But no, he'd turned out to be quite the dark horse. From what Jonny had gleaned from Helena, and from the swirl of media coverage – Juliet herself had never spoken about it to him – Harry had had a younger, blonder bit-on-the-side for quite a while. But Fleur had not stayed on the sidelines. Harry had left Juliet for her, married her and fathered two children with her, all within three years of walking out, which was going some for a man who looked and acted like a small-town librarian. Unfortunately for Juliet, Harry's new spouse was big on social media so photos of their loved-up life had been, and still were, everywhere. Their speedy, lavish wedding in the Cotswolds, their honeymoon in the Cayman Islands, their beautiful converted barn, complete with matching Afghan hound. And very soon a beautiful, bouncing baby girl was added to these scenes of stylish marital bliss. Jonny did the maths and whoever had designed Fleur's floaty, fairy-tale wedding dress had done a good job. Baby Isla had arrived, early apparently, just in time for Christmas. Baby Arlo followed an indecent year later. His birth prompted another flurry of at-home-with-the-Dowdens features. Fleur and Harry and their flaxen-haired offspring got more coverage than some of the Chalice's best-selling products.

Throughout it all, Juliet appeared to cope well. If anything, Harry's betrayal seemed to galvanise her. Whereas she'd worked hard before, after the split his sister was even more committed, more invested, more motivated, more ballsy than ever. The not-so-covert message being – *I am a woman of intelligence, substance and seriousness . . . unlike some scheming, shallow bitches, whose names shall not be mentioned, and whose only role in life is chasing other people's husbands and popping out sprogs.*

Then out of nowhere came the bombshell. At the age of forty, and at the very moment when she was finally being viewed – by far too many commentators for Jonny's liking – as Geri's natural successor, Juliet had announced that she was five months pregnant, father unnamed. In fact, the subject of her child's father was totally embargoed, both in public and in private. Well, thanks to his wife, Jonny now knew why.

So in hindsight, perhaps the roots of Juliet's mental instability had been sown all those long months ago by weedy Harry's betrayal. Perhaps the frenzy of work, the massively accelerated drive to expand the Health and Well-Being division, the manic flying around the globe like some sort of international troubleshooter, were actually his sister's attempt to distract herself from the collapse of her marriage. Her decision to get pregnant, a deeply emotional reaction to finding herself alone and staring down the barrel of turning forty. And now that the reality of single motherhood was kicking in, the gun had gone off in her face. It was fascinating to see that even his bête noire of a sister was as prey to hormones as the next woman.

All of which was bad news for Juliet, but very good news for Jonny.

Watching Geri watch a hollow-eyed Juliet being guided away by Lena only served to support his view. This was a woman who was patently in no fit state to take on the onerous and high-profile role of CEO of the Chalice Group. Which meant – Jonny smiled and rewarded himself with a big yawn and a stretch – that he must now be a shoo-in. Surely?

With Juliet and her child gone, the mood around the pool began to settle into something altogether less stressful, but Geri had obviously decided that trying to work while others played, argued and emoted was not a good idea, because she began packing away her stuff. From his vantage point, Jonny saw that she went to the trouble of backing up whatever she'd been working on onto a memory stick. Surely that was an unnecessary precaution; she was on an island, in the middle of the Med, surrounded by her family. Geri's overzealous security piqued Jonny's interest. What had she been looking at that was so important? Briefcase packed, Geri announced that she'd see them for lunch. But she wasn't quite done. She made a detour round the pool over to Ian. At the foot of his sunbed she stopped and lowered her sunglasses. They all heard her say, loudly and very clearly, 'It goes without saying that you are not invited.' *Place* and *put*!

The minute Geri was out of sight, his father beckoned Jonny back over. Jonny wished that he could simply blank the old bastard and go sit with Helena, but that was too high-risk. Having him and Ben in cahoots was not good. Jonny would have put a sizeable chunk of change on Ben being Ian's informant. The fool obviously still thought that as the 'baby' of the family he had the closest relationship with their father. For Christ's sake, the guy was thirty-two.

But unlike needy Ben, Jonny made his father wait. He took his time towelling off, smoothing his hair into place and applying more sun cream.

Having the old bugger making waves was a complication that Jonny could do without; that they could all do without, but that had been true for years.

Their father had burnt his bridges, with a flame thrower, when he'd been removed as CEO of the Chalice Group. Any fleeting thoughts of protecting his family from the fallout of his sudden demise had been incinerated by his raging sense of injustice and his hatred of the Board ... but primarily of Geri. Jonny obviously hadn't said anything at the time, but secretly he'd been impressed and profoundly relieved when his aunt had taken her chance and plunged a very long knife into his father's back. He had become a liability. He had needed to go and Geri had been the only one with the power, and the balls, to do it. It had undoubtedly been the right decision, but his exit from the business, and the family, had not been without its problems.

The secrecy surrounding precisely why he'd been removed had spawned a blizzard of rumours. That speculation, allied with the widespread coverage of his father's very public and very messy implosion in the months, indeed the years, that followed, had contaminated the Chalice name. The court case, the stints in the Priory, the much-publicised trips to ashrams, interspersed with splashy appearances in the trendy hotspots of the globe where he partied with his famous friends whose reputations were often suspect – none of it had been good. Jonny sometimes worried that he could see the unasked question in the eyes of journalists, investors, even his own wife on occasion – did he take after his father or was he more his aunt's type of guy? *Sure*, the voices whispered, *Jonny Chalice has a reputation for being a ruthless, effective money-making machine, but is the taint of his father's flakiness simply biding its time, waiting to emerge when the pressure gets too much?* Jonny's carefully fashioned reputation as a rational, hard-nosed, in-control businessman was no accident. Some fathers provided role models by default.

And now that shadow was back, lying with its hairy belly out on a sun lounger on the other side of the pool, and it was threatening to fall across Jonny and his prospects once again. Well, Jonny wasn't going to let his father derail his rightful accession to the top of the Chalice tree.

Not now, no way – not when he was *this* close. Ian wasn't the only Chalice with hatred in his heart for a close relative. The difference was that Jonny knew how to harness his animosity and use it to his advantage. Hence his willingness to shoot the breeze with his good ol' dad. If Jonny could establish Ian's price for retiring from the fight then he would be in possession of some very valuable information. An accurate quote for getting rid of his father would make a great additional present for his aunt on her birthday.

Fully dried, sun-protected, hair combed, Jonny strolled over and channelled pleasant. 'Hi Dad. No ill effects from last night's little showdown, then? Other than being even more of a *persona non grata*.' Ben raised his eyebrows, but Jonny ignored him. Perhaps his father hadn't debriefed Ben. That was interesting.

Ian spread his hands arms wide and indicated his supine, fleshy body as if he was some sort of supersized Adonis. 'None whatsoever. I have the constitution of an ox and the heart of a lion.'

'What was that all about with Juliet?'

'Oh, nothing. You know your sister, she's always been highly strung.'

It was a low blow, but there was nothing to be gained from defending Juliet in the current circumstances, so Jonny let it go. He spread out a fresh towel and lowered himself onto a sunbed. 'So in amongst upsetting Juliet and pissing off Geri, you're enjoying yourself?'

'I am indeed. It's the most fun I've had in a while. You?'

'We're not really here to have fun.'

'No. You're all about the business, aren't you, my boy?' He reached across and actually ruffled Jonny's hair. It took an epic amount of self-control not to slap his sweaty hand away. 'Speaking of which, how is your painfully slow meteoric rise to the top going? Have you had the nod from the ice queen yet?' Jonny held back on making any comment. That didn't bother his father. 'Nah, I thought not. It's her last hurrah, isn't it? Why wouldn't she milk it for all it's worth? She's always got off on lording it over other people. She must be wetting her old-lady knickers with this.' Jonny winced, although he should've been used to his father's crudeness by now. Saying the unsayable was Ian Chalice's favourite pastime, as he proved with his very next comment. 'I reckon it's because it's the only excitement she gets. I sometimes wonder what she'd have been like if she'd ever had a decent shag.' Hate could evidently still burn hot and bright two decades on. Jonny let the silence stretch. His father really was an odious man, but even by his warped standards his next comment was very left-field. 'What's with Carla, the loyal old retainer, then? Has she been injected with monkey glands or something?'

Despite his better instincts, Jonny found himself asking, 'What're you talking about?'

'Her and the luscious young Luca.' Ian pointed. Jonny hadn't noticed that Luca was working on one of the flower beds on the far side of the garden. 'There's something going on there, if you ask me.' Jonny hadn't. He took a deep breath, trying to summon up the patience to hang in there with this nonsense. He instantly regretted it because he inhaled a lungful of his father. It was not pleasant. He smelt of warm flesh, stale cigarette smoke and something else – something meaty and unhealthy. This was precisely why Jonny was normally happy rarely, if ever, to see or speak to his father. In fact, the greater the distance between them the happier he was. 'Aunt and nephew, my ass. They're all over each other when they think no one's looking. But I have been. I see them a-hugging and a-squeezing down at the boatyard.'

Even Ben stirred himself enough to object to that pile of total cobblers. 'Dad! This is Carla we're talking about. She must be fifty, if she's a day.'

Their father made a grunting noise. 'Oh, trust me, the old ones can be real goers. Your aunt excepted, of course.' He switched tack again. 'Speaking of matters of the heart, how are things between you and your good lady wife these days?' The question was clearly directed at Ben.

Ben looked away and Jonny felt a rare spurt of sympathy for his half-brother. They had very little in common, but they did share the misfortune of having a poisonous old fucker for a father. Jonny stepped in and took the bullet by pretending that he thought the question was aimed at him. 'We're fine, thank you. Not that it's any of your damn business.' Jonny glanced over at Helena as he spoke. He was unnerved to find her staring straight at them. Surely she couldn't hear what they were saying from way across the other side of the pool? There was a fraction of a second when their eyes met before she went back to her book.

But his father was obviously enjoying his role as prime agitator and disruptor. 'That good, eh? Makes me glad I'm not shackled any more. You mark my words, boys, life is *so* much better without a wife. All they do is spend your money and drag you down.' Having pissed on both of their mothers, he closed his eyes and went back to sunbathing.

124

Jonny had had enough. His father was a complete shit. Always was, always would be. The problem was, he was a shit that had floated its way onto the island. Jonny got to his feet, taking pleasure in being tall and toned where his father was short and flabby. He smoothed his hair, ran his hand over his flat stomach, then bent over and spoke slowly and very, very clearly in his father's ear. 'There's one thing that you need to get straight in that addled, alcohol-pickled brain of yours. You are yesterday's news. You have no power. No allies. No one on this island can stand the sight of you. And I think, deep down, you know that. So go ahead, try to extract your last pound of flesh from Geri before she hands over the business. But if I were you I'd do it quickly. Because, know this, Dad. If you fuck this up for me – I will end you.' Jonny straightened up. He inhaled the air – it was so much cleaner up here – then smiled. 'Enjoy the sun while you can. But I wouldn't stay out in it too much longer, it looks to me like you're burning.'

Chapter 25

HELENA

Helena watched the men from beneath the brim of her hat. A book was always good cover for eavesdropping. The estranged father and his two adult sons shooting the breeze, as the sun shone and the waves whispered around their own private slice of paradise. Except that there was obviously still some of the same old Chalice poison in the balmy air. Helena had already witnessed the strange and distressing altercation between Juliet and Ian. She'd risen herself, intending to go to Juliet's aid, but she'd not. She'd been hampered, as always, by the belief that it wasn't her place to intervene in Chalice family matters. That it had been Lena, the nanny, who had defused the situation bothered Helena. It made her feel like a coward. Perhaps she was. Then, in the aftermath of the incident, she'd heard Ian ripping into Juliet, describing her as 'unhinged' and labelling Lena 'a jumped-up little bitch', which seemed grossly unfair – from Helena's conversations with the girl she seemed perfectly nice; so much for being the lovable old patriarch. By the time Jonny had wandered over, her father-in-law was on a roll of viciousness; he'd called Geri an 'ice queen' and speculated crudely about her sex life and now he was weighing in on Carla, for Christ's sake. And all the while Jonny and Ben sat there and let him, no word of dissent. Men were such lowlifes – when they thought no one was listening.

Or at least the Chalice men were.

When Helena heard the word 'wife' she realised that they'd moved on to her. She might be married to Jonny, be the mother of his children and be the person who'd put her own life and ambitions on hold in order to support his career, but to them all women were the same. Herself, Natasha, Juliet, Lena, Alice, Carla, even Geri – every one of them was fair game. And she, for one, was getting sick and tired of being in their crosshairs.

Jonny caught her looking. She didn't immediately look away. Why should she? It would do him good to realise that he was being seen.

That her husband could be as at ease with an old misogynist like Ian Chalice as he was with the great and the good was no surprise to Helena. She'd realised early on in their relationship that Jonny had a number of different skins that he could slip on and off as the occasion demanded. He'd told her as much himself. He'd explained it as one of the requirements of his high-powered job and his high-pressure family. At the time she'd been stupidly impressed – not by his ability to project different versions of himself, but that he'd confided in her. It had made her feel special, privileged, chosen. Her belief that Jonny trusted her with his true self, when he was naturally suspicious of everyone else, was one of the reasons she'd married him. The life he'd been able to promise her had also been a factor, but it genuinely hadn't been the main one – whatever people might think. What Helena hadn't bargained for was the niggling doubt that the husband-version of Jonny that she got was also a projection.

Sick of the sight and sound of them, Helena dropped her gaze and went back to the reassuring certainties of fiction.

Chapter 26

ALICE

Alice sent the instructions regarding lunch at 11.00 a.m., as per Geri's instructions.

Table at Blu Stone booked for 1.00 p.m. Please be ready and waiting down on the dock by 12.30 p.m., at the latest.

Juliet responded almost immediately with, **I will not be coming. Please send my apologies to Geri.**

Geri would not be happy, and Alice's job was to ensure that her boss was happy. Alice typed, **Bring Sophie with you.** On second thoughts, that sounded bossy and she had no desire to get on the wrong side of Juliet, so she added, **You know how much the Italians love babies. I'm sure they'll make a fuss of her. She is adorable.** Two seconds later she received a single-word response. **No.** Well, that told her.

Alice waited. She got nothing from the other two. Irritation rippled through her. She knew they were down by the pool, doing nothing. She gave it twenty minutes, then prompted them. This time Ben reacted immediately with a smiley face and a thumbs-up. Another ten minutes passed. She imagined Jonny taking pleasure in his petty non-compliance. Well, two could play at being passive-aggressive, and Alice had had lots of practice.

129

She messaged him directly. **Pls confirm attendance ASAP. Otherwise I will assume that you and Helena are not coming and will change the booking accordingly.** She liked the 'accordingly'. It smacked of the officiousness that she knew he so hated about her. She sat back, imagined him cursing her. If he didn't reply in the next half-hour she might just go ahead and do it – cancel him and Helena *and* not tell him. Oh, how she would love that. Alice spent a glorious few minutes fantasising about them all travelling over to Positano on the boat, the sea breeze in their hair, the salt spray on their faces. Disembarking like royalty at the marina, Jonny and his simpering wife strolling ahead along the harbour front, hand in hand, looking forward to being seated in the best seats at the best table on the terrace at the Blu Stone. Only to discover that Alice had been as good as her word and changed the booking. If only.

Alice's phone buzzed. **We'll be there.** Damn. The dream evaporated. She updated Geri, by email. Geri replied with thanks. She kept any thoughts that she might have on Juliet's non-attendance to herself, but she did surprise Alice by adding a PS: *Given there's a spare place now, you'd be welcome to join us. If you would like to.*

Lunch at the best seafront restaurant in Positano overlooking the sparkling waters of the Med, all expenses paid, what was there not to like? Well, the company. But for the pleasure of seeing Jonny's face when she rocked up at the dock to accompany them to lunch it would be worth it. She replied, *Thank you. That would be great.*

Chapter 27

LUCA

The *Black Swan* was a twenty-two-metre-long cruiser built in 1935. As befitted a yacht of such craftsmanship, elegance and expense, she'd been well cared for ever since she'd taken to the water. Her gleaming black hull was painted every winter and her teak deck and mahogany fittings were cleaned and polished on a strict rotation – a job that for the next few days fell to Luca. He was happy to do it. He'd never looked after such a beautiful boat before and was unlikely to do so ever again. But the *Swan* wasn't just beautiful, she was a joy to sail. She had a full rig and a Caterpillar engine so could go out in any and all weathers, and she cut through the water with an efficiency and grace that was exhilarating when she hit her top speed.

In Luca's informed opinion, the *Swan* was utterly wasted on the Chalices. Carla had told him that all they ever used her for was shuttling between the island and Positano and Capri, or, if they were feeling really adventurous, for a leisurely cruise around to Sorrento. Hence Luca's job for the week was little more than being a glorified taxi driver. His years spent crewing around the Amalfi coast, his knowledge of the tides and complex currents, his maintenance and mechanical skills meant nothing to them. All it had taken was for Carla to vouch for him when Marco, the usual guy, fell ill, and they'd given him the job. It would've served them right if he'd been an idiot who'd sailed them out to their deaths.

Today's excursion was typical – a half-hour hop across to the mainland for lunch. Of course, they would still want him to raise the sail; it was all about appearance in the marina at Positano.

Jonny and his wife were the first to arrive in the cove, followed by Ben. As Luca helped them down into the *Swan* he winced. He found skin-to-skin contact way too intimate. Ferrying the Chalices around was one thing, touching them was something else. As soon as they were on board he surreptitiously washed his hands in the sea. Then there was an awkward wait for the others to arrive. No one spoke to him. They all just sat and stared at their phones. Some people could be surrounded by beauty and never see it. Luca didn't mind being ignored, it was better than being required to chat. Ian Chalice hadn't stopped bombarding him with questions on the way over to the island: who came to the island the most, who with, what were the parties like *these days*? When Luca had told him he didn't know, that this wasn't his regular gig, he'd still not shut up, but instead switched to asking for recommendations about the best bars, with the friendliest girls. The man was a pig. To kill time while they waited Luca busied himself with some unnecessary rope-coiling. He knew from his short stint working for them that the Chalices hated to see staff idle. Thankfully Geri appeared next, trailed by Alice, the secretary.

Luca was unsure about Alice. She was an employee, like him and Carla, yet she lived among them and ate with them as if she was one of them. And, as Luca had discovered through her endless text messages, she was demanding on their behalf, very. But, to her credit, she was polite to him and Carla and always grateful for their efforts. As a result, Luca was wary of her. He simply didn't know whose side Alice Baxter was on.

Look at today. Surely she should be staying back on Isola dei Delfini, locked away in her office, working on whatever it was she did for Ms Chalice, and yet here she was, all dressed up in her floaty summer dress and floppy hat, heading off for lunch at the Blu Stone with them. That didn't sit right with Luca. And yet when he handed her down into the boat she was the only one who looked him in the face and said 'thank you' like she meant it. They were mind-fuckers, the lot of them. Luca waited. There was still no sign of Juliet Chalice, the last member of their exclusive gang.

Ms Chalice looked at her watch. Luca asked if they should wait, but Alice said, 'No, Juliet won't be joining us for lunch.' There was a ping-pong of glances between the brothers and Alice. Luca didn't wait to be told twice. He cast off. The quicker he could get them over to Positano, the quicker he could be shot of the lot of them.

Chapter 28

JULIET

Juliet heard them pass the Cottage on their way down to the *Swan*, glad to her bones not to be going with them. The panic of the morning had to be boxed up and the lid nailed shut and to do that she needed to have some time on her own. Such flakiness was not her, and it really hadn't looked good. If she was going to prove to her father that he could not fuck with her, to Geri that she was still her best bet and to herself that she was the same person she had been before she'd had Sophie, then it was imperative that she got her shit together.

Her first step was to tell Lena to take a break. The girl looked hesitant at first, but Juliet insisted. 'It was just the shock of seeing him holding Sophie. I should have told you that my father and I do not have the best of relationships. And that's something of an understatement.' That was all Juliet could bring herself to say. Talking about her father made her think of her mother and that would not help. 'But I'm fine now, honestly. I'm going to take Sophie up to the House with me. I think we could both do with a siesta. Please, take some time off. You've earned it. Explore the island. Go for a swim. The rest of them will be gone for a few hours, at least, so no one will bother you.' Lena's, *Well, if you're sure. It would be nice to have a break*, made Juliet realise how indifferent she'd been to Lena's needs since they'd left London. The girl must be tired. She certainly looked it. Maybe it was that glimmer of empathy that made Juliet feel a sudden urge to hug Lena goodbye. Or perhaps it was her own need for physical contact and comfort. Either way, she didn't. It was weakness to rely on one's staff too much.

It felt strange having Sophie up at the House with her. Strange, but nice. It made the room feel more hers. Juliet laid her daughter on the bed, slipped off her sandals and settled down beside her. And joy of joys, Sophie seemed content, for a change. She gazed at the ceiling and cooed. Seduced by the calm and the quiet, Juliet allowed herself to do nothing but breathe and be. This was what she wanted – to be at peace with her child. Sophie drifted off to sleep. Juliet lay beside her and watched her.

She was on the woolly brink of sleep herself when her phone pinged. The sound startled her alert. It was another photo, another extreme close-up; this time of Sophie in Juliet's arms, down by the pool, when she was having her meltdown. The distress of the situation was evident in Juliet's anguished face and in the dark circle of Sophie's screaming mouth. Juliet scrambled upright. The message read: **Isn't she precious?** Juliet's sense of being calm and in control drained away. She waited, expecting and dreading more. It came. **The question is . . . how precious, Juliet? Because, make no mistake, you are going to have to decide what price you are prepared to pay to keep your daughter.**

Would he really stoop this low? A normal father wouldn't, but this was Ian Chalice and he had proved, time

135

and time again, that people, even his closest family, were nothing more than resources to him. But how on earth had he found out about Sophie's conception? No one, not even the clinic that carried out the procedure, knew that Juliet had committed a crime to have Sophie. A terrible one, in some people's eyes; a necessary one, in Juliet's – which just went to show how subjective morality was. Juliet had gone to considerable lengths to cover her tracks, and her father was not known for his diligence, yet somehow he appeared to have sniffed out the truth. No, that didn't make sense.

An awful alternative bloomed like mould in Juliet's brain. There was another candidate.

Geri.

Once contemplated, the fear that the messages might be coming from Geri rather than from her father mushroomed. Alice's comment about Geri having found something out about one of them came roaring back to her. That triggered an avalanche of suspicion. Ever since they'd arrived on the island Geri had been off with her. The insistence that Juliet stay in the House, the irritation every time she checked her phone for messages from Lena, the look of thinly veiled disgust on her face down by the pool when Juliet had panicked. It was a litany of judgement, and on each and every occasion Geri appeared to have found her wanting. Then there was their awkward early-morning conversation in the Cottage and Geri's sudden interest in her state of mind, her remark about motherhood *requiring sacrifices*. Had that been Geri's warped way of letting Juliet know she was not happy that she had chosen motherhood over her career and that there would be consequences for displeasing her?

No! Geri had always championed Juliet's success. She'd believed in her vision for the future of the Chalice Group. So much so that she'd supported Juliet's efforts to expand and modernise the business, to the tune of millions of pounds of investment. And she had implied, many times, that she saw Juliet as her natural successor.

But perhaps Geri thought Juliet had betrayed that faith in her by getting pregnant? Perhaps she saw Juliet's decision to have a child as disloyal? Stupid, even? She patently thought she wasn't coping and Geri had no time for failure. Could this be some sort of punishment for Juliet not living by, and up to, Geri's singular vision of how a woman had to be to get on in business? It was possible.

Her father or her aunt? Whatever the grim truth, Juliet needed to find out, and what better opportunity would she have than now?

Alice had gone with the others to lunch. The top floor was empty. She slithered off the bed and looked down at her daughter, sleeping peacefully. It seemed cruel to wake her, but Juliet had no choice. Geri would not have invited her father to the Blu Stone, which meant that he was somewhere on the island, which meant that there was no way Juliet was going to leave Sophie alone in an unlockable room.

Whispering 'Sorry, sweetheart', she picked Sophie up and took her with her.

The marble on the landing was cool beneath Juliet's bare feet. She climbed the stairs up to the top floor quickly. There were no guarantees that she'd find anything, but she had to try. The door to Geri's office was closed. Juliet shifted Sophie onto her shoulder and knocked, expecting, but still

137

praying for no response. There wasn't one. But it could very well be locked – that would scupper her. Thankfully the handle twisted and the door opened. Juliet didn't hesitate. She stepped inside.

The study hadn't changed much since her father's day. Juliet was surprised that Geri had left the oppressive decor untouched; there was a lot of ponderous dark-wood furniture, antique ornaments and desk toys. It was a cliché of a study. Perhaps the infrequency of Geri's visits to the island meant that she simply couldn't be bothered to redecorate, although such laxness was unlike her. Or maybe she enjoyed working surrounded by the props of male power. Juliet had noticed how Geri liked to keep the comparison between herself and Ian top of mind. Ousting her brother hadn't been enough for Geri; she seemed to take pleasure from reminding people of it. The only change that Geri had made was to the pictures. Ian had gone for a job lot of horses and English pastoral scenes. Geri had dumped these homages to old money and filled the walls with a cacophony of modern art. The overall effect was disorientating. It was like standing in the middle of a particularly badly curated art gallery, although Geri's collection was probably worth a fortune – she rarely made a bad investment.

The study had been off limits to Juliet as a child, despite her father rarely using it, but that hadn't stopped her sneaking into it from time to time. When Jonny was being particularly boisterous she used to collect up her dolls, climb up to the top floor and slip inside the room in search of some peace and quiet. She'd play happy families in here for hours – as a child she'd had a vivid imagination. She'd needed one! Being inside the study again evoked the same sense of guilt all these years later, but whereas as a child Juliet had been hiding, now she was seeking. She scanned the room, looking for cameras. What she was about to do was risky. It could be fatal to her prospects if she were filmed doing it. Feeling her heart rate rising, Juliet tried to reassure herself that she was not being observed. Although Geri was obviously not averse to keeping tabs on other people, Juliet couldn't imagine that she'd want her own behaviour recorded. Sod it. Needs must – somewhere in this study was the information that Geri had obtained on Juliet. She simply had to find out how much she knew.

Logic dictated that the innocuously described 'due diligence' that Alice had referenced would be on the MacBook that sat on top of the ugly big-ass desk. Juliet looked at the apple with its distinctive, pristine bite-mark. If only transgressions in real life were so neat and contained. The temptation to lift the lid and try to log on was powerful. But that would be a fool's errand. She would never be able to guess Geri's password. Juliet had to hang on to the slim hope that if Geri had incendiary information she would go for old-school security.

She crossed the room, crouched down and stared at the picture that was propped up on the floor in the corner of the study. As she did so Juliet could have sworn that she felt her daughter turn her heavy little head as if trying to get a look as well. It was almost like they were a team. It was the ugliest painting that Juliet had ever seen; a parade of monstrosities complete with a skeleton wielding a scythe, a monster with horns and a huge human head that had an anus instead of a mouth. Not art suitable for a child, or anyone else really. With another apology, Juliet laid

Sophie down on the rug. Avoiding the multitude of eyes looking at her, Juliet carefully moved the picture aside. She pressed the panelling and a section of the wall swung open to reveal the safe. (Juliet had found it quite by accident one day when she was playing. She'd simply leant back and the panel had popped open. What was more impressive was that she'd watched and waited a further six months before she finally got her hands on the combination. Her father obviously hadn't thought his young daughter wily enough to be paying attention when he checked that he had it right one day when she was in his study.) Juliet now did what she remembered her father doing all those years ago; she went over to the desk and picked up the globe. She unscrewed the base, and inside the hidden compartment was the familiar, tatty curl of paper – the combination to the safe. Geri probably didn't even know it was there. She'd have no need for a reminder. She was the type of person who would be able to recall perfectly a six-digit sequence, with left and right instructions, but there again she wasn't a barely functioning alcoholic, unlike Ian. Juliet grabbed a pen and wrote the sequence on the top of her left hand then returned the paper to its hiding place. She was fully aware that if Geri had changed the combination then she was screwed. She clicked her way through the numbers on the old rotary dial. It seemed to take an inordinate amount of time. Sophie made a small croaky noise, then another. Sweat trickled down Juliet's back, but she kept going. She wasn't going to get another chance to find out what Geri knew. There was a clunk. Juliet pulled open the heavy door.

The safe was empty.

That made no sense. Geri must have all sorts of sensitive commercial information that she needed to keep secure. Juliet's heart banged in her chest. Sophie's croaks were louder now. It sounded as if she was struggling to breathe. She needed her mother, but her mother was busy – trying her best to protect her. Did Sophie not understand that? Of course she didn't, she was a two-month-old baby. Frantically, Juliet swept the bottom shelf with her hand. Nothing. Sophie stopped croaking and began to cry in earnest. Juliet had to go to her. If Carla heard them, she would tell Geri. As she swept the top shelf, her hand connected with something solid. She lifted it out. It was an old-style cashbox. She opened it and was confronted by tight rolls of notes: euros, dollars and sterling. Money was no use to her. She slammed down the lid and shoved the cashbox back into the safe. She'd put herself in this vulnerable position for absolutely no reason. But as Juliet withdrew her hand something clattered to the floor. A memory stick. Thank fuck!

Stick retrieved, dial spun, safe locked, hideous picture restored to its propped-up position – Juliet scooped up her daughter and fled.

Chapter 29

LUCA

Having dropped off the Chalices at the restaurant jetty, Luca secured the *Swan* and headed below deck. He had 'permission' to go into the town, but he had no desire to do so. Although many of Luca's generation had moved away from the coast to find better, more regular employment, or simply for a new start – there were still a lot of the old-timers around, running the same old restaurants and bars that they had in his teenage years. Did he want to run into them and risk being recognised? Did he want to feel their stares and face their questions? There was always someone who prided themselves on 'saying what other people were thinking'. Why should he have to explain himself? To them, or anyone.

So as the world clamoured and clashed in the bright sunshine outside, Luca made his way down to the staff quarters in the dark belly of the boat. He kicked off his deck shoes, lay on the narrow bunk bed and closed his eyes. The *Swan* rose and fell as other craft entered and left the harbour. Part of it, but separate and secluded, just as he liked it, Luca rode the swell and felt at peace.

Chapter 30

JULIET

Juliet put her crying daughter on the bed, then took the chair from her dressing table and wedged it against her bedroom door. Next she pulled the shutters to. The resulting gloom helped a little, but she was still rattling with stress. Juliet was aware that barricading herself inside her own bedroom was not normal behaviour; it betrayed a siege mentality, but that was precisely how she felt – under siege. The memory stick in her hand was small, but it weighed heavily on Juliet. If Geri found out that she'd been in her office and broken into her safe that would be the end of their relationship, and of Juliet's career. She hated the thought of losing either; they were the most important things in her life. Or at least, they had been until she'd had Sophie. Juliet's heartbeat stuttered. Should she sneak back into the study and return the memory stick to the safe? Simply await her fate? But that was too passive, too cowardly. She couldn't not take a look. This was no longer simply about herself, she had to protect her daughter.

Her daughter . . . who now sounded as if she was choking. Juliet put the memory stick down and picked up Sophie.

Fifteen minutes later, calm was restored. Juliet had succeeded in wrestling a dirty nappy from her daughter and in getting her to take a full bottle of milk. It had been straight out of the fridge rather than at the recommended 37°C, but that seemed to make no difference to Sophie. She guzzled it. Juliet even managed to burp her on the first attempt. Not bad for someone vibrating with strain.

With Sophie sorted and settled in a nest of pillows by her side, Juliet fetched her laptop. She needed to know. She pushed the memory stick into the port and without hesitating clicked on the file marked **JJB**. There was a rapid flicker of activity as the documents began to appear on the screen. Juliet watched, breath held. Knowledge was power and Juliet needed to know how much power Geri had.

The answer was, a lot.

There was a file on each of them: herself, Jonny and Ben. So Geri had gone digging for all their skeletons, not just hers. The volume of information was staggering, the topics wide-ranging, the nature of some of the files deeply personal. It was clear that Geri's 'audit' went way beyond anything that could be considered remotely reasonable. It was a gross, thorough and devastating invasion of their privacy. But Juliet's indignation was of no use to her. What she needed to establish, and quickly, was what Geri knew about Sophie's conception. The rest of it could wait. She took a breath and clicked on her name.

A long list of folders appeared. She went straight to the one marked Medical History. There was a menu of subfolders. She skipped over *Mental Health*, *Illnesses and Injuries*, *Medication* and found *Fertility Treatment*. She clicked. There was another list of headings, dated in chronological order. A cold, unremitting catalogue of her long struggle to become a mother.

The investigators, whoever they were, had uncovered and detailed every step of her battle with infertility. They'd tracked down the payments she'd made to the clinic in Hertfordshire that she and Harry had originally used, and had listed the even heftier sums they'd paid to the Harley Street practice that they'd moved to for their fourth and fifth IVF attempts. The total cost ran into the tens of thousands of pounds. As Juliet scanned through the inventory of invoices for 'services rendered', the trauma of that time resurfaced. Each date and debit represented a staging post on her long, tortuous journey of public denial and private anguish. Ten years, a hundred-plus months, thousands of days and nights of hope and despair – all of which she'd kept hidden from sight behind the polished lie of Juliet Chalice, the woman for whom career was far more important than family.

So Geri knew that Juliet been trying, and failing, to have a baby for over a decade before finally falling pregnant with Sophie – and yet she'd not uttered a single word of interest, sympathy, support or reproach. Juliet scrubbed at her face to prevent the tears that had been building up from falling. The pressure was appalling, but there was no point in succumbing to it. What she needed to do was keep going. She went back to the finance trail. The fertility treatment payments stopped at the same time as her marriage. That made sense, but, of course, that was not the end of the story.

Juliet's eyes sought, and found, the file she feared. *Fertilas, Zurich*. Geri, or more accurately Geri's bloodhounds, had followed the trail that far. Had they got further? Had they managed to breach patient confidentiality at one of the most exclusive, expensive and successful fertility clinics in the world? Had Geri's wealth and influence trumped her own? Juliet was terrified that it had.

She took another deep breath then clicked on the *Fertilas* file – and fell down her own intensely personal, supposedly private rabbit hole.

Chapter 31

BENEDICT

Sea bass spaghetti with lemon gin mousse and prickly pear, seared octopus with provolone, linguine with hazelnut and anchovies, risotto with saffron and red prawns. It wasn't surprising that everyone passed on dessert. Instead they threw down their linen napkins, leant back and admired the view. It was the most relaxed Ben had seen Geri in a long while. She even faked delight when a bottle of champagne and a *torta della nonna* were presented to her and the whole restaurant sang 'Tanti Auguri, Geraldine'.

It was all so chilled that it didn't matter, well, not much, that Geri assumed it was Alice who had alerted the restaurant to the fact that it was her birthday, or that Jonny made a thing of not-so-surreptitiously paying the bill. It was fine with Ben. If his big brother wanted to play at being Billy Big Bollocks, let him.

After lunch they lingered in the gardens at the Blu Stone, almost like a normal family who didn't want to say their goodbyes after having a lovely time together. But the illusion didn't last long because Geri announced that, *unfortunately*, she needed to head back to the island as she had a conference call at 4.00 p.m. To Ben, she didn't look too unhappy about getting back to work. Jonny's Mr Cool persona slipped noticeably when he asked, 'Who with?'

Maybe it was the wine, but Geri actually answered him. 'The lawyers. To sort out this nonsense with your father.' So whatever their father had threatened, it had been enough to prompt Geri to seek legal advice. That was interesting. 'But you guys stay for a while. Luca can come and fetch you when you're ready. See you all later.' And with that Geri broke up the party. Alice trotted after her. The words to 'Mary had a Little Lamb' ran through Ben's brain.

The spirit of harmony departed with Geri. Jonny swung his jacket over his shoulder. 'Back at the quayside for, let's say, 5.00 p.m. Don't be late.' Ben watched Jonny and Helena disappear into the labyrinth of backstreets that clung to the hillside above the bay. He vaguely remembered Helena mentioning that they had something to pick up from the jewellers on Via Del Mulini. An expensive gift for Geri, no doubt. Hands in his pockets, sun on the top of his head, Ben set off in the opposite direction. Present-shopping would have to wait; his priority was restocking his stash.

Aldo was waiting for him in the bar just off Via Monte, as agreed. They did the deal in the toilets then had a drink together, caught up on the gossip. Given Aldo's trade, they had a lot of mutual acquaintances. The world was a big place, but it was surprising how the same names and faces kept cropping up.

Finding a present for his beloved, stinking rich, all-powerful – for now – aunt turned out to be more tricky than scoring. What do you buy for the woman who has everything? Geri's lack of passion for anything other than respect and success was the problem, and she certainly had no need for any more 'stuff'. She already had more than she could ever want, all of it tasteful and most of it very high-value indeed. Another painting, another helicopter, another piece of priceless jewellery would make no difference to her. As Ben wandered aimlessly and pleasantly through the shady of streets of Positano he smiled. Ha, his stupid brother was about to blow a stack on some exquisite, hand-crafted necklace or bangle that Geri wouldn't like, wear or want.

Which left what? A break at a luxury hotel or spa? An experience? An all-expenses-paid trip to one of the most amazing, remote, inaccessible locations that the world had to offer? But Geri could already go anywhere and do anything she wanted and she never did – not unless it was on business. Which was just plain sad, when you stopped to think about it. Perhaps it was because Ben's own family was drifting ever further away from him that he was suddenly struck by how fundamentally alone Geri was. She'd never shown the slightest interest in men, or women – for sex, partnership or friendship – at least not as far as Ben could see. And as for children of her own – that had never seemed to be a consideration. She'd always appeared content with her light-touch relationships with Jonny, Juliet and himself. She had, to all intents and purposes, lived the life of a nun – just one that was dedicated to Mammon, not God. Christ, a whole life lived without sex or companionship sounded bleak. All of which hazy, wine-softened musing left Ben with only one option. Sentimentality. He would get his aunt what no one else would – something

149

silly, personal and sweet. The question was, what? And whatever it was, Ben would have to find it in one of the local shops, in the next half-hour.

Chapter 32

JULIET

Switzerland. Juliet's last-ditch attempt to become a mother. It was all there in the *Fertilas* file. Her mouth dried.

Somehow – through bribery, no doubt – the investigators had got hold of the details of Juliet's trip. They had copies of her initial correspondence with the clinic and of the contract that she'd signed – hard proof that she'd engaged their services. They'd also researched what those services were. Juliet skimmed through that information quickly. She knew that the Swiss clinic was famous for succeeding where other fertility clinics had failed. Why else would Juliet have chosen them? That, and their reputation for the utmost discretion. But the 'evidence' in the file went much further than that. They had the date she'd arrived in Zurich and the number of days she stayed. Her alibi at the time had been that she was in Switzerland to look at a state-of-the-art collagen patch lab. She'd pretended to discount it as right for Chalice Well-Being on her return, for cost reasons. So much lying. It was a wonder that she hadn't slipped up. But she hadn't – it had taken Geri's forensic autopsy to uncover what Juliet had done. The bastards that Geri had hired had certainly been thorough. The file even included a copy of her hotel bill. Juliet remembered eating barely anything of the room service meal she'd ordered; she hadn't been able to sit in a dining room full of happy, holidaying couples. She read on, but she could find no further hard evidence, just a summary of the findings. A summary that made the case that – given the dates and the purchased services – *it could be fairly safely assumed that Sophie had been conceived on that trip to Fertilas*. A separate file followed that detailed the timeline of Juliet's pregnancy and Sophie's eventual safe delivery.

Juliet began to scroll even faster, clicking randomly on different documents in different folders. Her heart rate ticked up. What she'd found so far was invasive and cruel, but it wasn't game over. Not yet. She was searching for one word and one word only. She read the notes on her maternity care and on Sophie's birth. Nothing. She went back and reread everything relating to her dealings with Fertilas. She made sure that she hadn't missed a single damning line. But no, there was nothing. She hardly dared believe it, but it appeared that for all their digging around in the darkest recesses of Juliet's life, for all their gross invasion of her privacy, Geri's snoops had failed to discover the one thing that could really hurt her. Namely, the identity of Sophie's father.

Then she saw it: a subfolder entitled *Paternity*. With adrenaline coursing through her system, Juliet clicked on the file. It didn't have a lot in it, but there was one clear statement, which read, *Numerous attempts were made to ascertain the identity of the biological father of Juliet's child [please see attached], but the stringent security protocols at the Fertilas Clinic proved impossible to breach. We were forced to abandon direct approaches to staff due to the risk of detection. However, given that the conception event occurred twenty-six months post-separation from the husband and given the bespoke donor service that Fertilas provides, and that JC enquired about this service, it seems reasonable to assume that donor sperm was used.*

Juliet sat back. Her efforts at concealment had worked. Her secret was safe. Sophie was safe. The text messages were not from Geri, they were simply her snake of a father chancing his luck. She bent down and kissed her daughter's downy head. Sophie gurgled in response. This meant that she could fight on. She could, and would, prove to Geri that she, Juliet Chalice, could be both a mother and the CEO of the Chalice Group.

Reassured that Geri didn't have any ammunition that could fatally wound her – donor insemination wasn't a crime; in fact it was barely news any more, the rich and famous were always doing it – Juliet lifted Sophie onto her knee. Together they sat and watched the rest of the files download onto her laptop. Appalling as Geri's audit was, knowledge was power. It would be useful for Juliet to know what Geri had found out about her brothers.

Files downloaded, Juliet removed the memory stick, slid her laptop under her pillow, and picked up Sophie. She whispered, 'One last little trip, sweetheart', then she removed the chair and opened the door.

Juliet hurried up the stairs, along the corridor and back into Geri's study. Having put Sophie down on her spot on the rug, Juliet popped the panelling and laboriously went through the combination sequence. But this time there was no clunk. Knowing full well it was still locked, Juliet tried

153

the door anyway. It wouldn't open. Shit. She checked the sequence on her hand and entered it again, this time with sweaty fingertips. She was beginning to panic now. What if the safe had some sort of lockdown system after a certain number of failed attempts? Again, no clunk. Juliet rocked back on her heels and told herself to calm down. She wiped her palms on her dress and went through the motions one more time, checking as she went that each number was correct. She could not get 'three strikes and you're out' out of her head. Sequence complete, she held her breath. There was a dull clunk. The safe opened. Thank Christ.

She put the memory stick back on the top shelf next to the cash box, shut the safe, closed the panel, returned the picture to its original position and readjusted Geri's chair. Then she scanned the room for any sign that she'd been there. She couldn't see any. She picked up Sophie and stepped out into the hallway. Had the door been open or closed? Closed! It had been closed. She pulled it shut behind her.

'Juliet!'

Geri was standing there, at the top of the stairs, not ten feet away from her. It wasn't a greeting, it was an interrogation. What Geri really meant was, *what the hell were you doing in my office?* Behind her stood Alice, who appeared to be silently asking the same question. Juliet needed to bluff this one out, and quickly. 'Sophie and I had a little siesta.' Geri said nothing, nor did she move. The pause went on for what felt like an hour. Juliet glanced down at Sophie. The combination! Shit, shit, shit. She swiftly slid her hand out of sight behind the folds of Sophie's dress. 'I was looking for you. I'd forgotten that you were all out at lunch.' That didn't sound very plausible, but perhaps the accusations of baby brain could finally be put to some use. Juliet scrambled around for a valid reason why she'd had a sudden, urgent desire to speak to her aunt. A thought occurred to her. She went with it, for the want of anything better. 'I wanted to confirm my return-to-work date.' That was utter rubbish, but it was the best she could come up with under such intense pressure.

'Okay.' Geri's expression was sceptical. 'And . . . ?'

'Sorry, what?'

'The date?' Geri prompted.

'Oh, yeah. I'll be back on the 1st June.' Two weeks away. Two months earlier than planned.

'Full-time?'

No! 'Yes.' At this point Juliet would have said anything to get the hell out of there.

Geri moved to go past Juliet. 'That's great. Alice, can you log that and liaise with the relevant parties, please.' Thank Christ, she was being dismissed. 'Now, if you'll excuse me, I have work to do.' As she glided by she said, 'It's a shame you couldn't make lunch. It was exceptional, wasn't it, Alice?'

In response, Alice flashed Juliet a sly smile and said, 'It was.'

Chapter 33

LUCA

Ms Chalice and Alice travelled back to Isola dei Delfini after lunch, as planned – Ms Chalice obviously liked to stick to a schedule, even on holiday – but the others decided to stay on in Positano. This meant that Luca would have to go back over to the mainland to collect them later in the afternoon. He didn't really mind. It meant extra time at sea. The *Swan* was a pleasure to sail, even more so when Luca had her all to himself. So for one way, at least, he would be in his element. To make himself useful while he waited, Luca set to work sorting out the household waste. The Chalices generated a lot of rubbish. Consume and discard was what rich people did. Luca was on his second trip down to the compactor when he heard the scream.

Luca didn't assume he was hearing things.

He didn't dismiss it as a seagull or a snatch of video on somebody's phone.

He knew it was a real scream because he'd heard such panic and fear before.

He dropped the rubbish and ran.

Chapter 34

GERI

Geri closed the door on Juliet and her child and settled herself in the God-awful study that would forever remind her of the God-awful men in her life. She needed time and space and quiet in which to think. There was definitely something wrong with her niece. Her behaviour was becoming more and more erratic. Geri suspected that she knew what was wrong, but Juliet was not her immediate priority. Ian was. More specifically, how she was going to get rid of him.

Even though she'd requested the meeting, Geri was struggling with her decision to notify the lawyers about Ian's challenge to the legality of the original settlement. Once they got involved it would become a tangible problem. 'Tangible' meant substantive, and that was the last thing Geri wanted Ian's threats to become. Loath as she was to cave in to his tawdry attempt at blackmail, perhaps the wiser course would be to pay him off on the q.t. – yet again. How much would he want? Geri dreaded to think, but she knew it would be exorbitant. Ian's demands always were. He was greedy to his rotten core. And this time he believed he had additional leverage. His claims of mental trauma at the time of the original deal were, of course, utter rubbish, but in the current climate they might be enough to cast doubt on his fitness to sign away control of the business. The last thing Geri needed was for him to stand up in a courtroom. Ian could be horribly convincing when he saw fit. He'd played the victim enough times before. Even she'd fallen for it on occasion. Geri felt her usual sangfroid disintegrating. She might pretend otherwise in front of the family, but she genuinely feared that Ian could, yet again, cause her a heap of trouble, and now really was not the time for her brother's peculiarly grubby brand of exploitation.

Geri picked up a pen and twirled it in her fingers. Montblancs were always so nicely weighted. As she teased at the problem, another smaller thought nudged its way into her brain. She stilled, concentrated on the niggling. The pen had been on its rest when she left the study. Everything had a proper place in Geri's life. Micromanagement led to macro results. The niggle sparked and ignited.

Geri scanned the room. It all looked as it should, until she spun her chair around. She noticed it immediately – the Seven Sins picture had been moved. Only a fraction, but it was enough to confirm what she already suspected. Juliet hadn't been looking for Geri, she'd gone hunting for information.

Geri smiled. That was more like the Juliet she respected and admired.

Chapter 35

BENEDICT

Ben knew that his search for a birthday present for Geri was over the minute he clapped eyes on it, sitting there all alone on the top shelf of a little shop off Viale Pasitea. It was the perfect gift for the woman who had everything – except love. And at only twelve euros, it was an absolute bargain.

He paid in cash and wandered out of the shop on a high that for a change was not chemically induced.

Chapter 36

LUCA

Quick as he was, Luca was not the first person to reach the source of the scream. Carla was. She was already in Lena's room when he arrived. But confusingly, the nanny herself was nowhere to be seen.

Ian Chalice, however, was impossible to miss. He was rolling around on the floor, moaning and cursing.

Carla's breathing was uneven and her face looked different. Her familiar features appeared sharper and more defined. Maybe it was simply that Luca's senses were on high alert. Something bad had happened in this room. The question was, what?

'Where's Lena?' he asked.

'Safe. She's in the bathroom.'

'Good.' Luca would help Lena once he'd dealt with Ian. Carla raised a hand to her face to tuck away a strand of hair and Luca saw that her fingers were bloody. He felt savage. He moved towards Ian Chalice, fists clenched, not knowing what he was going to do, but sure as hell that it was going to hurt. As Luca approached him, Ian cried out and shuffled backwards on his arse. He got as far as the bed, which blocked his path. Marooned against the cotton bedspread, he yelled something that sounded like, 'Get the fuck away from me!' It was hard to tell, given the damage that had been done to his face. His nose was clearly broken and both of his lips were split. He was a mess. The extent of his injuries made Luca hesitate. But not for long, the old bastard was in no position to demand anything. Luca stood with the tips of his shoes touching Ian's hip and leant in close. He was pleased to see this blubbering, blustering apology of a man curl in on himself with fear. Blood bubbled through his teeth and dripped onto the rug as he whimpered and whined. Ian Chalice was at Luca's mercy and that felt good.

Chapter 37

GERI

There was a knock on the study door. Geri's first response was irritation. She was working – no one disturbed her when she was working. What the hell was Alice playing at? She was supposed to be her gatekeeper. Geri had already wasted over two hours having lunch with Jonny and Ben, then she'd frittered away more time pondering the conundrum of her brother and the possibility that her niece was a thief – and the call with the lawyers was in forty-five minutes. There was another burst of knocking. Geri barked, 'Come in!'

The door swung open and there stood Carla. She spoke quietly but firmly. 'I'm sorry, Ms Chalice, but you must come. Now.'

Carla's uncharacteristic assertiveness was all Geri needed to convince her that whatever this was, it was serious. She rose from her desk, put the errant pen back on its rest and followed Carla down the stairs. Carla moved soundlessly. Decades spent delivering unobtrusive service to the family and their guests had rendered her effectively mute, in movement and speech. Geri found herself treading lightly as well. The inclination towards stealth appeared to be catching. They left the House and took the path to the left. So they were heading to the Cottage. It must be Sophie. Babies could fall ill quickly, couldn't they? But if Sophie was sick, why would Carla seek out Geri? Child-rearing was not one of her areas of expertise.

The door to the Cottage stood open. Once inside, Carla raised her finger to her lips then made a small patting gesture with her hand. Geri was shocked to see that her fingers were bloodstained. Geri nodded, instruction understood – whatever lay in wait, she needed to react calmly. Carla led Geri upstairs. Without hesitation she opened the door on the right a fraction, Lena's room, then she disappeared inside. Geri followed her.

The breeze off the sea was stirring the curtains. For a second Geri was distracted by the view through the open window, but a wet guttural noise pulled her focus back onto the mess inside the room rather than the beauty beyond it. Luca was standing guard over by the bed, his arms crossed. At his feet sat Ian, head in his hands. There were bloody handprints on the rug and the bed. Luca appeared unharmed.

For a second no one said anything. Geri looked around Lena's room. She was data-gathering. Facts before emotion; it was an approach that had never failed her in the past. But although she saw a victim and a perpetrator, the motive for the violence was unclear. And what possible reason could there be for Luca and Ian even being in Lena's room? Her brother was groaning, a loud, wheezy mix of self-pity and pain. On seeing Geri he added some actual words to the torrent of moist noise. 'I'm telling you there's something wrong with her. She's not right in the head.

She's a fucking lunatic.' The effort of speaking triggered a coughing fit. More blood and phlegm oozed though his fingers. Disgusted as she was, Geri knelt down beside her brother and tried to assess the damage. He was bleeding from his nose and mouth. His features were swollen and had a purple tinge in the bright sunlight; a precursor of the bruising to come.

'What happened?' She directed the question to the room, curious to see who would answer it. To her surprise, it was Carla.

'He attacked Lena.'

Ian started denying it, vehemently. Geri ignored him. Christ, there was another player in the mix. 'Where is she?'

Luca answered that one. 'In the bathroom.'

Leaving Ian to his blustering, bloody indignation, Geri got to her feet and went over to the bathroom. If Ian was bleating, he was breathing. Geri knocked. She heard Lena step closer to the door. 'Lena! It's Geri. Open up.'

But the bolt was not shot back. Used to swift compliance with her demands, Geri had to remind herself that the girl was probably traumatised by whatever had happened. She tapped more gently. 'It's okay, Lena. I understand you're frightened, but I really need you to come out so that I can talk to you.'

'Is he still here?' Her voice was muffled by the door.

Geri looked at Ian and made a swift decision. 'I can make him leave. Is that what you want?'

'Yes. It is.' That was clear enough.

Geri paused, thinking fast. There were options. Not good ones, that much was evident, but there was always some sort of choice to be made. She could not allow this mess to derail her plans. She had come too far and put too much effort into ensuring that the next couple of days played out as she intended. 'Okay. Luca will take Ian away. I'll let you know when he's gone.'

She turned back to the crime scene that had once been Lena's pretty, sea-view bedroom. 'You heard what Lena said, Ian, she wants you out of her room. Luca, please escort Ian back to the Hut and stay with him until I come.'

Her instruction seemed to invigorate Ian, at least enough for him to object. 'I'm not going anywhere with that thug. I need medical attention. Look at me!'

Geri did, and she didn't like what she saw. 'And you shall get it, but first you need to get out of Lena's room. Luca, if you please.'

Ian waved his arms around, warding Luca off – 'Don't you fucking dare lay a hand on me' – but his indignation was mixed with resignation. After a few more curses, he flopped forward onto his hands and knees and lumbered around in a circle. It was like watching an injured walrus. He then proceeded to haul himself upright, using the bed for leverage. He looked even worse standing up, but at least he was on the move. After some more wheezy moaning he limped out of the room, with Luca close on his heels. It sounded like slow progress down the stairs.

Geri looked at Carla, but as always, Carla's expression gave little away. What she did do was put her hands behind her back. 'I want you to leave the talking to me.' Carla nodded.

This time Lena opened up at Geri's request. If she'd been crying, she'd stopped. She did, however, look warily around

165

the room as if expecting Ian to materialise out of the wardrobe or to emerge from beneath the bed. When she saw the state of the rug and the bed, Geri could have sworn that the shadow of a smile flitted across the girl's lips. On first impressions it would have been hard to tell that she'd been on the receiving end of any kind of assault – unlike Ian. Geri had a moment of doubt. Evidence – that's what she needed, or in the absence of evidence, a compelling testimony. She kept it simple. 'Sit down, Lena. I want you to tell me what happened.'

But Lena seemed unwilling to settle to her tale, or to be told what to do. She walked around the room, clutching the towel she was wrapped in with one hand and her mobile in the other. Eventually she said, 'I need to get changed. Juliet has been texting me. She's getting impatient. I need to go and collect Sophie.'

'Juliet can wait. What you need to do is tell me what has taken place in this room.' Geri heard the authority and the lack of sympathy in her voice, but in her experience, kind words were just that – words. Actions were what mattered. Finally Lena sat down, on the chair, not the bed. Geri didn't blame her. Her gaze kept sliding away from Geri to the bloody bed linen, then back to Carla. Geri was running out of patience and time. 'Lena!'

At last she took a deep breath and said, 'It's not Luca or Carla's fault. They saved me.'

'From?'

Now Lena did look Geri in the eye. 'From being sexually assaulted, possibly from being raped, by your brother.' It was ballsy.

Geri didn't flinch. 'Tell me.'

'He's been bothering me ever since we arrived on the island.'

'What do you mean, "bothering you"?'

'Paying me too much attention. I'm just the nanny, why would he be interested in me? He kept staring at me.'

'And?'

'It was making me really uncomfortable.'

Geri nodded, but an older man looking at a pretty young woman inappropriately was hardly news and it wasn't a crime. She prompted, 'And?'

'Juliet said I could have some free time this morning. She took Sophie up to the big house with her. I went for a swim, sat in the sun for a bit. I had permission, Juliet said she didn't need me until 3.00 p.m.' She was so defensive. Geri got that a lot from staff – the assumption that she was unreasonable. 'I came back here and was about to get changed ready to go and collect Sophie when there was a knock at the door. I thought it was Carla. No one else comes to my room.' There it was again, the prickliness. 'When I opened up, it was your brother.' Geri disliked the stress on the familial link. Again, suspicion bloomed. Was Lena building up to a demand for something? Hush money? It was a logical assumption. She became, suddenly, surprisingly articulate. 'I didn't know why he'd come to my room. I said I was busy, but he said he needed to speak to me about Juliet. He came in, without being invited. It was obvious that I didn't want him in my room. He didn't care. He started talking about how upset he was that his relationship with Juliet wasn't good. He asked me how I thought she was coping with motherhood. I thought that was none of his business. I told him so. He didn't like it. He said he loved Juliet and his granddaughter, that he wanted to have a better relationship with Sophie than he had with his other grandchildren. Then he looked sad, like he was going to cry. I just wanted him to get out of my room. He apologised, called himself... a sentimental old fool. I thought he was going to leave. But no. He went over to the window and looked out, started talking about being here when Juliet and Jonny were little, happy times. Then he went quiet. He turned around and there was something in his face. His expression was different. I knew I was in trouble. He crossed the room, said something about *women these days*, then he grabbed me. Here.' She put her hand to her breast.

She was telling the truth.

'I tried to push him off me, but he just squeezed harder. He forced me up against the wall.' She looked over at the spot. Geri followed her gaze and saw fifty-five-kilogram Lena in her swimsuit, trapped by her ninety-kilogram, pawing, pushing brother. 'He broke the strap on my bikini top. I started shouting. He told me to *shut the fuck up*. I didn't. He had an erection. He was going to rape me.'

Geri saw Lena glance at Carla. Geri needed clarification. Facts mattered. 'But he didn't.'

There was another slight pause, then Lena raised her chin and spoke quickly. 'Only because Carla and Luca arrived. They saved me. They pulled him off, told me to go into the bathroom and lock the door.' She stopped talking.

Her return to inarticulacy made Geri wonder. Was she faltering because she was too upset to go on, or was it because she didn't want to incriminate Luca? Whatever the cause, something felt off. Geri pushed. 'Sorry. They arrived at exactly the same time?'

This time Lena answered assertively. 'Yes.'

'And?'

'And what?'

'What happened after you'd locked yourself in the bathroom?'

'How would I know?'

'But you must have heard something.'

Lena stared at her. 'I heard shouting and your brother swearing and some thuds.'

So the only witness to the assault was Carla. But had Carla merely been a witness? If so, why were her hands covered in blood? They eyeballed each other. Geri blinked first. 'Okay. If Carla and Luca corroborate your version of events – ' Geri saw Lena stiffen, but she carried on regardless – 'I promise you that Ian will be off the island within the next hour.' The beginnings of a plan began to form in Geri's mind. Awful as this was, it could be the solution she needed to be rid of her brother, if she handled it correctly.

Lena nodded, then asked, 'And Luca . . . and Carla?'

Geri met her gaze. 'That depends.'

'On?'

Geri paused. 'On whether this is a police matter.' Ball in Lena's court. Geri let the air between them settle. She didn't want Lena to feel she was pressuring her – although she patently was. What happened next was very much in this young girl's hands. She had every right to kick up a stink, to demand that the alleged assault be investigated, but if she went down that route there would be no end of trouble, for herself and Luca . . . and, of course, Ian.

After some careful thought Lena gave Geri the correct answer. 'I suppose it doesn't have to be.'

Geri nodded. 'I agree.'

'What about Juliet?' Lena gestured with her phone. 'She's just messaged me again.' The last thing Geri wanted was Juliet turning up with Sophie in tow. She needed to get this wrapped up, and quickly. And there was the call with the lawyers in – she glanced at her phone – ten minutes. Well, the events of the past hour had put a very different slant on that. Power balances – they never stayed the same for long. Hence Geri chose to play her next shot with finesse rather than power. 'I can't see what good it would do, her knowing. Juliet has been estranged from her father for years' – Geri paused, looked Lena in the eye – 'for good reason. And I'm not sure – whatever he said – that my brother is going to feature very much in little Sophie's life.' Geri felt a stab of shame beneath her ribs, but she ignored it. Damage limitation mode left little room for empathy.

Again Lena gave it some thought before answering. Her answer, when it came, was very direct. 'So you're asking me not to tell her?' Geri's respect for Lena went up a notch.

'I think that would be for the best.'

There was another pause, then Lena said, 'Okay. But you need to understand this. I'm choosing not to tell Juliet because it was her father who did this to me and she can do without any more trouble from him at the moment. But if you don't deal with your brother then I will. And that's a promise.'

Geri didn't like Lena's threat, but she couldn't help admiring her for having the chutzpah to make it.

And so it was settled. Geri breathed a little easier, but only a touch. She had put out one fire, but there was another far bigger one raging down in the Hut. She needed to decide how she was going to smother that conflagration before Jonny, Helena and Ben came back from Positano. In as considerate a tone as she could manage, she asked, 'Do you need anything?' Geri waited. Was money going to come into the equation?

Lena fiddled with the broken strap of her swimming costume and studied the developing bruises on her arms – she would need to think carefully about her wardrobe for the next few days – then she said, 'No. Not at the moment.'

Geri picked up the reminder that she had to stick to her side of the bargain, but their pact would have to do for now. As she turned to leave, she said to Carla, 'Perhaps you could replace Lena's rug and fetch her some fresh bed linen then come and find me. I'll be down at the Hut.' Carla nodded. Geri left her to it.

They both had a lot of clearing-up to do.

Chapter 38

ALICE

If Geri didn't turn up soon she was going to miss her call with the lawyers – a meeting that she'd insisted be set up ASAP. That Geri had snuck out of her study without a word to Alice was also very out of character. Where the hell was she? And why wasn't she responding to Alice's polite, but increasingly pointed, messages?

She wasn't in the main house because Alice had looked everywhere, and she wasn't outside on either of the terraces. Alice hadn't bothered checking the pool. Geri only ever swam first thing in the morning or late at night. Just at the point when Alice was about to phone her she spotted the distinctive figure of her boss on the path that ran along the front of the Cottage. That in itself wasn't so strange. This was her island, after all; she was free to go wherever she liked. What was striking was that Geri didn't seem to be doing anything. She was simply standing there, staring out to sea. Alice couldn't imagine that she'd gone down there to seek out Juliet. That relationship seemed to be deteriorating by the minute. Juliet getting caught leaving Geri's office would not have helped. Alice didn't call out – Geraldine Chalice lived and worked in accordance with the philosophy of swans; namely, always look regal and never let anyone know how much effort you're putting in beneath the waterline, and she expected Alice to behave likewise – but she did break into a jog. The effort made her slightly breathless, which unfortunately resulted in her *I've been looking everywhere for you* greeting sounding panicky. Alice then made matters worse by unnecessarily glancing at her watch. She already knew that Geri had precisely seven minutes until she was due on her call with Harrison and May. Alice took a beat, then said, as calmly as she could, 'We really need to get you back up to the House.' For a moment it looked as if Geri hadn't a clue what she was talking about. That troubled Alice. Geri's head swung back and forth from the sea to the Cottage. Alice had never seen Geri be indecisive. Ever. 'For the call,' Alice prompted.

After a pause Geri said, 'I need to postpone.'

Before Alice could stop herself, she blurted out, 'Why? You still have time.'

Alice's insolence seemed to wake Geri up. She went very still and her expression hardened. She blinked twice before she struck. 'Because I say so.'

Unnerved, Alice took a step back. 'Sorry. Yes. Of course.' Her boss's wish was her command and Geri had just reminded Alice that it would be prudent not forget that – not if she wanted to keep her job. And Alice really needed to keep her job.

But with the next breath Geri's face softened back into that of a human being. 'Sorry, Alice, that was rude of me, but there's something of a personal nature that I have to deal with before I can turn my attention to business matters. Please call Harrison and May and make my apologies.'

173

Alice absorbed the rebuke and the retraction. 'Shall I say that you've been delayed over on the mainland and that I'll be in touch with alternative availability from our end as soon as your diary stabilises?'

Geri nodded. 'Yes. Do that. Thank you.' There was another fraction of a pause, then she added, 'Well go on, then.'

Hallelujah. The swan was back, but Alice hadn't a clue what the hell was going on beneath the surface of the water.

Chapter 39

JONNY

Jonny was pleased to see that Ben was on time for a change. Whether his half-brother was habitually late on principle or simply because he was a slack bastard was hard to ascertain. Regardless, the effect was always the same – irritation. Helena slid her sunglasses down her nose and said, 'What on earth is he holding?'

From a distance it was hard to tell, but whatever it was, it was large, black and had horns. 'God knows. Some tourist tat, by the look of it.'

Ben spotted them. He shifted his furry burden into the crook of his arm and saluted them with his free hand. 'Hi. All present and correct . . . as per your instructions.'

Close up, it became apparent that what he was clutching was a huge toy bull. Jonny had to ask, 'And your companion? Did you pick him up in one of the bars?' Ben had the look of someone who had spent the remainder of the afternoon indulging rather than sightseeing.

The insult slid off him. He grinned. 'This? This magnificent beast is Gerry.'

He was so bloody juvenile. 'You're not seriously intending to give that to Geri for her birthday?'

Ben turned the monstrosity around and held it up to his face. 'I am. I think she'll love him. He's a fellow Taurus. The embodiment of all Geri's most dominant traits: stubbornness, prodigious hard work and ferocity.' He spun the bull around and waggled it in Jonny's face. 'Oh, and cute to boot. Why? What have you got her?'

Jonny ignored Ben's question and instead checked his phone, but that only served to cause him more frustration. Luca wouldn't be back to collect them for another fifteen minutes, at the earliest. Jonny was going to have a word with Geri about that lad. He didn't seem suited to the job; too much self-worth, not enough deference. 'Luca's going to be late. I had trouble getting hold of him.'

Ben shrugged. 'So?'

'So, it's not acceptable. He's paid to be on hand to take us where we want to go, when we want to go.'

'No. I meant . . . so, what have you bought her?'

Helena had obviously had enough of their petty sparring. 'A rather beautiful handmade necklace. It's very elegant. Very Geri.'

Ben dumped the bull on the bench beside him. 'Can I see?'

Jonny said 'no' at the same moment as Helena reached into her tote bag and took out the branded gift bag from Preziosa. It was wise not to stroll around Positano advertising your wealth if you didn't want it ripped from you by some youth on a moped. Helena sat down on the bench on the no-bull side of Ben. She took the box out of the bag and snapped it open. Jonny liked that she showed the necklace to Ben, but didn't hand it over to him. He wouldn't have put it past his brother to suddenly develop butterfingers and for the 1,400-euro gift that Jonny had deliberated over for quite some time to end up in the harbour.

Ben whistled. 'Very fancy. I'm sure she'll adore it.' He was such an insincere bastard. And a nosey one. Ben peeked inside the bag. 'Ooh, do I spy more giftage?'

Helena flushed. Jonny was happy to lean into this one. 'It's just a small token of affection for my darling wife, to say thank you for fifteen happy years together.' It was Ben's fault that his own marriage had imploded. As intended, Jonny's reference to his enduring relationship put an end to any further conversation. The other, surprise item that Jonny had bought on the sly in Preziosa was hidden safely away in his jacket pocket. Neither of them needed to know about that particular purchase.

Chapter 40

GERI

Geri got down to the dock just in time to see Luca heading out on the *Black Swan*. She shouted, but he obviously couldn't hear her above the noise of the engine. There was a voice note from him on her phone; he sounded stressed. *Jonny and the others want collecting. I will be as quick as I can. The Hut is locked. I took the key. Just in case.* Geri noticed that Luca made no direct reference to Ian. The boy was smarter than he looked.

Luca's departure took the wind out of Geri's sails. She wanted, no, she needed, to get this mess cleared up before anyone else found out about it, but there appeared to be little she could do given that she couldn't get inside the Hut. Still she felt compelled to check on her brother. She always worried when he was near and she didn't know what he was up to.

Geri approached the squat two-storey building at an angle. She wanted to stay out of Ian's eyeline. She suspected that he would be watching out for her, keen to get his side of the story across, no doubt at volume. Being locked in by Luca would not have gone down well. The woodstore to the side of the building afforded Geri some cover. She stood in its shade and listened. She could hear Ian roaming around inside like a caged animal. The Hut was cramped, so there wouldn't be much space for him to vent his evidently prodigious sense of injustice and disgust. From what she could hear his anger appeared to be directed at all of them: Luca, Lena, herself, even Carla. They were all *bastards* and *bitches*, and worse. Listening to him rage made Geri feel tired. It was a familiar fatigue. Whatever happened it was never Ian's fault; it never had been. As a child it had always been *an accident* or *a silly misunderstanding*. As an adult, either jealousy or a *baseless, malicious allegation*. She was sick to death of having to deal with his shit.

Loath as she was to admit it, Geri was relieved that her showdown with Ian would have to wait. She was wary of tackling him on her own, which was embarrassing to admit, but understandable given that he currently wanted to *smash in her smug, patronising, arse-ugly face*. Her decision to have Luca escort him away from the scene and stand guard had obviously rankled deeply. That she'd been willing to listen to Lena's side of the story must also have driven him mad. Ian really didn't like having his words or deeds challenged – no matter how egregious they were. The stark reality was that her little brother had always been predisposed to anger and indignation. Depressed by a truth that she'd known, deep down, for decades, Geri turned her back on the Hut and edged away.

She got as far as the dock, where she sat down. She closed her eyes for a moment. She wasn't meditating, she was too riled up for that, but she did need time to regroup. What was always going to be difficult had now become so much more complicated. The regular slap slap of the sea against the old wooden pilings and the breeze on her face helped. After a few minutes, she opened her eyes and allowed herself to take in the beauty of where she was. Because Isola dei Delfini was undeniably beautiful – when there was no one else around. She let the moment settle, allowed her breath to deepen, felt her pulse slow. As if rewarding her composure in the face of such provocation, a dolphin and her calf soundlessly broke the surface of the water barely a hundred metres away from her. Geri watched as they swam a leisurely loop around the cove, the calf sticking close to its mother's side for protection, before slipping back down out of sight.

The sight brought Geri some solace, but no solutions. In under an hour Jonny, Ben and Helena would be arriving back and stepping onto this very dock. What if they heard Ian ranting and raving inside the Hut? How would she explain him being locked in? And what would he tell them if and when she let him out? Because she was going to have to release her brother at some point. She couldn't leave him in there and simply wait for him to starve to death. He was too well covered. It would take weeks!

Reluctantly, Geri got to her feet. Now was not the moment to be contemplating the beauty of the natural world and the nastiness of the human one. She needed to get control of the situation, one way or another. Resolve renewed, she set off in search of Carla who had keys for all the buildings on the island.

Chapter 41

JULIET

Back in her bedroom Juliet settled Sophie in her nest of pillows on the bed, then she went through to the bathroom. There she scrubbed the safe combination off the back of her hand. Had Geri seen it? She couldn't be sure. Geri had obviously been deeply pissed off that she'd had the audacity to set foot in her office. Juliet didn't want to think about how incensed she'd be if she discovered that she'd broken into the safe and stolen the memory stick.

As Juliet was drying her hands there was a knock at the door. Alice, come to firm up the details of her return to work? Or Geri, come to challenge her about what she was really doing in her study? A guilt trip either way. Or Lena – who had never made Juliet feel guilty? She hoped to God it was Lena.

And, for a change, God was listening.

'Is everything all right?' They said it simultaneously, but Lena waited for Juliet to answer first.

'Yes. Fine. She's been changed and fed. A full bottle. Some sleep, but not lots.' For a moment it felt like their roles had been reversed. It wasn't a bad feeling. 'You?'

Lena hesitated. 'Yeah. Fine. I went for a swim.' That would explain the damp hair. 'Shall I take her?'

Juliet looked back at the bed. She could see Sophie's little arms waving around. It looked like she was trying to catch the breeze that was finding its way in through the shutters. Juliet was tempted to say no, then she saw the edge of her laptop poking out from underneath the pillow, its lid closed on so many secrets – her own and her brothers'. 'Yes please. For a while.'

'I was going to take her for a walk around the gardens to get some fresh air.'

Now it was Juliet's turn to hesitate. Lena must have picked up on her anxiety. 'I promise that if I so much as catch sight of your father I'll be back in the Cottage with the door locked before he's had time to haul his fat arse up off his sun lounger.'

Lena's comment overstepped the line by miles, but Juliet let it go. Lena had earned the right to be rude about her father after his behaviour by the pool. Juliet was torn. Should she tell Lena about her fears? Confide in her? It would be a relief. But she couldn't bring herself to do it. It sounded insane that any father would use his grandchild to exert pressure on his own daughter for his own ends. It was. And . . . she still didn't know for certain that the texts were from him. But regardless of where the real threat lay, Juliet wanted Sophie to be safe, and inside the Cottage was as safe as it got on the island because it was away from every member of her family. 'I'd like you to take her straight back, please. I think she's had enough sun for one day.' Juliet turned and walked away from Lena's slightly crestfallen expression. She picked up Sophie, planted a kiss on her daughter's head and handed her over. 'Thank you. I'll be down later.'

Lena carried Sophie off along the hallway, talking to her as she went. Juliet watched them disappear down the staircase and listened until Lena's footsteps had faded to silence. Once they were gone she returned to her room. She wedged the chair against the door once more and retrieved her laptop. It was time to find out what Geri had dug up on Jonny and Ben.

Chapter 42

GERI

Much to Geri's frustration, Carla, who was always there or thereabouts, waiting to fulfil their every need at whatever time of the day or night, had suddenly disappeared. Alice was clearly disconcerted by Geri's insistence that she be found ASAP. She obviously sensed that something was going on, but thankfully she was too well trained to ask what. So, as instructed, she dropped what she was doing and joined in the hunt.

Unfortunately Alice had no more success than Geri. She reported that Carla was not in the kitchen or the out-house laundry, nor in her garden. Carla had a veg and herb plot tucked away on the south side of the House which she tended diligently and with considerable success in amongst her many other duties. The woman seemed to sleep as little as Geri.

Having drawn a blank at the House, Geri was forced to retrace her steps back to the Cottage. Alice offered to go, but Geri didn't want her heading down there. The last thing she wanted was anyone else knowing about what had happened, or nearly happened, in Lena's bedroom. But Carla wasn't at the Cottage either. Although she must have been there recently, because Lena's room no longer looked like a crime scene. The bed had been remade with fresh linen and the rug had been replaced. There was even a small vase of fresh flowers on the bedside table. As Geri headed back down the stairs the front door of the Cottage opened and in walked Lena, carrying the child. She looked refreshed in a simple summer dress with her hair tied back from her seemingly serene face. As much as Geri didn't have the time for pleasantries – the others would be back soon, which would put them down on the dock, close to the Hut and a no doubt still-raging Ian – she knew she had to speak to the girl. After mutual 'hello's were exchanged there was a pause. Lena jiggled Sophie in her arms and whispered to her, giving the child her full attention.

Geri felt uncomfortable. 'I've just been up to your room. It's all sorted now.'

'I'll say thank you to Carla next time I see her.'

She really was chippy. 'And how are you feeling?'

Lena looked up at that. 'Angry and bruised.' Geri was silenced. 'But if what you're really asking me is whether I kept my mouth shut with Juliet' – she paused – 'then you'll be relieved to hear that I did.' And with that she went to leave.

Geri stopped her with a hand on her arm. She was plainly not happy being touched so Geri quickly relinquished her grasp, but not before saying, 'When you have a moment, please can you come up to see me at the House. My office, not Alice's.'

'Why?'

'I have a little something for you.' An envelope of cash to encourage discretion. It had worked in the past.

Geri waited, curious to see what Lena's response would be. Principled or pragmatic? After a second or two she begrudgingly said, 'I will . . . if I get a chance.' It was all the tacit acknowledgement that Geri was going to get, but she was glad to get it. Although plainly the girl wasn't done. She stared at Geri and added, 'But what I said earlier still stands. If your brother's not off this island, and away from me and Sophie and Juliet, in the next couple of hours then I will start making myself heard, "little something" or not.' Lena set off up the stairs without a goodbye or a backward glance.

Geri had just been put in her place by a twenty-one-year-old nanny. However, Lena was right about one thing: Ian needed dealing with, and now. But as Geri opened the door to do just that she heard voices. She quickly stepped back inside and pulled the door to. Jonny, Helena and Ben were back from Positano. Geri listened, her mind spinning rapidly with the ramifications of everyone becoming aware of Ian's actions and Luca's reaction. But as they passed the Cottage their conversation seemed natural enough. They couldn't have heard Ian raging around inside the Hut, which meant they were ignorant of the afternoon's events – which meant that Geri's plan might still work.

Chapter 43

JULIET

Did she feel guilty about looking at her brothers' files? She did not. If they had got their hands on Geri's secret dossiers neither of them would have hesitated. What that said about them all as siblings didn't bear dwelling on.

Juliet looked at Jonny's file first – her big brother and her fiercest competitor. The next generation of brother and sister rivalry; it was the Chalice way. When you thought about it, neither of them ever really had a choice. Which made doing things like this easier. As with her own file, Jonny's was divided into subfolders. Freed from the anxiety about being discovered mid-theft, Juliet was able to take more in this time. The list of folders was long:

- Financial Audit
- Career/Professional Performance
- Non Profit/Charitable Activity
- Known Associates
- Medical History, including Mental Health
- Relationships/Sexual History
- Social Media Audit
- Non-Corroborated Issues

Juliet opted for *Financial Audit*; Jonny's area of expertise and his main motivation. With no rhyme or reason she opened various files. A blizzard of documents snowed her screen, including bank and investment statements, copies of UK and international BACS transfers, and what looked like the deeds for properties, including one in Nice and another in Ibiza. She quickly realised that she hadn't a clue what she was looking at. It would take a forensic accountant weeks to decipher the story told in the documents. And this was just one file. If the other folders had even a tenth of this volume of information in them it would take her months to go through Jonny's financial portfolio, never mind Ben's and her own. It was classic Geri – impressive and at the same time obsessive. Juliet 'got' not trusting everything that Jonny said, he was prone to inflating his own successes and downplaying any failures, but this went beyond suspicion and tipped into paranoia. Overwhelmed, Juliet closed it all down. All she had learnt was that her big brother was even richer than she'd thought.

Driven more by curiosity than anything more rational, she moved her cursor onto Jonny's *Medical History* and found the *Mental Health* tab. She clicked. She couldn't stop herself. In contrast to the financial folder, there wasn't that much in this file, but what was there was far more interesting. At least, it was to Juliet, who felt that she had never really understood her brother. There was a copy of a handwritten psych assessment from back in the day when Jonny was in the Territorial Army that assessed him as *driven, motivated and wholly lacking in empathy* and went on to endorse him for promotion to the rank of Sergeant First Class; a Chalice Group Human Resources report from over two decades ago, about a complaint made by a junior executive that included a highlighted mention of *anger management issues when confronted with challenges to his authority*; then in another document Juliet stumbled across what looked like the prescribing history of Jonny's own Harley Street doctor. She found herself scanning down the list. Her reward was a surprisingly short inventory of her big brother's minor ailments and sight of a note from the unnamed assessor that *there was little to no evidence Jonny had ever struggled with his mental health in his childhood or adult life.*

This upbeat assessment of one brother's psychological strength prompted Juliet to look at what the audit had to say about the state of mind of her other sibling.

Within ten minutes it was clear that the investigators had also left no stone unturned when it came to Ben. His acrimonious spilt from Natasha was covered in detail, including his ongoing custody battles, as was his escalating drug use. Juliet hesitated before clicking on Ben's *Mental Health* file. Poor Ben, he'd never been as robust as her or Jonny. Did she want to read about his inner demons, did she need to see, in black and white, that he had Daddy issues and that these lay at the root of his neediness and his risk-taking behaviours? (Juliet did know something about basic human psychology; how could you not, growing up in their fractured family?) On reflection, she decided she did not. Ben was no threat to anyone, other than himself. She was about to click back and delve into the world of Jonny's extramarital affairs when suddenly she stopped.

What she was doing was grubby. She had stolen the memory stick in an effort to protect her daughter, not to go rifling through dark corners of her brothers' lives and minds. She was better than this. Better than Geri.

Juliet had got to where she was by virtue of her intelligence, her diligence and her business acumen and she was proud of her success. Her career mattered because it had been honestly earned. She had never cheated or lied or resorted to dirty tactics before, and she wasn't about to start now. If she was going to win the final prize and become CEO she was going to do it fairly and on her own merit.

Reinvigorated by her own superiority, Juliet set about closing it all down; every last invasive, distressing fact about the three of them.

Chapter 44

GERI

To Geri's surprise it was Carla who opened the door to the Hut. She made no apology for going AWOL – she simply said, 'They're in the sitting room.' The second surprise was that the place was quiet. Perhaps it was this dissonance between what Geri had expected and what was actually happening that stopped her from registering that Carla was walking away.

'Wait. Where the hell are you going? I've been looking for you everywhere.' Carla froze and turned around. Geri saw her gaze flick behind her. She spun around fearing Ian, but finding Luca.

He answered on Carla's behalf. 'She's going back to the House to start preparing your birthday dinner.'

Geri snapped, 'No she isn't. I need to speak to her.'

Luca crossed his arms. 'And you can do, later, but for now she needs to be getting on.' Luca switched his attention from Geri to Carla. 'You go. I'll sort everything out here.'

Geri was for the second time that day shocked into silence. Carla seemed torn, but after a moment's hesitation she adjusted the basket on her arm, did a strange little bob, almost like a curtsey then hurried away. Staff making up their own minds – Geri didn't like it. Her dismay increased when Luca said, 'You'd better come in', as if the Hut was his property.

Geri hadn't actually been inside the Hut for years, she'd had no reason to. It was used as overflow accommodation for the additional staff that were shipped in when the Chalices hosted parties or held events on the island. She had forgotten how dark and shabby it was. She nearly knocked herself out when she misjudged the height of the archway through to the small sitting room. Ian was lying on one of the sofas. He was flat on his back, totally inert. On the low table by his elbow sat a bottle of Scotch and a glass. The bottle was two-thirds empty. So this was why the others hadn't heard anything – he'd passed out. Which had solved one problem, but created a bigger one. Namely, her inability to bawl him out. Geri needed him awake if she was going to impress on him the precariousness of his situation and get him to leave without a fight – and empty-handed this time. Her days of paying her brother to go away were over. Anger flared. She went for the sober target first. 'Why in God's name did you let him have alcohol?'

'I couldn't stop him.'

'That's patently not true. You put him on his backside easily enough in Lena's room, I'm sure you could've taken a bottle of whisky off him.' Luca stared flatly at Geri. She had no choice but to let it go. She approached the sofa and looked down at her brother. He was a disgrace. His shirt had ridden up, revealing the leathery, hairy paunch of his stomach. One hand cupped his balls, the other trailed on the floor. His beaten face looked like melted wax. His mouth hung open. Grotesquely, Geri could see down his throat. Unbidden, a vision of this lump of heavy, sagging flesh bearing down on Lena rose in her imagination. She felt nauseous and furious. She reached out, intent on shaking the bastard awake, but her hands were wrenched away. Luca had hold of her wrists. Geri was stunned by his audacity. 'Let go of me! This instant!'

But Luca held on. They stared at each other. 'There's no point. He's dead.'

Geri looked again and this time she saw the truth of Luca's statement. She wasn't looking at her brother, she was looking at a corpse. The tension went out of her and Luca let go. Geri backed away and lowered herself into an armchair. Luca remained standing and silent.

Instead of a rush of thoughts Geri's mind cleared completely, leaving a cool, grey blank. She didn't feel or think anything other than, *He's dead*. She waited . . . *Dead and gone*. Luca went to say something, but Geri held up her hand. She needed to see what her instincts wanted to tell her before she took the handbrake off her brain. *Gone for good*.

There it was. The truth. Her brother, the bane of her life – and that of almost everyone who'd ever had contact with him – was gone *for good*. It was no loss. It was a relief. She was finally free of him.

She released the brake on her thoughts and set off again. The facts, that's what she needed. 'What happened?'

Luca kept it simple. 'I brought him here, as you asked me to. He was pissed off, making all kinds of threats. He wanted a drink. I wasn't going to stop him. I stayed away from him. Then, as you know, I had to go and pick the others up from Positano. I locked him in. When I arrived back, I secured the *Swan* then I went to see if Carla was at home.' Luca must have sensed Geri's disapproval at him prioritising his aunt rather than her instructions, because he defended his actions. 'I was worried about her, after what went down in Lena's room. Anyway, she wasn't there so I came here and found him like this.'

'Did you try and revive him?'

'No. I didn't want to touch him.'

Reluctantly Geri returned her gaze to her dead brother. Had he had a heart attack? A stroke? Ian was out of shape and overweight. A heavy drinker. Natural causes, then? The sad but inevitable consequence of a dissolute life? There was no way of knowing for sure. Not without a post-mortem. Her brain picked up speed. But a post-mortem would flag up that Ian had been on the receiving end of a beating an hour or so before his death, which would prompt questions. Questions that would inevitably lead to the discovery that he'd assaulted Lena and that Luca had intervened. It would become a police matter, for sure. The press would have a field day. Her reputation for cool, calm, calculating control would be smashed to pieces. The old but persistent stories about Chalice rivalry and ill-will would breathe again. There was no upside to this becoming public, for anyone. *So?* the voice in her head demanded.

So . . . the challenge was to keep the ripples as small and contained as possible. The only people who knew that Ian was dead were herself, Luca and, presumably, Carla. Geri was confident that Carla could be trusted to keep quiet. She had in the past. She knew where her loyalties lay.

What about her nephew? He was an unknown quantity to Geri. But – her brain began clicking through the gears more quickly – Luca had an even more compelling reason to keep his mouth shut: his fingerprints were all over this, all over Ian. The route out of this was clear now. The others hadn't seen Ian since before lunch. A story could be spun that they would swallow. None of them had wanted Ian hanging around on Isola dei Delfini confusing things. The brutal truth was that there was no love lost between Ian and his children. He had frittered that away over the past twenty years. Ben might be a problem; foolishly, he seemed to still harbour hopes of having some sort of a relationship with his father. But even Ben wouldn't be surprised by Ian doing another midday flit. All she needed to do was hint at money changing hands and Ian's exit would make perfect, if depressing, sense. He got what he came for and he left. If they were lucky, it could be months before anyone noticed that, this time, Ian Chalice had disappeared for good.

Geri stood up. She needed to make her intentions and her expectations clear. But not in words. That would be tantamount to admitting her involvement in one crime, very possibly two, and she wasn't prepared to do that. Instead she met Luca's steady stare with the steel of her own. 'We promised Lena that he would be off the island by the end of the day. So I think that's what should happen.' Luca looked at Ian's corpse, an expression of utter disgust on his face. Geri waited. Then he nodded. Message received and understood. The secrets, the lies and the indebtedness – Geri was well aware that they would all have to be faced in the fullness of time, but for now they had a workable solution.

She glanced at her watch. 'Goodness. Look at the time. I don't know where today has gone. I really must be getting back to the House. You will be okay to take care of this, won't you, Luca? I'm relying on you.' She waved her hand around the room, but she kept her eyeline high. Luca nodded again. She said, 'Thank you.'

At the door she stopped. 'I'll let you know when the birthday party starts and everyone is present and occupied.' She hoped Luca understood that she was telling him that she would text him when the coast was clear. He simply stood, unmoving, looking down at her brother's body. She left, closing the Cottage door quietly behind her. She had delegated, efficiently and effectively, as was her habit. Ian was Luca's problem now.

Chapter 45

JONNY

Helena was already asleep when Jonny let himself into their room. She'd gone on up ahead when they arrived back from Positano. He'd said he'd a few calls to make and that the signal was better outside. His father had mocked him for being *a busy boy*. Well fuck him, busy boys were the ones that got shit done. Jonny took a deep breath and left thoughts of his father at the door with his shoes.

It was the golden hour on the island. Perfect for a late siesta. Jonny dropped his trousers, unbuttoned his shirt and lay down on top of the sheet next to Helena. It was nice to be able to watch her sleep. Normally it was him who crashed out first – another consequence of being busy. The wine and the champagne they'd drunk at lunchtime had obviously helped Helena to relax; that, and the very pleasant few hours they'd just spent wandering around Positano. Asleep and gold-tinged, his wife looked different – her face younger, her body sleeker – almost like a stranger. Jonny felt desire stir, but he didn't want to do anything to spoil the gentler mood between the two of them, so he kept his distance.

Instead he lay on his back, stared at the ceiling and listened to her slow, steady breathing. He loved Helena and he needed her; surely that was as decent a basis for a marriage as you were going to get after this long together. Jonny imagined he heard Helena's familiar, sceptical tut inside his head. Perhaps, after years of trying, she really could read his mind, even when she was fast asleep. God, that was a horrifying thought!

Of late Helena had stopped implying and started telling Jonny that their relationship needed work. Her clear message being that if he didn't invest more time and effort into their marriage, it might not survive. Jonny hadn't liked being threatened, but he had taken heed of her warnings. If work was required he would put it in – now was not the time for his marriage to be anything other than rock solid. Which was why he'd brought Helena with him to Isola dei Delfini. And it was working; she was softening and – Jonny yawned – by the end of the day he was confident that all Helena's talk of emotional effort and investment would be put to bed. Then he would be secure.

Chapter 46

LUCA

Luca had never disposed of a body before.

First there was the problem of weight. Ian Chalice must tip the scales at a hundred kilos. Luca could bench-press eighty, but he wasn't confident that he was going to manage getting Ian's corpse out of the Hut, down to the dock and onto the *Black Swan* without help. And he was on his own with this. Geri had made that very clear. What he needed was a plan of attack and some tools.

His first move was to go down to the boatyard for supplies. He collected a pair of work gloves, a ball of twine, a sharp knife, some rubbish bags and the strongest but thinnest tarp he could find. Then he went back to the Hut and locked himself in with the dead man.

He started small, by going upstairs and clearing Ian's bedroom. Even with gloves on, Luca found touching Ian's worn underwear difficult. It looked like he'd simply stepped out of his underpants and left them where they lay, in the middle of the bathroom floor. Ian Chalice was obviously used to having his mess magicked away by others. Well, this was the last time that some faceless, poorly paid lackey was going to have to tidy up after him. Luca sped up.

He dumped Ian's clothes, his toiletries and a stack of paperwork held together with a bulldog clip that he found in the bedside-table drawer, into Ian's big leather holdall. The bag was monogrammed, which was just typical. Luca remembered to unplug Ian's phone charger, which reminded him that he needed to find the phone itself. He then looked under the bed. It was a good job he did, because there was a pair of sandals stained with the clear imprint of Ian's feet under there, along with a comb and some clumps of tissue. Luca didn't want to imagine what the tissues had been used for. Gagging, he slung everything into the bag. He left the bed unmade, the towels on the floor and the sink full of toothpaste spit – exactly how Ian would have left it – then he headed down to the sitting room. He dropped the bag beside the sofa and collected the tumbler that Ian had been drinking out of. He took it through to the kitchen, washed and dried it, and returned it to the corner cupboard. He left the snacks, soft drinks and the array of alcohol that Carla had provided untouched, and returned to the sitting room.

Time was ticking. Luca had a corpse to get rid of, but first he needed a breather. He picked up the whisky bottle and went to sit on one of the saggy old armchairs. The room was full of death. Not the smell of it yet; just the absolute, definitive absence of life. All that remained of the awful person Ian Chalice had been was a repulsive slab of flesh that was now Luca's responsibility. Luca turned the whisky bottle around in his hands. What little was left sloshed and splashed around inside. Something was eating at Luca. And that something was Geri. He didn't understand why she'd been so lacking in curiosity about how her brother had died. One minute Ian was alive and shouting the odds; the next, he was stone-cold dead – and yet she hadn't seemed affected by his death or interested in what had killed him. The blows to Ian's face and his pride hadn't been enough to end him, and the man drank heavily all the time, so surely that couldn't have been a factor in his sudden demise. And yet there he lay – life extinguished. Luca had more curiosity. He unscrewed the bottle, raised it to his nose and sniffed. Did it smell wrong? It was hard to tell, Luca was no spirits drinker. He screwed the cap back on, stood up and walked over to the window. He held the bottle up to the light and agitated the liquid inside. Fine flecks of white powder swirled in the whisky then slowly settled, like a light dusting of snow, or dandruff. Luca's suspicion that someone had got into the Cottage and tampered with Ian's whisky grew. It was looking increasingly likely that the question wasn't *what* had killed him, but *who?* Luca shook the bottle again. As he watched the adulterated whisky slosh around inside, he thought about the people on the island with reason enough to kill Ian Chalice, and accepted that Carla's name would be on that list.

Luca took the bottle through to the kitchen and emptied what was left down the sink. He rinsed the bottle out, then he whacked the cold tap on, full force. He wanted to be certain that he'd washed away all traces of the white sediment. He dried the sink with a tea towel. The empty bottle was added to Ian's bag. Geri had asked him to 'clean house', so that was what he was doing. Evidence, if that's what the whisky had been, spirited away, Luca turned to the next job. There was no putting it off any longer. He was going to have to touch him.

Again Luca relied on speed to make the job bearable. He tugged off Ian's shoes, but left his socks alone. He couldn't face touching his bare feet. Then he removed Ian's belt, his watch and, after a struggle, the chunky gold signet ring on the little finger of his right hand. The fleshy thwack of his knuckles hitting the tiled floor when the ring finally came off was grim. Luca found Ian's phone and wallet in his trouser pockets. That was another gag moment. He stuffed Ian's personal belongings into a bin bag and tied the top tightly. The plan was to separate the body from its identifying possessions. Luca might be a novice accessory to murder, but he had a grasp of the basics. There remained the issue of Ian's teeth. His mouth was open, but Luca simply couldn't contemplate such intimate violence. That would be a step way too far. His task had a grim momentum now. He moved the coffee table and spread the tarp out on the floor. Without ceremony he dragged Ian's body off the sofa onto it. It made a wet thud as it hit the floor. Working fast, Luca wrapped Ian's corpse inside the tarp and used the twine to bind it. When he'd finished it looked like a neatly wrapped, gruesome gift. Luca straightened up and felt a twinge in his back. A sure sign of hard graft.

Next he went to the door and stepped outside into the glorious early-evening sun. The coast was clear. He shouldered Ian's holdall and the bin bag and took them down to the dock where the *Black Swan* was moored, ready and waiting. For a second Luca paused. He didn't want Ian's possessions polluting the *Swan*, but that was a sentimentality he couldn't afford. He jumped on board and stowed the bags in the cabin. There he took a moment to press the palms of his hands against the smooth teak of the yacht's pristine interior: wood that only yesterday he'd waxed and buffed. The fleeting contact with something so untainted and beautiful helped. Then he made himself disembark, walk up to the Hut and go back inside. Loath as he was to be alone with Ian's corpse, Luca locked the door behind him, went over to the armchair and sat down. There was nothing he could do now other than wait for Geri's message that her birthday party had begun.

Chapter 47

JONNY

When Jonny asked Helena to come for a walk with him before dinner she looked surprised. 'I thought you'd have work to do or more calls to make.'

'No. That stuff can wait. Today has been lovely. The two of us having some time on our own.' He smiled at her. 'And I don't know about you, but I'm in no rush to be back on duty. Besides, it's a glorious evening and we've barely seen anything of the island.' After a slight pause she put down her book.

He was pleased that she let him hold her hand as they made their way downstairs and outside. He realised that he was nervous. It was an unfamiliar emotion, but a good one. Jonny was determined to prove to Helena that he loved her and that he was capable of being the man she wanted him to be. He was acutely aware that his marriage protected him. If he lost that protection, he would be vulnerable in ways that Helena couldn't begin to imagine. The key to the chapel was heavy in Jonny's trouser pocket. He liked the feel of it banging against his leg as they walked along the path. The old brass key spoke of time and endurance. He smiled. Helena smiled back, somewhat hesitantly. She obviously had no idea what was coming.

The chapel was set apart from the rest of the buildings on Isola dei Delfini. It had been built – one assumed with some difficulty – on the rocky apex on the southern tip of the island. Its location was presumably a bid to bring the congregation closer to God. Not that the chapel could ever have accommodated many worshippers – it was tiny. There were only six pews either side of an aisle that was so narrow that you had to approach the altar in single file. On the simple stone altar sat a brass crucifix on which hung a crudely cast Jesus. There was no stained glass, no vaulted ceiling, very little decoration at all. It was essentially a cool, white box of nothing – all the better for the contemplation of one's sins. Not that anyone had used the chapel for much soul-searching for a very long time. But for Jonny's purposes, it was perfect.

He had, of course, had to run his idea past Geri; such micromanagement was one of the many reasons that his beloved aunt needed to step aside. Why in God's name did she need or want to know what Jonny had planned for his nearly wedding anniversary? Well, he hadn't actually spoken to Geri, but he had emailed the omnipresent Alice in advance, to ask for the key and to arrange for Carla to dress the altar with some flowers. He was a fully grown man, and yet he needed his aunt's permission to use the family church to renew his own wedding vows. It was ridiculous, but he'd suffered the indignity – for his wife.

Said wife must have sensed that he was up to something because she suddenly let go of his hand and stopped walking. The soft evening light hit her face. She looked good, the backdrop of milky-blue sky and denim-blue sea throwing her familiar beauty into relief. 'Come on. Spill. What's really going on? You never want to go for a walk.'

'Please, just trust me.'

'Okay, but I want to know where we're going.'

He pointed up the rising path to the chapel. She shrugged and started walking again.

When they arrived in the shady porch he produced the key, unlocked the door, then ushered her inside.

The cool interior of the church after the effort of the climb was welcome. Jonny closed the door and the thud echoed though the small space, then the air settled once again. You couldn't hear a thing, not the waves or the gulls or his niece crying or Ben's incessant bloody music. Carla had done a good job. The altar was flanked by two small vases of wildflowers and grasses. It was modest, but apt. There was a scent in the air that Jonny couldn't identify, but that reminded him of the gardens at the back of their childhood house in Holland Park. He headed down the aisle. Helena followed. There were two cushions on the front pew with their names hand-embroidered on them in silver thread. That was a nice touch. Not his. He sat and beckoned Helena to sit beside him. The silence expanded. Helena was waiting for him, as she often was.

'I've brought us here because there are some things that I want to say to you. Things that, as you rightly pointed out, I should have said before.' She looked apprehensive. Or was she suspicious? Jonny found it hard to tell what women were thinking. Even after fifteen years of marriage and three kids, Helena was no exception. He sat up straight. 'I know I ask a lot of you. That my job sometimes' – she shot him a look, he back-pedalled – 'that my job *often* seems to take precedence over our family. Over us.' She didn't argue with him. 'But I wanted you to know that I couldn't do any of it without you.' That didn't sound as romantic as he'd intended; it made her sound like a valued employee rather than his wife and lover. He hurried on. 'I'd be nothing without you, Helena.' That was better. More wholehearted. 'I love you. Now as much as when we first met.' He stood, picked up his cushion and dropped it on the stone floor, then he lowered himself down onto one knee. This was better. She looked genuinely taken aback. 'Helena Mia Chalice, will you do me the honour of staying married to me for the rest of our days? If you say yes, then I promise that I'll be more deserving of your love from this day forward.' Was that a bit pompous? No, it sounded genuine. He slipped his hand in his trouser pocket, pulled out the ring box and held it aloft. She hadn't seen all his purchases in Preziosa. The sepulchral quiet, the light filtering in from the single, simple high window and hitting the naked body of Christ on the cross – for a moment Jonny felt like a knight in an Arthurian legend. He looked at Helena and was shocked to see that she was crying. He panicked. 'Is that a "yes"?'

Still she didn't say anything. Instead she wiped her eyes and slowly reached out, not to take the ring box, but to stroke his cheek. She stared into his eyes as her fingers traced the contours of his face. It was unnerving to be so studied, but he held her gaze. She was obviously searching for something. Jonny held fast, fearful of, but luxuriating in, her gentleness. Whatever it was she was looking for, she must have decided, or convinced herself, that she'd found it because, ever so quietly, she said, 'Yes.' Ring forgotten, they embraced. It was Helena who pulled away and kissed him, hesitantly at first, then with more urgency. Jonny felt passion flicker and flare. Real, full-blooded desire took root and grew. His hands moved down Helena's neck onto her breasts. He pressed on, tenderness replaced by urgency. She met his need with her own. And in that moment, in that chapel, on the cool stone floor, all the knotty complications of their relationship dissolved, washed away by the glorious simplicity of lust.

Chapter 48

GERI

Instead of a formal dinner party, Carla suggested that she lay out supper in the garden, *given that it was such a lovely evening*. The revised arrangements came through Alice. She seemed wary of Geri's reaction to the change of plan – as well she might be; the world was going mad, the domestic staff were now deciding how things should be run – but Geri simply shrugged and said, 'That's fine.' Alice backed out of the study with a concerned look on her face. The reason for Geri's acquiescence? You couldn't see the bay or the dock from the garden and an informal supper would be over and done with much more quickly than a sit-down meal. Unsurprisingly, Geri wasn't really in the mood for socialising. What she really wanted was to go through to her yoga studio, lie on the floor in child's pose, with her forehead pressed against the floor, and stretch out her body and her thoughts, but that wasn't an option. She needed to gather everyone together – to provide Luca with a window of opportunity to act, and so that she could broach Ian's disappearance. So face them she must.

Ian's death was troubling Geri. Not emotionally. She felt no grief over his demise – to pretend otherwise would be hypocritical – no, what was disturbing her was the true nature of his death. Beating or no beating, her brother had sounded robust enough when he was raging around the Hut cursing them all. And yet less than an hour later he was dead. Geri wanted it to be natural causes, the self-inflicted consequence of having lived his life as if there was no tomorrow, but she wasn't naive enough to discount foul play. A cushion pressed against his face as he lay on the shabby sofa in his drunken stupor? A hand covering his mouth and pinching his nose? A sharp blow to his heart? It was possible. Ian being on the island had represented a threat to them all.

He'd certainly proved to be a threat to Lena.

Geri picked up the Montblanc and began doodling on the jotter. Ian assaulting Lena had been a nasty shock, but Geri couldn't say that it was wholly out of character. Her brother had always been sexually indiscriminate and indiscreet. She'd realised that years ago when she saw him rest his hand on a waitress's backside as he ordered himself a drink at her eighteenth birthday party. He'd been fifteen at the time. The inky spiral on the jotter expanded. Other incidents came to mind. There were the claims made by another waitress at one of the Chalice Christmas work dos – that girl had been paid off – and Geri remembered the owner of a hotel complex in the Cotswolds that they used to book regularly for company awaydays, who declined to have them back after another *misunderstanding* with a junior member of staff. Then there was the secretary at head office who left when she fell pregnant. She later claimed that the child was Ian's. He denied it, of course, while refusing to take a DNA test. That had been an expensive negotiation. Geri had had to get involved, as their father had retired by that point. There were many reasons Geri had never married, but the behaviour of the men in her family was definitely on the list. That Ian's heavy footsteps had beaten a path to Lena's door wasn't, therefore, a huge surprise. Perhaps she should have been more alert to the risk that he would misbehave in more ways than one, but she'd assumed that at the ripe old age of sixty-seven her brother had quit his old tricks.

Geri felt her first flush of emotion since realising that Ian was dead – and that emotion was guilt. She'd accepted Ian's blustery pleas of innocence and, while not wholly believing them, she'd not challenged him either. It had been easier that way. And she had colluded in making those women go away. Why? Because that was what had been best for the business, in those male-dominated, phallocentric, *boys will be boys* days. But it was not *those days* now. So yes, Geri believed Lena's tale. Her brother had, in all probability, made a hideously inappropriate pass at her and when she'd rebuffed him he'd attacked her.

But something about the events of the day that still didn't sit quite right with Geri. Lena had been remarkably composed for someone who had just been sexually assaulted. When she'd spoken to Geri she'd seemed more enraged than upset. Defiant – that was the right word for her demeanour. But surely Sophie's softly spoken, slightly built nanny hadn't been angry enough to slip down to the Hut and wreak revenge on her attacker? In theory, she had had the opportunity. She could have called in on Ian before heading up to the House to collect Sophie, but even if she'd been brave enough to go anywhere near Ian, how had she

211

killed him? Geri had a sudden very clear image of Lena's small, strong hands – that tended to Sophie so gently and diligently – pressing down a rose-patterned cushion on Ian's battered face and him stirring and starting to resist, only to realise, too late, that he'd finally met his match.

The scenario was no more preposterous than thinking that one of Ian's own children might have done it. Because that was another theory Geri was entertaining – patricide. Given their family history, it wasn't beyond the realm of possibility.

The jotter was now a riot of interconnecting swirls and whorls. If Geri was going to contemplate her nephews and niece as suspects then top of the list would have to be Jonny: the primary contender for her crown, in his own estimation. Jonny was impatient, ambitious and ruthless, as he loved to keep reminding her. But could he really be that cold-hearted? Perhaps. Especially having found out that Ian was planning on derailing the succession process. Would Jonny really murder his own father to secure his place at the head of the company? Insane as it sounded, it was possible. Then there was Juliet. She'd never forgiven Ian for leaving her mother and, in the process, her. When Joanna took her own life, that sense of abandonment had curdled into hatred. Becoming a parent herself did not appear to have changed that; indeed, it seemed to have intensified her disgust. Just look at her behaviour when Ian simply picked Sophie up when they were down by the pool. She'd been raging, but surely not enough to want him dead.

The more Geri thought about it, the more they all appeared to have an entirely plausible motive for want-ing to see the back of their father. Even Ben? But that one didn't compute. Geri crossed out one of her spinning circles. It must have been Ben who invited her brother to the island in the first place and he was the only one who appeared to want a relationship with his father. So why would he kill him? It couldn't have been Ben.

No, the only other candidate for murderer – if murder it had been – that made any sense, was her. She was the one with the very public lifelong antipathy towards Ian and, given his recent threats, the one with the most pressing motivation for wanting rid of him. She'd also had the opportunity. She had come back to the island early from lunch, before the others. Yes, if someone had offed Ian then that person was most likely her!

Geri's phone pinged. It would be Alice, chasing her up. She was deviating from the agreed schedule yet again. It was becoming a habit.

Geri stood up, smoothed her dress and at the same time tried to calm her agitation. She glanced again into the mirror above the mantelpiece, looking for any tells as to her inner turmoil, and was reassured that she couldn't see any. She took three deep breaths, channelling her inner swan, and headed down to celebrate her birthday with her likely suspects.

Chapter 49

HELENA

It was idyllic in the garden – the temperature balmy, the views soothing. Helena sipped her Bellini and enjoyed the moment. The ring that Jonny had bought her from Preziosa glittered on her finger. It was beautiful: a twist of white gold set with three small but piercingly blue sapphires. It was understated rather than extravagant, her style rather than his. A thoughtful gift, a token of his enduring love, or another bribe? Marriage to Jonny was so fucking complicated. How was it possible that at the same time she was acting and, intermittently, feeling like Jonny's cherished wife, she was secretly speaking to a law firm who specialised in high-net-worth divorces? Was he the hypocrite or was she? She heard him laugh at something Ben had said, or simply at Ben; it was hard to tell. She looked up at her husband – a man at ease with himself and the world. So not so fucking complicated for him. Ben joined in with the joke, but his laughter sounded forced. There were so many undercurrents between the three of them, it was a wonder they didn't all drown.

Juliet, the last of the dysfunctional trio, had yet to put in an appearance, which was unusual. Conflicting demands are the definition of motherhood, but it was all new to Juliet. Helena hoped that she'd make it down before Geri arrived. Tardiness was one of the many things that Geri did not tolerate. Not for the first time, Helena thanked her lucky stars that she hadn't come from a wealthy family. At least the dynamics in her own family were the normal, messy mix of love, loyalty and petty rivalries rather than the grand dramas of the Chalices.

As if summoned by Helena's thoughts, Juliet emerged from the House and hurried down the steps to the garden. Even from a distance it was obvious that she was still not herself. It was there in the hunch of her shoulders and the speed of her approach. She fixed herself a mineral water, glanced at Jonny and Ben, clocked Helena, then chose to avoid them all by walking off to look at the view. Hurt, Helena left her to it. It was hard to help someone who was so sealed off.

Suddenly, out of nowhere, Helena was hit by a wave of longing for her own kids. Isola dei Delfini might be idyllic, but it wasn't home. In that moment she would have gladly swapped the sapphires and Bellinis to be on the sofa in the snug watching crap TV with Aaron, Amy and Rory. Normal family life might be dull, but it was comforting. She dropped a message into the family WhatsApp group, the one that didn't include Jonny, then stared at her phone willing one, or ideally all, of her children to respond.

The sound of the front door opening shattered Helena's yearning for her children. Geri emerged from the House, sleek and elegant in a simple but stunning emerald-green dress. The birthday girl – not that there was any doubt that Geri was most definitely a woman, not a girl – had arrived and so the party could begin. Helena got to her feet. It was time to push thoughts of her children to the back of her mind and fulfil her role as the loyal wife of the future CEO of the Chalice Group.

Chapter 50

GERI

The atmosphere down by the pool seemed relaxed. Guilty consciences or not, they must all have had a better day than her, although that wouldn't have been difficult. Jonny was positively ebullient – an adrenaline rush? And Helena, whose inclination to silence rather than speech Geri found hard work, seemed more sociable than normal. Her welcoming kiss had been a new development. Geri couldn't work out what Jonny saw . . . and kept seeing . . . in Helena. If she'd been a betting woman she'd have wagered that it would have been Jonny's marriage that would have ended in divorce rather than Ben's. Jonny didn't normally linger where there wasn't something to be gained. Speaking of Ben: she sought him out, conscious that he would be the one most hurt by Ian's 'sudden departure'. He toasted her arrival with his Campari and soda – not his first, by the look of him. There was music coming through the speakers. She guessed that was Ben's doing as well. Even Juliet eventually wandered over and mustered a smile.

They were expecting a party and so a party she would give them. She must behave as if nothing had happened if she was going to facilitate Ian's last voyage and continue with her own journey. A monstrous lie to facilitate a truth. She could live with that.

Geri indulged in a few minutes of small talk before she tackled the thorny issue of her brother. She did it in as measured a way as possible, by crossing her long legs, glancing at the sunset, taking a sip of her drink and simply saying, 'Before we eat, I want to let you know that your father has left Isola dei Delfini.' They responded in a ripple. Jonny asked, 'When?' with an edge of ill-concealed relief, Ben said, 'Really!' with what sounded like genuine surprise and Juliet exclaimed, 'Good', with such venom that the bubble of worry lodged in the centre of Geri's chest expanded. Had Lena broken their pact and said something to Juliet? Surely not. Geri had been very clear that that was not advisable, for everyone's sake. Worryingly, the girl hadn't 'found the time' to collect her 'incentive' yet. Geri might have to stoop to deliver it herself at this rate.

Geri pushed her concerns about Lena away. In the here and now her priority was 'disposing' of Ian. She rolled over their reactions smoothly. 'As you know, the fact that he turned up here purely to see what he could get infuriated me. Jonny, you heard him last night, he was talking all sorts of nonsense. He had no grounds whatsoever for his complaints, but, as always, he was happy to throw around threats and make cruel insinuations in a bid to muddy the waters and cause division between us. On balance I decided that it was better for all of us to advance him yet more funds from my personal account, and surprise, surprise, that did the trick.'

She paused, curious to see their response. It was, as she had hoped, muted to the point of silence, only Ben asking, 'Where's he gone?'

Geri could at least answer truthfully. 'I don't know, and I didn't ask. Because, if I'm going to be honest with you all, I don't care, as long as he stays away . . . at least until we get things settled.' She was slightly ashamed to be pleased by her last comment. She hadn't strayed into the past tense, she'd reminded them all why they were together on Isola dei Delfini in the first place and she'd communicated her faith that their father would reappear, as soon as the latest tranche of money ran out. As far as they, and she, were concerned, Ian was still alive.

With impeccable timing, Carla chose this moment to emerge from the House carrying a huge platter of risotto. They all watched her make her way carefully down the steps. The smell of saffron was amazing. 'Shall we eat?' Geri asked. They rose in unison. So they were all happy to gloss over Ian's departure. Should that concern her? Probably. But for now she was simply glad to have put out the fire. That she didn't know who was responsible for setting the blaze was another matter, for another time.

Chapter 51

CARLA

Carla left them feasting on the meal that she'd managed to throw together, despite everything that had happened. The risotto was poor – gluey and over-seasoned. You couldn't cook rice properly when your mind was somewhere else. It needed love and attention and she'd felt neither as she'd cooked Ms Chalice's birthday supper. They wouldn't notice. If they needed anything else they would have to fetch it themselves. She had other priorities, and for a change she was going to address them.

Chapter 52

LUCA

With nothing to do but watch over a gift-wrapped corpse, Luca struggled to keep his mind from wandering. Unsurprisingly, given the events of the last few hours, it meandered back into the past and to Carla.

Luca's childhood had been full of love. In that he knew he was lucky, because without it he wasn't sure he would have survived, grown strong, learnt to be himself. Carla had been his rock when he was young. She still was now. Unconditional love was an anchor and no matter how much you might tug and strain against it, it was the only thing that stopped you getting swept away. But Carla was also a source of profound frustration for Luca. She was a conundrum that he'd never managed to work out. He loved her, but after all these years he still didn't understand her.

As a child Luca had been fascinated, but unnerved, by Carla's ability to shape-shift. When she was working, she was so submissive and quiet that at times she hadn't seemed human at all. Yet when she was with him she was funny and fierce, with strong views on all sorts of things, from politics to the length of his fringe. Seeing her switch between these two versions of herself had been deeply confusing. Of course, as Luca had grown, he'd begun to understand that her behaviour around the Chalices was a requirement of her job and that it was her job that kept a roof over their heads. But when he was a teenager that appreciation had become tinged with frustration, then embarrassment and ultimately judgement. Carla was, effectively, a twenty-first-century servant. Sure, it was to uber-rich people, but she still spent her days cleaning their toilets and washing their bedsheets. That she was still beholden to them, still cleaning up their messes, troubled Luca even more now. He had been able to move on and yet she hadn't.

He was startled back into the present by the sound of knocking. Fuck! Could he have been seen through the window? It was impossible to tell. There was another knock. He was going to have to answer. As Luca approached the door he heard Carla's voice. 'It's okay. It's only me.' Speak of the Devil, although Carla was hardly that.

He opened the door a crack and she slid inside. Luca locked it behind her. 'What are you doing here?'

'I came to help you move his body.' Her directness surprised him, although after what had happened in Lena's room perhaps it shouldn't.

Luca had been taken aback when he'd reached Lena's room and found Carla breathing heavily with the exertion of having dragged Ian Chalice off Lena and beaten him into submission. Ian must have been equally shocked, which was how a slightly built, five-foot-four-inch woman had been able to put down such a lump of a man. The ferocity of her attack had been shocking. Ian's face had been a mess. Carla and such violence did not compute, but there had been no time for Luca to unpack what the hell was going on, or how he felt about it, because by that point Ian had been making a move to stand up and Luca wasn't risking that. He'd planted his foot on his chest and pushed him back down. 'You. Stay. If you move a muscle I'll start on you.'

Ian dealt with, for the time being, Luca had turned his attention to Carla. She appeared to be coming back into herself, but Luca had still been wary. 'Are you all right?'

'Me? Yes.' She had looked down at her hands and seemed puzzled to find them covered in blood.

'Where's Lena?' he'd asked. 'Is she all right?'

'Yes. She's okay. She's in the bathroom.' Ian had started saying something, but he'd shut up when Luca raised his fist. That's when Carla had looked Luca direct in the eyes and said simply, 'I had to stop him.'

Luca had looked back at her, trying to make sure that his gaze was steady and unwavering. 'And you did.'

Carla had nodded and rubbed her knuckles.

Now what? Luca really hadn't had a clue. Ian whimpered. Time wasn't standing still. It was ticking away at a rate of knots. It was Carla who had decided. 'I'll go and fetch Ms Chalice. She'll know what to do.'

And Carla had been right: Geri had known exactly what needed to be done, including, thankfully, blaming him for Ian's beating. But as a Chalice she'd obviously had no intention of doing any of the dirty work herself.

Which was why Carla was back offering to help drag Ian's body down to the boat. 'This isn't what we agreed. You need to stay out of it.'

She actually smiled. 'That's very considerate of you, my dear, but it's a bit late for that.' She walked past him into the sitting room and he followed. They stood and looked at the bundle on the floor. 'You've done a good job.' It was an odd thing to say, but the praise still felt good. 'Come on then, let's get him shifted. They're busy stuffing their faces with my badly made risotto.' She moved towards the head end, but Luca couldn't have that. 'Okay. But you take the feet and let me know when you need a rest. He's heavy.'

Without looking up she said, 'I know.'

They braced themselves, lifted, and began the slow haul down to the boat.

Carla only needed three short breaks on the cumbersome journey. Luca sometimes forgot how much a long life of domestic drudgery built up your strength. He himself was glad to take a rest to let the blood flow back into his arms. Having finally hauled Ian's body down onto the dock, they both straightened up. The sun was setting, streaking the sky purple and red. Carla watched the colours, seemingly unperturbed by the fact that they had a dead member of the Chalice dynasty lying at their feet. Having been soothed by the sky, it was Carla who said, 'Let's get him on board, then.' They took up their positions.

'On three,' Luca advised. 'One, two, three.'

They heaved, swung as best they could and let go. Ian's head caught one of the gunwales and he crashed awkwardly onto the deck below. Luca felt for the *Black Swan*. She'd not been built, with such craftsmanship and care, to ship waste. 'I can take it from here. You go back. You don't want them noticing that you're missing.'

She ignored him. 'How will you get him over the side on your own?'

'I'll be fine. I can winch him, if I need to.'

She still seemed reluctant to leave. 'Have you got something to weigh down his body?' Luca nodded. 'What?' she asked. He understood her need for reassurance that Ian Chalice's body wasn't going to come bobbing back up to the surface any time soon, or ever. Luca pointed. His dumb-bells lay ready and waiting on the deck. She laid a hand on his arm. 'Sorry.' Carla knew how important they were to him. Weight training was *the* thing that kept him sane.

He shrugged. 'It's fine.' Some sacrifices were worth making.

She smiled with such gentleness that he had to look away. 'Take care out there.'

He kissed her cheek, climbed aboard and pushed off, impatient to get this over and done with.

When the sails were set and the *Swan* was under way Luca looked back at the island and there she was, contrary to his advice, standing on the dock, watching him. He waved and she waved back.

Chapter 53

GERI

After the meal Ben suggested that they retire to the sun loungers. Although Geri would have been happier to retreat to the haven of her suite, she complied. While they were lounging by the pool, weighed down by risotto, Caprese salad and vanilla panna cotta, they couldn't be anywhere near the Hut or the jetty. After about ten minutes there was some stage-whispering and the four of them struggled to their feet. They urged her to stay put, before they headed up to the House. Geri closed her eyes for a few minutes. Fatigue nibbled at her. She hated being tired; it made her feel weak. This is what families did to you; they frayed your perfectly tailored seams. She expected to hear the gentle clink of crockery as Carla materialised and started to clear the debris from their supper, but there was only the fizz of the sea hitting the island and the occasional clatter of wings. Not birds – there were no birds on Isola dei Delfini – only bats. They didn't bother Geri. It was as much their island as hers. It was, in some ways, a compliment that they were happy flitting around catching mosquitoes above her head – normally, they stayed hidden in the eaves of the House when there were people about.

Before long she heard footsteps and voices. The bats departed. She envied them. She opened her eyes and saw Jonny, Helena, Ben and Juliet making their way down to the garden – Greeks bearing gifts. She sat more upright; she didn't want them detecting any hint of weariness in her. Once back down on the terrace they pulled the sun loungers into a semicircle around her. It was obviously birthday gift time. She really could do without this, but she smiled and obliged with a 'you really shouldn't have'. Sibling hierarchy kicked in, meaning that Jonny was the first to lay his offering at her feet, or more accurately on her lap. Jewellery from Preziosa, could he have less of an imagination? She dipped her face and untied the ribbon, withdrew the box and, in deference to the cost, if not the thought, she paused. Then she snapped open the lid. Nestled on its bed of signature purple velvet was a hand-beaten silver necklace. It was a thing of craftsmanship and beauty – that she would never wear. What part of a seventy-year-old body did most women *not* want to draw attention to? Their crepey necks. She snapped the lid shut, dropped the box back into the bag and murmured her thanks. Juliet thrust her present at Geri next with all the grace of a moody teenager. It was obviously a book, wrapped by the store judging by the neat execution of the corner folds. Geri eased the paper off. It was a hardback biography of Catherine the Great. A ruler that, to her knowledge, she'd never expressed the slightest interest in, and who was infamous for being harsh and unscrupulous. More insincere thanks were offered. Then it was Ben's turn. For a moment it looked as though he was empty-handed, but that was just a jolly wheeze – Jesus, she was exhausted – because he jumped up and went to fetch her present from where he'd hidden it behind one of the bushes. It was large and very badly wrapped, in plain brown paper. Sourced, Geri suspected, from the kitchen in the House. Ben passed his gift to her with a big grin on his face. 'I saw this and thought of you.' Whatever it was, it was light despite its bulk. She ripped off the layers of wrapping. It turned out to be a soft toy. She was so exhausted by them by this point that she couldn't be bothered to disguise her confusion. Why on earth had he bought her a child's toy? Ben looked crestfallen. He took the furry lump from her and held it up for her to get a better look.

'It's a bull.' As if that explained anything. 'He's called Gerry. After you.' He laboured on. 'You know, Taurus. Your star sign.'

The thing was hideous. She forced a smile. 'Why thank you. It's certainly . . . different. Thank you all.' Surely now she could leave. But no. Carla was back. There was the rasp of a match and a pause while they waited. The only saving grace was that they hadn't gone for the full seventy candles. It still took Carla a while to light the seven stuck in the thick layer of cream. Lunch and dinner, cake and presents, the death of her brother in suspicious circumstances – birthdays really were a marathon. Candles lit at last, Carla picked up the tray and carried the huge chocolate and whipped cream confection across the lawn towards them. As she approached, Jonny, Helena, Juliet and Ben broke into a ragged rendition of 'Happy Birthday'. Would this day never end?

What struck Geri, as she took a deep breath and prepared to extinguish her birthday celebrations, at long last, was how young Carla looked in the candlelight.

Chapter 54

BENEDICT

Well, that hadn't gone as planned. Geri had hated Gerry. She'd not got why he'd bought her a furry bull for her birthday at all. So it plainly wasn't the thought that counted.

Everyone else drifted back to their rooms once Geri had departed, but Ben stayed down by the pool. Not because he didn't want the night to end, but because he didn't want to have to head to bed on his own. Loneliness didn't feel quite so bad out in the open air.

He waited until Carla had finished clearing away before he had a bump. This trip was proving to be a lot less entertaining than he'd hoped. It was also way too quiet for Ben's liking. What was it that women were always saying about feeling lonely in their marriages? Well, boo hoo, Ben felt lonely most of the fucking time. He needed people around him and he needed those people to be radiators. His family were all fucking drains, including his own father. Another bump. Why not? Yeah, why the fuck not. He had plenty to be going at after his rendezvous with Aldo. If it hadn't been for Ben the old man wouldn't even have known that they were travelling to Isola dei Delfini or what was on the agenda. Ben was the only one who'd had enough loyalty to let him know. Christ, he'd actually felt sorry for his dad, having seen how disrespectful and dismissive Geri had been of him. That comment by the pool about him not being welcome at her birthday lunch! That had been brutal. Ben had even gone down to check that the old bastard was all right before they'd set off for Positano.

And what thanks had he got?

Nada! Zilch! Nothing but gibes and low blows. His father's last words to him? Something encouraging? Maybe even, God forbid, something kind? No, his last words to Ben had been, 'Don't you worry about me, son. I'm doing just fine.' He'd taken Ben's face in his hands and squeezed, hard. 'It's you who needs to sort themself the fuck out.' Parenting Ian Chalice style – indifference spiked with abuse. Good riddance to the old bastard. Ben never wanted to see him again. Christ, this was a one-way trip to Gloomsville! But Ben was on the highway now, so there was no turning back. Perhaps Aldo had slipped him fentanyl instead of coke. That always brought Ben down for some reason. The snarky bastard. If he had, he'd . . . Ben couldn't muster the energy to think what he'd do to Aldo. It required too much effort.

The mosquitoes were committing mass suicide in the pool. Ben watched them crash-land, become waterlogged, struggle and drown. Their corpses floated on the surface of the water like tiny used condoms. Luca would have to fish them all out in the morning. Ben hoped that some escaped his net. Geri might, hopefully, end up swallowing a few when she took her dawn dip. How could she not like Gerry? Gerry had been bought with real affection. Ben had another bump.

What he really needed was a hug, but there was fat chance of that. His yearning for some human contact felt shameful, pathetic and overwhelming. Ben couldn't remember his father being physically affectionate with him – ever – and his mother hadn't stuck around long enough to provide much in the way of love or support either. The thought depressed him further, but it didn't lessen his craving. And sex was off the table. He giggled at the thought of himself having sex on the dining-room table slap bang in the middle of their 'big' meeting tomorrow. Now that would really disrupt the agenda! But even that daydream fell apart. There weren't any eligible candidates on the island. Well, there was Lena, but loaded as Ben was, he knew that turning to his baby niece's nanny for a shag smacked of some deeply Freudian shit. He should've hung onto Gerry! Geri clearly hadn't wanted him. At least Gerry would have taken up the empty side of the bed. Christ Almighty, he was boring himself with this self-pitying shit.

Ben staggered to his feet, dropped his phone on the sun lounger – see, he wasn't that high, he had enough functioning grey cells left to preserve his tech from damage – and before he could change his mind, he took a running jump and dive-bombed into the pool.

Chapter 55

JONNY

It had been a successful day in a number of ways, some of Jonny's own making, some not. To celebrate, he wandered over to the chest of drawers in the corner of the room and opened the third drawer down. Hidden beneath his shorts was a box. He took a cigar out of the box and smelt it. There was something about a good cigar; it encapsulated success. He was about to wander over to the window and light up – Helena disliked him smoking around her, but he felt confident that she wouldn't begrudge him one tonight – when he spotted Helena's phone. She was in the bathroom, no doubt working her way through her skincare regime; it took a while. Presented with the opportunity, Jonny took it. He scrolled through the pictures she'd taken since arriving on the island. There were some nice shots. He smiled, sent a couple of the best ones to himself. His expansive mood spread. Yes, it had been a good day that was going to be followed by an even better one.

He ambled across the room, pushed open the shutters and the windows and lit up. The first puff was the sweetest. Periods of abstinence really did sharpen your appreciation of life's pleasures.

Their room had a panoramic view of the coastline. In the darkness the lights of Positano appeared to hover and sway above the solid black expanse of sea. The mainland looked both near and far. This was the true magic of Isola dei Delfini, the sense of being secluded but connected; it was, literally, the best of both worlds. Jonny took another puff. He held the smoke in his mouth, savoured the rich, heady taste. Tomorrow he was going to get what he deserved. Finally. He knew it. Not because he was arrogant, although he was happy to admit that he was, but because he'd earned it. He was a self-made man. Sure, people would scoff, but look at his lineage: a fat, greedy baker of a grandfather from Scunthorpe (his grandmother a blank, all he remembered of her was a strong Yorkshire accent), a borderline degenerate of a father and a mentally fragile mother. Jonny had travelled a long way under his own steam. His character, his drive, his ambition were his and his alone. And now, crucially, there were no obstacles in his way. He'd repaired his relationship with Helena, his father was no longer a problem and Juliet, his only real rival, was in as weak a position as she'd ever been. One last nudge and she would fold; he was certain of it. He was now, inarguably, the only person capable of becoming the next CEO of the Chalice empire. Helena emerged from the bathroom. Jonny slid his phone into his pocket out of sight and smiled at her.

A movement down in the garden drew his attention back outside. Poor old Ben. He was really stupid enough to think that he could have been a contender. But perhaps you didn't have to look too far to see where he got his delusions from. Ben shared their father's misapprehension that charm alone was enough. How wrong-headed did you have to be to live in such denial? As if to prove the point, the daft bastard suddenly leapt up, set off running and threw himself, fully clothed, into the pool. The splash drew Helena to the window. She slipped in beside Jonny with a rustle of silk and a waft of face cream. 'Is that wise, given the state he's in?'

They both watched the dark shape that was his half-brother lying at the bottom of the spotlit pool. Jonny took another hit of his cigar. He courteously blew the smoke away from Helena. 'I doubt it, but when did Ben ever do what's sensible?' After what felt like an age underwater Ben finally drifted up to the surface. He languidly flipped over onto his back and began floating aimlessly around the pool. Perhaps he could see Jonny and Helena watching him, perhaps not. Either way, he didn't seem to care.

Regretfully, Jonny stubbed out his cigar on the window-sill – he didn't want to push his luck. 'Are you ready to turn in?' Helena nodded. Jonny slipped his arm around his wife's waist and guided her towards the bed. He left the window open – on the off-chance that Ben might hear what he was missing out on.

Chapter 56

JULIET

Juliet waited until the House had settled, then she slipped on a robe and slippers, shoved what she needed into a bag and made her way down to the Cottage. She was not going to stay away from her daughter for the sake of appearances, not any more. There had been no more messages, her father was gone and Geri did not know who Sophie's father was, but Juliet still couldn't relax without her daughter close by.

She was reassured to find the front door to the Cottage locked. She thought about knocking, but she didn't want to freak Lena out, so she sent her a WhatsApp instead. Lena responded almost immediately, with **I'll be down in a sec**. She looked flustered when she opened the door. 'Is everything all right? Sophie's fine. She's fast asleep. I checked in on her not more than twenty minutes ago.'

Juliet appreciated Lena's rush of reassurance. She decided to be honest with her, for a change. 'I know. You said, in your text. But I can't sleep up at the House. I don't like being so far away from her.'

As they climbed the stairs Lena whispered, 'You can take my room, if you want to. I'm happy to sleep in the nursery.'

Juliet stopped on the small landing. 'Thank you, but I want to be in with her. I'll bed down on the sofa.'

Lena afforded Juliet the courtesy of not arguing with her. 'Okay. If that's what you prefer, but let me fetch you a pillow and a throw.' Lena returned swiftly. In the dim light of the landing Juliet noticed that she looked tired. She had every right to be; she was bearing the brunt of Sophie's care and her own erratic behaviour. As Lena passed Juliet the bedding their hands brushed. Neither of them pulled away. Lena said, 'Let me know if you need anything – I'm just across the landing. I'm a light sleeper.'

Juliet's 'Thank you' was heartfelt. Lena nodded, turned away and disappeared into her room.

Juliet crept into the nursery. The nightlight was plugged into the socket in the skirting board. It gave off just enough light to let Juliet see Sophie, who was, indeed, fast asleep. Juliet stood beside her daughter's cot for a few minutes, allowing herself to feel love without panic or self-reproach. It felt good. Simple. Real. She matched her breathing to her daughter's. It was calming. So calming that Juliet let the tiredness that she'd been holding at bay sweep over her. She pushed her bag under the sofa, made up her makeshift bed and lay on her side so that she could still see Sophie through the bars of her cot.

She was woken by the rattle of her phone on the wooden floor. She had no idea whether she'd been asleep minutes or hours. She grabbed her handset and the screen flared harshly into life. The backlight hurt her eyes; the content hurt her heart. It was another photo. This time it was a long-distance shot of Lena sitting out at the front of the Cottage with Sophie in her arms. Judging by the soft light

Juliet guessed that it must have been taken early evening, when everyone else had, allegedly, been getting ready for Geri's birthday celebrations. Everyone apart from Ian, who had already left Isola dei Delfini by this point and who, therefore, although still an abject apology for a father and grandfather, categorically could not be the person waging this deeply unsettling campaign of intimidation. The text accompanying the photo read, **Have you decided yet Juliet? Because the clock is ticking. Not your biological clock this time, a real one. And it's attached to a bomb that's about to go BOOM!**

Juliet scrambled off the sofa and ran over to Sophie's cot. In her haste she banged into it. The jolt woke her daughter, who began crying. Juliet scooped her up into her arms. It made no difference to the volume of her daughter's distress. The next thing Juliet knew the door to the nursery banged opened. A torch beam blinded Juliet for a moment. She froze.

'Is everything all right?' It was Lena's voice. She lowered her phone so that at least Juliet was no longer blind. Lena came halfway into the nursery then stopped, obviously uncertain of the etiquette of the situation. She went for deference. 'Sorry. I heard Sophie crying. I thought I'd better check on her. On you both,' she hastily added.

Juliet heard herself screech, 'Get out! I'm perfectly capable of looking after my own child.'

Lena was the person with 24/7 access to Sophie. Was she knowingly allowing someone to get close enough to her daughter to take these shots? Was she part of this sick campaign? No, that didn't make any sense. Lena had gone above and beyond to help Juliet. And she was in the photos. Think, Juliet! Think! But it was impossible to form a rational thought with Sophie squirming and bleating in her arms. The door was closing. Lena was leaving. No, no, no. The last person Juliet wanted to alienate was Lena. Lena had saved her sanity. Lena was good with Sophie. Lena would never let any harm come to her. Lena was not family.

'Lena!' The door swung open again and Lena's troubled face reappeared. Juliet needed an ally, even if it was a paid employee. 'Please. I had a nightmare. I dreamt that someone had got into the nursery and they were going to take Sophie. When you came into the room I panicked. I wasn't thinking straight. I didn't mean to shout. I'm sorry.'

Lena paused then asked, quite justifiably, 'Juliet, what's going on?'

Chapter 57

GERI

Tiredness was no excuse for foregoing your routine; if it was, Geri would have retired long ago. Endurance and commitment were the two key pillars of her success. She had learnt young that she couldn't always defeat her competition, but she could outlast them. But tonight even Geri was tempted to throw in the towel. Her seventieth birthday had been testing – and that was an understatement.

Make-up removed, dress replaced with comfortable leggings and a soft brushed-cotton tee, Geri started her vinyasa flow. It would be a short, gentle one, chosen to flush some of the silt of the day out of her system. Geri wasn't a yoga zealot, but her practice had improved the quality of her body and mind for the past fifty years and she had hopes that it would extend it for a good many more. Whatever the slogans said, age was undeniably a number, but you could and, in Geri's opinion you should, defy it.

Geri was nearing the end of her session when she heard Juliet's bedroom door open and close. Geri cut short her Virabhadrasanas and went along the hall. She watched her niece sneak down the staircase like a demented ghost. Why couldn't any of them stay put and behave rationally for longer than ten minutes? Ben jumping fully clothed into the pool. Jonny smoking a cigar in his room, despite any form of nicotine being strictly prohibited anywhere in the House. Carla appearing and disappearing at will. Luca flatly defying her. Chess pieces were not supposed to have wills of their own. Every time Geri looked at the board they had all moved, and that made executing her strategy all the more difficult.

Thank God for Alice.

Alice had arrived in Geri's life at exactly the right moment. She'd brought with her efficiency, professionalism, dedication and something else, something that Geri had badly needed – a mirror . . . that she'd held up to Geri and her family. Geri had rejected Alice's gift at first – no one wanted to see a true reflection of themselves, warts and all – but now that she had accepted Alice's offering there was no going back. Unflinching scrutiny – Geri Chalice was famous for applying it to competitors, suppliers, partners and employees, but she'd been remiss in its application to her own family. Well, her myopia had been corrected now.

Because today was only the start. Tomorrow was going to be even more challenging, and by the end of the day Geri suspected that no one would be happy. Apart from Alice.

Chapter 58

LUCA

It was gone 2.00 a.m. when Luca got back to the island, but Carla was still waiting up for him.

She held his face in her roughened hands and looked into his eyes for a moment, then she placed a kiss on his forehead. The tenderness released the tight screw of tension that Luca had been using to help propel himself through the awfulness of the day. Wordlessly, she pulled him into her embrace. He leant his head on her shoulder, reassured as always by her warmth and strength. After a few moments of comfort she gently pushed him back onto his own two feet. As she bustled around the small kitchen he sat at the table, swaying with tiredness. It was the smell of fresh bread that brought him round. She placed the loaf in front of him and watched as he tore off a lump, poured oil on it and crammed it into his mouth. He chewed and swallowed, filling his belly. He hadn't eaten anything since breakfast. He'd been too busy dealing with the problems of the living, and the dead.

Only after he'd eaten half of the loaf did she speak. 'He's gone?'

'He has. Straight to the bottom.'

She reached behind her and picked up a bottle of red wine. She pulled out the cork and poured them each a glass. They clinked glasses and drank in silence. No toast was needed; they both knew what they were celebrating.

Day Three

Chapter 59

JULIET

Surprisingly, Juliet overslept. She pushed herself upright, stiff from the lumpy sofa, but pleased to have finally got some rest. Unburdening herself of her fears and suspicions to Lena had helped, that and being close to her daughter. She glanced across at Sophie's cot. It was empty. For the second time in a few hours she scrambled across the room, her heart in her mouth. There was a handwritten note on the crumpled white baby blanket. Juliet snatched it up. It read, *Sophie is with me. She woke early. She's been fed and changed. I'm going to take her out for a walk. I thought you needed to sleep. Lena*

Juliet clung onto the cot rail and swayed. She couldn't go on like this.

And she wasn't going to.

She was stronger than this, smarter than this, more in control than this. She was not a passive woman, so why was she behaving like one? Motherhood wasn't a disability. She wasn't powerless. And what she needed to know was what Geri wanted – because the texts had to be from her aunt after all.

Juliet grabbed her phone and typed, **I've had enough of this. What do you want?** and pressed send.

She waited, her heart thudding. The response when it came was longer than any of the previous texts.

At long last you've done it Juliet. After all that heartache. All that money. All that cloak and dagger jetting around Europe for treatment. You're finally a mother. Sophie is lovely and wonderful and precious. End of text. Juliet was gripping her phone so hard it was a wonder it didn't shatter. **The question is . . . how precious? Is Sophie more valuable to you than your career?** Another pause. Then, **Because you can't have both. You do know that, don't you Juliet?** Another few seconds, then finally Geri showed her hand. **Withdraw, Juliet. It's the only thing you can do . . . if you want to keep your daughter.**

In a curious way Juliet felt relieved. Geri had named the price of her silence. She must have worked it out, despite the gaps in the information that her spies had gathered. What a bitch! What an astute, ruthless, cruel bitch.

She knew that Harry was Sophie's biological father.

Juliet sat on her makeshift bed and reflected on the perversity of her aunt using her desperation to have a child against her. It was monstrous.

What Juliet had done wasn't. Harry had betrayed her. He'd claimed to love her and for years they'd shared, or so she'd thought, the trauma of trying and failing to have a child together, but he'd left her the minute a better, easier, prettier, younger option had presented itself. Juliet had, through sheer willpower, recovered from that treachery, but when she found out that Fleur was pregnant something had snapped inside her.

And that's when she started to plan. Her first step was to push for the divorce to go through as quickly as possible. She refused to let her lawyers get into lengthy wrangles over the division of their assets or the final settlement. The brief was for a clean break; if it cost her, so be it. The lawyers obviously thought she was mad, but they did as asked; she was paying their fat fees, after all. Through those seemingly interminable months of negotiation Juliet waited, breath held, for Harry to raise the issue of their remaining fertilised embryo. But he was obviously much too busy creating an easy-peasy, instant family of his own. Had he really forgotten that there was one last chance of a child sitting in a freezer in a clinic on Harley Street? Apparently he had. Which was as shocking as it was deeply hurtful. But it helped. Harry didn't deserve to be consulted about what happened to the remaining embryo. He relinquished that right when he abandoned her and their potential child.

But Juliet hadn't given up on that chance at motherhood – despite the many obstacles.

Not least of which was reproductive legislation. The embryo was legally the property of both of them and could only be used with joint consent.

And so began Juliet's journey into criminality.

She had to use every ounce of her influence to lean on the clinic in London to facilitate the transfer of the embryo to Switzerland. She remembered sitting in the Director of Client Services' cool, grey, minimal office – unflinching and insistent. He wasn't happy about her request – her acrimonious divorce was a matter of very public knowledge – but he obviously didn't want to stand in the way of the wishes of one of his A-list clients. Instead he got her to sign some hastily drafted 'release' papers that he clearly hoped would exonerate his unimpeachable clinic if the case ever went to court. He then charged her an exorbitant amount to transport the precious last embryo, by specialist courier, to Switzerland, a country with a justified reputation for excellent fertility services and for doors that swung open with the swipe of a Platinum Amex card.

Discretion guaranteed, though not success, Juliet flew out to the Fertilas clinic two days after her decree nisi came through and went through with the procedure. No questions asked. She flew home guilt free, but, yet again, full of desperate hope.

And then the miracle. The embryo took, the pregnancy progressed and nine months later Sophie was born. She had her child, at last. Her child – no one else's.

And now Geri was threatening to reveal what she had done. She knew that Sophie's conception and birth involved the breaking of many laws, whichever country you were in. The damage that Geri could do with such information was huge. It would be reputation- and career-ending. But way more frightening was what would happen if the truth about Sophie's biological heritage got out into the public domain. Juliet's parental rights would be challenged, she could be prosecuted, she might end up in prison and if that happened Sophie, the precious child that Juliet had gone through so much to have, would be taken away from her.

Juliet shuddered so violently that she dropped her phone, not with fear but with rage. The question in the text was a valid one. Just how precious was Sophie and how far was Juliet prepared to go to keep her?

Chapter 60

JONNY

Decision day broke cool and clear.

On the doorstep Jonny paused. Isola dei Delfini really was a special place. Sure, it was beautiful, but more importantly, it was the tangible evidence of his family's success. With the purchase of the island his grandfather had secured the Chalices' entry to the exclusive club of the uber-rich. The island proved just how far they had come. No wonder it was the place that Jonny felt most himself. And soon it would be his.

His route took him past the Cottage. There were no signs of life. He wondered if Juliet was inside and, if she was, what sort of state she was in. He loved his sister. He wished her well in her new role as a mother. He really did. He wasn't a monster.

He skirted around the back of the Cottage and took the narrow path that ran up between the rocks. He had to scramble up the last hundred metres on all fours, through the bastard gorse bushes. The Drop might be a pain to get to, but the climb was worth it. It was a rock platform that jutted out over the bay like a stubborn chin. Breathing hard with the exertion of the climb, Jonny walked out onto it and looked down. It was a sheer twenty-metre drop. Hence the name. Jonny instinctively stepped back from the edge. The dive was a test – which was precisely why he'd come to do it this morning of all mornings. Fear was an essential ingredient in pleasure, at least it was for Jonny. The sense of making oneself take the leap, the need to be decisive. As in business, so in life. If you hesitated when you launched yourself off the Drop there was a real danger that you would smash into the unforgiving skin-and-bone-breaking cliff face. But nothing worth having was without risk.

Jonny took off his flip-flops. He wedged them together and hurled them. They arced high in the sky before disappearing out of sight. He stepped back up to the edge, positioned his toes on the lip. The rock was uneven and rough beneath his bare feet. For a second or two he fought the swinging, swaying sensation that heights always brought on. Precarious; it was just a word unless you were the type of person who was actually prepared to put yourself in a situation with real jeopardy. Jonny had been fourteen the first time he'd jumped. He'd been on his own then as well – unsure whether he'd have the bottle to go through with it. As a foolhardy but ballsy teenager he'd simply taken a running jump and thrown himself into the void. When he'd hit the water that first time he thought he'd broken his back, but when he'd finally resurfaced and realised he wasn't irreparably damaged, he'd felt a rush of invincibility that had been intoxicating. Over the intervening years Jonny had taken the test a number of times – here and in other places and in other situations. He'd passed every time.

He would again, today.

He tensed, raised his arms above his head and took a steadying breath. He looked down at the water that would save or swallow him, then up at the sky above him, then he flexed his knees and propelled himself into the void.

Chapter 61

BENEDICT

The sunlight woke him. It was a rude awakening. He should have closed the shutters, but of course he hadn't. He hadn't been in a fit state. Ben vaguely remembered going for a dip in the pool. That would explain why he was stark bollock naked. He didn't move, knew it would be unwise. No sudden movements, no rash faith that if he stood up he wouldn't fall straight back down. Small increments were the way to go after a heavy night. Instead, he stared at the Moroccan tiles on the ceiling. The mosaic was beautiful, a repeating pirouette of tiny aqua and dark-green tiles. But this morning the pattern made him feel nauseous. He closed his eyes again.

Today was the day – Geri's grand exit and Jonny, or Juliet's, ascension to the throne. His chances? Nil. Ben did use a lot of mind-altering drugs, but he wasn't delusional. He knew that Geri would never give it to him. It was for the best. Who would want a depressed addict as CEO?

The sickness receded slightly. He sat up, experimented with some slow blinking. Then he stretched his arms out wide, wrapped them around his body and hugged himself. It helped. He could now keep his eyes open for prolonged periods. He imagined he looked like a sloth. The thought nearly made him smile. Things were on the up. He spied his wet clothes on the floor, a line from doorway to bedside. He suspected that had been a strip with very little tease.

A long shower, some breakfast and he would be as good as he ever was these days. Yeah, he reckoned he could make it to the bathroom. He swung his legs over the side of the bed and put his feet down, onto something sodden. His boxer shorts. Undeterred, because if Ben was used to anything it was setbacks, he carried on up to standing. Ta-dah! I thank you! His first achievement of the day – getting out of bed. He would have taken a bow, but that would have brought back the vertigo.

All he had to do now was get through the rest of the day. The fun was over, it was time for the serious stuff.

Chapter 62

JONNY

It was a good omen. Not only had Jonny executed the dive perfectly – he'd entered the water like a knife – but he'd even found his flip-flops floating a few metres away from him on the surface of the flat, calm water.

After a leisurely swim round to the next bay he scrambled onto the rocks and made his way back up towards the House. The sun was higher now, warming his wet skin. His adrenaline was pumping. He felt anointed. Blessed. Zinging with energy. Fourteen or forty-four, Jonny knew that he had what it took to get what he wanted.

As he climbed the steps to the garden he heard singing. A lullaby, sung in Polish. Lena with Sophie. Jonny stepped quietly off the path, crossed the flower bed and peered through the balustrade. His eyeline was directly level with the lawn. Lena had spread a blanket out under one of the pine trees. She was lying on her stomach with Juliet's baby beside her. Lena's legs were waving in the air. Her feet bare. Jonny was close enough to see the soft skin on the soles of her feet. He could even hear Sophie's soft, snuffly baby breathing. The sound catapulted him back to his own twins as babies. He remembered holding them after they'd been born. Helena had been taken away to be stitched up and he'd had a glorious hour on his own with his newborn son and daughter. A baby's breath – it was a sound that reached inside you and hooked itself into your soul. Feelings heightened by the dive, and sharpened by the sight of Juliet's child, Jonny experienced a sudden overwhelming yearning to be a father again. To experience that rush of unadulterated love. To reassert his virility. To expand the Chalice dynasty with his progeny. To ensure its longevity and increase his offspring tally: Juliet on one, Ben on two, Jonny, front of the pack with three, would be the outright winner if they had four.

It wasn't such a mad idea. They had plenty of money, and they were about to come into a lot more. As CEO he would probably have to put in fewer hours, and Helena wasn't *that* old. They'd had no trouble whatsoever conceiving the twins. Another child would put the seal of permanence on their relationship. True, Helena had said they were done with babies, but perhaps now that they were on better terms, it might be something she'd reconsider. He would offer inducements. Besides, Helena wouldn't have to bear the brunt of the child-rearing. Another live-in nanny or au pair would be the way to go. There were always plenty of young French or Italian girls with maternal instincts who wanted to spend a year or two in a nice house with a nice family. It had worked well in the past. New babies didn't have to be hard work. He was on a roll now. He imagined commissioning a family portrait, soon after the birth – something relaxed and modern, nothing stuffy. Him in an open-necked shirt, smiling, his hand on Helena's shoulder, her holding their new baby, the older kids forming a tight knot around them.

Lena shifted and the movement broke into his thoughts. She rolled over, sat up and lifted Sophie up onto her knees. She bent over the child, her thick blonde hair falling either side of her tanned legs like a tent. Jonny imagined what being within that embrace must feel like. Lena was chatting to Sophie as if they were actually having a conversation. It was enchanting.

Something snapped under foot. Lena looked up and for a second her gaze met his. He wished that she hadn't caught him peering at her from behind a garden wall like some old perv. He raised his hand, waved and turned away, casually, but not before registering that she didn't wave back.

Jonny made as much noise as possible as he stepped back onto the path and continued on his way up to the House. This was Chalice land and, whatever the views of an uppity Polish nanny, he owned it and would do what he liked when he was here.

Chapter 63

LUCA

Luca woke early, but still not early enough to be moving before Carla. She was obviously already up at the House, running around, sorting breakfast for them all. His arms ached, but not from lifting weights. One more night and they would be free of the lot of them. Luca couldn't wait. He planned to stay on for a few extra days after they'd left, have some real time with Carla, without the constant demands of the family, but he would need to leave by the Friday. He had a job lined up. Taking day trippers out to the Blue Grotto. It would be mind-numbing, but it was guaranteed work for the whole summer and it was close enough to let him get back to see Carla regularly. Because, sadly, the Chalices would return to the island – they always did. And once Jonny got the keys to the kingdom there'd be no stopping him. Luca felt a wave of guilt. Carla would never leave. She would never be free of them.

He took his pastry and coffee down to the dock and ate his breakfast there, breathing in the silence. The sea was crystal clear, flat calm, utterly benign. That was good. Storms had a habit of stirring up what lay at the bottom of the ocean, and they could do without that. As Luca chewed and swallowed he wondered how long it would take before he could gaze at the sea and not see Ian Chalice's corpse. Probably as long as it would take for the salt water and the currents and the fishes to nibble away at the rope, then the tarp, then the copious amounts of flesh. Luca suspected that Ian's bones would be rolling around on the seabed for many years to come. The Chalices' power to pollute other people's lives and minds was one of the many reasons he detested them.

Luca's phone buzzed. He looked at the message with dread. What task did they want him to perform now? But it wasn't Alice or any of the Chalices. It was Carla. He had to shade the screen with his hand to see her message. It read: **They're meeting in the dining room at 10.00 a.m. We should know who it's going to. Please come. I want you here with me.**

Luca's instincts screamed flee, but his sense of indebtedness was stronger. He rose to his feet slowly. If Carla needed him, then he had no choice but to be there – that's how families worked.

Chapter 64

JONNY

Jonny dressed casually for their meeting – he didn't want to look too much like the CEO-in-waiting. Light-blue linen trousers, a loose-fitting white shirt – if anything, Carla had given it too fierce a press. The sleeves had sharp creases in them like a bloody airline pilot, but there was nothing he could about that this late in the day. A generous spritz of his favourite cologne and Jonny was ready to go. He felt, smelt and, despite the shirt, he looked good. Even Alice's redundant message reminding him, and the others presumably, to *be punctual* didn't dent his mood. He was happy to comply; no one wanted to be late for their own coronation. Her follow-up edict asking them *NOT to bring their phones into the meeting* was mildly irritating, but again, what the hell. Such nonsense would be a thing of the past very soon.

He was the first to arrive. He poured himself a coffee and took a turn around the sitting room, sipping and planning as he strolled. There were so many changes he wanted to make in the business. Geri had steered the ship well, but she was risk averse, something you couldn't afford to be in today's climate, especially in terms of alternative investment streams. But he would start with personnel. He was going to need a like-minded team around him. Ms Alice Baxter would be the first person he'd be having a word with. It was time to move Geri's pet monkey into a role more suited to her conspicuously narrow talents – payroll would be perfect. She'd be handing in her resignation before he'd had time to email her the job spec. The thought made him smile. It was unfortunate that Juliet chose that precise moment to rock up. She must have seen his lips twitching, because her reaction on seeing him was extreme. She scowled and stormed past, out onto the balcony, where she began pacing up and down. His sister always had been a sore loser. Everything about her shouted defeat. The lack of attention to her appearance; she was dressed in a saggy sundress that, unlike his shirt, was screaming out for an iron. Then there was her posture; the slump of her shoulders, the way she kept clenching and unclenching her hands. She really did look on the edge. Jonny took a seat, crossed his long legs, picked an imaginary piece of fluff off his trousers and savoured his composure and his coffee.

He was, appropriately enough, down to the dregs by the time Ben arrived. If it was possible, he looked even worse than Juliet. Better dressed, that was true, but very green around the gills. Ben's faith that a sharp haircut and a designer T-shirt could mask his habit was bordering on tragic. He did at least acknowledge Jonny. 'Any left?' He indicated Jonny's coffee.

'Yeah. Plenty. On the side.'

Ben wandered off to add caffeine to the concoction of stimulants that was no doubt whizzing around his system.

The stage was set. All they needed now was Geri, the kingmaker.

Chapter 65

JULIET

Juliet still didn't know what she was going to do. How was that any kind of plan? Always have a clear objective and stick to it, no matter how much dust other people kicked up. It was the first rule of business. A rule inherited from Geri. Yet here she was about to go into the most important meeting of her life unclear about her aims and, more importantly, her actions. Never before had she been so paralysed, but then she'd never been as scared as she was right now.

Juliet kept her back to Jonny. She glared at the sea and stewed in her own private tsunami of anger and indecision. Even out on the terrace in the fresh air, as far away from Jonny as she could be, the overwhelming smell of his cologne was oppressive. Ambergris and oud; the dominant, cloying, unmistakable scent of male superiority. Despite her impossible situation, Jonny's assumption of success made her want to keep on fighting him. She'd been doing it the whole of her life. She *was* better than him, smarter than him; she could have beaten him – if her hands hadn't been tied behind her back. But she wasn't free to fight any more. Geri had seen to that.

The injustice of it made her want to scream. Her daughter or her career? The future of her own fragile family or that of the Chalice Group? It was a simple choice and a very complicated one. And she was going to have to make it in the next hour.

Chapter 66

BENEDICT

Ben poured himself a double espresso. There was little point in him being there, given that he had no real skin in the game, although – as he added two lumps of brown sugar to his coffee – it struck him that he should perhaps have given a little more thought to the likely implications for himself of one or the other of his siblings becoming CEO. Neither of them liked him. At best they tolerated him – both in the business and within the family. The question was, which of them would tolerate him for the longest and at the highest salary? It was a tough one to call, which made worrying about it pointless. Ben took a swallow of his bittersweet coffee. Aw, what the hell, he was still a Chalice. He would always have a seat at the table, it just might be one right down at the bottom end. So bring it on and get it over with. Ben couldn't wait. He, like his father, had had enough of Isola dei Delfini and his family.

Chapter 67

GERI

Geri looked around the study, with all its ridiculous trappings of power and status, and thought, not about its next incumbent, but about herself. She'd been CEO of the Chalice Group for twenty years. It was nowhere near long enough. She wanted to go on working, increasing the Chalice Group's wealth and reach, forever. Whatever people thought of Geri, or no doubt would say about her after this, she always put the needs of the business first. Hence what she was about to do.

On cue, Alice knocked and entered. Geri suspected she was wearing a new suit, not that it looked very different to her other grey outfits, but there was something in the cut and the material that spoke of quality. It was clearly a statement of intent. Geri could respect that. Or perhaps the difference was that, despite her best efforts to disguise it, her PA was obviously excited. The one miscue was that Alice was clutching the files containing their investigations into each of the candidates to her chest. Geri understood that she was proud of her work, but as a tell it was a huge one and Geri didn't want the meeting to escalate too swiftly. 'Perhaps a briefcase might be less . . . on the nose.'

Alice flushed. 'Of course. Sorry.' She hurried out and returned with the files zipped out of sight inside a soft leather document folder.

'Are they gathered?' Geri asked.

Alice fired off a text and got an immediate response. Geri assumed that would be Jonny, chomping at the bit. 'Yes. Ben has just arrived.'

Geri stood up. She checked the fall of her silk vest across her shoulders and the fit of her soft jersey trousers across her hips, then she ran her hand over her scalp. Satisfied, she came out from behind the desk. 'Right,' she said, 'let's do this.'

Chapter 68

HELENA

Helena hadn't expected to be invited to the meeting. Why would she be? This was business and she was merely Jonny's wife. According to Jonny, it was a foregone conclusion anyway. You certainly couldn't accuse her husband of lacking confidence.

She looked through her swimming costumes. Most of them were new. She'd bought them especially for this trip. That embarrassed her. After all these years, and despite the innumerable times Jonny had let her down, Helena couldn't stop wanting to look good for him. The pathetic truth was that she still wanted him to desire her. She craved that power; she had precious little influence over him otherwise. Hence her reaction yesterday evening. She felt her cheeks flush at the memory. At the same time as a solicitor in London was *exploring her options*, she'd been having sex with Jonny in the little chapel at the top of the hill – with Jesus watching. Helena knew she was leaving herself wide open to disappointment, but when Jonny was this attentive, this thoughtful, this committed to making her feel loved – then he *was* the man that she wanted to be with. And the island was playing its part as well. Isola dei

Delfini was beautiful, secluded and undeniably romantic. A private fantasy utterly divorced from reality. Who could resist being seduced by it? For a few days, at least.

But the possibility of, at some point, leaving Jonny still held some allure. The promise of freedom kept circling Helena, whispering in her ear, telling her that she had choices, that she could live a good life . . . if she unchained herself from her husband. If Natasha could rid herself of Ben, why couldn't she jettison Jonny? She was tempted. Because once they returned to London Helena knew that the sunlit bubble they had been living inside on Isola dei Delfini would burst and they would fall back into the old routines. Jonny would once again be busy, preoccupied, impatient, and she would be stuck at home, underoccupied and frustrated. Would him becoming CEO change that? No, it would not. He might, as he claimed, have less actual work to do, but she couldn't imagine him being at home more – not willingly. Her husband was hard-wired to roam and perform; it was in his DNA. And as CEO he'd have more dinners to go to, more press commitments to fulfil, more trips abroad to make, bigger and better audiences to dazzle and manipulate. All of which would be the perfect excuse for him to escape the boring demands of his family and his marriage.

The only difference?

They would be richer, a lot richer.

Should she stay or should she go? The decision wasn't simple.

Choosing a swimming costume was.

In the end Helena went for the teal bikini, reasoning that it would look good against her developing tan.

Chapter 69

GERI

Jonny and Ben stood up and Juliet came in from the balcony when Geri entered the room. 'Shall we?' They followed her through into the dining room. Carla had set it up like a board meeting, complete with jotters, pens, a decanter of iced water and a cluster of glasses. There was even a bowl of fresh fruit. That wasn't going to be touched, but the aesthetic was nice. Geri took her seat at the head of the table. Her rightful place. Alice silently stood to the side.

They sat. Jonny to Geri's right, Juliet to her left, so that they were facing each other. Ben, ignoring the blotters, took the unset place at the end – the one vacated by his father. Geri swerved that thought. Deal with a problem and never look back. Well, Ian had been dealt with and there had been no blowback. So far. The nagging question of who had provided the solution remained, but perhaps some puzzles were best left unsolved. Jonny repositioned his pen and shot his cuffs, Juliet reached for the water; neither of them looked at one another. Ben simply sat back and waited.

After the settling came the tension. They were all study-ing her now – openly, brazenly, expectantly. The time for

268

scheming and subtlety was over. She had uncovered their secrets and their sins.

She had thought long and hard about what the business needed – and it was not them.

Where to start?

Years ago, was the honest answer to that, but there was no going back; the only thing Geri could do now was shape the future. 'You all know that there is *nothing* more important to me than the health and wealth of the Chalice Group. It is my life. Contemplating a future in which I'm no longer in control of the business has been difficult. But, as has been pointed out to me by more than one person, it is time to decide if there is someone better equipped to drive us forward, to bigger and, hopefully, better things.' She paused. 'The CEO of the Group must, it goes without saying, be a Chalice. We are a family business to our core.' She took another beat. 'But having such a short list of candidates for the top job is not without its challenges. It pits family member against family member and it severely limits the talent pool.' There was a general shuffling in their seats. Had she just insulted them? Oh yes, she had, and there was plenty more of that to come. 'When I was assessing your individual suitability for the role I realised how little I really knew about each of you. Given the importance of my decision, I set about rectifying that ignorance.' More shuffling. 'Hence . . .' Alice was ready and waiting. She unzipped the folder, stepped forward and passed the first file to Geri. Geri placed it on the table in front of her. 'I did some research. Which, if you'll bear with me, I'd like to share with you.'

Geri watched Jonny and Ben's attention ping-pong around the room, bouncing from her to the file to each other and back again. Neither of them had the presence of mind to look at Alice. They both looked shocked and worried. As well they might. In contrast, Juliet's gaze was steady. She stared at the file on the table, but not in shock. Why would she be shocked? She already knew that Geri had a dossier on each of them because she had cracked the safe and accessed the memory stick. Points for initiative to her niece. No one said anything, but that was unsurprising; they really didn't have any other option but to hear her out.

It was time to take each of them apart, starting with the one she loved the most.

'Ben.' They all jumped at the sound of her voice. 'Shall we begin with you?'

Chapter 70

CARLA

Luca wasn't happy. He never was when he was inside the House, but Carla needed him to be here for this. It would, she hoped, help him to understand. He was chafing at being asked to crouch at the bottom of the scullery steps beside her and eavesdrop on the Chalices. He thought it beneath him, and he was right, but it was the only way they could participate in the proceedings – until Ms Chalice invited them upstairs. Because that was the important thing that Carla knew and Luca didn't. Their invitation to take a seat at the table was coming; they just had to wait for the signal.

Chapter 71

GERI

Ben smiled at Geri.

They all thought Ben was stupid, but he wasn't, he was just stunningly unfocused. Irrespective of his many failings, Ben was the most likeable of the three of them, as a human being, but it was precisely his humanity that lay at the root of most of his problems. He was impulsive, compulsive, reactive and random. The gambling, the partying, the craven pursuit of popularity and profile at whatever cost; it was all so immature and wasteful. Ben was only ever going to amount to something if he applied himself, and sadly he never did – not to his marriage, his children or his career.

You didn't need to be a psychologist to diagnose the problem. Ben was a little boy in a designer T-shirt, wandering around searching for approval in all the wrong places. Ben's craven need to fill the void of not being loved as a child – wherever Geri looked she saw the collateral damage caused by her brother – rendered him utterly unsuitable to be the CEO of any business. He simply lacked the backbone. In truth, Ben was lucky that the Group employed him at all. They certainly wouldn't have if he hadn't been family. Head of Consumer Research and Market Insight! The irony was obviously wasted on him. It was a job that had been specially created to keep him as far away as possible from any real decisions. Let him predict trends and chase the latest TikTok fads to his heart's content. They could always ignore his 'insights'.

Geri smiled back at her youngest nephew and did him the kindness of putting him out of his misery quickly. 'I'm not giving it to you, Ben.' In rapid succession she took in his shrug of acceptance, Jonny's smug nod and Juliet's lack of reaction. Geri really needed to stop fixating on her niece; her time would come, soon enough. 'You're not suited to it. You don't have the ruthlessness.' She was sugaring a bitter pill. He sat back, looked relaxed, thinking himself safe; he had inherited some traits from his father. And such appalling, ingrained complacency was precisely why Ben was due some much harsher medicine. He couldn't continue to live life like a spoilt child in a sweetshop, because Geri genuinely feared that if he was left to his own devices, he would gorge himself to death. She opened his file. It was time for Ben to 'open wide'. 'On top of your lack of business acumen and ambition, there's your habit of using company resources as your personal trust fund.' She pretended to peruse the top sheet. She didn't need to; she knew what was in all their files. 'In fact, there are quite a few habits that you need to kick, Ben.' He stopped smiling. She didn't. She went on, relentlessly, for his own good. All of Ian's offspring were going to hear some unpleasant home truths over the next hour. 'The partying, the drugs, the drinking, the gambling – the playing at life. You're thirty-two, Ben. You may no longer have a marriage, but you do have children, a job and lots of life ahead of you. Don't you want to live it? And better than you currently do? Wouldn't it feel good to have a reputation for being something other than a playboy? If you're going to do that then you have to start behaving like an adult. Boring, I know, but so much safer in the long run – for everyone. The gambling and the drugs, they have to stop.' Ben's expression had morphed from indifference to discomfort, but Geri still couldn't detect any contrition. He was going to need a push. 'To encourage you, I want you to look at this.' She slid a couple of pages of figures across to him.

Ben scanned them. Despite his tan, he seemed to pale. 'How the hell?'

'Research, Ben.' It was a cheap shot, but it landed. 'We' – none of them were sharp enough to pick up on the pronoun and look at Alice – 'weren't able to establish the full extent of your debts; many of your creditors aren't listed at Companies House, obviously, so the figure for your "Drug Expenditure" is, I confess, a best guess – based on current prices and on what you appear to be inhaling and swallowing every month. By the way, your regular dealer in London is ripping you off. And there, sadly, we have another reason why you could never be allowed to run the business – you're far too trusting.' She let that sting for a moment, then continued. 'After all your debts are settled, and I appreciate that the company may be the last to be paid, given that we're less likely to break your legs than some of your other creditors, you will invest a portion of your considerable remuneration for the job you are paid to do, but could do so much better, into something useful. I suggest some cognitive behavioural therapy to help you regulate your emotions and a detox programme to rid you of your addictive tendencies.'

'I'm not an addict.'

'Yes, Ben, you are. And, although I'm no expert, I think you're depressed. You need to accept the extent of the problem and actively do something about it if you want to hold on to your job and, more importantly, your kids.' She stopped. Cruel to be kind. But it was still cruelty. Ben was rubbing at his face like a child trying to hold in a sob. The rasp of his hands across his stubble sounded like sandpaper. When he starting pulling at the skin along his jaw Geri decided to step in. 'Ben. Listen to me. It's going to be okay. We can get you the help you need. All I want for you is . . . better.'

Finally he stopped trying to erase his own face. He put his palms flat on the table and took a deep breath, then he stood up abruptly, knocking over his chair in the process. 'Fuck you, Geraldine,' he spat. He looked to her right and to her left, at his brother and sister, added, 'And fuck you two as well', then stormed out.

Well, that had gone exactly as Geri had expected and planned. He would calm down eventually and when he did he would come to her and they would make their peace. He always did.

Geri closed Ben's file, passed it to Alice and turned her attention to Juliet.

Chapter 72

LUCA

Luca and Carla both jumped when Ben's chair hit the floor. They listened to his footsteps as he strode out of the room. Carla whispered, 'I told you it was worth listening in.'

Luca shrugged. He had no feelings either way about Ben; as Geri had said, he was an irrelevance, but in spite of his initial reservations, Luca was now hooked on hearing the rest of the meeting. Because Jonny and Juliet's fates did interest him. One of them would replace Geri and become Carla's boss. As such they would have control over her life, just as previous generations of Chalices had. The thought thoroughly depressed him. He reached out to take Carla's hand and was, once more, about to raise the prospect of her leaving the island and their employ, when she raised her finger to her lips.

Geri had started talking again.

Chapter 73

JULIET

Geri's evisceration of Ben had been savage, but her arguments and her evidence had been irrefutable. And Ben was supposed to be the one she liked.

Now it was her turn.

Juliet tried to swallow, but found that she couldn't. She was parched. Alice passed Geri her file. Geri placed it carefully on the table in front of her and flipped through the dividers to the middle. Juliet noticed that each tab was neatly labelled in Alice's tiny, precise handwriting. Alice's cryptic comment to Juliet in the office about Geri doing her *due diligence* and *certain factors coming to light* had been false modesty. Alice obviously knew exactly what was in each of their files, which surely went way beyond her pay grade. Geri patently trusted her PA more than her own family.

Geri traced her short, polished nails across the open page. Juliet saw the heading – *Fertilas* – and shouted, 'No! Wait.'

Her aunt was obviously irritated by the interruption, but she did lean back just a fraction, indicating that Juliet should proceed.

Juliet blurted, 'I don't want this.' Geri studied her.

Up until that moment Juliet had been debating whether to fight on, to lay claim to her crime and defend herself. Her old self had argued that it might be worth a try. Jonny was hardly a saint. If Juliet's reading of his file had been even remotely accurate, he was lining his own pockets to the tune of hundreds of thousands of pounds. Geri would not be impressed by that. But Geri's text messages had been explicit; she wanted Juliet to give up on becoming CEO and if she didn't there would be consequences. Such vindictiveness made Juliet's stomach curdle. Geri and Jonny were staring at her. Juliet dropped her head. Let them wait, she needed a moment. She'd earnt it. This was her life hanging in the balance.

Say she dug in and fought Jonny for CEO, that she let it get bloody and nasty and messy. And say, by some miracle, that Geri was impressed by her balls, that she realised that Juliet the mother was the same woman that she used to admire and trust. And say Geri switched horses just before the finishing line and Juliet got to be in ultimate charge of the Chalice Group . . . what exactly would she be winning? She would be signing up for a life where people were commodities, where worth was purely a metric and where profit was the be-all and end-all. Life would be just more of the same: making more money than they knew what to do with – other than buy up more businesses and expand into more territories and thereby make more money. On and on, ad infinitum, until she ended up like Geri, playing vicious power games with the very people she was supposed to care about. It wasn't worth it.

Juliet lifted her head. 'I withdraw. I don't want to be the next CEO of the Chalice Group.'

Geri stared. 'Sorry? What?'

Juliet looked into Geri's eyes and repeated herself. 'I withdraw. Let Jonny have it.' The sense of release was powerful.

'Why?' Geri asked.

She really was enjoying this cruel charade. What to say? Certainly not *the whole truth and nothing but the truth* – that was what Juliet needed to keep buried. But her daughter was still her only credible reason. 'Sophie.'

There was a loaded pause. Perversely, despite everything that had happened, a part of Juliet hoped that Geri might argue with her, but all she got was a sigh and a small tap of a finger on the incriminating paperwork, then Geri simply flipped shut the file. Her face was a mask. 'So be it. If that's your decision, I respect it. Sophie is obviously your priority at the moment. I just hope that the sacrifice will be worth it.' It was the exact same phrasing as the text messages. She really was a malevolent, two-faced old bitch.

Why go to all this trouble? Why commission all this invasive, costly research into every nook and cranny of their lives? Why drag them all to the island to toy with them so cruelly? Why not simply name Jonny as her successor in London and be done with it? Juliet was glad to be out of it. Her family was an abomination. She looked across at her big brother. He had given up any pretence of politeness and was grinning from ear to ear. They were as bad as each other, which was why they were a perfect fit. Geri knew that Jonny had been secretly building up a huge portfolio of investments and properties, in his own and Helena's name, using funds siphoned off from the business and that he'd been exploiting his position and his contacts to manipulate the markets, and she simply didn't care. She was always going to go for Jonny because he played the game the way she did, ruthlessly. His crime was greed and Geri respected greed. What she would never understand was love.

With as much dignity as she could muster, Juliet rose to her feet and followed in Ben's footsteps, out of the room.

Chapter 74

JONNY

Sixteen minutes – that was all it had taken. He was going to be the next CEO of the Chalice Group. Halle-bloody-lujah.

And yet Geri didn't say a word to him after Juliet's departure.

The silence stretched. Jonny was very aware of Alice standing there, behind Geri, holding his file. Surely that was irrelevant now. Still, he felt a twinge of unease. His file was thick. Thicker than Ben's or Juliet's. He had a good idea what was in it. If Geri had uncovered the full extent of Ben's debts and tracked down his suppliers then it was a dead cert that she'd done a deep dive into Jonny's own brand of 'sin'. But hey, she always said she wanted someone enterprising to take over from her. Well, she couldn't say he wasn't that.

Finally Geri turned to him and said, 'And then there was one.'

It was hardly a ringing endorsement, but it didn't matter. He could put up with Geri's posturing and power plays for a few more months while they sorted out the transition, then she would be out of the door and he would have a free hand. Now was the time to appear statesmanlike and magnanimous: the classic qualities of a good CEO. 'I just want to say . . .' He had prepared a speech. It was important to do these things properly.

But Geri held up her hand and rudely stopped him in his tracks. 'There'll be time for that later. If you'll excuse me, I feel I should speak to them both – smooth things over, as best I can, before they leave.' She passed Juliet's file back to Alice. The implication that he would have been tempted to take a sneaky peek if she'd left it out on the table was offensive and wholly accurate. 'I suggest we reconvene after lunch. We have a lot to discuss.' And with that she stood up and left. Alice trailed after her, clutching her brief-case as if contained the codes for a nuclear missile launch. What the fuck! Jonny sat back and looked at the empty seats around the table. This wasn't how he'd imagined it going. There'd been no back-slapping, no champagne, no recognition whatsoever. He was at a loss about what to do next.

But only briefly.

Helena. That's who he needed. His wife would be happy for him, even if no one else was.

Chapter 75

CARLA

So the power was being handed back to a man. Jonny Chalice was going to be her boss. Carla wasn't surprised. It was the way of the world.

Before Luca could start up the familiar refrain about her leaving the island and finding a normal job with normal people, she told him to go and get the *Black Swan* ready. He hesitated, but she reminded him that the sooner he dropped Juliet and Ben back on the mainland the sooner he would be back. Reluctantly, he did as asked.

After he'd gone Carla went out into her garden. She took her basket and her gardening knife with her. She cut some sprays of slender, silvery eucalyptus and a few of the heavily scented *giglio*. She needed an excuse to be wandering around upstairs. Things were starting to fall apart and she wanted to witness that disintegration first hand. Armed with the fresh stems, she hurried back up the kitchen stairs into the main body of the house then on up to the upper floors. On the first-floor landing she set about refreshing the floral display on the chest at the end of the hall. She could hear Juliet banging around inside her room, talking. She was obviously on a call to Lena, issuing rapid-fire instructions about them leaving. Carla slipped the knife into her apron pocket and left her basket on the side.

She knocked. Juliet didn't hear her, so she knocked again, louder this time. The door was wrenched open. Carla kept it simple. 'Can I help?'

Juliet looked about to say no, then seemed to think better of it. 'I'm leaving, with Sophie. Now.'

'Yes. I know.' These people never stopped to think about how much 'the staff' knew about them; about their secrets, their fears, their vulnerabilities, their intentions. 'Luca is getting the *Swan* ready for you.'

'Good.' Juliet seemed to lose momentum.

'Perhaps some assistance . . . with your packing?'

Juliet looked behind her. The bedroom was in chaos. 'Yes, please. That would be appreciated.'

Ten minutes later Juliet's bags were packed and stood ready to go by the door. Juliet picked up one, Carla the other. Juliet pulled the door closed behind them with a decisive thud. 'Just give me a minute.' She ran along the hallway and hammered on Ben's door. 'You coming?'

Carla heard Ben reply, but not what he said. Without waiting, Juliet marched into his room. Cautiously, Carla crept along the hallway.

'Oh for God's sake, Ben!' Carla risked a peek inside. Ben was sprawled on the bed. The bag of drugs that normally lived in the hidey-hole under his bed was resting on his stomach. Carla had found it years ago. She was a good housekeeper, and a good housekeeper looked under beds as well as changing them. Juliet was in full flood. 'You have precisely fifteen minutes to get your shit together and get down to the dock. I'm not messing, Ben. If you're not there, we're leaving without you. And don't you dare bring *that* with you.'

Ben muttered, 'Okay, okay. I'll be there.'

Carla stepped away. Luca was right, listening at keyholes was tawdry, but it was informative. She resumed her docile position, minding Juliet's luggage. After another barked instruction to Ben to *get his arse into gear*, Juliet re-emerged. Together they made their way to the stairs.

Halfway down the staircase Juliet stopped. Carla saw why – Ms Chalice was standing in the hall, by the front door. Her voice, as always, was calm and clear. 'Juliet. I'd like a word with you before you leave.'

Juliet descended the last few steps. She walked briskly up to Ms Chalice. Carla watched through lowered lashes, fascinated. Juliet dumped her suitcase on the marble floor and squared up to her aunt. 'Would you? Well, tough. My days of listening to you are over.'

Ms Chalice seemed momentarily thrown. That was something Carla had never seen before. When she next spoke, it sounded very much like she was struggling to keep her tone civil. 'I'm concerned because I sense that you are angry.' Juliet didn't say anything, but Carla saw her whole body stiffen. Ms Chalice carried on, regardless. 'Your decision to withdraw was . . .'

Juliet sliced her off. '*My* decision! That's rich. It's hardly been up to me, has it? The only thing that has surprised me has been your utter cowardice. It's not like you to be so underhand. Why not just tell me that you weren't going to give it to me?' Ms Chalice went to say something else, but Juliet was having none of it. 'I thought you said that this process wasn't going to be personal. Well, it feels fucking personal from where I'm standing. And don't think that I don't know the depths you've descended to in pursuit of your fucking due diligence! I do! What I don't understand is why!'

'Juliet, please. I know that my actions may seem some-what . . . excessive, but given what was at stake I had to know what I was dealing with. I needed to know the truth about each of you. Your real selves, warts and all, not the touched-up version that gets presented to the world. And, regrettably, what I found was deeply troubling. You may disagree – you plainly do – but I'm afraid that the business matters more than any one individual.'

Juliet roared, 'Can you even hear yourself?' She mim-icked Geri's measured speech. '*The business matters more than any one individual! Dealing with!* My fertility problems, my divorce, my daughter are not *things* to be dealt with – by you! They are my life.'

Ms Chalice's voice remained calm, but Carla could see a tinge of red creeping up her neck. 'I agree that a woman's fertility *is* a private matter, but I believe that your zeal-ous pursuit of motherhood has affected you, and your judgement.'

Juliet laughed. It was an ugly sound. 'Private! You don't know the meaning of the word. Nothing is sacrosanct to you, is it, Geri? Not even family. It's all just data to be crunched, analysed and utilised. Well, I'm sorry. I've had enough. I'm done.' Ms Chalice tried to speak again, but Juliet talked over her, her hands chopping through the air as she did so. 'You've got the CEO you deserve. I just hope that you, and your beloved business' – she spat the words – 'survive long enough to regret it!' With that, she bent down, picked up her case and straightened up to her full height.

Ms Chalice looked stunned, but she didn't make any attempt to stop her niece leaving. As Juliet stepped over the threshold Carla heard Ms Chalice say, more to herself than her niece, 'This isn't over, Juliet. I still have to speak to Jonny.'

It was impossible to know whether Juliet didn't hear her or no longer cared, but either way she didn't break stride as she disappeared out into the sunshine.

Chapter 76

HELENA

Helena was on the top deck of a bus. She'd nabbed the best seat, the one at the front where you could look down the weird mirrored tube at the driver's hands on the steering wheel. Helena knew she must be dreaming because she hadn't been on public transport for years, but she felt perfectly happy sitting there on her unreal bus watching the world of her imagination slide by. It was raining in her dream. The hammer of raindrops on the roof every time the bus passed under a tree was loud. The bus juddered to a wheezy stop at each set of lights. Helena didn't mind, she was in no rush to get anywhere. She heard a voice calling her from the bottom deck, but she didn't want to leave her seat – someone might nab it.

'Helena!' Not someone. Jonny. She was not on a bus, she was on Isola dei Delfini. She pushed herself upright, blinking at the harsh sunlight.

'You were away with the fairies there!'

She needed to tune back into reality. Something important had happened while she'd been happily riding around listening to the rain. The meeting. She looked at the position of the sun. It didn't help at all, she had no sodding idea what time it was. 'You're finished? Already?'

He said, 'Yeah.'

Something was up. He didn't look pleased or puffed up, nor was he angry. He was nothing, and that was not a good sign. 'And?' She was fully awake now.

'Oh, she gave it to me. You're looking at the next CEO of the Chalice Group.'

That was her cue for excitement, but his strange mood was inhibiting. Still she tried. 'That's fantastic news. Congratulations, darling. Well done you!' She leant over and kissed him, somewhat self-consciously. She wasn't looking her best – she was hot and sticky and her mouth was gluey with sleep. 'Tell me all about it. How did Juliet react to the news?' She would be rightly furious; pipped at the post because she'd had Sophie. Biology screwed it for women who worked. Helena kept that thought to herself, of course. To prove she was interested she swung her legs off the sunbed and faced him, making sure that her arm was covering her stomach.

Jonny stroked her leg absent-mindedly, his mind still on the meeting. 'Juliet said she didn't want it.'

'Oh.' Wasn't that good news? 'But that helps, doesn't it? Going forward, I mean.'

'Yes.'

It was not like Jonny to be so circumspect. 'And Ben?'

'Oh, that was brutal. She basically tore him a new one. She told him that he needed to sort his shit out, that he was lucky to be working at all. She'd dug up all sorts on his personal life. She knew all about his gambling debts and the extent of his drug habit.'

289

Jonny had never cared for his half-brother, so Helena was surprised at how little glee there was in his voice. Jonny normally liked seeing other people brought low. 'So it went just as you'd hoped, then.'

'Yeah.' There it was again, that curious flatness. A tiny niggle of suspicion blossomed in the back of Helena's brain.

'And yet you seem' – she knew that she needed to choose her words carefully – 'a little bit deflated.'

He looked up at the House. 'It was all a bit of an anti-climax.'

She moved across so that she could sit next to him. She draped his arm around her shoulders and snuggled into him; Jonny liked to feel big and strong. 'Maybe that's only to be expected. You have been waiting for this for a very long time. But you've done it now. No more kowtowing to Geri. The company is rightfully yours. Jonathan Mathew Chalice, CEO of the Chalice Group. It has a nice ring to it.' She kissed his cheek. He pivoted, took hold of her and kissed her on the lips. This was more like the Jonny she knew. 'So, when do we start celebrating?'

'This evening.' His voice was slowly returning to its normal, confident strength. 'We just need to work through the details of the handover. We're going to do that this afternoon. I want it all agreed and signed off properly; that way there'll be no chance of any last-minute changes of heart on her part.'

Helena laughed. 'She wouldn't dare.' She stroked his back, forced herself not to react to the dampness. Jonny sweating was another rarity. She didn't add that Geri also now had no other candidates for the role. A race with only

290

three competitors had never been much of a contest in Helena's opinion.

He lifted his chin. 'No. You're right. She wouldn't.'

Another kiss, this time with his tongue in her mouth, then he stood up. He held out his hand. So that was her sunbathing and bus-riding at an end. It was time to start behaving like the wife of a CEO of a multinational corporation.

Chapter 77

JULIET

The *Black Swan* was carrying them away from Geri and Jonny, and everything they represented. Isola dei Delfini was now nothing more than a rock surrounded by water. Skimming along on top of the waves, Juliet was finally able to breathe. The pressure that had been building up inside her head for the past three days began to ease, which allowed her to think, and what she thought was simple and reassuring – she was free.

That clarity brought release. Juliet stopped gripping the side of the boat and sat down. She felt the sun and the sea spray on her face. She relaxed. She listened without speaking, felt without hurting, existed without planning. Just was – for at least five minutes.

It was the sound of Sophie sneezing that made her switch back on.

Lena was sitting opposite Juliet holding her daughter. Their eyes met and they both smiled. Lena hadn't questioned their abrupt departure from the island; in fact, she'd seemed more than happy to leave. Paradise could be purgatory, in different ways for different people. Their shared desire to be home, in no doubt rainy London, back to order and calm, made Juliet feel a warmth that had nothing to do with the sun beating down on the boat. That was one good thing that had come out of the debacle on the island; Juliet had gained a new perspective on what loyalty, care and kindness really were. Lena wordlessly offered Sophie to Juliet and she took her.

As they whipped along with Luca at the helm, the sails snapping in the wind, the wide blue ocean smoothing their passage, Juliet looked down at her daughter. Sophie lay placidly in her arms, her blue eyes open. Juliet knew that she wouldn't always be this content. That at times, probably this very day, Sophie would throw up or have an inexplicable tummy pain, that she would grizzle miserably – for what felt like hours on end – and that for the rest of her life she would demand more than Juliet could give. But now there was a crucial difference – Juliet knew that she would cope. Not excel, perhaps, but not fail either. She was Sophie's mother. She had chosen her daughter over her ambition. Surely that was proof that her maternal instincts were strong.

But despite that epiphany, Juliet hadn't had a personality transplant.

Being a mother did not have to be her only job. The world of Chalice might have chewed her up and spat her out, but there were other, more humane businesses, where she would be able to work and make a difference. With Lena's help she should be able to have a good career *and* be a decent mother. And the best way to do that was for her to take back control of her life. The minute they reached dry land she would find a café with an Internet connection and she would formally tender her resignation. Besides,

Juliet knew that if she tried to hang on to her current role it wouldn't be long before Jonny started to manage her out – he wasn't a *keep your enemies close* merchant, and Juliet was done with defining herself by her brother. Let him have it. All of it. She would stand back, fold her arms and watch, with satisfaction, his every misstep and cock-up. Because there was no way that Jonny was ever going to come close to their aunt. Geri might be a cold-hearted bitch, but she had been a stellar CEO.

Career thrown away with a one-sentence email, Juliet then planned to find a nice little trattoria and order lunch, because the other thing that was coming back, the further away she got from Isola dei Delfini, was her appetite. She had been starving herself for far too long and for all the wrong reasons. The thought of a big bowl of ravioli alla caprese strengthened Juliet's resolve even further. Leaving was the best thing she could do. She would find something better suited to her talents and her needs. She might even set up a business of her own; she had the skills and the contacts. But, and this would be part of her new approach to life, she would take her time deciding. There was no rush. She had plenty of money in the bank and elsewhere. Hell, she might work part-time. The world was still her oyster. It was amazing how energising it was to say no!

Having a plan in her head and the stirrings of happiness in her heart, Juliet became conscious of Ben. He'd thrown himself and his bag onto the boat like a teenager in a strop and not said a word since they'd set sail. She shifted around so that she was facing him. He might be quiet, but he wasn't still. He was flipping his phone over and over in his hand. It was a tic that she'd seen a thousand times, but she'd never before registered it as anything other than irritating. Tics and tells could be misleading if you didn't know their cause. She shifted Sophie in her arms. 'Hey. Sorry, I was MIA there for a while. I needed some time to process what's just happened. It's all a bit of a headrush, isn't it?' The meeting had been bad for her, but it had been far worse for him. He'd had his dirty linen dragged out from under the bed, strewn across the table and held up to an unforgiving light.

His response was a grunt, but at least he shoved his mobile away in his trouser pocket. 'We got royally screwed. That's what happened.'

The closer Juliet looked, the more she saw that her half-brother was in a bad way. She'd known he hadn't been firing on all cylinders for a while. She'd heard the rumours floating around the business about his unreliability, his lack of focus, his general subpar performance, but she'd been too preoccupied – too self-obsessed? – to care. And, in truth, when had Ben ever been anything other than mediocre? But at least in the past he'd been a happy-go-lucky also-ran. Not recently. No, recently, she now realised, he'd been struggling. Tough love or no love, Geri had been right about one thing – Ben needed to sort his life out, before it was too late. Perhaps the best place to start was with some more straight talking from her. 'What is it to you?'

He did a double-take, bristled, sat up straight. 'Well, and I repeat, in case you actually are deaf, not just chronically insensitive like the rest of the family, fuck you too, Juliet.'

She didn't flinch. 'No, seriously. I want to know. Why are you letting it get to you so much?'

He paused, scratched his palm, looked over her shoulder

at the waves then finally said, 'Because no one ever takes me seriously.'

It was a classic Ben reaction – self-pity, and that never got you anywhere. She didn't hesitate. 'That's because you don't take yourself seriously.'

'Yeah, well, being an uber-serious suck-up hasn't worked out so great for you, has it?' he snapped.

She didn't bite. 'No. You're right. But that's because it was never a level playing field. And I ... and you ... should have realised that sooner. Much, much sooner.' Sophie started to wriggle. Juliet lifted her up onto her shoulder. A change of perspective was sometimes all she needed. 'Anyway. I'm done with all the games and the politics. I'm going to leave.'

'What?'

'I'm going to resign.'

'You're letting Jonny win if you walk away.'

'Ben! Wake up! He has won.'

'Well, I'm not going anywhere. Geri didn't say anything about sacking me. Let him try and get rid of me! Then he'll have a fucking fight on his hands.'

Beneath the bravado, Juliet could hear the edge of desperation in Ben's voice. Sophie yawned. Her breath was sweet. Juliet softened her approach. It took time for poison to work its way through your system. 'It's your call. Only you can decide whether it's worth it, but I'd be careful. It didn't pan out too well for Dad, did it? Hanging on? He got kicked out eventually, and on Geri's terms, not his.' She risked one more step into the dangerous swamp of the Chalice family saga. 'You don't want history to repeat itself, do you?'

Ben didn't say anything. For a few minutes they both watched Luca lowering the sails in preparation for their approach into the marina. The more immediate question was whether Ben would disappear into the backstreets of Positano and go on a bender or whether he would start as he meant to go on – by travelling with her to Naples and onto the first available flight home.

'Please don't leave me on my own with him,' he suddenly blurted. He sounded like the child Geri had accused him of being.

Concerned as she was about Ben, there was no way Juliet was going to stay in the family business just to keep him company. 'Sorry. My mind's made up. I can't be around Jonny or Geri. They're bad for my health.'

Ben stood up and went to stand at the front of the boat, his hands in his pockets, his shoulders hunched. It took Juliet longer than it should have to realise that he wasn't sulking, he was crying. Juliet glanced over at Lena. Out of politeness Lena pretended not to have noticed Ben's breakdown, but she did hold out her arms to take Sophie from Juliet. But Juliet was learning that to successfully negotiate life you often had to take your child with you, sometimes literally. She went and stood next to Ben. They watched Positano draw closer in silence. After a minute or so, he wiped his face roughly with the back of his hand. Luca switched on the engine in preparation for docking.

Ben didn't look at her. 'Sorry for being a dickhead.'

'That's okay. It's been a rough day.'

'More than just a day. A whole fucking life.' She had nothing to say to that. Luca guided the *Swan* into its berth.

'Can I come and stay with you when we get back, just for a bit, while I sort myself out?'

His request took her by surprise, but what was even more surprising was that she found herself considering it. Ben needed someone, she was his sister and there was no one else. But she wasn't a sucker. 'What do you mean by . . . *sort yourself out*?' If he fudged his answer that would be it.

'Full detox.'

'The booze and the drugs?' she asked.

'Yeah.'

What the hell was she playing at?

'Please.' The boat pulled alongside.

He was desperate. She had one further condition. 'With counselling, on a recognised programme, with a sponsor.' He nodded, miserably but hopefully. Luca hopped off the *Swan* onto the pontoon and began tying her up. 'You bring so much as a grain of coke or anything else into my home and you're out.'

Ben nodded again and held out his hand. He was flickering back to life in front of her eyes. 'Tell me again why you're packing it in. You do know that you're quite good at this hardball negotiation shit, don't you?'

She smiled back. 'I'll do you a deal . . . if you stick to the plan, scrupulously, I'll tell you.'

'Promise?'

'I promise.' They shook on it.

Chapter 78

GERI

The coast was clear. Juliet, Sophie, Lena and Ben were gone. It would have been good to get rid of Helena as well, but Geri hadn't been able to think of a way to engineer that. Helena shouldn't have been on the island in the first place, but Jonny had insisted. Of course he had; he was a man who was accustomed to getting his own way. Helena was a complication, but, on reflection, Geri thought that it was probably for the best that she was present. She should know what sort of man she was married to.

Through the open study door, Geri could hear Alice pacing around her office. She, understandably, wanted them to crack on with the next phase of the plan, but Geri had said they should wait. She was stalling, but it was not due to hesitation, she was simply being sensible. She wanted Luca back on the island before they reconvened, especially after what had happened with Ian. The ramifications of her next move weren't going to be entirely within her control. The only thing she knew for certain was that Jonny was going to be incensed.

Chapter 79

JONNY

Fucking Helena had improved Jonny's mood no end, as had the sight of the empty, abandoned bedrooms of his sister and half-brother as he made his way downstairs to find something to eat. Sex always made him hungry.

Carla was not, as expected, in the kitchen. Jonny sincerely hoped that she had something lavish planned for the evening. His ascension warranted a proper celebration. He went hunting and was reassured to discover that there was plenty of good stuff in the larder and the big fridge; there were a couple of fresh lobsters, still waving their eyes around, in the bucket, some huge juicy prawns, a pack of smoked trout and a jar of beluga caviar along with plenty of salad and fresh vegetables. Carla would be able to get a banging seafood stew on. And there was plenty of champagne and beer left. Yeah, there was ample for a very nice supper for three. He messaged Alice and said as much. The thought of her irritation at him bossing her around demanding a feast and uninviting her in the process only added to Jonny's pleasure. Let her moan to Geri about his presumption and his rudeness, if she dare. It would be another excuse for handing the stuck-up bitch her P45.

Jonny ate his cobbled-together lunch of bread and cheese sitting on an old dining-room chair that he found, positioned perfectly, on the step just outside the back door. Carla's little garden at the side of the House was beautiful; full of flowers, tall grasses and herbs. The sea breeze whispered through the treetops that were just visible at the edge of the plot where the land fell away to the sea. It was a lovely spot, with a breathtaking view that was currently sadly wasted.

Jonny spent the next half-hour contentedly making plans for how he would change Isola dei Delfini once he was in charge. The House, like the business, was long due a makeover. Perhaps Helena could get involved. She did have a good eye for design and it would keep her usefully occupied. Yeah, that might pan out quite nicely; her back at home, in London, planning and ordering and spending and him having to make more frequent trips to the island to oversee the work. Jonny warmed to his remodelling vision. It would make sense to move the kitchen into a new, purpose-built annex. That would increase the separation of staff from the family and guests and – genius thought – it would mean they could put in a deck with a bar and a hot tub on this very spot. Jonny swallowed the last mouthful of burrata and wiped his mouth with the back of his hand.

Yeah. It was definitely too good a view to waste on the staff.

Chapter 80

LUCA

Luca got back to Isola dei Delfini in record time. He headed straight up to the House, but as he approached the garden gate he stopped. Jonny Chalice was sitting on Carla's chair, with a bottle of beer in his hand. He looked perfectly at home. Perfectly at ease. Perfectly smug and self-satisfied. He took a swallow of his beer, put the bottle down on the step and tilted his head back.

Luca was sorely tempted.

Jonny's Adam's apple was sliding up and down in his tanned throat. He was always clean-shaven – it was one of his 'things'. That, and rich cologne. The sight made Luca physically nauseous. Jonny was literally ripe for the taking. One swift blow across his windpipe and he would be down and choking, totally vulnerable, and Luca would be able to do whatever he wanted to him.

But he'd promised Carla – and himself – that he would behave, so he backed away quietly, leaving Jonny oblivious to the danger that was so close to home.

Chapter 81

JONNY

Jonny strolled around the dining room. He was back on form. Helena's adulation, midday sex, his lunch, his genius deck-and-hot-tub plan; they had all repaired his spirits. His initial disappointment at how Geri had handled the announcement was a thing of the past. A moment of personal weakness. He didn't need his aunt's glowing endorsement. She'd recognised that he was the only one who could fill her shoes and that was all that mattered. Jonny smiled at the simultaneous inappropriateness and aptness of the saying. For a tall woman, Geri had tiny feet, whereas his were a respectable size ten. It would be good to have a man back at the helm. Good for him, obviously, but also good for the business. Successful as the Chalice Group had undoubtedly been over the past couple of decades, they had missed out on certain opportunities under Geri's leadership. The old boy network was still alive and well, and as influential as ever, although it was more circumspect than it had once been – and Geri, for all the respect and admiration afforded her, had never been a member of the club.

On his third lap of the room Jonny stopped by the drinks

trolley. He settled on a martini. He felt the need for something more celebratory after his casual beer. He toasted himself and drank.

'Started without me?' Geri appeared in the doorway. She was on her own and she wasn't carrying a file. Jonny relaxed even more. She'd also changed into a simple, sleeveless black dress. Old as she was, there was no denying that Geri was phenomenal for her age – a cross between Jamie Lee Curtis and Jane Fonda with the brain of Ruth Porat. She smiled as she came towards him.

'Can I make you one?'

She shook her head. 'No thank you.'

'Oh, please. I know we have things to discuss, but surely a drink is in order.'

'If you insist. A glass of champagne.'

There wasn't any on the tray, but unbidden Carla emerged from the kitchen stairwell carrying a bottle. So she was tuned into Geri's needs, just not his. Perhaps Carla was another one who needed to be put out to pasture. Long serving equated to long memories and Jonny had every intention of sweeping away as much of the past as possible. Carla crossed the room and passed the bottle to Jonny, then left. No ice bucket, no flutes. He was about to call her back, but Geri stopped him.

'It's fine. Well, don't just stand there. Open it.'

Jonny unwrapped the foil, unwound the wire cage and eased out the cork. Firing it across the room was a Ben-style affectation. Geri must have seen him hesitate because she picked up a tumbler and held it out. He poured. The champagne fizzed. They both watched the bubbles climb up inside the glass then slowly subside. Geri kept her hand extended. For an uncomfortable second it reminded him of her stand-off with his father. As requested, Jonny topped up her glass and then poured himself one. Beer, martini and champagne. It wasn't his usual combination, but this wasn't a usual day.

'Shall we?' She indicated that they should take a seat. Jonny obliged. It was time to get down to the nitty-gritty. Discussions with the Board, the exact wording of the announcement, how to handle the City, who to talk to first in terms of the press, plus setting in motion the labyrinthine legalities; Geri might have named him her successor, but there were still a multitude of issues to discuss, not least, her substantial shareholding. The transition of power was going to need careful handling. It was a golden PR opportunity, but even Jonny could see that Geri's departure, much anticipated as it was, was a critical moment for the Group. He needed her to be seen to fully endorse him if it was to go smoothly. Hence, he was going to have to keep her sweet until she was gone. Jonny raised his glass to his aunt. She inclined her head. There was the shadow of a smile on her face. Jonny began, 'In all the drama of this morning I didn't get a chance to express my genuine appreciation that you've decided to entrust the future of the Chalice Group to me. It means a lot. Thank you. I promise that I will do my utmost to make sure the business goes from strength to strength under my stewardship. I know I have a class act to follow.'

Geri kept half-smiling at him, but there was something in her eyes that was making Jonny nervous. He drained his martini and swallowed a mouthful of champagne. It wasn't chilled properly. Then it struck him – she was waiting for some contrition. She might not have the file with her, but she had scrutinised his life as much as she had Ben's and Juliet's. He briefly wondered what Geri made of Juliet's unorthodox path to motherhood, but he dismissed the thought quickly – his sister was no longer a threat. The 'investments' he'd made could, in a certain light, be seen as suspect. Insider trading was really just another word for being better informed, and being bold enough and wealthy enough to act on that information. Geri was still studying him, waiting for him to speak. 'With regard to' – shit, he should have thought of the correct form of words before embarking on this hair-shirt section of their conversation – 'some of my financial dealings.' At that, Geri raised her eyebrows. Bugger. He hastened on. 'My aim was simply to ensure that Helena and the children would be secure, whatever happened to me.' Her eyebrows rose higher. He was going to have to front this up. 'Okay.' He held his hands up. 'I won't insult your intelligence. I confess. I have been feathering my nest.'

She put down her drink. 'For years, to the tune of, at a conservative estimate, eight million pounds sterling, once it's all converted back into UK currency.'

He risked it. 'You know me, Geri, I'm not afraid of risk . . . if the return is worth it.'

The moment held. The atmosphere teetered. Then she said, 'The shady side deals, the tax avoidance and the blatant misuse of offshore accounts, in Helena's name, are a concern.' She paused and stopped smiling. 'But your insatiable financial greed isn't what I want to talk about, Jonny. There's another, far more troubling issue that I need to raise with you.'

All Jonny could think was . . . bring it on. He was tired of her game-playing. There were only the two of them in the room. Between them, they'd seen off the other three. If Geri wanted to throw one last hissy fit, he would let her. He'd waited the best part of twenty years for this moment; another twenty minutes of her grandstanding wasn't going to make a great deal of difference.

Chapter 82

HELENA

Helena woke from her second nap of the day to find Jonny gone. That was the effect Isola dei Delfini had on you; it seduced you into indolence. She stretched, starfished, took up all four corners of the bed. The sheets smelt of Jonny. She had worked her magic, made him feel like the titan of industry that he so desperately wanted to be. Daddy issues! She wondered if there was a man in any boardroom anywhere in the world that had a healthy relationship with his father. But she felt satisfied, not sexually perhaps, but emotionally. If it continued like this, with Jonny turning to her more, then there might be a future for them. But if Jonny wanted her to play Melania to his Donald, then he was going to have to talk to her as well as sleep with her. Yes, she decided, after his negotiations with Geri were complete, Jonny was going have to sit down and talk terms with her. Marriage was after all, as Jonny was so fond of saying, a partnership, and it was time that theirs was a more equal one.

She showered, slipped on a sundress and collected her book and sunglasses. She decided to skip lunch. Her new wardrobe would look better if she lost a few pounds.

She would go and sit in the garden and read. She was still surplus to requirements, until he was finished with Geri. Helena had wanted to go and speak to Juliet to check that she was okay, but Jonny had said that she'd already left the island. Perhaps it was for the best. It would have been hard to know what to say to her. Seeing Jonny get the job she'd been working towards for so many years must have hurt. Perhaps that was why Jonny made Helena feel disloyal if she spent any time with Juliet, and why he was so keen to know what they talked about. Petty jealousy. It was another one of Jonny's less attractive traits.

Helena heard his voice the moment she opened the door, but it wasn't coming from downstairs. It sounded much closer, above rather than below her. She went to the end of the landing and looked up the staircase. Yes, the voices were definitely coming from the upper floor. Helena had never ventured up there. She'd had no reason to and she'd sensed, rather than been told, that it was off limits. Without really thinking about what she was doing, Helena found herself climbing the stairs. Jonny's voice grew louder and more insistent. She followed it.

The upper floor was a series of closed doors, with one exception. She approached the room at the end with the open door. It sounded as if Jonny was inside, but at the same time she had the distinct feeling that the room was empty. She saw the flicker of a TV. Curiosity piqued, Helena slipped inside.

One wall of the room was covered with screens. At a glance Helena could see most of the house, including Jonny and Geri, sitting facing each other, a bottle of champagne between them, in the dining room. There must be hidden cameras everywhere, because she could also see the sitting room, the terrace, her own room and Ben and Juliet's rooms. Jonny's voice rattled around the small space drowning out her thoughts, as per usual. She scanned the complicated-looking console and eventually found the volume button for the dining room. She muted him – if only she could do that in real life. As she watched her husband setting out his stall, Helena tried to process what she was looking at. She'd always known that Geri was controlling, but this took things to a whole new level. Jesus, was this what she'd really been doing when she'd claimed to be working in her study – spying on them, watching them, listening to their every word? It made Helena's skin crawl. She scrambled backwards into her memory, trying to recall the conversations that she and Jonny had had, what had been said and whether any of it had been incriminating. And not just her conversations with Jonny. She'd talked to Juliet about things that Helena was confident Juliet would not have wanted her aunt to hear, and she'd chatted with Lena by the pool and down at the Cottage about Sophie and Ian. Thank God she hadn't phoned her solicitors while she'd been on the island. That would really have put the cat among the pigeons.

As Helena watched her husband waving his hands around, silently carving out his future in the air, she reflected on what a fucked-up family she'd married into. Geri's surveillance of their every move was an atrocious invasion of their privacy. But there was an upside. It meant that Helena now had a rare chance of being in the room where the decisions were being made. And there wasn't a cat in hell's chance that she was going to pass up that opportunity.

Helena dropped her bag and her scruples on the floor. She crossed the room and shot the bolt on the door. Then she returned to her position at the console and turned the volume back up.

Chapter 83

JONNY

Geri was still studying him. She corrected herself. 'Or, to be more accurate . . . there's a serious issue that *we* need to raise with you.'

Jonny knew from the mouse-like patter of footsteps that the other person Geri was referring to was Alice. What the fuck did Geri's PA have to do with any of this? And yet here she was, yet again, sticking her pointy beak into things that had nothing to do with her. Geri welcomed her with a nod. She took the chair next to Geri, her demeanour self-effacing, her expression composed. Jonny looked from one to the other, his blood pressure rising. 'What's she doing here?'

Geri kept her eyes on him. 'Alice is here because she's the person who helped me collate all the information on each of you. She knows what's in those files better than I do.' So Alice was Geri's PA with an emphasis on the *personal*. Jonny was going to have to look into getting a watertight NDA for Ms Baxter before he let her go. 'And it was Alice who made me see that there were some gaping holes in my research, especially with regard to you.'

Jonny refused to look at Alice. 'What are you talking about?'

Geri smiled coldly. 'I'm talking about the sort of crimes that leave no hard evidence, other than an indelible imprint on the people affected.' Jonny shrugged – WTF. Geri went on, 'It doesn't matter whether you have selective amnesia or not, because, luckily, we have Alice here to remind you.' Then, to add insult to offence, Geri nodded at Alice and the mouse began to speak.

'Your memory must be bad, because you genuinely don't remember me, do you, Jonny?'

Jonny's stomach muscles twitched, and Jonny had learnt that a man should never ignore his gut, even if he wasn't sure what it was trying to tell him. He pushed back his chair and stood up. 'When you're ready to have a serious conversation, Geri, then let me know and I'll happily sit down with you. But I refuse to participate in whatever this affirmative-action bollocks is.'

Geri calmly said, 'Sit down.'

Jonny stayed on his feet. 'No. I won't.' He heard more footsteps, this time on the kitchen stairs. Luca emerged, followed by Carla. Carla closed and locked the door behind her. Luca crossed the room and went to stand in the archway through to the sitting room. This was getting ridiculous. They'd actually encircled him. It was so preposterous that he laughed. 'I don't know what the fuck's going on here, but if you think that I'm going be questioned by the bloody staff about my appropriateness for a role that is mine, by birth, right and skill, then you must have finally lost your marbles.'

Geri simply repeated, 'Sit down, Jonny.' Her tone was

level, but uncompromising. 'I'm still in control of the business and, therefore, of your future, so I strongly advise you to do as I ask.'

Jonny swore again, but he had little choice but to thump back down in his seat. He folded his arms and glared at Alice. 'Go on, then. Let's get this charade over with.'

Alice tilted her head slightly and studied him. 'I want you to think, Jonny. Are you sure you don't remember me?'

'What do you even mean by that?' Jonny snapped. He was pissed off with the whole carry-on. He took a deep breath, signalling his disgust, and said, 'I vaguely remember you joining the company, but I haven't a clue when that was. You've been with Geri for what . . . eighteen months? Two years? It's not something that I think about – administrative staff.'

Alice sat back. 'No, Jonny. I'm not talking about my time at Chalice. I'm talking about before.' He shook his head. 'I'll help you out, shall I? Davidson Laing.' He remembered the name. They were an ad agency they'd used a few years ago. They'd parted ways after a disagreement over fees and a number of niggling personnel issues, but back in the day they'd done a number of campaigns for the Chalice Group, mainly for the retail side of the business, the division that Jonny had been put in charge of when he got his first full directorship at the age of thirty-three. 'I remember them. Decent outfit. They did some good work for us, before they got greedy. And they used to throw great Christmas parties.'

Antipathy rippled across Alice's face, but she kept her tone light. 'Yeah, that was their reputation, *work hard, play hard*. I worked there for a short while, on the in-store rollout campaign.' Jonny did the maths. They'd set up the partnership between the bakery arm of the business and Tesco midway through his stint in Retail, so it was possible. She must have been some lowly junior at the time. But why would someone go from working in an advertising agency to secretarial work? Maybe that's what she'd been at Davidson Laing, some sort of admin bod. When he said nothing further, she carried on. 'It was my first job out of university. I was twenty-two. I was one of three graduate trainees they took on that year. I couldn't believe I'd got a place.'

Jonny was bored. He looked at Geri. 'What is this all about?'

'Just listen.' Her gaze was steady, unnerving.

Jonny turned back to Alice. 'Look, I don't remember you. If you were there, I didn't notice you.'

'Oh, how I wish that were true.'

The way she said it made Jonny's scalp prickle. He looked at her more closely, trying to dredge anything up, but nothing came.

Alice's expression hardened. 'I thought that me being back on Isola dei Delfini might help to jog your memory.'

Did she just imply she'd been to the island before? The prickling sensation intensified. 'Why would it?' he stonewalled.

'Because I've been here before. With you.'

Shit, this wasn't good. Jonny's brain started scrambling. So Alice had been here before, in her early twenties, when she worked at Davidson Laing. The nagging in his gut pulsed. He tried to ignore it. He was the next CEO of

315

the Chalice Group; what harm could a lowly PA do him? He jumped when Geri slammed her hand down on the table.

'You are a disgrace.' She enunciated every word. 'Tell him, Alice.'

Alice didn't shift her position or change the low, calm register of her voice. 'You *must* have noticed me at the time, because out of the blue I got asked to travel here, to the island, with an updated version of some storyboards for the campaign we were working on. You'd requested some minor changes, things that could easily have been signed off remotely, but you said no, you wanted to see the actual artwork, not a digital copy. You specifically asked the agency to send me . . . as a thank you for all my hard work. And those were the days when if an agency's biggest client demanded something slightly weird and totally unreasonable, then that agency said, "Yes, no problem, of course we'll send a graduate trainee on a wild goose chase, on her own, to a private island off the Italian coast, no questions asked."'

Shit. Shit. Shit. No, it couldn't be. Could it? He remembered that girl, but she'd looked nothing like Alice Baxter. She hadn't even been called Alice. Or had she?

Alice's gaze didn't leave his face. 'Yeah, I know what you're thinking, Jonny. You're thinking that I've changed. And you're right, I have. And that change has, in no small part, been down to you.'

Chapter 84

HELENA

Helena felt light-headed, but she couldn't stop watching. The edge of the console was cutting into her stomach because she was leaning so far forward. She welcomed the pain. It was grounding. It reminded her that what she was seeing and hearing on the small screen was real.

Chapter 85

ALICE

Alice had been SO excited when she'd found out where they were sending her. She hadn't flown anywhere on her own before, and never for work. Her flatmates had been jealous. She'd downplayed it, saying she was little more than a bag-carrier, but inside she was buzzing. Italy, a yacht transfer to a private island, a meeting with the boss of one of the agency's biggest clients; it was the stuff of fantasy. She remembered worrying about what to wear for her thirty-five-hour round trip to how the other half lived.

It was the wrong worry. Her outfit of choice hadn't proved to be a problem, nor did the trip last thirty-five hours. In the end Alice didn't get back to her flat in Acton until the early hours of Monday morning, four days after setting off.

It had been fun playing at being a high-flying exec, at first. Alice had chatted happily to the woman in the seat next to her on the plane, telling her all about her job, and she'd enjoyed eating her pretzels and drinking her one glass of complimentary white wine. She'd got a kick out of swishing her way through Naples airport with her Davidson Laing branded art bag, and a buzz from seeing a driver standing in the arrivals hall with her name written on a piece of cardboard. Before she'd had time to draw breath, she'd found herself whizzing through the Italian countryside with the air con cooling her bare legs. Then, as if by magic, she was in Positano, looking around at the picture-postcard houses and the boats in the harbour that presumably never saw a fish, but spent their time ferrying wealthy people up and down the coast. Capri was, apparently, within spitting distance. But again, there wasn't much time for sightseeing. The driver had handed her onto the Chalices' boat and another ridiculously good-looking Italian man – she didn't catch his name either – cast off, started the engine and steered her out to sea.

As Alice watched Positano shrink from view she remembered thinking what a lucky girl she was.

'You came down to meet me off the boat.' Jonny was looking slightly flushed now. She hoped it was a sign that the effort of keeping up appearances was beginning to take its toll. The sense of finally being in control flared and crackled inside Alice, but she tried to damp it down. She'd waited too long and worked too hard for this to blow it now.

'You behaved like the perfect gentleman. You carried my bag and asked me how my journey had been. You thanked for me for travelling such a long way.' His eyes were flicking from Alice to Geri now. Geri was obviously still his main concern – which was typical, people like Jonny only ever cared about the opinions of those with power. They believed that the old levers of mutual self-interest and wealth would keep them safe. In the past they had. But the times they were a-changing – as Jonny Chalice was about to find out. 'Carla was waiting on the terrace with a tray of drinks. Campari and soda. I still can't stand the smell.' A movement in the background distracted Alice. Carla had raised her hands to her face. She was trying to cover her shame. Alice wanted to reassure her that she had nothing to be ashamed of, that this was a man-made plague, but she didn't want to break off from her retelling. 'You gave me a tour of the House. We took our drinks with us. I remember being surprised at how quiet it was. You said your wife was flying out the following day with your kids and your au pair. I was waiting for you to ask to see the storyboards. When I mentioned them you said you'd take a look in the morning, that I should just relax and enjoy the island. That threw me. I'd expected to get your approval and leave. I had a hotel room booked in Positano. You insisted that I stay.'

Jonny leapt in. 'Look, I apologise for not recognising you, but to be fair, you've never mentioned that we'd met before. And it was a long time ago.' He was remembering her now. Colour was creeping up his neck to his cheeks. Brick red wasn't a good look on him.

'Seven years, four months and twelve days, to be precise.'

He changed tack. Tried appealing to Geri. 'Look, Geri. Is this really necessary? It has no bearing on my becoming CEO.'

Geri stared flatly at him and said, 'Yes. It is. And it does have a bearing on your fitness to lead the business.' She turned to Alice. 'Alice, if you're okay to do so, please can you *remind* Jonny what happened next.'

'You gave me another drink.'

His face flushed a shade darker. 'Oh, come on now. I know where this is going. I'll say it, if you're going to string it out like this. We had a good time together. We shouldn't have, but we did. I'm not proud of it, but it happens.'

Alice stayed outwardly calm. This was about power and control and she was determined to have both – at long last. 'No, Jonny, that's not what happened. You lied to me. Helena wasn't coming to the island, the following day, or at all, I'm guessing. You set it all up so I would be on my own, trapped, with no way of escape. You wanted me vulnerable.'

'Oh, this is rich. I remember now. I lent you some of Helena's clothes. You went for a swim. We ate supper on the terrace. The next day we had a wander around the island and I showed you the chapel. Yeah, I do remember it now. We had a very nice weekend in the sun.'

She stared at him, appalled all over again by his arrogance and entitlement. 'No. I had a truly awful time. I was petrified every second I was on the island. I went to the chapel to get away from you, but you wouldn't leave me alone. You followed me up there.'

'This is utter nonsense, Geri.'

Alice kept going. 'You forced yourself on me that first evening and again the following day, and that night and the day after. And in between you talked to me as if nothing had happened. And I was powerless to do anything about it. When you'd had enough of me you packed me off. I remember that the guy piloting the boat didn't look at me once on the way back to Positano. I didn't blame him. Because even then I knew that I wasn't the only one. I *knew* that there'd been others before me, and that there'd be more after. Because men like you, Jonny, are ... well – men like you.' Alice had to stop and take a breath. She would not break down, not over him, not now she had him in her sights. She resumed. 'The boat guy just abandoned me at the harbour. I had to make my own way up to Naples, all my original travel arrangements were ruined. I had to find a train and a flight and get back home – all in a state of shock. You used me then discarded me. And, to my knowledge, you never did look at those storyboards.'

'Geri, you can't believe this. She's obviously got some sort of vendetta against me.' He was blustering now. 'And anyway, if I did do as she claims, why didn't she report me?' He pivoted around to face Alice, barely repressed fury in his eyes. 'Because you never did, did you, Alice? Not to the police, not to the agency, not to anyone. In fact – ' he was gathering steam – 'you stayed on at Davidson Laing. I do remember you now. You were in some of the meetings for that DM campaign we did with, what was she called – ' he clicked his fingers – 'that loud-mouthed Geordie . . . Vicki Patterson! And that was after you came here.' He sat back, seemingly happy to have made his case.

'I did. That's true. I needed that job. I was worried the agency wouldn't believe me and that, even if they did, they wouldn't do anything about it. And at the time, I was ashamed. You're correct; I did wear one of Helena's bikinis. I did swim in the pool and drink your drinks and eat your food, BUT I DID NOT CONSENT TO BEING RAPED.'

The ensuing silence held his anger and hers, but only one was righteous. It was Geri's turn to pick up the baton now. When she did speak, it was with her usual authority. 'The problem you have, Jonny, is that I do believe Alice. I believe every single word of what she's just said.'

'Oh, come on! Think about the timing, Geri. This is

obviously some sort of ploy to extract money from the pair of us.'

'No, it isn't.'

He wasn't listening. 'I assume she lied about who she really was when she applied for the job with us – I believe that's a criminal offence, actually – so it's not much of a stretch to think that she's lying now.'

'Alice didn't lie. She omitted some details, for good reason.'

He blinked, realisation finally dawning. 'So how long have you known who she really is?'

Geri looked at Alice. 'Six months.'

'What the fuck! And you didn't say anything? You didn't even think to ask my side of the story?'

'I didn't need to.'

'Why not?'

'Because Alice had done her homework. She didn't just come to me with her story, she came with the stories of eight other women who have had similar experiences with you.'

'Oh, come on. You know as well as I do that you can run anything up a flagpole these days and someone will rally around it, especially on women's issues.'

Geri looked at him with unveiled disgust. 'This isn't a "women's issue". It's a man's issue, or more specifically it's a "you issue", Jonny.' She bent down and extracted her laptop from her briefcase. 'I, of course, asked for further corroboration and Alice found it.' Geri opened her laptop, clicked on the separate dossier on Jonny. She turned the screen towards him. He refused to look at it. Geri was undeterred. 'It's a pity that Alice didn't make it as an ad exec, she has excellent research skills and a real way with people.' Geri continued to click on the different documents that it had taken Alice years to put together, making the point that they had their 'evidence', and plenty of it. 'She convinced women to talk to her who have never told anyone about your abusive, exploitative, sexually predatory behaviour. Five of them are prepared to go on the record. I suspect that others may follow suit when they hear that charges have been made against you.' He shook his head in denial. She went on, 'We have statements from two former employees of the Group, from a female exec at another ad agency that worked with the business and one from poor Patrice, the au pair who was unlucky enough to be employed by you last summer.'

'So you're buying this bullshit.'

Geri rested her hand on the table. 'It's not bullshit, Jonny. Although I confess that I took some convincing, initially. I thought that particular problem had been root-ed out of the business, and the family, when I got rid of your father. How wrong I was. I suspect that you're simply much better at covering your tracks. Ian was never circum-spect. Everyone knew he was a dirty old man. Times were different then, of course, but that's no excuse. And I know, before you say anything, that I don't come out of this squeaky clean either. I never bothered to look too closely into his behaviour, I just wanted rid of him. Perhaps if I had been more curious I would have been more alert to the pos-sibility of it happening again on my watch.' She paused and looked at Alice. 'God forgive me, I thought that the staff who left did so because you were difficult to work with, that it was because you were arrogant and overbearing.

I didn't notice that the majority of those leavers were female and young. Or perhaps I didn't want to. And I admit it ... if Alice had come to me any earlier I might have dismissed what she was saying because it would've presented me with a problem, and my *raison d'être* has always been to smooth over problems and protect the business at all costs.' She shook her head. 'But not any more. Not now that I have so little time left to make amends. So you are, in one way, right, Jonny. Alice did pick precisely the right moment to make her case.'

Jonny was now crimson, not with fear, but with anger. He still wasn't getting it, as he proved with his next utterance. 'So, what now? You have "proof" that I shagged around in my twenties and thirties. So what?'

'And your forties. And I suspect that if nothing is done, you'll go on into your fifties and your sixties and beyond.' Alice saw Jonny clench his fist. Geri had been right to have Luca with them.

'I know you're not personally a fan, Geri, but sex isn't a crime.'

'No, it isn't, but what you do *is* criminal. It's coercion. It's sexual assault. It's rape. It blights women's confidence, their careers, their sense of themselves – sometimes for the rest of their lives.'

'Bullshit!'

Somehow Geri maintained her cool. She rolled on and over him. 'We have the victim statements of the five women who are prepared to go to the police.'

He snorted. 'Let me guess, that includes Ms Baxter here, despite *her* faulty memory and absolute lack of any physical evidence.' Alice hated the thought of having to make a formal allegation, but she nodded. You can't lead a pack from the back.

Geri continued as if he hadn't spoken. 'I will support these women's attempts to raise a prosecution. I will let any investigation have full access to our HR files and your diary. And I will make sure that every press outlet gets the story. Unless' – here it came, Geri's version of justice, which was not the same as Alice's – 'you step down, with immediate effect, you sell all of your shares in the company and you sever all ties with the Group and all our subsidiaries.'

Jonny stared at Geri. 'No. I won't do it.' He wiped his mouth with the back of his hand. 'And neither will you do what you're threatening. Because if you go public with this, it will be a disaster. Our value would go into free fall. You would never allow that. And besides, who's going to run the business, Geri? Ben is a fuck-up and Juliet has fucked off.'

'I will. I never wanted to retire, and once I started digging I realised that none of you, least of all you, Jonny, are fit to take over from me.'

'Now I really have heard it all. You're delusional, Geri. I've already let people know it's me. Harry and Vincent and Ray.' His key allies. 'The Board won't stand for it. You're seventy, for God's sake. Everyone wants you out.'

Geri shook her head. 'I think you're underestimating my support and overestimating your own. Besides – better an old woman at the helm than a rapist.'

Jonny took a breath, then said slowly and with absolutely chilling conviction, 'If you want a fight, bring it on. Every single one of those women was willing and they were all of age. If they come forward with their baseless allegations, I will refute them all. Alice wasn't the only one to have a nice little break in the sun, in the lap of luxury, in exchange for some sexual interaction. They all gained from their association with me, one way or another. This "every woman is a victim, every man a predator" is such horseshit – and people are sick of it. So, go ahead. Try and make this stick. See how far you get with a handful of historic allegations from a few bitter, financially motivated women with an axe to grind.' He sat back.

Alice hated him more in that moment than she had ever hated him before. He thought he was untouchable. Her fear was that he might be right.

They had reached an impasse. Female outrage versus male entitlement.

To Alice and everyone else's surprise, it was Luca who made the next move.

He approached the table at speed. No one seemed to know what to do, not even Geri. Luca was not part of the plan, other than as muscle. He stopped behind Jonny's chair and without pausing, he yanked it around. Then he grabbed hold of Jonny's neck. Still no one moved. Luca bent down low in Jonny's face and yelled, 'Liar! They weren't all willing.' He tightened his grip on Jonny's airways. Jonny's face went puce. 'And at least one of them *was* underage.' He pushed Jonny away. 'Me!'

Jonny coughed dramatically and started to bleat, but his complaints were drowned out by another, much louder noise, a high-pitched keening that was coming from Carla. Alice was confused, until she looked at Luca and saw what they'd all missed.

Luca was a survivor as well.

Chapter 86

HELENA

Helena cut off the sound of Carla's screams. They were too much to bear. The room on the screen fell silent. The room in which Helena sat was equally quiet. It was a moment of such stillness that Helena couldn't bring herself to break it. If she moved so much as a finger she thought she would shatter. Instead she stared, waiting for them to make a move.

She was married to a rapist. She made herself use the word, as a punishment and as a spur. If she did nothing else from here on in, she would do this, she would face the truth and name it for what it was.

For most of their married life Helena had suspected Jonny of being unfaithful. She'd accused him of it many times. He'd always denied it; steadfastly, passionately and, in a deeply warped sense, truthfully. Because Jonny hadn't been lying to her, he hadn't been *having affairs*; what he'd been doing was systematically assaulting and abusing women and young girls. Images of the au pairs who had lived with them over the years flickered through Helena's mind. Had there been five or six of them? All nice girls. All fresh-faced. All young. Marina, Claudette, Christina,

Valeria, Amelia and Patrice, the quiet dark-haired girl who had only lasted a month and had gone home early last summer because she was so homesick. Not homesick at all, terrified. How could he? In their own home? Those girls ate with them, went on holiday with them, watched TV with them. They had looked after their children. They had been part of the family. How could she not have known?

If what Alice and Geri were saying was true, then her husband of nearly fifteen years was one of *those* men. Rich, privileged, entitled; men for whom sex was something that they took as, when and where they wanted. It was not something to be mutually enjoyed. Except – her stomach lurched – with her. Jonny had shared a 'normal' sex life with her, and she with him. Why had he chosen her to be his wife rather than one of his victims? Was it because he really loved her? Or was it because he'd seen in her a gullibility and, more importantly, a culpability that he knew he could work with? Had he identified her desire for the nicer things in life, and for him, and known that such hunger would keep her in line?

Jesus . . . and she'd thought that they'd been starting to understand each other better, that he was beginning to respect her for standing up to him.

The chapel came back to her in vivid, sound-tracked detail. The shame was overwhelming. And the shock. Alice had said he'd taken her there as well, or followed her there. Helena's hand flew to her belly. It ached. This was the man she'd fallen in love with, married and had three children with. He was Aaron and Amy and Rory's father. She felt a wave of nausea. Jonny had a twelve-year-old daughter who was on the cusp of womanhood. Jonny loved Amy. He was protective of her. He worried about her growing up in a world of Andrew Tates, online bullying and misogyny. And yet he'd done this, over and over again, then he'd come back to her and the children and lived like a normal man.

She'd known from the beginning that he was egotistical, selfish, driven, but she'd not realised that he was capable of this.

She'd lived with her suspicions for years, but she had not suspected him of this.

She'd forgiven him for many things, but she could never forgive this.

Chapter 87

CARLA

'Me!'

Luca's words blew Carla's world apart.

Jonny Chalice had abused her child, just as Ian Chalice had abused her. It made perfect, awful, irrefutable sense. And the thought had never crossed Carla's mind.

Not when Lucia had gone from being a happy-go-lucky child to a diffident teenager. Not when her previously even-tempered daughter had started flying into sudden inexplicable rages. Not when Lucia went from wanting to live on the island with Carla whenever she could to making excuses to stay away. Not when their relationship went from easy and straightforward to complex and difficult. There's none so blind as those who will not see. Carla had initially thought that the changes in her daughter were simply the sad but natural process of Lucia growing up and away from her. She'd been wrong. Lucia had not wanted to leave her or the island, she'd been driven away by Jonny.

Then Carla had got it wrong again when at eighteen Lucia, her beautiful, restless daughter, had summoned up the courage to tell her that she felt different to other girls, that she didn't feel like a girl at all. Carla had been upset, but she'd also been relieved. She'd thought she'd found the key to her child's unhappiness. So began a journey that had taken them both a long time and a lot of heartache to travel – the journey of Lucia becoming Luca. And not once during those difficult, at times confusing, ultimately life- and love-affirming years, had Luca ever breathed a word about the abuse he'd suffered as a child.

Why?

Was it because he'd thought she wouldn't believe him? Or had he thought that she'd fight him about transitioning? That she would blame the abuse for his identity? Or was it that he simply thought she wouldn't understand? That she couldn't understand because she'd lived such a closeted, isolated life?

Carla had condemned her child to silence by maintaining her own.

The noise coming out of her was that of a wounded animal. But animals protected their young and she had put hers in harm's way. She and Luca loved each other, they'd laughed and cried and comforted each other as any mother and child would for the past twenty-four years and yet between them lay a secret so damaging and life-changing that neither of them had been able to speak of it.

And that was the Chalices' fault.

Carla slid her hand into the pocket of her apron. Like father, like son. Ian and Jonny were one and the same, the same deviance had been passed from one generation to the next and she had not been on guard for it.

She launched herself across the room, pushed Luca out of the way and plunged the knife into Jonny. She felt the blade press against his flesh, the moment of resistance, then the give as it entered his body. He yelled. She screamed. She pulled the blade out so that she could stab him again, but there were hands on her, dragging her away. Luca. He was angry with her. He had every right. Her fury was far too little, far too late. Where had she been all those years ago when he'd needed her protection? Luca was speaking, but she couldn't hear what he was saying, her head was too full of rage. Spit and snot ran down her face, her arms whirred and stretched. She still had the knife in her hand; she wanted to go again, and again. She wanted to kill Jonny Chalice, but Luca was holding her back. Her child was protecting his abuser. The fight drained out of her. Luca was no longer holding her off, he was holding her up and pleading with her.

'Please, Mum. Stop. It's okay.'

Carla pressed her face against Luca's chest. She felt his heart through his shirt, beating hard and fast. It was not okay. It would never be okay.

Chapter 88

HELENA

Helena found herself back in their room. She couldn't look at the bed. Her indecision was physically painful. She'd never felt so lonely and frightened, and yet she didn't cry. She didn't allow herself that indulgence; she'd indulged too much already. What she needed to do was think and act. She scanned the room and her eyes fell on Jonny's phone. He was never without it. Well, now he was. She picked it up and entered his passcode. What was she looking for? Evidence of the man who had left this room as her husband and the father of her children and was now downstairs, a sexual predator.

There was nothing incriminating on his phone. But there wouldn't be, would there? Men like Jonny didn't leave clues. She threw it at the wall, was pleased to hear the screen crack. Then out of nowhere a thought pushed its way through her confusion. Last night – Christ, had it only been last night, when Jonny had been smoking by the window, watching Ben? – she'd seen him with a different phone. He'd slid it into his trouser pocket when she came out of the bathroom. She went over to the wardrobe, found the trousers he'd been wearing the previous evening and

334

felt around in the pockets. The phone was still there. Same password. He was predictable in some areas of his life. Still not sure what she might find, Helena went to his messages.

It made no sense.

There was only one active text 'conversation'.

It was with Juliet.

Chapter 89

GERI

When Carla attacked Jonny, Geri didn't react. Carla's fury was powered by love. Geri was immobilised by ignorance. It was carnage, on her watch, under her roof – because of the men in her family.

Luca was the only one who appeared still to have any agency, and enough presence of mind to exercise it. Having pulled Carla off Jonny, he led her away into the sitting room. Geri looked at Jonny. He was holding his hand against his left side. She approached him, crouched down and tentatively touched his bloody fingers. 'Let me see.' There was a small patch of blood on his shirt. She unbuttoned it. The wound in his side was dark red, sticky and small. It looked like a leech. Alice appeared beside her and passed her a cloth. It took Geri a moment to realise it was one of the linen napkins they used for formal dinners. 'Can you lift your arm?' Jonny could, though he blanched and quickly lowered it. He was obviously in some pain, but he wasn't screaming and the wound was oozing rather than gushing blood. The evidence was mounting that Carla had done only superficial damage. 'Here. Press this against it.' She passed him the napkin. He did as he was told, but as she began to get to her feet he grabbed her with his free hand and pulled her towards him.

'This has gone too far. You need to get me and Helena off this island. Now!' he hissed in her ear.

She looked into his face and saw that nothing had changed. Jonny still thought he was in charge. His assumption disgusted her, but it didn't surprise her. Power was never relinquished without a fight. 'Let go of my arm, Jonny.' He hesitated. She pulled. Reluctantly he released her. She stood up. 'You stay where you are. If you move a muscle I will send Carla back in here to finish the job. Do you understand?' Jonny started swearing. She asked Alice to keep an eye on him, then she made her way into the sitting room.

Geri approached Luca and Carla carefully. They were sitting side by side on one of the sofas, not talking. She sat down opposite them, respected their stunned silence. She noticed that the backs of their hands were touching. She wanted to help, but the only help she could think to offer was immunity, and even that felt wrong. It would be yet another Chalice deciding their futures and both of them had had a lifetime of that. 'Do you want me to leave you alone?' she asked.

Her voice startled them. Carla shook her head. Luca simply sat taking deep breaths, in through his nose and out through his mouth. He was obviously trying to regulate his feelings. It would have been impressive, if it hadn't been so distressing to watch.

Carla was the one who eventually said, 'No. Stay . . . and listen. It's time the truth about our two families was told, and heard.'

So she wanted Geri to bear witness. There was punishment in that. It was fair. Geri nodded and waited.

It took Carla another couple of minutes before she starting speaking. 'The most important truth is . . . that Luca is my son and I love him more than life itself, but I have failed him.'

Geri looked from Carla to Luca. A thousand pennies dropped into a thousand slots. How had she been so blind? The hormones had wrought huge changes, but the basic bone structure was the same. She could see it now, in the shape of Luca's eyes and his lips, in the curl of his hair. This was the child who used to follow Carla around the kitchen 'helping', who used to slide across the parquet flooring in the hall when they thought no one was looking. This was the child whose illegitimacy was never mentioned, the teenager who had disappeared at the age of eighteen, apparently to go to university, and never returned.

Luca began saying something in her defence, but Carla gently cut across him. 'No, please don't come up with any excuses for me. I have failed you. I didn't tell you about Ian because I was ashamed, and I wanted to forget. That was wrong of me. But worse than that – I didn't think to guard against it happening again . . . to you. I left you in harm's way. I will never forgive myself for not protecting you from Jonny.'

Luca's breathing sped up. Geri saw him grab hold of his mother's hand and squeeze it. 'Tell me now.'

'Okay, I will, but that doesn't mean that you have to speak about your experience. You do not have to do or say anything you do not choose to. If you want me to stop, just say, and I will.'

Luca blinked. 'I need to know.'

Carla began hesitantly, but she was unflinching in her telling. 'Ian started abusing me when I first came to the island with my mother to help out when the family were visiting. I was fifteen. It didn't begin with abuse. It began with presents. Fabric to make dresses, cheap bits of jewellery, and he paid me compliments. A lot of compliments. I was flattered by his attention. He exploited my naivety. He took my virginity when I was sixteen. Whenever he was on the island after that he came to me. I never resisted. I never fought him off. I never said no. But I hated it. It finally stopped when I was twenty-six. I think I was too old for him by then. Or perhaps he was simply bored with me. I got pregnant with you not long afterwards.' Luca looked horrified; he started getting to his feet, but Carla stopped him. 'Ian was *not* your biological father. I promise, that is the truth. As I told you, Antonio Ricci was. Antonio was a sailor.' She briefly smiled. 'He was a decent man. He wanted to marry me. He asked me many times. I said no. I told him to leave me alone. My parents never understood why I rejected him. He came back for me, and you, after you were born, but I still refused to marry him. I didn't know what I wanted, but I knew I didn't love him and that I wasn't the type of person that a man like him should be with. But the other thing I knew for certain was that I wanted a child. And I was blessed to have you. You are, and always have been, the best thing in my life.'

'Why did you keep working for them?' Luca's voice sounded raw.

'I was an unmarried mother in a Catholic country. My only skills were cooking and cleaning. We had somewhere to live here and I had guaranteed employment. And they accepted that I had a child, no questions asked. Most employers would not have been as forgiving.' Geri winced at Carla's choice of words and wondered why her father had been so accepting of Carla's circumstances. She was appalled by the only logical answer. Gerald must have assumed that the child was Ian's. Carla looked exhausted, but she soldiered on. 'We were happy here. This was our home. And I thought we . . . I thought you . . . were safe. Ian had stopped. I made myself forget.'

Luca appeared to steel himself, then he said very quietly, 'But Ian had a son.'

Geri swallowed.

Carla lowered her head. 'Yes.' The silence yawned.

What was there to say? Nothing. Nothing could express the utter wrongness of Ian and Jonny's behaviour. After a few moments Luca shifted in his seat. He let go of his mother's hand. There was another beat. Then he reached out and touched Carla tenderly beneath her chin with his fingertips. At his prompting, she lifted her face. Luca smiled at her. 'Jonny Chalice means nothing to me because I refuse to let him.'

Carla inhaled deeply. The breath seemed to strengthen her. 'I couldn't be prouder of you. You have taught me so much. And one of those lessons is that you have to stand up for yourself.' Geri could feel a shift in the atmosphere and sure enough Carla's next words were directed at her. 'This' – she indicated the room, Geri, Jonny, maybe even the island itself – 'is bad and there will be consequences, I know that, but that's okay. Finally some justice has been served to two men who got away with appalling behaviour for far too long because women like me kept their secrets. But I refuse to be silent any more.' Geri realised what Carla was about to confess a second before she said it. 'It was me who killed Ian. Seeing him behaving like that again: an old man, a young girl – the same grasping brutality – was too much. It released a rage inside of me that I couldn't control. Hurting him wasn't enough. I knew I had to finish him off. While you were taking the other Chalices over to Positano I went up to Ben's room and stole some of his pills. A lot. I ground them up and put the powder into a fresh bottle of whisky. I didn't know what it was and I didn't care. I took the whisky down to the Hut. I let myself in and gave him the bottle. He didn't question my motives. He was used to me providing for his every need.' Carla switched her focus back onto Luca. 'My only regret is that I got you involved. You should never have come back to the island. It was selfish of me. I wanted you here for old times' sake, for the happy memories.' She swallowed a sob. 'I'm sorry. I've made so many mistakes.'

Luca simply stroked her face and said, 'No regrets, Mum. It's the only way.'

Geri sat back. Her brother and her nephew, two generations of harm, and all of it taking place on the island. She didn't even want to contemplate what her father's role in any of this might have been. Who knew how far back this corruption went?

Alice cut into Geri's thoughts. She was standing in the archway between the dining room and the sitting room. She must have heard it all. 'Geri?'

'What?'

'I really think we need to decide what we're going to do with Jonny.'

'Yes. I know.'

Alice's eyes flicked from Jonny to Geri to Carla and Luca and back again. 'And?'

'And at this precise moment, I haven't got a clue what to do with him.'

'Might I suggest that you start by letting me speak to him.' They all started and turned towards the door. Helena stood there; the jigsaw piece that no one had noticed was missing.

Chapter 90

HELENA

Helena didn't wait for Geri's permission, she simply strode across the sitting room, keeping her eyes from falling on Carla and Luca. She couldn't look at them. Their pain was too much. She brushed past Alice, into the dining room. If she lost momentum she would crumble. The real, flesh-and-blood Jonny – not the monster on the screen – looked up at her with relief. He was a mess. His face was ashen and sweaty, his shirt unbuttoned, and he was holding a bloody napkin against his side. So Helena's eyes hadn't been deceiving her; Carla had been holding a knife and she had stabbed her husband.

Jonny got to his feet and held out his hand to her. 'Thank God. They've gone insane – the lot of them. We need to get out of here.' After a fraction of a hesitation Helena took it. His fingers were tacky with blood. Close up, he smelt bad. The Jonny Helena knew was always fresh, clean and doused in expensive cologne; this man was rank with desperation. His hand gripped hers. He needed her more now than he'd ever done before, and they both knew it.

When she turned around she saw that Geri, Alice, Carla and Luca were all lined up in the archway, blocking their path. Jonny actually stepped behind her, seeking her protection. It was a stand-off in which Geri and herself were the lead antagonists.

Geri, of course, spoke first; even with something as fucked-up as this she had to be the one in control. 'Helena. I know this looks bad. I won't deny that things have got out of hand, but there's a very valid reason for what's happening here. Jonny has things to answer for. He is not the innocent party in all this. He is not free to leave.'

Helena didn't hesitate with her response. 'Leave?' She laughed. She sounded far more in control than she felt. 'How would we leave, Geri? We can't get off the island without your permission. There may be a valid explanation for all this.' Jonny made a noise behind her; she ignored him. 'But as ever, I appear not to have been copied in on the memo.' She looked along the line of his accusers. 'Therefore, I think it's only fair that you allow me to speak to my husband for a few minutes – in private.' She stared at Geri and Geri stared back. As silent conversations went, it was a robust exchange.

Eventually, and surprisingly, it was Geri who conceded. 'Okay.' The rest of her words were drowned out by a storm of protest from the others. Geri waited until they'd shut up before she continued, 'You can have ten minutes, out on the terrace, but Luca' – at this point she sought agreement from Luca – 'will be on hand. As will I. I do not want him leaving my sight because, believe me, we are not done here.' She directed that barb at Jonny. 'And I warn you, Helena, he will spin you a tale, most if not all of which will be untrue.'

Helena nodded. Geri was right about one thing – they were far from done.

There was another beat, then Luca stepped aside to let them pass. For once Helena led the way. Jonny was chuntering and moaning behind her, but she stayed focused. Her goal was to get them outside.

They walked to the edge of the terrace. The beauty of the wide blue sky after so much claustrophobic ugliness was therapeutic. For a moment Helena let herself breathe and look and listen. The crash of the waves against the island provided a rhythmic, hypnotic soundtrack. Helena could have stayed there forever, suspended between her past and her future.

Chapter 91

JONNY

Jonny had never been so glad to see Helena.

Instead of spending the afternoon fashioning his triumphant future, he appeared to have fallen slap bang into the middle of some sort of perverted feminist revenge tragedy. And it had started to look ominously like there was no way out for him – until Helena had wafted into the dining room in her kaftan and sunglasses. As he watched her stand her ground against Geri and argue for his release Jonny had vowed many things; he would treat his wife better, he would stop his extracurricular activities, he would be faithful. This debacle wasn't, as he'd begun to fear, the end. It could be a whole new beginning.

True, the terrace wasn't much of a getaway, but it was a start.

'Do you need to sit down?' Helena asked.

Jonny nodded. Of course he did, he'd been stabbed, for Christ's sake. Luca had taken up his position on one of the rattan sofas and Jonny wanted to put as much distance between himself and this disturbing reincarnation of Carla's daughter as possible. So Luca was . . . or had been, Lucia! Jonny was struggling to comprehend that piece of madness in the midst of everything else that had imploded in the past hour. 'Let's sit on the wall.' As he lowered himself onto the parapet that ran around the edge of the terrace he had a flashback to young Lucia. He remembered dark eyes, delicate features, a slim waist, small breasts. It hardly seemed possible. And yet, apparently, it was. Behind Luca the spectre of Alice Baxter floated. All his ghosts had come to haunt him at the same time. He blinked and concentrated on the pain in his side to ground himself in the middle of all this madness. It hurt like fuck, but it appeared that Geri was right, he wasn't in immediate mortal danger.

Helena declined his offer of the space beside him and remained standing. 'So –' she took a breath – 'talk.' It was hardly the shock and sympathy he'd been expecting. He'd been accused of unspeakable behaviour then knifed, and yet he was the only person who seemed to think the world had gone insane. The precariousness of his situation hit home. He was trapped on an island surrounded by crazy women and his only hope was his wife. He reached out to grasp Helena's hand, but she moved away from him. Her expression was worryingly guarded. 'You have precisely five minutes to tell me what's going on. When you left me to go and speak to Geri you were king of the hill. I want to know why Geri is so incensed with you. Why Carla attacked you. And what the hell Alice has to do with any of it. And Jonny, I want the truth.'

Jonny was taken aback. He stalled. 'Geri said ten minutes.'

She stared at him. 'Yes, but after you've told me exactly what the hell you've been up to, I'm going to need time to decide what I'm going to do about it.'

Mea culpa. It could work. He confessed to the financial sharp practice, briefly but honestly. There was plenty to confess, but most of it had, as he'd told Geri, been done for their family's future. 'There are some properties and investments in your name that I've never told you about. To the tune of about fifteen million.' It was best she knew the scale of their wealth. It was a tick in the positive column.

Her expression didn't change. 'And that's why Geri is angry with you?'

He paused. His confession didn't seem to have moved the dial. Helena might never have had a real job, but she was by no means stupid. His defence needed to be credible. The kangaroo court of random members of staff and Carla attacking him needed explaining, and quickly. 'Yes, and no. Alice has got into her head and filled it with a load of nonsense.'

'About?'

Straight talking was his only hope. 'She accused me of coming on to her.' He waited.

'When?' That was helpful.

'Years ago. When she was working at an ad agency that we used.'

'And you're saying that you didn't try it on with Alice?' She glanced at her watch. 'You have two minutes left.'

'No, of course I didn't. It's total rubbish. She's doing it to make a quick buck because she knows I'm going to fire her once Geri's gone.' He thought he saw a tremor in her right eye. Helena had challenged him on his fidelity before, and had accepted his lies before. The jury was out as to whether she would do it now that he was on the cusp of everything they'd worked towards for all these years. It appeared she might, but then she asked, 'How come Carla and Luca are involved? I presume Carla didn't attack you over your financial affairs.'

This was a tougher sell. But Jonny reminded himself that Helena didn't know what he and his father had been accused of in relation to Carla and Luca, so he was free to put his own spin on events. He just had to hope that Luca was sitting far enough away that he couldn't hear their conversation. 'That bit of this madness is sad. It transpires that my father behaved inappropriately with Carla when she was young. I think it's festered over the years. Him turning up like that obviously triggered some bad memories. Somehow Carla got it into her head that I'd done the same with her daughter.' He had a sudden thought. 'Perhaps Alice planted the seed.'

'What daughter?'

It was too complicated to explain, so he lied. 'Exactly. How would that even be possible? Her daughter has been living in Portugal for years, as far as I know.' Jonny couldn't stop himself glancing at Luca. He couldn't have heard, because he didn't react.

Now all Jonny had to do was agree to whatever nonsense Geri demanded and get off the island. Everything else could be dealt with when they were back in the land of the sane. He'd get the wound seen to in Positano, then get them home ASAP. Once back in London he'd speak to his lawyers. He still couldn't believe that Geri would really risk the business over a few minor indiscretions, but it was best to be prepared. His chances of becoming CEO were slimmer, but there was no way he was giving up. Geri's behaviour these past few days only served to underline that it was time she stepped down. And he had leaked her decision to appoint him to his supporters on the Board. He was looking forward to seeing how she was going to wriggle out of that without substantial collateral damage. All he needed was for Helena to believe him. Or at least, to be willing to pretend that she did, for the sake of their future.

She tapped the face of her watch. 'Ten seconds.'

Jonny shrugged. He felt a trickle of blood seep from the wound in his side. He needed off this island, and fast. 'That's it. I swear.' He wanted a fierce Helena in his defence, not in his interrogation.

She pushed her sunglasses up her nose. It didn't help that he couldn't see her eyes. He waited. Then she said, 'One last question.'

'What?'

'Have you been blackmailing Juliet?'

Chapter 92

GERI

Silhouetted against the sky, Jonny and Helena looked like a couple posing for a travel ad, but appearances could be deceptive. Geri had considered the impact of Jonny's sudden fall from grace on Helena, but it hadn't been a priority. Geri had reasoned that it was up to Helena what she did with a deposed, furious, disgraced, out-of-work husband. Stick or twist? Her choice. Her gamble. As always, Jonny appeared to be doing most of the talking out on the terrace. He would be spinning Helena yet more lies and Geri's best guess was that they would work. Helena was a woman who had survived on a fiction-heavy diet for years.

Should she tell Helena the true extent of her husband's offending?

No. Even with the revelation of Jonny's abuse of Luca, Geri was focused on outcomes, not revenge. Her nephew needed to be stopped, and the best way to do that was to remove every last bit of power and privilege from him. The loss would neuter him far better than any possible, but in no way guaranteed, prosecution might. Rich men had wriggled out of similar allegations before, and no doubt would again. Jonny's disinheritance, although less dramatic, would hurt him. And it would also be less damaging for the business. Not that that was a priority, but it was a factor. Geri was still responsible for the fortunes of the Chalice Group.

Their conversation seemed to be drawing to a close. Jonny the charmer appeared to have made short work of getting his loyal wife on side.

Helena's involvement in the afternoon's events complicated matters, but there would be some sort of workaround; there always was when it came to tricky negotiations. Geri imagined that Jonny would want Helena out of the picture when they talked. He wouldn't want her around to witness his capitulation. Because Geri was confident that he would capitulate – now that they had Luca's testimony. At least, he would if he knew what was good for him.

She watched Jonny rise slowly to his feet. He was still clutching his side, making the most of being the poor, wounded soldier. How she despised him. He held out his hand to Helena.

What happened next happened quickly.

Chapter 93

HELENA

He thought he was safe, that she would buy his bullshit, because she had in the past.

But not any more, because she now knew it *was* bullshit. She could see it pouring out of him, the stench and splatter of it contaminating her, their marriage, their lives together; a never-ending river of filthy lies.

He was incapable of telling the truth, not because it was too awful; he would have to have some degree of self-awareness and contrition to recognise how appalling his behaviour had been, but because he simply didn't think he'd done anything wrong.

There was no hope for a man like that. None. He was dangerous and deluded and powerful. She raised her hands. He looked at her and started to smile. Confident, complacent, cunning old Jonny was back. She put her hands on him. She knew that the feel of his skin under her fingertips and the beat of his heart inside his chest would haunt her forever. She gave him one hard, decisive shove.

Jonny's smile died. Shock and disbelief flickered across his face.

He shouted something. One last, lying denial?
Then he was gone.

Chapter 94

LUCA

Luca was glad to be out of the House and out at sea. It was where he felt safe and in control – whatever the conditions.

The decision to go and look for Jonny had been Geri's. She'd said they should. No one had disagreed with her, although their rescue mission had begun with a marked lack of urgency. Luca had retrieved the bloodstained napkin from the terrace and his mother had tidied the dining room. As she washed the glasses and poured away the wasted champagne, he'd burnt the napkin in the stove. When they finally reconvened in the hall, Geri had been upstairs to collect her sunglasses and a shawl, Helena had changed out of her kaftan into a T-shirt and a pair of shorts and Alice appeared to have used the time to take off her suit and restyle her hair. It suited her down. It made her look younger.

They walked down to the dock together. As Luca helped the women onto the boat they all said thank you. Each of them seemed to hold on to his hand a little longer than was necessary. In those touches Luca felt a kinship that he'd never experienced before. It was good to be part of a group – albeit one united by violence and damage.

Luca sailed the *Swan* around the island to the section beneath the terrace where Jonny had gone in. He didn't weigh anchor. Jonny would either have hit the rocks, which he couldn't have survived, or drifted out to sea. He might, conceivably, if he'd been exceptionally lucky, have swum away from the point of entry into the water and found somewhere further around the island to scrabble ashore, but there were very few places to climb out on this stretch of coastline; the rock face was too sheer. Helena couldn't have picked a better – or a worse – spot, depending on your perspective, to cast off her husband.

There was no sign of a body on the rocks so they focused their search on the water. Geri got to her feet first, followed by Alice then Helena. His mother remained seated. He knew why; Carla didn't want Jonny to be rescued, she wanted him dead. They took up their positions at different points around the boat and stared out or down. Luca piloted the *Swan* in elegant, lazy, ever-widening figures of eight, stopping every now and again so that they could listen and stare. No one shouted. No one moved. No one saw anything other than blue sea and blue sky and a single cormorant that flapped loudly and slowly overhead.

After an hour of searching Geri turned and said, 'I think we should head back.' Gladly, Luca set a course for the bay.

Back at the House they gathered in the kitchen. Alice made tea and Carla put pastries, bread, creamy butter, salty cheese and sweet honey on the table. They fell upon the spread, filling their mouths and their bellies. Helena ate with the same gusto as the rest of them. When their stomachs were full, they sat back. Luca moved his chair over to the open back door and lit a cigarette, without asking

356

permission. Alice fetched a bottle of brandy from the larder. She poured a generous measure into each of their cups. No one declined.

Geri's first question was directed at Luca. 'What will happen to his body?'

Luca took a drag, thought, answered as best he could. 'It's hard to say. The currents should take him out to sea, initially, but there's no guarantee that he won't come back in at some point.' Helena reached for her cup and drained it. Alice leant over and refilled it, without being asked.

Geri nodded. 'So, we only have a small window of time to come up with an explanation for how Jonny ended up in the water. What time is it now?'

Alice checked. 'Seven p.m.'

Luca shrugged. 'Yeah, I guess we do.' He had no desire to steer this particular ship. Thankfully, it appeared that Geri did.

Chapter 95

GERI

Geri took a sip of her brandy. They were all waiting for her to speak. She wasn't surprised that it fell to her to construct a credible narrative from the tangle of sin, shame and violence of the past few hours, but perhaps the fact that they all were up to their necks in this mess was a good thing. Joint complicity meant joint jeopardy.

'So . . . a tragic accident.' No one nodded – not yet. She was going to have to convince them of their own alibis. She took another hit of the brandy and warmed to her tale. 'We start by rewriting today. Okay. How about this . . . Jonny, Alice and I spend the afternoon working. We keep going until suppertime. The transition of power – because we must act as if that was going ahead – is a complicated thing, lots of moving parts and interested parties. We are keen to get Jonny's move into the role right. Alice and I will create minutes of our discussions that will prove that we carried on working into the evening. We will break at about 9.00 p.m. After a simple supper of bread and cheese, Alice and I will away to our beds, tired after a long day, and Jonny will stay up with a drink. He will make himself a martini.' So far, so nearly true. Someone famously said that the best

358

lies were those that only deviated from the truth by small degrees. But who? It didn't really matter, but it bugged Geri that she couldn't remember. 'You, Helena, spend the day swimming and reading. You have a light supper, the same food as us, at about 7.30 p.m., in the garden, on your own. Jonny comes out to see you, briefly, to apologise for his prolonged absence. You will recall that his mood was upbeat, excited. Carla, are you getting this?' Carla nodded her understanding. Carla would need to be on top of the domestic details in terms of who was served what and when. Geri thought that the police would be more inclined to trust Carla's timeline than anyone else's. Why would they suspect the housekeeper of having any reason to harm Jonny?

Irritatingly, Helena didn't seem to be paying much attention to Geri's improvised script. 'Helena!' Geri spoke her name sharply. Helena jumped. She did look shattered, but now was not the time for sympathy. It was a time for clarity. 'A text home to the kids from you to that effect would be useful here . . . a comment about how well things are going and how much you and their father are looking forward to coming home. Sign off by saying that their dad has some exciting news. Send it at about . . . 8.00 p.m.' Geri ignored Helena's shudder at the mention of the children. 'You will say, when asked, that you didn't realise Jonny never came to bed because you fell asleep. When you wake in the morning you assume that he's slept in one of the guest rooms to avoid waking you. Claim he's done that before. You join Alice and me at breakfast and that's when we realise no one has seen Jonny since the previous evening. We look for him, in the House first then further afield. Luca and Carla join in the search of the island. But we can't find him anywhere. Not a trace. Where are his wallet and his phone?'

They all looked at Helena. 'His wallet will be on him. His usual phone is up in the bedroom.'

'Well, that needs ditching at sea.' She looked at Luca. He nodded. But then she circled back. 'What do you mean, his "usual phone"?'

Helena slid her hand into the pocket of her shorts and pulled out Jonny's other phone. 'I found this in the pocket of one of his other pairs of trousers.' She placed it on the table.

They all stared at it. Geri pushed the conversation forward. 'And you got into it?'

'Yes.' Helena tucked a strand of hair behind her ear.

'Well?' They really didn't have time for Helena's stalling.

She said, 'It wasn't what I thought.' Then she trailed off.

Geri grew even brisker. She picked up the phone and threw it at Luca, who caught it. 'It gets dumped in the Med with his other one.' She didn't have time for any more nasty surprises. Jonny was gone; any evidence of his wrongdoing needed to disappear with him. She picked back up on their joint alibi. 'Luca takes the *Swan* out after breakfast, just in case Jonny has gone for a swim and got into difficulties.' A thought struck Geri. 'Does he still dive?' Helena mutely nodded. 'Okay. We'll hold that in reserve. If it becomes necessary, I'll mention it to the police. No one else! Just me. By midday there's still no sign of him. We become worried. That's when I raise the alarm. After that it will be in the hands of the Italian authorities. I suspect they'll take it seriously given who we are and the fact that there's no way off the island other than by boat or helicopter.' That was it. It was all mapped out for them. All they had to do was commit the details and the timings to memory and stick to them.

'And then we lie through our teeth for the rest of our lives.'

Geri swung her attention back onto Helena. 'Yes, we do and so will you if you want your children to have at least one parent around to watch them grow up.' It was brutal, but necessary. Helena was the one who'd turfed Jonny into the surf. Although, to be fair, Carla had tried to kill him, Luca must have wanted to and who knew what Alice might have done if she'd been left alone with him. But it was Helena who had acted and, as a result, she was going to have to learn to live with what she'd done, and fast. The role of the grieving widow was going to be pivotal if they were all going to walk away from this unscathed. Momentum and belief, that's what they needed. Geri carried on, 'We'll have to stay on the island for a while after we report him missing. It would look uncaring not to, and the police will want us here, but I suspect, given the circumstances, that you'll be released to go home to be with the children, Helena. And Alice, I can't see them keeping you here after they've taken your statement. I will stay for as long as I can, but eventually my work commitments will necessitate my return to the UK. Then we wait. We say nothing . . . other than how shocked and saddened we are by Jonny's inexplicable and untimely disappearance and how tragic it is, coming so soon after him being chosen as the next CEO of the Chalice Group. I'll get the PR team to draft a statement on behalf of the whole family. We have to be prepared. Whatever we say, the press are going to be all over this.'

'What about Juliet and Ben?' Helena asked.

'Well, that's the good thing about them leaving when they did. They'll be in the clear.'

'I meant when are you going to tell them that their brother is missing...presumed dead.' Helena again. At least she was listening now, although her relentless focus on the truth really wasn't helpful.

'I'll call them tomorrow lunchtime, when we...determine that he is, in fact, missing.'

'Then what?' Killing Jonny had definitely increased Helena's confidence.

'As I said...then we do nothing. There will be a lengthy investigation that – we have to hope – will be unable to ascertain what happened with any degree of certainty. Death by misadventure would be the best result for everyone.'

'Unless he washes up.' This time it was Alice throwing up obstacles. It was almost as if they didn't want to believe that they might get away with it. But what would be the point of it all coming out: Jonny's crimes, their outing of him, Helena's fury, the push? Jonny had been her nephew; she had known him man and boy. True, she had never loved him, but finding out what sort of man he really was had convinced her that his death was no great loss to the world, the business or, sadly, his family.

'If and when they find his body, they'll conduct a post-mortem. They'll find alcohol. We have to hope the working hypothesis will be that he slipped and fell into the sea while under the influence. I will mention him drinking the last time I saw him. Like I said, a dreadful accident.'

'And the knife wound?' Now it was Carla's turn.

There was a pause into which Luca stepped. 'The water, the salt, the motion of the waves and the fish, will do a lot of damage. The longer he stays in the water the better the chances that they won't find the wound. And even if they do, they might think it came from his body snagging on a rock or some passing debris.'

Helena raised her hand to her mouth and she began to sway. Before her eyes, Geri saw the reality of what she'd done to her own husband take hold. Awful as it was, it was better that this happened now rather than later. Geri carried on speaking, making sure that Helena realised her words were aimed at her. 'I'm not happy that Jonny is dead, but I'm not sorry either. He needed to be stopped, and you stopped him. It wasn't what I had planned, but it is a solution and one that I can live with. How the others feel is for them to say.'

Geri looked at Alice. She lifted her chin. 'I'm not sorry either. He was a predator. He saw women as a commodity. He used and abused them, and I think he would have gone on doing so until the day he died, just like his father.'

Next Geri turned to Luca. He took another drag on his cigarette, reluctant as ever to voice his thoughts. They waited. He had more right than any of them to be glad that Jonny was dead, but when he spoke his voice was calm and utterly lacking in passion. 'I don't feel anything about him. I didn't when he was alive and I don't now he's dead.'

Which left Carla.

Having watched Luca say his piece, she stood up and walked around the table. She knelt down in front of Helena, stretched out her arms and embraced her. Then she said,

'I'm deeply sorry for your loss, but I'm not sorry he's dead either. He deserved to die for what he did.' She rocked back on her heels and took Helena's face in her hands. 'But you shouldn't have been the one who had to do it. It should've been me. What you've done for me and Luca and Alice and Lena, and all the other women that men like Ian and Jonny have hurt, was brave and right. And I thank you from the bottom of my heart.'

The dam broke, and Helena started to cry.

Chapter 96

HELENA

The crying hurt, but the sense of purging herself helped. Helena hauled up bucket after heavy bucket of shock, confusion, grief and anger, and all the while Carla held onto her tightly. There was strength in Carla's thin arms and in her solid support. She was a mother. She knew better than anyone. That she could forgive Helena for living with and, yes, loving, the man who had abused her child meant a lot. It meant that there might be a way for Helena to make peace with what she'd done *and* what she'd been blind to. At the bottom of the drained well, Helena found a small, shallow pool of relief. The world was free of him, as was she.

Carla brought her a wet cloth and Helena wiped her face. She scrubbed at her smudged make-up and what she knew was the first of many layers of guilt. She was under no illusion that living the rest of her life as Jonny's killer was going to be easy, but she also knew, with a growing certainty, that it was better than living the rest of her days as his wife. She looked around the kitchen and the others looked back at her. It was the first time in years that Helena felt truly seen. The truth was that Jonny's abhorrent behaviour and his brutal death had united them in a way that nothing else could have done. The five of them would be bound together forever by what they'd experienced, what they knew and what they'd done. The thought brought Helena comfort, and something else: a sense of, if not power, then at least not powerlessness. It was a start.

Luca, who had steadfastly remained by the door while she'd had her breakdown, chose this moment to stand up. He smiled at her and said, 'Come and see.' They all trooped outside into Carla's garden.

The sun was setting, not with a blaze, but with a sigh. Daubs of peach and turquoise streaked the sky. It was nature at its most majestic and indifferent. There was no storm. If God was in his heaven, he had nothing to say on Jonny's violent demise nor on Helena's hand in it. Everything was calm, still and utterly benign. They each found somewhere to perch. Geri offered Helena the only chair and she took it. For a good while they sat, without speaking, watching the light fade from the sky and listening to the breeze stir the grasses. Nobody's phone rang. No one came. In that moment they were all safe on the island.

The Aftermath

Chapter 97

LUCA

After Geri reported Jonny missing, Isola dei Delfini was invaded.

A couple of *polizia* officers were the first to arrive, but as soon as they realised who and what they were dealing with they quickly called in reinforcements, including the *guardia costiera*. The *polizia* scoured the island for clues as to Jonny's whereabouts and, presumably, for evidence of misadventure or worse, and the *guardia* searched the shoreline.

While the uniforms did the seeking, two detectives conducted the interviews. Luca and the others were each taken into separate rooms and asked the same questions over and over again. Luca kept his responses simple. He hoped the others did too. The sea search went on into the darkness. The huge lights on the *guardia* boats strafed the island throughout the night at irregular intervals. No one slept.

When there was still no sign of Jonny the following day, dead or alive, the *carabinieri* got involved. Despite police assurances, word had obviously got out that Jonny was missing, because the journalists began to turn up at first light. It started with a trickle that rapidly turned into a flood. Soon there was a small battalion of boats surrounding the island. The glint of the photographers' telescopic lenses added to the sense of invasion. Every time Luca went out on the *Swan* to ferry officials back and forth to the mainland or to pick up supplies, he had to run the gauntlet of their shouted questions. In the absence of a member of the family, many of the photographers took photos of him. He hated to think that his image might appear anywhere in relation to the Chalices. Some of them offered him ridiculous sums of money for information about what was going on and, more specifically, 'how the family were coping'. Luca ignored them. Thankfully, the *Swan* was able to outpace most of their boats.

At lunchtime on the third day the senior *carabinieri* officer, who was now overseeing the recovery operation, asked Geri and Helena to join him in the dining room. Luca, Carla and Alice listened in as best they could down in the kitchen. After detailing the extensive search efforts, the officer broke the news that, sadly, he believed they were now looking for a body. Helena broke down and cried. Geri maintained a dignified silence. In a strange way it was a relief that other people now thought that Jonny was dead. It was progress, of sorts. The officer said that Helena was free to return to the UK to be with her children. Geri said she would stay on.

It fell to Luca to smuggle Helena and Alice off the island unseen.

They set off after midnight when all but the most committed paparazzi had given up for the day. A full moon illuminated their passage. As soon as they were out of the bay Luca killed the engine. He set sail stealthily and smoothly, using what little wind there was to glide them over to the mainland. There was a car waiting for them in Salerno. They'd not headed for Positano; the risk of them being spotted had been too high. Alice had arranged it all. The plan was for them to be driven to Rome and to fly home from there. Once back, Helena was to hunker down with her children while Alice coordinated things for Geri from head office. Luca was surprised that Alice wanted to keep working for the Chalices. She'd achieved what she'd set out to do, so she had no reason to stay. Perhaps her pact with Geri went further than anyone knew.

Luca was not sorry to see them go. Alice and Helena reminded Luca of events and emotions that he had no use for. Revenge, retribution, anger – no matter how righteous those feelings might be – kept you trapped in the past. Jonny's death was deserved, but Luca had no intention of dwelling on it. He hoped that the others wouldn't either.

With Alice, Helena, eventually the police and, for the most part, the press gone, the island settled down once more – but not into the old ways. The hierarchies and habits of the past had died along with Jonny and Ian. Luca, his mother and Geri inhabited the island quietly, living along-side but not on top of each other. They circulated through the House and around the island like currents, independ-ent of each other, but connected. Without discussion, Geri no longer expected to them to look after anything more than their basic needs. Luca made sure that there was always food in the larder, and sometimes his mother cooked a risotto or a pasta dish for them to share, but she no longer waited on the lady of the house. Carla was most often to be found sitting in her garden, staring out at the view. Luca still took out the trash – someone had to – but he also swam in the pool and went off exploring around the island as he used to. Luca was aware that Geri was working as normal. She still spent long hours in her office every day, presumably running the business and trying to manage the fallout from Jonny's disappearance, but she always kept the study windows and the door closed. It was as if she was conscious of their need for peace and quiet. Luca was glad; he had no desire to listen to Geri spinning the ever-widening web of lies that was all that was keeping his mother, himself and Helena out of prison.

Over dinner, Geri did occasionally update them on the ongoing investigation into Jonny's disappearance, but Ian's fate was never mentioned. That pact of silence held, a secret within a secret. And so, with each sunrise and sunset, they edged further away from both deaths.

During those suspended, languid, oddly peaceful weeks Luca saw his mother tentatively begin to unfurl. He kept his distance from her at first. He respected her need to heal, but couldn't share in her pain. Ian had happened to her, as Jonny had happened to him. The abuse and its consequences were not their fault. The only guilty parties were the men themselves, and they were both at the bottom of the sea – that was enough for Luca. In time, he hoped it would be enough for her.

But the hiatus couldn't last forever.

It was Geri who eventually called time. She came down to see Luca at the Boathouse one morning when he was oiling the deck of the *Swan*. 'Have you time for a quick chat?'

Luca wiped his hands. 'Yeah. Sure.' They sat on the dock.

Geri didn't leap straight in. Luca was fine with that. After a while she said, 'I saw a dolphin with her pup last time I sat here.'

Luca nodded. 'They like the bay. It's sheltered. Not so many predators.' He hadn't intended to make any sort of point.

She gave no sign that she'd noticed. 'We need to think about what happens next.' He nodded. 'I'm going sell the island. Not straight away. It'd be better to wait until things are . . . clearer, but there's too much history here, so much of it bad that I can't imagine wanting to stay here ever again.' Idly, Luca wondered what the surviving Chalice heirs would make of her unilateral decision; from what his mother had told him Juliet was still blocking Geri's calls. Carla's views on the fate of the island would also not be a factor. Despite everything that had happened, her well-being still didn't count for much when compared to a piece of real estate that was probably worth in excess of 100 million euros. But he was wrong – because in her very next breath Geri said, 'I'm very conscious that this is your mother's home.'

'Yes. For the past thirty years.' Luca shuddered to think that she might be in some way part of the sale – a live-in cook and housekeeper. Those days had to be over, surely? Which is why he added, 'But I think it would do her good to leave Isola dei Delfini. She'll find it difficult, but if she stays here she'll never learn to live for herself. And I want that for her. I want her to have a good life.'

'I agree. I think she deserves to have a place of her own where she can feel safe and secure.' Geri paused. 'Which is why I intend to provide the funds for her to buy somewhere to live on the mainland.' Luca stopped himself saying thank you; this was payment of a debt that could never be settled. 'We will have to be careful. I wouldn't want it to come back on your mother later down the line. A sudden transfer of funds, after what's happened; well, it could trigger some awkward questions, but there are ways around that . . . if you're happy to leave it with me?'

Luca nodded. He didn't like Geri, but he was confident that she would know how to route money through different channels better than most. 'Do you want me to tell her?'

'I think that would be best.'

Luca fell back into silence. It was all coming to an end. He was glad.

'And what about you?' Geri asked.

'What about me?'

'What will you do?'

'With no due respect, Geri, that's none of your business.'

She absorbed his rudeness. He respected her for that. He thought she'd leave then, but she didn't. She stretched, did some shoulder rolls and sat placidly next to him. It was uncomfortable at first, but as the sea slapped against the dock he relaxed into it. He would get back to the decking once she'd left. Unbeknownst to Geri, Luca already had a job lined up; skippering day trips to the Blue Grotto for Vincenzo.

Eventually Luca sensed rather than saw Geri smile. 'Do you want her?'

'What?'

Geri gestured at the *Swan*. 'It would be nice for her to sail further than Capri and back. I think she's earnt an

adventure.' Luca was stunned. It was a ridiculous suggestion. The *Swan* was a rich man's boat. She was elegant and
glamorous and she must be worth three million euros, very
possibly more. But the thought of owning her opened up
such an intense yearning inside him that he couldn't speak.
Geri was properly smiling now. 'She's yours, if you want
her' – she paused – 'and I'm guessing, by the look on your
face, that you do.'

Chapter 98

HELENA

Helena was nervous. Although she'd spoken on the phone to Juliet a few times since Jonny's disappearance, their conversations had been brief and mired in so many complex and conflicting emotions that her only objective had been to end each call as quickly as possible.

And yet here she was, sitting in a coffee shop in Hampstead, waiting for her sister-in-law, of her own volition. She'd chosen the venue because it was neutral territory, it was equidistant from their homes and it was anonymous. The press were still obsessed with the story of the missing Chalice heir and the last thing Helena wanted was to be snapped by someone with a phone, an eye for an easy buck and the number of someone who worked at one of the news outlets. As she waited for Juliet, Helena rehearsed what she was going to say. The fragile friendship that had begun to bud between the two of them when Juliet announced she was pregnant had been frozen solid by the events on Isola dei Delfini. She'd heard the hesitation in Juliet's voice when she'd suggested they meet. And yet here she was, pushing her way through the door, a child's car seat hooked over her arm. So she'd brought

Sophie with her. Helena wondered whether that was as a distraction or a defence.

Helena helped Juliet settle Sophie's car seat on a spare chair, then she hurried off to fetch their drinks. As she waited in line her heart thudded in her chest. What the hell was she playing at? She could have left this alone.

When she returned to the table Juliet was standing up, shrugging off her jacket, but there was no hug of greeting. Helena could have done with one. Objectively, Juliet looked well, which, given the circumstances – the loss of her career, her brother and her relationship with Geri – might seem odd, but Helena got it. Despite what she'd discovered about Jonny, what she'd done and the ongoing uncertainty hanging over her future, she had been feeling better herself.

Juliet sat down and twisted her cup around on its saucer so that the handle was just so, but she didn't take a drink. Helena bottled it and turned her attention to Sophie. The little girl, like her mother, looked well. She'd filled out and her features were emerging from the blur of generic baby podge. Helena caught herself wondering who Sophie most looked like. That question returned her directly to the purpose of their meeting. 'Thank you for coming.'

'That's okay.' Juliet's guard was still well and truly up.

Helena knew that she had only a small window to convince Juliet to hear her out; Juliet, like Geri, did not tolerate indecision or delay. 'I wanted to see you because there's something I need to tell you. About Jonny . . . and about me.' If it was possible, Juliet's expression became even more guarded. Helena reached inside her handbag. That day on the island she'd broken all manner of moral codes. Asking Luca to give Jonny's secret phone back to her had been small beer, in the context of murder. She put the phone on the table between them. 'After Jonny went missing I found this, in the pocket of a pair of his trousers.' Sophie blew a spit bubble and Juliet dexterously wiped it away with the corner of a muslin cloth. She didn't say anything, but she was obviously interested. 'I thought it might provide some sort of clue as to his state of mind.'

'Did it?'

'See for yourself.' Helena entered the code and passed the handset to Juliet. It took all of two seconds for her to realise what she was looking at. Watching Juliet's expression switch from indifference to shock to anger was unnerving. Before she could stop herself, Helena blurted, 'I'm sorry. I had no idea.'

Juliet was scrolling through the photos and messages with a look of intense concentration, although she obviously knew what they were – she'd been on the receiving end of them. 'I thought it was Geri.'

'I know. She told me. That's why I wanted us to meet today. I thought … think … it's important that you know the truth. I don't want you blaming Geri for something she didn't do.' The hysteria that Helena had been pressing down for the past few weeks fizzed and buzzed inside her.

Juliet finally looked up. 'The bastard!' she spat. Then she checked herself. 'Sorry, that was inappropriate … given the circumstances.'

Helena shook her head. 'It's okay. It's not you who should be apologising. It's him. He had … he has … so much to apologise for.' Juliet lowered her head and went back to scrutinising Jonny's messages. Helena watched her, waiting for her heart rate to steady. She could leave it at that. No, she couldn't. About her part in this chapter of the nightmare she could, at least, come clean. 'It's my fault.'

'What is?'

'I think it was me who gave him the idea.'

'To blackmail me?' Juliet was looking at Helena now.

'No! Of course not. I wouldn't do anything to hurt you or Sophie. Ever. Not deliberately. But I did tell him more than I should have. And for that I am *so* sorry. I thought he was asking after you because he was genuinely interested in why you'd decided to have a child on your own and how you were coping.'

'Go on.' Juliet's voice had a hard, glittering edge to it.

Helena ripped the Band-Aid straight off. It was the only way. 'I told him that you'd used a fertility clinic. I remember he made some crack about it being "typical you" to cut out the man from the process. I only told him because I wanted him to see how strong you were. I said I admired you, going it alone. He assumed that you'd used a donor.' There was a moment of silence between them. 'But . . . I think I may have said something about you using the last of the embryos that you'd had frozen.' She tailed off. Juliet continued to glare at her. 'I'd been drinking and I'd taken a sleeping pill.' Juliet's expression didn't soften. She was right, there was no excuse. 'It obviously lodged in his mind and from that one inadvertent comment he must have worked out that Sophie was Harry's biological child. It never occurred to me that he'd use it against you.'

Juliet's reply was sharp and to the point. 'But he did. He turned it into this.' She gesticulated with the phone. 'A nasty, vicious campaign to get rid of me.'

Helena had to tell it all. 'There's one last thing.'

'What?'

'I took the photos that he sent you. He must have taken them off my phone.'

Juliet simply shook her head in disbelief. 'For fuck's sake, Helena! Why did you take them in the first place?'

Helena flushed. 'You were obviously struggling with being apart from Sophie and with Geri's demands, then your father turning up clearly upset you, so I thought I'd take some pictures of Sophie – as a memento of her first trip to the island. I was going to send them to you when we got home.'

Juliet dropped the phone on the table and sat back. 'Wow, Helena. Just wow.'

Around them people chatted and laughed and drank their coffee while she and Juliet sat and pondered her stupidity and Jonny's awfulness.

She had confessed, to something, and who knew, that might help. She stood up. Juliet let her. 'I'll leave now. I hope, in time, that you might be able to forgive me.' Helena picked up her bag. 'And although I'm sure you don't care, I do now see what sort of man Jonny really was. And I want you to know that, whatever happens, he and I are done.'

Chapter 99

JULIET

Juliet caught a glimpse of a different person in Helena's eyes when she said, 'He and I are done.' Not a grieving soon-to-be widow, but a relieved woman. As she watched her leave, Juliet found herself reassessing her sister-in-law. Helena could have kept her mouth shut and avoided Juliet's anger and judgement, but she hadn't. Missing husband or not, she had done the right thing and for that Juliet was grateful. She did forgive Helena. Her crime was trusting her husband and that was hardly a capital offence.

Juliet picked up the offending phone and took one last look at the handful of photos and messages that had changed the course of her life. Did she feel cheated out of her rightful inheritance? No, she felt disgusted; that Jonny had stooped so low *and* that she hadn't spotted it. Mother-hood had made her soft, which was no bad thing in life, but was a distinct disadvantage in the swirling shark pool of her family. She should have known that Geri would never be that underhand. If she'd had doubts about Juliet's com-mitment she would just have said so. That did not change the fact that her aunt had paid people to excavate the most painful and supposedly private areas of Juliet's life, or that she had patently been very unhappy that Juliet had chosen to prioritise becoming a mother. So much for Geri Chalice, the Rolls-Royce model for female empowerment! It had only ever been about her own success and power, not anyone else. Juliet would simply have to live with the fact that she would never know whether Geri would have used Sophie's conception against her or not. Sophie gurgled and an older woman sitting at the next table smiled at them both. Unless, of course, Juliet asked her outright, and she had no intention of doing that. She'd found peace in her decision to walk away from everything Chalice-related. It was a peace that was worth more than anything her aunt or the business could ever offer her. Juliet deleted the stolen photos of her daughter and Jonny's threats, pushed thoughts of Geri to the back of her mind and instead chose reality. A quick gulp of cooling coffee, another mop of her daughter's dribbly face and they were good to go.

On their way across the car park Juliet threw the phone in the bin, consigning the issue of Sophie's conception to the trash. Paternity was not being a parent. Sperm was not fatherhood. Juliet dropped a kiss on the top of Sophie's head as she slotted the baby seat into the car and checked that it was secure. Sophie gurgled and waved her fat little fists at her. Sophie would do just fine without a father in her life because she had a mother who had wanted her more than anything else.

Chapter 100

GERI

It was a textbook take-off. Neat, controlled, smooth. For a second or two after lift-off the island was shrouded in dust, but by the time the helicopter had climbed to a hundred feet Geri's view was clear and uninterrupted. She was leaving Isola dei Delfini for good. But instead of banking and heading north, Geri took a turn around the island, for old times' sake. Perspective; it was always good to review your situation from on high.

So far, their alibis had held. The huge amount of work that she and Alice had put into creating the fake minutes of the non-existent transition meeting with Jonny on the day he 'disappeared' had also paid off. Alice's meticulous documentation had lent credibility to their story. And Carla had played a blinder, placing all the key players in all the right places at the right time. Such precautions had been necessary. The police investigation had been thorough. The Chalice name had obviously helped to keep the questioning civil, as had the low-key but persistent involvement of Harrison and May, but inevitably there had been a lot of suspicion. It had lingered like a bad smell in the background of every conversation that Geri had with the *carabinieri* officers. They had, as she expected, questioned her about the cameras, but eventually, begrudgingly, they'd accepted her assertion that they hadn't been switched on. Why would they be on? It had been a family gathering for her birthday. Despite all the questions, no direct allegations had been made nor any evidence of foul play presented, because none had been found. And, crucially – there was no body. Of course, that was going to cause problems with regard to settling Jonny's estate, but there was no rush to do that. It wasn't as if Helena was short of funds. In fact, she and the children would be set up for life once Jonny was declared dead – he'd seen to that with all his nefarious investments. Yes, for now, they were in the clear.

Geri flew another circuit around the island.

The press and the online conspiracy theorists, of course, were making the most of it. She and Alice had decided that the blizzard of rubbish that was swirling around what had really happened on the island could be made to work in their favour. Together they'd concocted a narrative about the blighted male line of the Chalice family. A new 'cursed uber-rich family' myth to add to the Grimaldis, the Guinnesses and the Gettys was bound to gain traction. There was, after all, plenty for people to feast on: her father's massive heart attack in the middle of his seventy-fifth birthday party – over 400 people had been present to witness his last, gasping breaths; Jonny plummeting to his death from Isola dei Delfini just at the point when he was about to take over as head of the company; not to mention Ian's colourful, dissolute life, and his disappearance coming so quickly after his eldest son's untimely accident – because Ian's absence would soon be news, whether Geri liked it or not. The Chalice Curse storyline would no doubt lead to scrutiny of Ben and his addictions, which wasn't good, but Geri hoped that, by that point, he might have started to turn things around. From what Helena had said, living with Juliet was already having a positive effect on her youngest, now her only surviving, nephew. Perhaps Ben would become the Chalice who changed the fortunes of the male side of the family.

That this narrative might appease Ian and Jonny's victims was, of course, also a consideration. Geri hoped that the unhappy fates of her brother and her nephew would satisfy any desire for retribution while at the same time keeping the real truth under wraps. At the end of the day it was a story about male fallibility and comeuppance, and at least half the population would go for that. Geri was acutely aware that she was walking a moral tightrope while spinning multiple plates, but her balance had always been good.

For some reason Geri didn't feel quite ready to leave Isola dei Delfini. She made a third circuit around the island, then a fourth, each loop wider and higher so that the island became little more than a dot of rock surrounded by the sparkling cerulean sea. As she flew, Geri realised that she was scanning the water for any sign of Ian and Jonny. They were both out there somewhere, festering beneath the weight of the waves. How did she feel about their deaths? Conflicted? Contrite? No. What she felt was that justice had been served and, to her at least, it seemed oddly fitting that it had been Carla and Helena, the two women with the least power, who had delivered the fatal blows. There was a neatness and a balance in that, if not in the execution.

Reassured that neither her brother nor her nephew had resurfaced, Geri finally felt ready to take her leave. On a whim she shifted the joystick hard left and headed south, away from, not towards land. She flew low and straight. The shadow of the helicopter raced ahead of her, tempting her on. The rush of adrenaline after so many weeks of caution and physical confinement was intense. She increased her speed and felt the helicopter rattle and strain to meet her demands. She sped along above the sea, revelling in the sensation of being simultaneously in control and on the edge. It was time she went back to what she did best – running the Chalice Group. Her age was an irrelevance. Let people speculate. Her performance spoke for itself. There was no one to succeed her. Not yet.

Another five years.

She flew even faster, chasing the horizon.

Another ten. Why not?

Reality awaited, and she was eager to get back to it. As for the future, well, a new candidate had emerged from the chaos of the past few weeks. One who might, under Geri's tutelage and guidance, be perfect for the role of CEO.

Alice.

Geri smiled. That would put the cat among the pigeons. Alice Baxter: young, female and, above all, not a Chalice – the Board would have apoplexy. Geri would need to build support for her, make sure she had an excellent financial director by her side, not one of Jonny's old cronies; but given time, and some not-so-gentle persuasion, it might be feasible. If Juliet could be persuaded to endorse her that would help, hugely. Alice's appointment would also make it possible for Juliet to stay on as an executive director without much, if any, real work to do – if she wanted to. Geri was rapidly warming to her own brilliant idea now . . . Who knew, should Ben really clean up his act, Geri might finally allow him a seat at the table – if he promised to always vote with Alice. It could work. Alice was analytical, focused, hardworking and smart. And she'd proved herself to be tough. She was already Geri's protégée; why shouldn't she be her successor? Geri laughed out loud at the thought of Ian and Jonny spinning in their watery graves. It was the perfect solution.

Mind made up, appetite for the fight whetted, Geri eased off the throttle, turned the helicopter around and headed north, back to the responsibilities that defined her: CEO of the Chalice Group and head of her dysfunctional, depleted, demanding family.

Acknowledgements

I readily acknowledge that I've never flown a helicopter, set foot on a private island, run a multinational company or looked like a cross between Jamie Lee Curtis and Jane Fonda, even on my better days. That's not to say I wouldn't love to! But that's the joy of fiction; it's an act of imagination and research.

What follows are my thank and yous to the people who allow me to pursue that joy.

First off, I want to thank my agent Judith Murray at Greene and Heaton for encouraging me to 'go big' and to release the darkness that plainly lurks within my soul. As ever, I've been cheered on and expertly steered through the choppy process of writing this book by my smart, supportive, eagle-eyed editor Sarah Hodgson at Corvus. She is the best *ballet instructor* any author could have! I'm also hugely indebted to Rachel Wright who stopped Jonny smelling of an orange paint and all Italian men having the same surname!

But conceiving and writing a novel is only the start of its publishing journey, so thanks also go to everyone on the dedicated, enthusiastic marketing, PR and sales team at

Corvus who have put so much time and effort into this, and my previous books.

On a more personal level, I want to give a special mention to my local powerhouse bookseller, Amanda, at Truman Books, for her energy, knowledge and passion. I hope to have many more food, wine and fun-filled book launches in your lovely shop with the irrepressible, ever-supportive Julie. And here's to me participating in the fabulous Farsley Lit Festival for years to come.

Shoutouts also go to Eleanor Chitham, the queen of sun salutations; to my fellow humble warriors in The Cabin; to Ian Hunt for his valuable insights into the world of privately owned companies and the vagaries of rich, powerful families; and to the extremely informative YachtWorld website. Sadly, my recent enquiries regarding the seventy-five-foot Gannon and Benjamin schooner with the teak interiors are unlikely to result in a purchase at this current time. And a special mention has to go to my sister, Sue Bond, for her one-woman marketing and sales campaign for my last book, *Happily Never After*.

Lastly, I want to let my family, Chris, Alex, Geena, Rachel and Lorna, know that I love them, a lot; and my friends, Val, Linda, Kath, Sam and Joss, that I'd be a lot less fit, in body and mind, without them in my life.